DARK
COMPANION

Baen Books by ANDRE NORTON

Time Traders
Time Traders II
Star Soldiers
Warlock
Janus
Darkness & Dawn
Gods & Androids
Dark Companion

DARK COMPANION

ANDRE NORTON

DARK COMPANION

This is a work of fiction. All the characters and events portrayed in this book are fictional, and any resemblance to real people or incidents is purely coincidental.

Copyright © 2005 by Andre Norton. *Dark Piper* copyright © 1968 by Andre Norton; *Dread Companion* copyright © 1970 by Andre Norton.

All rights reserved, including the right to reproduce this book or portions thereof in any form.

A Baen Book

Baen Publishing Enterprises
P.O. Box 1403
Riverdale, NY 10471
www.baen.com

ISBN: 0-7434-9898-4

Cover art by Bob Eggleton

First printing, April 2005

Library of Congress Cataloging-in-Publication Data

Norton, Andre.
  [Dark piper]
  Dark companion / by Andre Norton.
      p. cm.
  ISBN 0-7434-9898-4 (hc)
  1. Life on other planets--Fiction. 2. Governesses--Fiction. 3. Children--Fiction.
I. Norton, Andre. Dread companion. II. Title: Dread companion. III. Title.

  PS3527.O632D373 2005
  813'.52--dc22

                                                                    2004029943

Distributed by Simon & Schuster
1230 Avenue of the Americas
New York, NY 10020

Production by Windhaven Press, Auburn, NH (www.windhaven.com)
Printed in the United States of America

10 9 8 7 6 5 4 3 2 1

CONTENTS

DARK PIPER

ONE

✦

I have heard it stated that a Zexro tape will last forever. But even a second generation now may find nothing worth treasuring in our story. Of our own company, Dinan, and perhaps Gytha, who now work on the storage of all the old off-world records may continue to keep such a history of our times. But we do not run our reader now except for a pressing need for technical information, since no one knows how long its power pack will last. Therefore, this tape may keep its message locked for a long time unless, ages from now, those off-world do remember our colony and come seeking to learn its fate, or unless there shall arise here people able to rebuild machines that have died for want of proper repairs.

My recording may thus be of no benefit, for in three years our small company has taken a great backward leap from civilized living to barbarism. Yet I spend an hour each evening on it, having taken notes with the aid of all, for even young minds have impressions to add. This is the tale of the Dark Piper, Griss Lugard, who saved a handful of his kind, so that those who walk as true men should not totally vanish from a world he loved. Yet we who owe him our lives know so little about him that what we must in truth set upon this tape are our own deeds and actions and the manner of his passing.

Beltane was unique among the Scorpio Sector planets in that

3

it was never intended for general settlement, but instead was set up as a biological experimental station. By some freak of nature, it had a climate acceptable to our species, but there was no intelligent native life, nor, indeed, any life very high in scale. Its richly vegetated continents numbered two, with wide seas spaced between. The eastern one was left to what native life there was. The Reserves and the hamlets and farms of the experimental staffs were all placed upon the western one, radiating out from a single spaceport.

As a functioning unit in the Confederation scheme, Beltane had been in existence about a century at the outbreak of the Four Sectors War. That war lasted ten planet years.

Lugard said it was the beginning of the end for our kind and their rulership of the space lanes. There can rise empires of stars, and confederations, and other governments. But there comes a time when such grow too large or too old, or are rent from within. Then they collapse as will a balloon leaf when you prick it with a thorn, and all that remains is a withered wisp of stuff. Yet those on Beltane welcomed the news of the end of the war with a hope of new beginning, of return to that golden age of "before the war" on which the newest generation had been raised with legendary tales. Perhaps the older settlers felt the chill of truth, but they turned from it as a man will seek shelter from the full blast of a winter gale. Not to look beyond the next corner will sometimes keep heart in a man.

Since the population of Beltane was small, most of them specialists and members of such families, it had been drained of manpower by the services, and of the hundreds who were so drafted, only a handful returned. My father did not.

We Collises were First Ship family, but unlike most, my grandfather had been no techneer, nor bio-master, but had commanded the Security force. Thus, from the beginning, our family was, in a small measure, set apart from the rest of the community, though there was nothing but a disparity of interests to make that so. My father lacked ambition perhaps. He went off-world and passed in due course through Patrol training. But he did not elect to try for promotion. Instead, he opted to return to Beltane, assuming, in time, command of the Security force here that his father had commanded. Only the outbreak of the war, which caused a quick call-up of all available trained men, pulled him away from the roots he desired.

I would have undoubtedly followed his example, save that those ten years of conflict wherein we were more or less divorced from space kept me at home. My mother, who had been of a techneer family, died even before my father lifted with his command, and I spent the years with the Ahrens.

Imbert Ahren was head of the Kynvet station and my mother's cousin, my only kin on Beltane. He was an earnest man, one who achieved results by patient, dogged work rather than through any flashes of brilliance. In fact, he was apt to be suspicious of unorthodox methods and the yielding to "hunches" on the part of subordinates—though, give him his due, he only disapproved mildly and did nothing to limit any gropings on their part.

His wife, Ranalda, was truly brilliant in her field and more intolerant of others. We did not see much of her, since she was buried in some obtuse research. The running of the household fell early on Annet, who was but a year younger than I. In addition, there was Gytha, who usually was to be found with a reading tape and who had as little domestic interest as her mother.

It must be that the specialization that grew more and more necessary as my species entered space had, in a fashion, mutated us, though that might be argued against by the very people most affected. Though I was tutored and urged to choose work that would complement the labors of the station, I had no aptitude for any of it. In the end, I was studying, in a discontinuous manner, toward a Rangership in one of the Reserves—an occupation Ahren believed I might just qualify for—when the war, which had not affected us very directly, at last came to a dreary end.

There was no definite victory, only a weary drawing apart of the opponents from exhaustion. Then began the interminable "peace talks," which led to a few clean-cut solutions.

Our main concern was that Beltane now seemed forgotten by the powers that had established it. Had we not long before turned to living off the land, and the land been able to furnish us with food and clothing, we might have been in desperate straits. Even the biannual government ships, to which our commerce and communication had sunk in the last years of the war, had now twice failed to arrive, so that when a ship finally planeted, it was cause for rejoicing—until the authorities discovered it was in no way an answer to our needs but rather was a fifth-rate tramp hastily commandeered to bring back a handful of those men who had been drafted off-world during the conflict. Those veterans were indeed the halt and the blind—casualties of the military machine.

Among these was Griss Lugard. Although he had been a very close part of my childhood, the second-in-command of the force my father had led starward, I did not know him as he limped away from the landing ramp, his small flight bag seeming too great a burden for his stick-thin arms as its weight pulled him a little to one side and added to the unsteadiness of his gait.

He glanced up as he passed, then dropped that bag. His hand half went out, and the mouth of a part-restored face (easy to mark by the too smooth skin) grimaced.

"Sim—"

Then his hand went to his head, moving across his eyes as one who would brush aside a mist, and I knew him by the band on his wrist, now far too loose.

"I'm Vere," I said quickly. "And you are"—I saw the rank badges on the collar of his faded and patched tunic—"Sector-Captain Lugard!"

"Vere." He repeated the name as if his mind fumbled back through identification. "Vere—why, you're Sim's son! But—but—you might be Sim." He stood there blinking at me, and then, raising his head, he turned to give his surroundings a slow, searching stare. Now he gazed as if he saw more than his boots raising planet dust.

"It's been a long time," he said in a low, tired voice. "A long, long time."

His shoulders hunched, and he stooped for the bag he had dropped, but I had it before him.

"Where away, sir?"

There were the old barracks. But no one had lived there for at least five years, and they were used for storage. Lugard's family were all dead or gone. I decided that, whether Annet had room or not, he could guest with us.

But he was looking beyond me to the southwest hills and to the mountains beyond those.

"Do you have a flitter, Sim—Vere?" He corrected himself.

I shook my head. "They're first priority now, sir. We don't have parts to repair them all. Best I can do is a hard-duty hopper."

And I knew I was breaking the rules to use that. But Griss

Lugard was one of my own, and it had been a long time since I had had contact with someone from *my* past.

"Sir—if you wish to guest—" I continued.

He shook his head. "When you've held to a memory for some time"—it was as if he talked to himself, almost reassuring himself—"you want to prove it, right or wrong. If you can get the hopper, point her west and south—to Butte Hold."

"But that may be a ruin. No one has been there since Six Squad pulled out eight years ago."

Lugard shrugged. "I've seen plenty of ruins lately, and I have a fancy for that one." With one hand he fumbled inside his tunic and brought out a palm-sized metal plate that flashed in the afternoon sun. "Gratitude of a government, Vere. I have Butte Hold for as long as I want—as mine."

"But supplies—" I offered a second discouragement.

"Stored there, too. Everything is mine. I paid half a face, strong legs, and quite an additional price for the Butte, boy. Now I'd like to go—home." He was still looking to the hills.

I got the hopper and signed it out as an official trip. Griss Lugard was entitled to that, and I would face down any objection on that point if I had to.

The hoppers had been made originally to explore rough country. They combined surface travel, where that was possible, with short hops into the air to cross insurmountably rough terrain. They were not intended for comfort, just to get you there. We strapped into the foreseats, and I set the course dial for Butte Hold. Nowadays it was necessary to keep both hands on the controls. There was too apt to be some sudden breakdown, and the automatics were not to be trusted.

Since the war the settlements on Beltane had contracted instead of expanded. With a short supply of manpower, there had been little or no time wasted in visiting the outlying sites, abandoned one after another. I remembered Butte Hold as it had been before the war—dimly, as seen by a small boy—but I had not been there for years.

It was set on the borders of the lava country, a treacherous strip of territory that, in remote times, must have lighted most of this continent with titanic eruptions. Even the eroded evidence of these volcanoes was still spectacular. Of late years it was an unknown wilderness of breaks and flows, a maze of knife-sharp ridges with here and there pockets of vegetation. Rumor had it that, beside the forbidding aspect of the land itself, there were other dangers—from beasts that had escaped the experimental stations and found this forsaken range an ideal lair. No one actually had evidence of such. It was rumor only. But it had grown into tradition, and a man wore a stunner when he ventured in.

We left the road at a turn trace so dim by now that I could not have found it without Lugard's direction. But he gave that with the surety of one seeing markers plain in the sun. And very shortly we were out of the settled land. I wanted to talk, but I did not quite dare to ask my questions. Lugard was so plainly occupied with his thoughts.

He would find other changes on Beltane, less tangible than those of the abandonment of old landmarks but nonetheless sharp. The settlements had been drained of certain types of men: first the guard, and then scientists and techneers. Those left had unconsciously, perhaps consciously in some ways, changed the atmosphere. The war had not come close enough to make any great impression on our planet. It remained a subject of reports, of attrition of supplies and manpower, of growing irritation as men, buried in their own chosen fields of research, had been commanded to explore other paths for refinements in killing. I had heard enough to know that there had been a deliberate dragging of feet in sections that had been set to war problems. And there had been angry outbursts five years back, threats passed between the last commander and such men as Dr. Corson. Then the commander had been ordered off-world, and Beltane settled down to a peaceful existence.

The sentiment now on Beltane was pacifist—so much so that I wondered whether Lugard would find an accepted place among these men bent so strongly on keeping matters as they were and had been. He had been born on Beltane—that was true. But, like my father, he was of a Service family, and he had never married into one of the settlement clans. He spoke of Butte Hole as his. Was that literally true? Or did it mean that he was sent here to make ready for another garrison? That would not be welcome.

Our trail was so badly overgrown that I reluctantly took to the air, skimming not far above the top of the brush. If Lugard was the forerunner of a garrison, I hoped they would number among them some techneer-mechanics with training in the repair of vehicles. Already our machines had become so unpredictable that some of the settlements talked of turning to beasts of burden.

"Take her farther up!" ordered Lugard.

I shook my head. "No. If she parts at this height, we have a chance of getting out in one piece. I won't chance more."

He glanced first at me and then at the hopper, as if he really saw it for the first time. His eyes narrowed.

"This is a wreck—"

"It is about the best you can find nowadays," I replied promptly. "Machines don't repair themselves. The techneer-robos are all on duty at the labs. We have had no off-world supplies since Commander Tasmond lifted with the last of the garrison. Most of these hoppers are just pasted together, with hope the main ingredient of that paste."

Again I met his searching stare. "That bad, is it?" he asked quietly.

"Well, it depends upon what you term bad. The Committee has about decided it is a good thing on the whole. They like it that off-world authority has stopped giving orders. The Free Trade party is looking forward to independence and is trying to beam in a trader. Meanwhile, repairs go first for lab needs; the rest of it slides. But no one, at least no one with a voice in Committee affairs, wants off-world control back."

"Who *is* in charge?"

"The Committee—section heads—Corson, Ahren, Alsay, Vlasts—"

"Corson, Ahren, yes. Who is Alsay?"

"He's at Yetholme."

"And Watsill?"

"Drafted off-world. So was Praz—and Borntol. Most of the younger men went. And some of the big brains—"

"Corfu?"

"He—well, he killed himself."

"What?" He was clearly startled. "I had a message—" Then he shook his head. "It was a long time reaching me—out there. Why?"

"The official verdict was minor fatigue."

"And behind that verdict?"

"Rumor has it that he discovered something deadly. They wanted him to develop it. He wouldn't. They pressured him, and he was afraid he might give in. So he made sure he would not. The Committee like that rumor. They have made it their talking point against off-world control. They say that they will never put weapons into anyone's hands again."

"They won't have the chance—into former hands, that is," Lugard replied dryly. "And they had better give up their dreams of trade, too. The breakup is here and now, boy. Each world will have to make the most of its own resources and be glad if someone else doesn't try to take them over—"

"But the war is over!"

Lugard shook his head. "The formal war, yes. But it tore the Confederation to bits. Law and order—we won't see those come again in our time, not out there—" He motioned with one thin hand to the sky over us. "No, not in our time, nor probably for generations to come. The lucky worlds with rich natural resources will struggle along for a generation or two, trying hard to keep a grip on civilization. Others will coast downhill fast. And there will be wolves tearing all around—"

"Wolves?"

"An old term for aggressors. I believe it was an animal running in packs to pull down prey. The ferocity of such hunts lingered on in our race memories. Yes, there will be wolf packs out now."

"From the Four Stars?"

"No," he answered. "They are as badly mauled as we. But there are the remnants of broken fleets, ships whose home worlds were blasted, with no ports in which they will be welcomed. These can easily turn rogue, carrying on a way of life they have known for years, merely changing their name from commando to pirate. The known rich worlds will be struck first—and places where they can set up bases—"

I thought I knew then why he had returned. "You're bringing in a garrison so Beltane won't be open—"

"I wish I were, Vere, I wish I were!" And the sincerity in his husky voice impressed me. "No, I've taken government property for my back pay, to the relief of the paymaster. I have title to Butte Hold and whatever it may contain, that is all. As to why I came back—well, I was born here, and I have a desire that my bones rest in Beltane earth. Now, south here—"

The traces of the old road were nearly hidden. There had been a washout or two, over which the quickly growing guerl vines had already laid a mat. Now we were coming to the lava country, where there were signs of the old flows. The vegetation rooting here was that fitted to the wastelands. This was midsummer, and the flowering period was nearly over. But here and there a late blossom still hung, a small flag of color. There were ripening yellow globes on the vines, and twice spoohens fluttered away, at the approach of the hopper, from where they had been feeding.

We circled about an escarpment and saw before us Butte Hold. It was a major feat of adaptation, the rock of the mountain carved away and hollowed to make a sentry post. It had been fashioned right after First Ship landing, when there was still doubt about the native fauna, meant to be a protection against what lay in the saw-toothed wilds of the lava country. Though the need for such a fort was soon known to be unnecessary, it had served as a headquarters for all the outland patrols as long as they kept watch here.

I set down on the landing strip by the main entrance. But the doors were banked with drifting sand and looked as if they had been welded so. Lugard got out, moving stiffly. He reached for his bag, but I already had it, sliding out in his wake. By the looks of it, he was traveling light, and if there were no supplies within—well, he might change his mind and want to return, if only temporarily, to guest in the section.

He did not deny my company but went on ahead, once more in his hand that metal plate he had shown me at the port. As he came to the sand-billowed doorway, he stood a long moment, looking at the face of the stronghold, almost as if he expected one of those now shuttered windows to open and himself to be hailed from within. Then he stooped a little, peering closely at the door. With one hand he brushed its surface and with the other fitted the plate he carried over the locking mechanism.

I half expected to see him disappointed, my belief in the durability and dependability of machinery having been systematically undermined by the breakdowns of years just past. But in this case I was wrong. There was a moment or two of waiting, to be sure, but then the seemingly solid surface parted into two leaves, rolling silently back on either side. At the same time, interior lights glowed, and we looked down a straight hall with closed doors to right and left.

"You ought to be sure of supplies," I ventured. He had turned to reach for the bag I still held. Now he smiled.

"Very well. Assure yourself, come in—"

I accepted that invitation, though I guessed he would rather be alone. Only I knew Beltane now as he did not. I would have to leave in the hopper, and he would be, could be, disastrously on his own—marooned here.

He led the way straight down the hall to a door at the rear, raising his hand to pass it in a swift, decisive gesture over the plate set into its surface. That triggered the opening, and we stood on the edge of a gray shaft. Lugard did take precautions there, tossing his kit bag out. It floated gently, descending very slowly. Seeing that, he calmly followed it. I had to force myself after him, my suspicions of old installations being very near the surface.

We descended two levels, and I sweated out that trip, only too sure that at any minute the cushioning would fail, to dash us on the floor below. But our boots met the surface with hardly a hint of a jar, and we were in the underground storeroom of the hold. I saw in the subdued glow shrouded machines. Perhaps I had been wrong to think Lugard would miss transportation when I left. But he was turning to the right and some alcoved spaces, where there were containers and cases.

"You see—I am well provided for." He nodded at that respectable array.

I looked around. There were weapon racks to the left, but they had been stripped bare. Lugard had gone past me to pull the covering off one of the machines. The plastic folds fell away from a digger, its pointed pick nose depressed to rest tip against the surface under us. My first hopes of a command flitter, or something like it, faded. Perhaps, just as the weapon racks had been stripped, so had such transports been taken.

Lugard turned away from the digger, and there was a new briskness about him.

"Have no doubts, Vere. I am well situated here." His tone was enough to send me to the grav, and this time he signaled reverse, so we rose to the entrance hall. I was on my way to the door when he stopped me:

"Vere—?"

"Yes?" I turned. He was looking at me as if he were hesitant to say what was in his mind, and I had the impression that he fought to break through some inner reserve.

"If you find your way up here again, look in." It could not be termed a warm invitation; yet, coming from him, I knew that it was as cordial a one as I would ever have, and it was honestly and deeply meant.

"I will that," I promised.

He stood in the doorway, a light sundown wind stirring up the drifted sand, driving some of it over the threshold to grit in the bare hallway, to watch me go. I deliberately circled once as I left and waved, to see his hand raised shoulder high in return.

Then I headed to Kynvet, leaving the last of Beltane's soldiers in his chosen retreat. Somehow I disliked thinking of him alone in that place, which must be for him haunted by all the men who had once trod its corridors and would never now return. But that it was a choice no one could argue against, I knew, Griss Lugard being who and what he was.

When I put the hopper down at Kynvet, I saw the wink of lights through the summer dusk.

"Vere?" Gytha's voice called from our house. "Annet says hurry. There is company—"

Company? Yes, there was the other hopper with the Yetholme code on its tail, and beyond it the flitter Haychax kept in flying order—almost as if we were entertaining half the Committee. But—why? I quickened pace and for a space forgot about Butte Hold and its new commander.

TWO

✴

It might not be a full meeting of the Committee gathered under Ahren's roof that night, but the men whose voices murmured behind closed doors were those who would dominate any such meeting. I had expected to have to answer for the presence of the hopper and was prepared to stand up for Lugard's rights, only to discover that had I presumed to take a flitter, it would not have been noted then.

Annet, busy at dishing up before summoning the men now entrenched in her father's study, informed me of the reason for such an unusual convocation. The ship that had brought in Lugard and the other veterans had, in addition, a second mission. The captain had been contacted, as he came out of hyper into orbit, by a ship now above Beltane, of whose presence we had not been aware. And a plea had been delivered to the Committee.

It was as Lugard had predicted, though his view of the matter had been gloomy. There were ships now without home ports, their native worlds burned-out cinders or radioactive to the point that life could not exist on their deadly surfaces. One such load of refugees now wove a pattern in our sky and asked for landing rights and settlement space.

Beltane had, by the very reason for its settlement, been a "closed" world, its single port open only to certified ships. But that enclosure vanished with the end of the war. The truth was

15

that the sector settlements occupied so little of the continental masses that we were not even a true pioneer world, in spite of the permanence of the hamlets that radiated from the port. The whole eastern land mass was empty of any colonization at all.

Did the old restrictions still prevail? And if they did not—was the welcome signal out for any flotsam of the war? I thought of Lugard's dire prophecy that wolves ranged or would range the star lanes—that those without defenses could be looted, or even taken over. And would these men now conferring with Ahren think of that possibility? I believed not.

I picked up a platter of dunk bread and took it to the long table. Servo-robos were long gone now, save for a few in the labs. We had returned to the early state of our species and used our two hands, our feet, and the strength of our backs to work. Annet was a good cook—I relished what came out of her pots and pans more than the food at the port, which was still running by robo. The appetizing odor of the dunk bread made me realize it had been a long time since noon and that my port meal had been even less satisfactory than usual.

When I returned for a tray of dunk bowls, she was looking out of the window.

"Where did you get the hopper?"

"Portside. I had a passenger into the outback."

She looked at me in surprise. "Outback! But who—?"

"Griss Lugard. He wanted to go to Butte Hold. Came in on the tramp."

"Griss Lugard—who is he?"

"He served with my father. Used to command at Butte Hold before the war."

"Before the war" was even more remote to her than to me. She had hardly been out of a sector crèche when the first news of the conflict had come to us. And I doubted if she could remember the time before.

"What did he come for? He is—was—a soldier, wasn't he?"

Soldiers, men who made fighting their profession, were as legendary on Beltane now as any of the fantastical creatures on the story tapes of the young.

"He was born here. He was given the hold—"

"You mean there are going to be soldiers here again? But the war is over. Father—the Committee—they will protest that! You know the First Law—"

I knew the First Law—how could I escape it? It had been dinned into my ears, and supposedly my head, long enough. "War is waste; there is no conflict that cannot be resolved by men of patience, intelligence, and good will meeting openly in communication."

"No, he's alone. He is no longer with the forces. He's been badly wounded."

"He must be wit-addled too"—she began ladling the stew into the waiting tureen—"if he plans to live out in that wasteland."

"Who's going to live in the wasteland?" Gytha bobbed up, a collection of bowl spoons in her suntanned hands.

"A man named Griss Lugard."

"Griss Lugard—oh, Second-Commandant Lugard." She surprised me as she was so often able to do to all of us. Her mouth curved in a smile at our astonishment, and her two side braids of hair swung as she nodded vigorously. "I can read, can't I? Don't I? Well, I read more than story tapes. I read history—Beltane history. It's all in the old news tapes. And there's more, too. All about how Second-Commandant Griss Lugard brought artifacts from the lava caves—that he found Forerunner things there. They were going to send someone here from Prime Center to see—then the war came. And nobody ever came. I read a lot of tapes to find out if they did. I bet he's come back to look for treasure—Forerunner treasure! Vere, couldn't we go out and help him look?"

"Forerunner artifacts?" If Gytha said she had read it in the news tapes, it had been there. In such matters she made no mistakes. But I had never heard of any Forerunner remains on Beltane.

When our kind had first broken out of the solar system that had nourished our species, we soon learned that we were not unique in our discovery of the worlds of far space. We met others already free of the lanes between system and system. And, as the galaxy counted time, they, too, were newcomers, though they were centuries in advance of our own first timid star steps. Yet there were those who had gone before *them*, and others before and before—until one could not count the empires that had risen and fallen or know how many generations of creatures, many much longer lived than we, had passed since some of those Forerunner ships had planeted on long-forgotten worlds.

There had once been a brisk market in Forerunner finds, especially in the core planets of the inner systems where VIP's had wealth and wanted curiosities to spend it on. Museums bought, too, though the story was that a better deal could be made with a private collector. If the tape Gytha quoted had the truth, then I could understand Lugard's return to the Butte. Having been granted it, he would have legal title to any find thereabouts. But that such a luxury trade would be of use to him now—No, if conditions were as bad as his pessimistic account made them, one could tumble into a whole Forerunner warehouse and get no good of it.

However, there is always a pull to the thought of treasure, and I cannot deny that Gytha's reaction was mine—to go look for such. The thought made one's blood run a little faster.

The lava caves were no place for the prudent to venture unless a man knew something of the territory and went well equipped for all emergencies. They are not formed like usual caves by the action of water, but rather are born of fire. A tongue of lava flows down a slope and congeals on the outer surface, but the interior remains molten and continues to move, forming a passage. After ages, the roof of such a tube may collapse, opening it to the outer world. These long corridor caves can run for miles. The landscape around them is ridged with trenches where some cave ceilings have entirely collapsed, and in places natural bridges of rock span them. There are craters, broken volcanic cones, hazards that close the country to the casual traveler.

"Could we, Vere? Perhaps the Rovers could go?" Gytha clattered her spoons against each other in rising excitement.

"Certainly not!" Annet whirled around from the cook unit, a ladle dripping in her hand. "That is dangerous country; you know that, Gytha!"

"Not alone," Gytha returned, none of her excitement in the least dampened. "Vere would go and you maybe. We'd abide by the rules, no straying. And I never saw a lava cave—"

"Annet," Ahren called from the other room, "we're in a hurry, daughter."

"Yes, coming—" She went back to filling the tureen. "Take the spoons in, Gytha. And, if you please, Vere, the preserve crocks."

Her mother had not come in. This was not unusual, since

experiments in the lab did not wait on meal hours, and Annet was long resigned to sending over a tray or keeping back a portion of a dish. Consequently, she most always gave us food that could be reheated or set out successfully for a second or even a third time.

The visitors and their host were already seated at the head of the table, and we took the hint to sit at the foot, not to interrupt. Not being truly one of their number, I usually found the conversation at such gatherings of little interest. But tonight might be different.

However, if I had hoped to hear more of the refugee ship, I was disappointed. Corson ate mechanically, as one whose mind was entirely elsewhere. Ahren was as taciturn. Only Alik Alsay paid Annet compliments concerning the food and finally turned to me.

"Good report you turned in, Collis, about the north slope."

Had he been Corson, I would have been pleased, even flattered a little. But I knew very well that my report was of small interest to Alsay, that he was merely making conversation. I murmured thanks, and that would have been that had not Gytha taken a hand for motives of her own. When she chose to fasten onto some project, as I might well have remembered, she generally, sooner or later, got her way.

"Vere was out to the lava beds today. Have you been there, First-Tech Alsay?"

"Lava beds." He paused in raising his cup of caff in open surprise. "But why? There is no authorized mapping in that direction—simply wasteland. What took you there, Collis?"

"I took someone—Sector-Captain Lugard. He is at Butte Hold."

"Lugard?" Ahren came out of his preoccupation. "Griss Lugard? What is he doing on Beltane?"

"I don't know. He says he was given Butte Hold—"

"Another garrison!" Ahren set down his cup with a clatter that slopped a little of the caff over on his fingers. "We will *not* have that nonsense here again! The war is over. There is no need for any Security force!" The way he said "security" made it sound like an oath. "There is certainly no danger here, and we will not have any of those controls foisted on us again. The sooner they learn that, the better." He glanced from Alsay to Corson. "This puts another light on the whole matter."

But what matter he did not explain. Instead, he demanded of

me a full accounting of what I had learned from Lugard, and when I had given that, Alsay cut in.

"It would seem Lugard has the hold as a pension."

"Which could be only a cover-up he used with the boy." Ahren was still aroused. "But his port papers—they ought to tell us something. And"—once more he turned his attention to me—"you might well keep an eye on him, Vere. Since he accepted your help in getting there, he could well understand your dropping in again—"

What he was suggesting I did not like, but I would not say that yet, not before these others and across the table where I ate by his leave, under the roof he had made mine. Something in Lugard's return seemed to have flicked Ahren on the raw; otherwise, he would not have gone to the length of hinting I should spy on a man who had been my father's good friend.

"Father"—once more Gytha cut in, still intent on her own wishes—"can't Vere take us with him. The Rovers have never been to the lava lands."

I expected Ahren to quell her with one of those single glances he used with effect. But he did not, and when he made no quick answer, Alsay spoke.

"Ah, the Rovers. And what has been their latest adventure, my dear?" He was one of those adults who were never at ease with children, and his voice took on a stilted note, used earlier to a lesser extent with me.

Gytha could be polite when the occasion, by her measurement, warranted it. She smiled at the Yetholme leader, and she could smile winningly when she chose.

"We went to the gullat lizard hatchery and made a recording of peep cries," she replied. "It was for Dr. Drax's communication experiment."

I applauded her cunning. To remind her father at this point of some volunteered aid in the past was a bolster for her present demand to widen horizons.

"Yes," Ahren agreed. "It really was an outstanding piece of work, Alsay, showing great patience and perseverance. So now you would like to see the lava beds—"

I was startled. Could he actually agree? Across the table I saw Annet stiffen; her lips moved as if they were already shaping a protest. But Alsay spoke again and this time to me.

"Quite a useful organization, Collis. You are supplementing the teaching tapes very well. It is a pity we have not been able to advance to off-world study. But now that the war is over, there will be opportunities for that."

Did he really believe so, I wondered. The Rovers were more Gytha's idea than mine, though she had drawn me into it and locked me to her purposes so well that I could not now have dropped the project even if I wanted to.

When the settlers had come to Beltane, they had intended to train their children into a science-minded caste. In fact, experiments in such education had been part of the original plan. However, the war had interfered with this as with so much else. Off-world science during those years might have made some great strides. We suspected as much. But our knowledge had become so specialized and narrowed that, lacking fresh imports of taped information, we generally still went over ground ten years old by planet dating, perhaps a hundred by advances elsewhere.

To counteract this stultifying effect had been one of the tasks of the educators. However, the cream of them had been drafted for service. Those remaining—like the sector people—tended to be conservative, the older ones. Then there was a drastic epidemic in the third year of the war (caused, said rumor—we always had rumor—by over-zealous experimentation for the Services that resulted in a battle between the sector chiefs and the commandant and the closing down of two projects). After that there were even fewer left to be concerned with the training of the next generation. By spasms parents came out of their labs and studies long enough to be excited for a moment over the lack of concentrated cramming for their children. Then some sudden twist in their own work, some need for complete concentration, took their minds off the matter.

There were never many children—at Kynvet now only eight, ranging from the seven-year-old twins Dagny and Dinan Norkot to Thad Maky, who was fourteen and considered himself—irritatingly at times—nearly adult.

Gytha early dominated. She had a vivid imagination and a total recall memory. Her use of every tape she could lay hand on, though she was barred from digging into lab recordings, had given her a wide range of the most miscellaneous and amazing information. But she differentiated clearly between fact and fiction, and she could spin a fantasy or answer a factual question in the space of a couple of breaths. To the younger children, she was a fountain of wisdom. They appealed to her general knowledge before they approached any adult, for the abstraction of their parents had become so much of a habit by now that this community was really split into two, marked by the difference in ages.

Having organized her followers, Gytha had worked upon me. And I found, whether I willed it or no, I was leading expeditions of the Rovers sometimes more than I was trying to further my own Ranger studies. At first I had rebelled at assuming such responsibilities, but Gytha's discipline held so well, her threat to any one of them of being left out was direful, that they did obey orders. And it came to be a source of pride to me that I was in part a teacher for those eager to learn.

Annet was not quite one of us. She always distrusted Gytha's enthusiasms and thought her sister very prone to reckless disregard for danger. But she did not give vocal vent to any worries when I was in command, for she knew I would not willingly lead them into trouble. Now and then she did join one of our expeditions, her role usually being that of managing the commissary. And, I will say this in her favor—she never made any complaint when on the march.

But to take the Rovers into the lava lands—no, that was where I joined with Annet and was ready to hold firmly to the negative. But Ahren leaned forward a little to question his younger daughter.

"Do you have a project in mind?" He at least knew how to talk to the younger generation, using the same tone of interest with which he would have greeted a remark from one of his colleagues.

"Not yet." Gytha was always honest. She never tried to conceal facts. "Only, we've been to the swamps, and up in the hills several times, and never there. It is to broaden horizons—" She fell back on her own general term for exploration. "We would like to see Butte Hold."

I noted that she said nothing of a hunt for Forerunner treasure.

"Broaden horizons, eh? What about it, Vere? You were in there today with a hopper. How was the terrain?"

I could not hedge, though I wanted to. He need only check the reading on the machine dial to know the truth, though I did not know why Imbert Ahren would do such a thing. Only, I did know him well enough to recognize a state of mind-made-up. He wanted us to go to the lava lands—or at least to Butte Hold. And the reason for that took little guessing—he wanted a report on Lugard. Perhaps he thought if he could not get it readily from me, he could from Gytha. Children's eyes are sharp, and they see much.

"Well enough around the Butte. I would not venture farther without a good survey."

"Gytha"—Ahren turned to her—"would a trip to Butte Hold enlarge horizons enough for the present?"

"Yes! When—tomorrow?" She demanded almost in one breath.

"Tomorrow? Well—yes, tomorrow might be very good. And, Annet"—he spoke to the older girl—"we shall be at the port. Your mother will accompany us. I think that the Norkots and the Wymarks will be going, too, for a general meeting. Why don't you make this a full-day outing? Take food for a—do you not say—cookout?"

Again I was sure she would protest. But in face of the firmness underlying that suggestion, she did not. Gytha gave an exclamation of delight. I thought she was already mentally listing supplies needed to uncover Forerunner treasure.

"Give my greetings to the Sector-Captain," Ahren said to me. "Say that we shall be very glad to see him at the port. We may be able to profit by his experience."

That I doubted. Ahren's opinion of the military had been stated so many times, forcibly for the most part, that I could not conceive of his listening to Griss Lugard on any subject without impatience and a closed mind.

Ahren was so eager to speed us on our way that he gave me permission to use the supply hopper, which I knew to be in repair and which would hold our whole company. Once supper was done, Gytha was off at light speed to warn her crew of the next day's promise.

I helped Annet clear the table and saw her frown as she fed the dishes into the one kitchen mecho that still ran—the infra cleaner.

"Father wants to know about Griss Lugard," she said abruptly. "He doesn't trust him."

"He need only go out and meet the man, and he'd know the truth." I was unhappy about the way we were being used. "Lugard is certainly not planning to take over Beltane! He probably only wants to be left alone—and I don't think he will welcome us too much."

"Because he does have something to hide?" she flashed.

"Because he must want peace and quiet."

"A soldier?"

"Even they can grow tired of war." I had skirted her prejudices before. They were rooted in what she had been taught all her life. My situation as more guest than family had made me talk and walk with circumspection ever since I had been sorrowfully and firmly put through a discussion session for defending my absent father's beliefs with my fists when I was all of ten.

"Perhaps." But she was not convinced. "Do you really think there is something in the Forerunner artifact story? That seems unlikely. There were never any traces of anything found on the surface."

"Not that we have searched very thoroughly," I countered, not because I did believe in any treasure, but to keep the record correct. It was true that we had aerial surveys of much of the western continent, plus the reports of all the early exploring parties, but although those made a network of the known across much of the land, it was a loose one, with perhaps something to be learned about what lay in the gaps between.

The land was wide and empty. Perhaps those of the refugee ship, were they permitted to settle, could even find a good place to the north, south, or farther west, without changing much the course of our pattern.

We prepared for an early takeoff in the morning, but we were still behind those who left for the port. I gathered that they were assembling not only the full Committee, but also as many of the others as they could to hear the petition of the orbiting ship. But for the children, this subject took second place. The lava country had been so talked up by Gytha that I feared there might be some disappointment later.

So I sat in the pilot's seat, half facing around as we readied to go, and made it most plain to my passengers that our destination was Butte Hold and *not* the rough country behind it, which we had no intention of entering. Also, they were not to fasten on

Lugard or enter the hold unless at his invitation, which secretly I thought would not be uttered. Were he wise and caught sight of us on any view screen when we landed, he would leave us to wander outside his wall.

Privately, I had also made it clear to Gytha that if Lugard did appear and be hospitable, she was not to mention Forerunners, treasure, or anything of the sort.

I was answered by her scorn. As if she did not know how to act! I was, she commented, getting to be as narrow-minded as Annet. And if that was what came of growing up, she would try to get some sort of retarding pills from one of the labs and be herself for years yet. She *liked* to be the way she was, and she didn't try to make people over either!

The flight-hop from Kynvet was shorter than that from the port. In the old days, Kynvet had been the first link in the chain tying the Butte to the other settlements. In less than an hour, we touched down on the blowing sand of the old landing. I fully expected to see the Butte firmly closed, but its door stood open to the morning sun and there was Lugard, entirely as if he had invited and expected us.

Obeying orders, the Rovers hung back as I went to explain our presence, but I heard some muffled exclamations. The veteran was not alone. On one of his thin shoulders perched a herwin, as if it had known him since its hatching. And by his boots crouched a rock hanay, while between his fingers he held a slender dark red rod. He did not speak or hail us, but rather he raised the rod to his lips. Then he began to pipe—and at that trickle of clear notes falling in a trill as might spring rain, the herwin whistled its morning call and the hanay rocked back and forth on its clawed digging paws, as if the music sent it into a clumsy dance.

I do not know how long we stood there, listening to music that was like none I had ever heard before, but which drew us. Then Lugard set aside the pipe, and he was smiling.

"Magic," he said softly, "Drufin magic." He gave one last note, and the herwin took wing, sailing straightway up into the sky, while the hanay seemed to see us for the first time, gave a startled grunt, and waddled into hiding among the rocks.

"Welcome." Lugard still smiled. "I am Griss and you are—?"

The children, as if released from a spell, ran to him, and each called his name as if he wished to claim instant recognition from this worker of magic. He gave them greeting and then suggested that they explore the Butte, making them welcome to any room with an open door. When they had gone into the corridor behind him, he looked at me, at Annet, and back to me, and his face was darkly sober.

"The refugee ship"—his question was a command for an answer—"what have they decided to do concerning that?"

"We don't know. They have a meeting at the port today."

He limped on into the sun. "Lend me your hopper." Again it was more order than asking. "They can't be so stupid as to let them land—"

I stood aside without a question, so compelling was the force of his preoccupation. It was clear he harbored some thought to the extinction of all else.

He was in the cabin, raised from the ground, when Annet cried out, "Vere! He's going off with all our food—leaving us here! When will he be back? Stop him!"

Since this was now a complete impossibility, I caught her arm and pulled her out of the miniature dust storm raised in his takeoff, urging her to the Butte. She turned on me then with demands to know why I had let him go. And to tell the truth, I had no real answer for her. But I did manage to make her understand that Lugard's supplies could certainly be used by us under the circumstances, and it might be well to see what the Rovers were doing inside.

THREE

"It isn't real magic!" We heard Gytha's voice raised from one of the rooms. "Don't you *ever* read tapes, Pritha? The vibrations, the sounds—they attract the animals and birds. I don't know what Drufin means—it's probably off-world. But it's the sound—and maybe a special kind of pipe to make it." As usual she was quick to distinguish the real from the unreal.

One of the thoughts I sometimes have crossed my mind then— what *is* real and unreal? Unreal to one people or species can be real to another. Beltane libraries are sadly lacking in information about other worlds—unless it deals with scientific matters. But I had heard stories from spacemen, and perhaps not all of those were tall tales told to astonish the planet bound. Drufin magic meant nothing to me either, but doubtless Gytha's explanation was right. But there were other things beside piping to start the thought of magic growing—

"With a pipe such as that," Thad broke in, "you could go hunting and never come home with an empty bag. Just pipe 'em up and stun 'em."

"No!" Gytha was as quick to counter such speculation as she had been to deny the supernatural. "That is a trap and—"

I moved on into the room. Gytha, her cheeks flushed, faced Thad, indignation expressed in every line of her thin body. Behind her the younger children had drawn together as if to form a support. And Thad had only Ifors Juhlan on his side. It was a clash that had occurred before, and I expected it at intervals. Perhaps someday such a difference of opinions would break Thad loose from the Rovers. He wanted action and more excitement than we could promise him.

"Second Law, Thad," I said now, though that sealed me away into the adult world. But the admonition was strong enough to keep his rebellion bottled.

Second Law—"As we value life and well-being, so does lesser life. We shall not take life without thought or only to satisfy the ancient curse of our species, which is unheeding violence."

There was no need to hunt on Beltane—save for specimens for the labs. And then sure care must be taken of them so that they eventually might be returned unharmed to the Reserves. These were scattered widely, each with its population to be studied. The prizes were the mutants of the over-mountain Reserves. Their intelligence had been raised, and a certain number of such animals had even gone to war, in "beast teams," aligned with human controllers. I hoped to qualify for work on such a Reserve. Since the breakdown of the educational chain, I thought I could persuade the powers in control that practical knowledge of the field type was as useful now as the stated requirements of off-world learning, which might never be in existence again.

I had gone a-hunting with a stunner, and I had shown visa-tapes of this to the Rovers. Perhaps that had been a mistake. Thad—well, we were a nonviolent world, with action mainly confined to cerebration and experimentation within four walls. There had been a case or two during the past few years of killing and pillage without cause. The perpetrators had been sent to the psyche lab at the port and the stories hushed up. But—perhaps not only machines broke under the circumstances that had gripped Beltane for the last decade. I had been thinking of the stalemate in education. If one did not go forward, one did not just remain still; one slipped back. Were we slipping back? We were still conditioned by the laws, intended to keep us at peace with each other and the life about us. But—

"Vere—" Thad changed the subject now, either because he wanted to escape Gytha's accusation or because he was really interested. "What is all this?"

He gestured to indicate the four walls of the room. Time

had set lightly here. I believed the Butte must have been sealed airtight. The walls were as bright under the diffused light as if they were newly painted. Three were unbroken; the fourth, with the door, was separated by that into two tall panels. And what they all displayed were maps, each covering a quarter of our continent, north, east, south, and west. All the settlements were marked with small bulbs, unlit. In addition, I picked out some of the long abandoned Security holds, most of them mere sentry posts.

Below each wall was a board with a range of levers and buttons, and in front of each board a chair that slid with ease along the full length of the controls. The center of the room was occupied by a square platform a step above the surface of the floor, and on it was a fifth chair, made to face any wall, as Dinan Norkot had discovered, sitting in it to whirl dizzily about.

Memories of the past when I was about Dinan's age stirred. I had been here once and had seen my father in that center seat—not whirling but turning slowly to watch lights winking on the board. Blue—yes, blue for the sectors, red for the Security posts, and yellow—no, green—for the Reserves.

"This is a com post," I told Thad. Not a com post either, but *the* com post—more important even than the one at the port. Butte Hold had been the most secure of all the posts, and so the most necessary installations were here.

Did it still work, I wondered? The lights were out, but that might only mean that the boards were closed down, not really dead. I went to the one facing north. The port light—I leaned over the board, discovered that that was too uncomfortable, so seated myself in the chair, and compared numbers on board and wall until I found the button to press.

Voices boomed into the room so that I heard Annet cry out, and we all stared at the wall map from which they seemed to break with a clarity that would have been more natural had the men speaking stood before us.

Dagny Norkot ran over to stand beside my chair. "That's my father," she declared. "But he went to the port—"

"—satisfied with their statements. Then—"

It faded as if Norkot had walked away from an open com mike or else that the power installation weakened. Annet was beside me now.

"We're not supposed to be listening in on a Committee meeting," she said.

That was the truth. But somehow I wanted to know just how effective the whole system still was. I snapped up the port lever and depressed that of Yetholme.

Again we had a pickup. Not clear voices as Norkot's had been, but enough to know that the old setup was partially effective.

"You know"—Thad pushed between Annet and my chair—"this Griss Lugard, he can about hear all that is going on—everywhere—and stay right here! Voice pickup anyway. Isn't there any visa-screen relay?"

Again I remembered. Getting out of the seat before the north board, I went to that center control chair where Dinan had been spinning moments earlier. It took me two false starts before I either remembered, and was not aware of it, or lit by chance on the proper combination of two buttons in the chair arms, plus a foot lever. A section of the wall slid up to disclose a screen.

"Yah!" Thad expressed his excited interest. "Now what do you do?"

I glanced quickly over the rest of the map, having no mind to look at any occupied sector house. The easiest choice would be one of the abandoned Security ports in the far north.

"Thad, press the first lever, first row," I ordered, holding the screen ready with my own fingers.

He did so. There was a flicker on the screen and then a picture, so dim at first that I thought the power was nearly exhausted. But as I continued to hold, it built up into a brighter display, and we were looking at another room. This, too, had banks of controls, a couple of chairs. But there was a great crack in the wall behind the control board and—

"Look—a wart-horn!"

For a moment it was startling. Crouched in the chair, which was still on an even keel, was indeed a wart-horn. Its warty skin, its froglike head and face with the forward pointing horns, made it anything but a pleasant-looking object. But the way it crouched in the chair, its webbed forepaws even resting on the arms as it seemed to lever itself up to meet our gaze, always supposing that our actions here had activated the appearance of a twin screen for reception there and two-way viewing, gave it a disturbing air of intelligence, as if it had been about some secret business of its own in our alien structure and had been surprised.

We watched its throat swell and heard, muted but still recognizable, its harsh croaking grunt. It leaned up and out even farther, its face filling the screen, and I heard Pritha cry out, "No! No!"

I released the com buttons, and the screen not only went dark but also the wall moved to cover it again.

"I don't like it! It looked at us!" Pritha's voice became a wail.

I swung around in the chair, but Annet had already taken her in her arms.

"You know wart-horns," she said soothingly. "They are nothing to be afraid of. And if that one saw us, he probably was just as startled as you were. That"—she turned to me—"was an old sentry post, wasn't it, Vere?" At my nod, she continued. "And it's been left empty for years. I bet the wart-horn may have a den there."

"It looked at us," Pritha repeated.

"And we looked at it," Annet answered. "So we're even. And that place where it is is a long way from here!"

"Two days by hopper, Pritha," I cut in. "Nobody goes there any more."

"Vere"—Gytha was beside Thad, her hand poised above the levers and buttons—"let's try another one—maybe this?"

"No!" Annet snapped before I had a chance to answer. "There's been enough of this listening and peeping. And since Sector-Captain Lugard made off with our lunch, suppose we try to find out what is in the cupboards here. As you said, Vere, he owes us that."

"Indeed he does." I backed her up. But I lingered to make sure I was the last to leave the room, Gytha and Thad going reluctantly, gazing back at the tempting display of possible peeps hither and thither across our world.

"Vere?" A small hand slipped into mine. I looked down into Pritha's almost triangular face. The families that had been brought in to settle Beltane had not been homogeneous in the beginning but came from widely separated worlds, since it had been their special talents and training that selected them. So we did indeed represent types of many kinds, some of which had mutated physically from the ancient norm of our species.

Pritha Wymark, within one month of Gytha's age, was hardly

taller than Dagny, five years younger. Her delicate bones and
slender body, though, were not those of a small child. She had
a quick mind, but she was timid, highly sensitive to things that
perhaps the others were never aware of or felt only lightly. Now
there was a shadow on her ethereal face.

"Vere," she repeated, and her voice was hardly above a whisper.
"That wart-horn—it—it was watching us!"

"Yes?" I encouraged, for behind that statement of fact something troubled her. Dimly I felt it also—that the way the thing
had squatted in the chair before the screen, its stance aping that
of a man minding the control board, had been disturbing.

"It—it was not—" She hesitated as if she could not put her
troubled thoughts into words.

"Perhaps it was just the way it was hunched in the chair,
Pritha. Wart-horns have never been submitted to the up-raying,
you know. They are too low on the learn-scale. And that was a
sentry post we picked up, way out in the wastelands. It was not
on one of the Reserves."

"Perhaps—" But I knew she was not satisfied.

"When we get back, Pritha"—I tried to reassure her—"I'll report
it. If by chance some wart-horn *has* been up-scaled and escaped,
they will have a record of it. But one does not have to fear even
an up-scaled animal—you know that."

"Yes, Vere. I guess it was just the way it sat there, looking
at us."

But still she kept her hand in mine until we reached the last of
the open doors and looked in upon a scene of activity as Annet
examined labels on ration cans taken from a case recently opened
and made choices to set out on the table that must once have
served the whole garrison for mess.

Lugard's cooking arrangements were simple. He had attached
two portable cooking units. And there was another case of mess
kits clipped together, which Thad now unpacked with no small
clatter.

Against the far wall were the huge units that were dial food,
but Lugard's plates were enough for our purposes. Gytha handed
the containers Annet selected to Ifors, who fitted them into the
heating clips. It was all very brisk and efficient.

"It would seem we are not going hungry," I commented.

Annet wore an excited expression as she turned to me.

"Vere, real catt! Not just parx-seed substitute! And a lot of off-world things. Why, here are camman fowl slices and creamed fass leaves—things we haven't seen for years!"

"Lugard must have been using officers' mess supplies." I crossed to read the labels on some of the cans. We ate well enough on Beltane—perhaps our common fare would have seemed luxury on some worlds, since the bio labs produced new strains adapted to growing here in great variety—but for a long time there had been no imports, and we had heard, if we had never had a chance to taste for ourselves, nostalgic mention now and then of some particular viand our elders remembered.

Prudence finally controlled Annet's selection, and she picked for our eating not the more exotic things she had found, but those that promised few if any upsetting reactions from stomachs unaccustomed to the unknown. We ate cautiously at first and then with our usual good appetites to be satisfied.

When we had done, Annet lined up a small company of containers and looked at me wistfully.

"Do you suppose he would trade?" she asked. "If I could have some of these for Twelfth Day feasting—"

"No harm in asking. He ought to like some fresh dunk bread, or your partin-berry preserves, or even a freeze dinner out of the deep store. Canned rations, even if they are from off-world, must get tiresome after a while.

"Now"—I spoke to the rest—"suppose we set this all to rights again."

Camp discipline held, though I knew they were impatient to go exploring. I had noted that the grav door was shut, and for that I was thankful. They would obey rules, I knew—no opening shut doors.

I was deswitching the heating units when something made me count heads and find two missing, Thad and Ifors. I repeated their names. Annet turned to count, but Dinan had an answer for us.

"They went out—after they packed the mess kits, Vere."

The com room? It would be just like Thad to experiment there, though I thought that the activation of the screens would be something even Thad could not do. But I started down the hall in swift strides, aware that Thad was becoming more the rebel—and I did not want the facedown to come between us here and now.

"—Griss Lugard!"

The volume was up, loud enough so that those words bellowed down the hall, echoing a little. I came into the room just as Thad's hand shot out to the button he had pushed a moment earlier. But, though he was apparently exerting pressure on it, the old fittings were now jammed, and the sound continued to roar.

"That is the situation, Gentle Homos." It was Lugard's voice now with a rasping, grating tone increased by the broadcast. "You cannot trust such treaties—"

"Perhaps you cannot, Sector-Captain." That was Scyld Drax. "The military mind is apt to foresee difficulties—"

"The military mind!" Lugard's interruption came clearly. "I thought I made it simple—the situation is as plain as the sun over you, man! You say you want peace, that you think the war is over. Maybe the war is, the kind we have been fighting, but you don't have peace now—you have a vacuum out of which law, and what little protection any world can depend upon, has been drained. And into this is going to spread, just like one of your pet viruses, anarchy. A planet not prepared to defend itself is going to be a target for raiders. There were fleets wrecked out there, worlds destroyed. The survivors of those battles are men who have been living by creating death around them for almost half a generation, planet time. It has become their familiar way of life—kill or be killed, take or perish. They have no home bases to return to; their ships are now their homes. And they no longer have any central controls, no fears of the consequences if they take what they want from the weaker, from those who cannot or will not make the effort to stand them off. You let this ship land—only one ship, you say, poor lost people; give them living room as we have a sparsely settled world—there is one chance in a hundred you read them aright.

"But there are ninety-nine other chances that you have thrown open the door to your own destruction. One ship, two, three—a home port, a safe den from which to go raiding. And I ask you this, Corson, Drax, Ahren, the rest of you. This was a government experimental station. What secrets did you develop here that could be ferreted out, to be used as weapons to arm the unscrupulous?"

There was a moment of silence. He had asked that as a man might deliver a challenge.

Then we heard Corson. "We have nothing that would serve as such—not now. When the authorities forced certain of us to such experimentation, we refused—and when that authority left, we destroyed all that had been done."

"Everything?" Lugard asked. "Your tapes, your supplies, perhaps, but not your memories. And as long as a man's memory remains, there are ways of using it."

There was a sharp sound, as if a palm had been slapped down hard on some surface.

"There is no need to anticipate or suggest such violence, Sector-Captain Lugard. I—we must believe that your recent service has conditioned you to see always some dark design behind each action. There is not one reason to believe that these people are not what they have declared themselves to be, refugees seeking a new life. They have freely offered to let any one of us come aboard while they are still in off-orbit—to inspect their ship and make sure they come in peace. We would not turn a starving man from our doors; we cannot turn away these people and dare still to call ourselves a peaceful-minded community. I suggest we put it to the vote. Nor do I consider that you, Sector-Captain, are so much one of us as to have a vote."

"So be it—" That was Lugard once more, but he sounded very tired. "'And when Yamar lifted up his voice, they did not listen. And when he cried aloud, they put their hands to their ears, laughing. And when he showed them the cloud upon the mountains, they said it was afar and would come not nigh. And when a sword glinted in the hills and he pointed to it, they said it was but the dancing of a brook in the sun.'"

The Cry of Yamar! How long had it been since anyone had quoted that in my hearing? Why should anyone on Beltane? Yamar was a prophet of soldiers; his saga was one learned by recruits to point the difference between civilian and fighting man.

There was another faint sound that might have been boot heels on a floor. Then a murmur and Ahren's voice rising above that.

"Now—if there are no further interruptions, shall we vote?"

As if Thad had at last loosed the button, though he had ceased to struggle with it some time ago, there was silence in the com room. Thad pushed the button again, as determined now to have it open as he had been earlier to close the channel. But there was no response.

"Vere?" Gytha stood a little behind me. "What was Griss Lugard talking about? Why didn't he want the refugees to land?"

"He was—is—afraid that they may want to turn pirate—or to raid here." Without thinking of my listeners, I gave her the truth.

"Which is simply stupid!" Annet said. "But we must not blame the Sector-Captain. He is a soldier, and he does not understand the kind of life we have here. He will learn. Thad, you should not have listened in on the Committee meeting—"

He looked a little guilty. "I didn't mean to—we were trying to see how many of the stations were still open. I hit that button by mistake, and it stuck there. Truly that is what happened."

"Now"—Annet glanced around the room as if she disliked what she saw—"I think we had better go. We had no right to come here—"

"He said we could go in any room where the door was open," Gytha promptly reminded her. "And this one was. Vere"—she spoke to me—"could we go up in the watchtower and look at the lava lands, even if we can't go out there?"

To me that seemed a reasonable request, and when we found that the door to the upper reaches of the Butte was one of the open ones, we went. There was a short climb and for the last part a steep one. Annet chose to remain below with the Norkot twins and Pritha, who disliked heights. We came out on a windswept sentry go. I unslung my distance lenses to turn them north and west.

Here and there were splotches of green vegetation native to Beltane, not the lighter, cultivated mutant off-world growth that lay about the settlements. In some places it formed odd shadows that seemed almost black. But the stretches of bare lava ran and puddled out in vast rough pockets. There were other runnels of the stuff, and I had never seen a land so forbidding and forsaken. Even if it had any life hiding there, a man could search for a year and perhaps never uncover so much as a trail.

"Yah—" Thad focused his own lenses. "Looks as if someone stuck a paddle down in seal-cor and turned it around a couple of times and then just let it cool. Where are the caves?"

"Your guess is as good as mine," I told him. When I visited the Butte in the old days, I had been too young to go exploring. I could not remember having seen this before, though I had probably been brought up to the lookout.

"Vere, how old is it—the lava flows, I mean?" Gytha asked thoughtfully.

"Read your geology tapes. I wouldn't know that either." I unslung my lenses and passed them to Ifors, who would hand them in turn to Sabian and Emrys.

"But old—very old—" she persisted.

"Undoubtedly that."

"Then the lava caves might have been here a long time, too—as long as Forerunner times?"

"Who knows when those were? And there were more than one lot of Forerunners." I was evasive, trying to catch Gytha's eye and warn her against the treasure-hunting story. But she had leaned both elbows on the parapet and was holding Thad's lenses, giving a searching survey to the wild lands.

"Forerunners?" Unfortunately Thad had heard. "Why worry about Forerunners? There weren't any ruins here—"

Before I could stop her, Gytha answered. "That's all you know! Griss Lugard found Forerunner relics back in a lava cave before the war. If you'd read Beltane history tapes, you'd know a lot more, Thad Maky. There were men coming from off-world to explore—then the war broke out and nobody did any more about it."

"Is that so, Vere?" Thad demanded of me. "Forerunners—here! Is that why Griss Lugard really came back? My father said he was getting the Butte ready for a new garrison and the Committee wouldn't let them in. They'd put the repel rays on at the port if they tried it. Lugard landed before they knew it, but they aren't going to let any more of his kind in. But if he came back just on his own after Forerunner treasure—Maybe he'd let us help him—or the Committee could make him—"

"Thad! Gytha read a rumor in an old news tape. That is all there is to it. We are not going to mention this to Griss Lugard or at home—understand? This is a *hold*—" I appealed to one of their own private rules. "Holds" were just that, information they kept to themselves, some even secret from me. And I had always respected their reticence. But this was important.

Thad looked steadily back, but there were no reservations and no hint of mutiny in his answer. "Agreed." He used their regular formula.

Then I turned to Gytha. "Hold?"

She nodded violently. "Hold!" And the others followed her.

"Vere." Emrys had aimed the lenses east. "There is something coming—a hopper, I think. And it must be on top circle speed—it's really shooting."

I took back the lenses and followed the pointing of his finger. Our hopper—with Lugard. Perhaps it would be better to make ourselves scarce as soon as we could, so I headed my crew down to the lower levels.

FOUR

If we had expected to see in Griss Lugard some reaction to the
dispute at the port, we were to be disappointed. Outwardly, he
was one on a holiday now. He limped toward us as we waited
by the door of the Butte, a smile on his face, though that was
pulled slightly awry by the reconstruction flesh on his left cheek
and jaw.

"My pardon, Gentle Fem." He spoke first to Annet, using the
courtly off-world address and sketching with his free hand a half
salute of courtesy. In the other one he carried the basket of food
she had packed that morning. "It would seem that in my haste
I carried off your nooning. I trust you found enough to make
up for it—"

"We did," she returned tartly. But then she, too, smiled and
added, "Better fare than was in that, Sector-Captain."

"No." He corrected her. "Not Sector-Captain. I have retired—
there is no one here to command, nor will there be. I am Griss
Lugard, and I own Butte Hold. But I am no commandant of any
new Security force. That will not be seen again on Beltane." His
tone, so light at first hail, was now serious, as if he uttered a
warning rather than gave an explanation of his presence. Then
his mood changed again, and his smile returned. "What think
you of my hold?" The question was not asked alone of Annet
but of all of us.

"I am afraid that we made too free, though you did say that the open rooms were for exploration," I spoke up. Best to have it clear that we had lighted on one of his possessions that he might not want to have common knowledge—the com system. "We activated the calls—"

But he did not lose his smile. "Did you now? And they worked? How well?"

Could it be true that he had not tried out the system for himself, that he had no curiosity about what could be a spy network across the sectors, did he want or need one?

"It worked. We got a little of your meeting with the Committee." Let him know the worst at once. If he then wanted to fire us out for meddling, well, we perhaps had that coming to us.

"My eloquence, which did not move mountains of prejudgment, eh?" Again he did not seem disturbed but rather as if he had known all along about our eavesdropping, though I did not see how that could be possible.

Unless—could he have wanted us to do just as we had done? Again—for what purpose? I guessed, however, that would be one question he did not want asked or answered.

Then Pritha stood a step or two nearer to him and looked directly up into his repaired face.

"We saw something too—"

"In the Committee room?" Still in that undisturbed voice.

"No. Vere said it was in one of the old security posts. There was a wart-horn sitting in a chair—acting—acting as if it were a man!"

"What!" For the first time his serenity was ruffled. "What do you mean?"

"We got the visa-screen working," I explained. "Picked up Reef Rough post. The thing was crouched in a chair in the com room, looking straight at the screen. It was just a coincidence, but a rather startling one."

"It must have been," he agreed. "But if the screen worked at its end, too, it must have been just as astounded, don't you think, Pritha?" He had remembered her name out of the mass introduction of the morning. "I don't believe we need fear an invasion of wart-horns—not wart-horns."

But refugees were different, I thought to myself. For all his surface unconcern, Griss Lugard was inwardly uncommitted to Beltane ways.

For the rest of that day, though, one would not have believed so. Annet was won over as easily as the rest of the Rovers. I think even Gytha's curiosity about the Forerunners was appeased by Lugard's flow of talk. He spoke freely of setting up a new type of Reserve wherein he intended to study native wild life, applying certain techniques he had learned off-world. He would not be working with mutant animals but with norms. And the stories and projects he talked of were engrossing enough so that we could believe he intended just such a life as he outlined.

He brought out his pipe once more, and the notes he drew from it, if they enchanted birds and beasts, could enthrall men also, for while he piped, we listened, and there was no idea of the passing of time until he put it aside with a laugh.

"You pay my poor music high honor, friends. But night comes with lengthening shadows, and I believe questions will be asked if you continue to linger here—"

"Vere!" Annet jumped to her feet. "It's almost sunset! Why, we've been here hours! I am sorry, Griss Lugard." She stumbled a little over saying his name. "We have imposed upon you far too long."

"But, Gentle Fem, it has not been any imposition. The Butte is lonely. A welcome for your guesting here, all of you, is ever ready. There will be no private latch upon this door." He reached one hand to his right and touched the portal with his fingertips, as if so to impress upon us his invitation.

"We can truly come again?" Gytha demanded. "When?"

He laughed. "Whenever you like, Gytha. All and any—whenever you like."

We said our good-bys and thanks. But I wondered as I set the hopper toward Kynvet if we would ever return to the Butte. Lugard's stand before the Committee would give them no good opinion of him, and Ahren and his colleagues would perhaps be now of the belief that close association with an ex-officer would corrupt their youth.

To my surprise, however, there were no comments made on Lugard's argument with the now rulers of Beltane. Some questions were asked concerning the day's activities. I did not think it was deception not to mention our inadvertent eavesdropping. And for once the unity of the Rovers was an aid, since they seemed to have decided among themselves that this was to be a *hold* as far as the adults were concerned. They were free enough on all else, talking a lot of Lugard's project on studying the wildlife of the waste. My own instinct was to question this, but he had already given it as the reason for wanting the Butte.

"So he asked you to return," Ahren commented when Gytha was done. "But you must not take advantage of his courtesy, daughter. He is here on a special grant—"

"Special grant!" I could not suppress that exclamation.

"Oh, yes. It is not at all what we suspicioned. He is, of course and unfortunately, apt to look at matters from the point of view of the Services, but he has severed all relationship with the forces. I gather his injuries made such severance mandatory. Now he is an accredited settler-ranger—with an archaeology grant into the bargain!"

"Forerunners!" Gytha cried with a triumphant glance at me. "I was right—"

But her father shook his head. "Not Forerunners, no. There was never any trace of such here. But before the war Lugard did find some odd remains in one of the old lava caves. There was no time for investigation thereafter—the universal madness had already burst. So the find remained unexamined since Lugard himself was drafted off-world before he could make any concise explorations. There had been a collapse of a cave roof that sealed off the portion he was interested in. Now that he is free, he has returned. Since we will no longer have a garrison here, he claimed Butte Hold and a section of lava lands for pay due him and was given the grant. He has entered that in the port records. I gather that it will take him some time to locate the portion he is eager to find. There have been further subsidences of the land thereabouts, and it may be he will never be able to uncover it again. Now, Vere"—he spoke directly to me—"I do not want the children to be a disturbance to Lugard. Poor man, he has had much to suffer. We cannot be impatient with his views. He has lived with violence so long that he expects to find it everywhere. If he wishes for company—perhaps that of younger people—" Now he looked thoughtful and added, "Did he say aught of what was done before the Committee this afternoon? Make some comment on the decision?"

"What decision, Father?" asked Annet, though I think she guessed the answer as quickly as I did—perhaps because it was more in keeping with her own views.

"It has been decided to extend the offer of friendship and homeland to the refugees," Ahren said a little impatiently before he returned to his main interest. "Lugard said nothing of this? Made no comments?"

I was able to answer no truthfully, for he had not to us.

"I told you." Gytha was inclined to be impatient when she was caught up in some idea of her own. "He talked about animals, and he said we could come again. And he piped—"

"Well enough. Yes, I see no harm in your going to the Butte again, but you will await some specific invitation from Lugard. On the other hand, Vere, you will go there tomorrow with a message from the Committee. We wish to affirm certain matters so there may be no misunderstandings later."

What the message was, I was not told. But I thought perhaps I knew part of what must be on the tape I took to the Butte the next morning. And when I handed it to Griss Lugard, the eyebrow on the normal side of his face twitched up and his wry smile curled.

He had crawled out from under a complicated piece of machinery I did not recognize, though it bore a small resemblance to a cultivator, save that where it should have sprouted a plow nose, this had an arm, now folded under, with a sharp point at its apex. And there were moving belts along its left side with bucket-shaped pockets.

Lugard flipped the roll of tape from one hand to the other, still smiling. "Official cease and desist?" But it seemed he asked that question more of himself than of me. "Or official grants to do as I will? Well, I suppose I better read so I can answer. What do you think of my monster here, Vere?" He seemed in no hurry to read his tape but now held it in one hand while, with the other, he traced along that belt of buckets, some upright, others reversed where the belt turned under. "Excavator." He answered my unasked question. "Made for this country—see her creep-treads? But still anyone mounting her is going to have a rough ride back there." He nodded to the lava lands.

"Then you *are* going to dig out a cave?" I do not know why I had continued to believe that Gytha's story of Forerunner treasure and Ahren's of archaeological exploration had seemed to me a screen. Had there really been a find of artifacts of some race preceding us on Beltane?

"Dig out a cave? But of course, probably more than one. It's all in my charter, boy." But I thought he gave me a quick, measuring glance as if he wondered now about me as I did about him. "She needs a good overhaul—has been laid up too long, though this was meant for hard labor under difficult conditions. Look her over, if you wish." He went into the hold with the tape.

Though I had never seen an excavator of this type before, I could understand most of the functions of the machine. The spearpoint on the now folded arm must be used to chip away at obstructions, the bucket band carrying the debris away from the work area. There were also two more attachments laid out on a plasta sheet, both smeared with preservative. One was a borer, the other a blower, both intended, I deduced, to fit on the end of the arm now carrying the pick.

It was a relatively small machine, meant to be handled by one man, mounted on elastic treads that should see it through the lava country. And it should be a very efficient tool. I wondered what other machines had been stored at the Butte. Lugard must have been owed a vast amount of back pay to gain all this. Or else there was another answer. If conditions off-world were as chaotic as he described, perhaps somewhere a bureaucrat saw no reason to keep on his books a hold on Beltane and had been ready to sign it away—perhaps even for some private consideration Lugard could offer him?

"So they did it, made their stupidly blind choice." Lugard came up behind me as I surveyed the excavator.

"You mean let the refugees in? But they may not be the menace you think them."

Lugard shrugged. "Let us hope so. Meanwhile, I shall make no attempt to corrupt innocent young minds with my off-world pessimism."

"Ahren gave you that warning?"

He smiled but with little humor. "Not in so many words, no, but it is implied. I am to be a responsible citizen, well aware of my duties as well as my privileges. Was there anything said about the children not coming again?"

"Just a warning to Gytha not to intrude if you were busied with your own affairs."

Now his smile was less of a grimace. "Good enough! And I'll play fair in return—no more warnings. I could not convince them even if I used a ply drug probably. They're as set in their own processes as that lava flow is glued to the mountain over there."

"They think the same of you," I commented.

"Which they would. But bring the children, Vere, if they want to come. The Butte is lonely sometimes. And they have quick minds. They might be far more of an aid than a hindrance."

"What are you hunting for?" I dared to ask then.

"I suppose some would say treasure."

"Forerunners really?" My disbelief must have shown. He laughed.

"No, I don't think Forerunners, though we cannot rule out any possibility until we uncover the ice cave—always supposing I can locate it again. Ten years—such as I have spent—is a long time, and there have been changes in the land, too—several landslips and cave-ins."

"What about this ice cave?" I persisted.

"We were exploring with the idea of developing storage centers," he said. "Time was running out. We knew we might be at war shortly. And then there was always a chance that Beltane would not be safely behind any so-called battle lines but right out in a fleet blast. We needed hidey holes then, or thought we did. Lava caves run like tunnels. We opened several new ones and were exploring them. The squad I commanded found ice and things in it, enough to show that we weren't the first to think of storing down there. There were supplies frozen in. But we had to close it off in a hurry. Security wanted no poking around at a critical time."

"Gytha found the story in an old news tape."

Lugard nodded. "Yes—men talk. Rumor got out. So your father decided to make as innocuous a tale as he could. We admitted a find and said it was sealed pending the arrival of off-world experts. Then we really sealed the whole section. I figure it will take some work to open it up now, perhaps more than is feasible."

"But if conditions now off-world are so bad—"

"Why do I want to go treasure hunting? Well, I have all the time in the world now, Vere. And I have no occupation. There is this equipment waiting to be used, and curiosity is nibbling at me, biting pretty sharply at times. Why not? Even if I am never able to find that cave again, or if I do, no one is going to be interested in my discovery except myself—but that is enough. Unless you and the children will—"

I was. There was no denying the surge of excitement in response to Lugard's story. And if he told the Rovers, there would be no holding them back. Help or hindrance, they would swarm to the Butte.

"So, let me get this old pick-rock to working and we're off—" He went to his knees and then lay flat to crawl under the excavator. "Meanwhile, if the children want to come, bring them, any time."

I repeated that invitation to Ahren when I returned to Kynvet, and to my surprise, he was receptive to the idea that the Rovers might visit the Butte and take part in Lugard's search. So in the weeks that followed, we did that several times. Once or twice Annet also joined us, always bringing food of her own to trade with Lugard for off-world supplies, an exchange that satisfied them both. In those weeks the refugees, having landed their ship, not at the port but well to the north in a spot they selected, settled quietly to their own affairs. Since most of our people were long conditioned to be concerned only with their work, there was little visiting between any of the settlements and the refugee camp. They came into port now and then, made requests for medical aid or supplies, and tendered in turn off-world products, some of which were eagerly welcomed by the sector people. It would seem that Lugard had been indeed wrong.

That Lugard himself would have some contact with the off-worlders I should have foreseen, though knowing his estimation of them, I was surprised to find a flitter, definitely not one from the port, on the landing space by the Butte when I brought the hopper in one morning. As it happened I was alone, for which I was glad, since, had there been any witnesses to carry the tale of what happened—

Lugard was at the door of the Butte, but he held no pipe in his hands. One hand swung idly at his side as he faced the two men standing before him; the other rested only inches away from a weapon leaning against the door, one that was not a conventional stunner.

The men both wore shabby tunics that had been part of uniforms, and their deep tans said they were out of space. They kept empty hands ostentatiously in sight, as if in no way wishing to alert Lugard.

I felt in the side rack of the hopper and loosed the stunner. Holding it in hand, I dropped out, to walk across the sand, my soft woods boots making no sound. But Lugard saw my coming.

"Good guesting—" He raised his voice in the Beltane greeting.

"High sun and a fair day," I returned. The men turned in a swift movement, as if they had been drilled. I fully expected to see weapons facing me, but their hands were still empty. They stared at me blank-eyed. I was sure that neither would forget me and that they had quickly summed up my potential in relation to the scene.

"The answer is no, Gentle Homos." Lugard spoke now to them. "I have no need for aid in my work here—save what is offered by the settlers. And I have no wish to be overlooked while I work either."

The taller of the two shrugged. "It was only a thought," he said. "We believed we might help a fellow veteran—a mutual-aid pact—"

"Sorry—no!" Lugard's voice was cool and final.

They turned and went, without a backward look. But still I felt a need to hold the stunner ready. I had never used even that defense save to control a man in such a temper as to unleash violence. But what I sensed emanating from the two now climbing into the flitter made a chill crawl between my shoulders. If I had been conditioned to nonviolence by my childhood training, then in that moment the conditioning cracked under an inheritance from generations of fighting ancestors. I could smell the cold promise of trouble.

"What did they want?" I asked when the flitter lifted in an upsurge that blew sand spitefully around us and into the half-open door to the hold.

"According to their story, employment." Lugard's fingers closed about the weapon he had had on display. He looked down at it, and his mouth was set. "We could not have expected they would not hear the treasure story—"

"And they may be back, with reinforcements?" I asked. "With you here alone—"

But at that Lugard laughed. "This is a Security hold, remember? I have devices to activate, if I wish, that will close this tight against anything they can bring up. No, this was just a try-on.

But I tell you, Vere, when the Committee invited them in, they opened the door to night, whether they believe it or not. Now, what can I do for you?"

I remembered my own news. "They're going to give me a post—in the Anlav Reserve."

"How soon?"

"Next month." It seemed to me that he had gone tense when I had told him of my luck, almost as if he feared to hear it. But why? This was, as he had known from all the talking I had done, the only future I had on Beltane. And to get the appointment now, with no more putting off because I had no formal schooling, was a triumph due to my continued persistence.

"Next month," he repeated. "Well, this is next to second Twelfth Day. Suppose on third Twelfth Day we do a little celebrating out here? The whole of the Rovers, plus Annet, if she can come, and urge her to it, Vere. I'm getting close to a find. Maybe we'll break through in time to make a double occasion of it."

I was distracted by his mention of a breakthrough. He would not say that unless he was sure of success, and again the excitement of a treasure hunt tingled in me. I agreed and spent some time working with him on a new machine, one meant to carry supplies but which he thought could be used to transport debris away from the promising cave he had just opened.

When I returned to Kynvet, I found again a convocation of transportation in the yard. But the drivers were already taking off, and Ahren waved me out of the hopper with haste, almost climbing over me to take his seat at the controls. I went in and looked to Annet for an explanation. For once she was not busy at any household task but stood at the window watching her father away, a worried look on her face.

"What has happened?"

"There are two more ships in orbit. They say they want to join the refugees—that they were promised a place here."

"I thought there was a treaty for one ship only."

"They say that is a mistake, that the first ship meant to treat for them all. The Committee is going to talk with their representatives. They came down in a lifeboat."

I thought of Lugard's disregarded warning, of the type of men who had visited the Butte, and of the undefended and now undefendable port. That sensation of danger I had had at Butte

Hold was again cold in me. But did Lugard know? And knowing, what could he do to defend people who would make no move to help themselves?

"Dr. Corson says they seem very reasonable," Annet continued. "After all, it is only just that they should want to be with their friends, and it could all be a misunderstanding. But they will have to put it to the full vote. Vere, what did Griss think of your news?"

I told her of the invitation, and she nodded. "I think we could go. If they have a full vote, all the sectors combining, it will come about then, so they won't mind what we do. It would be wonderful if he did find something and we had a chance to see it first!"

She did not mention the refugees again. It was as if she purposely avoided a subject too indelicate or unpleasant to discuss. But I knew that from that hour it was always in our minds.

FIVE

✵

Full vote was decided upon we learned, which meant that all the adults at Kynvet, as well as those of the other settlements, would gather at the port. And the Ahrens, as well as the parents of the other Rovers, welcomed our plan for going to the Butte. I gathered that this time there was divided sentiment over allowing the landing of new ships, and there might be protracted argument. Perhaps some of Lugard's warnings were beginning to make sense to the more suspicious members of the Committee. There were defenses at the port, but how much these had suffered from years of neglect no one really knew. And whether the handful of veterans who had returned could successfully activate them was also a question, not apparently that any move had been made to do this.

We left early in the morning of the third Twelfth Day—the whole of the Rover crew: Dagny and Dinan Norkot, Gytha, Sabian Drax, Emrys Jesom, Ifors Juhlan, Pritha, and Thad, as well as Annet. We carried our field kits since this was to be a real trip into the lava country; the hopper was loaded to the point that we had to make a low flight with many rest runs on the ground. Thus, it was past the ninth hour when we set down at the Butte. Lugard was waiting, sitting at the controls of what had once been a squad troop carrier. He was impatient, but he left the loading of our kits to us, going back to the hold himself for a long

51

moment just before we pulled out. When he returned, the leaves of the door clicked to behind him with so sharp a note that I turned my head just in time to see him slip the metal plate that locked them into the front of his coverall. So, did he fear that there might be visitors during our absence? I did not wonder at his precautions.

It might have been a tight fit in the squad carrier had we all been adults, but the children were reasonably comfortable as Lugard put it into gear and we rumbled out, Annet sharing the driver's seat with him. The rest of us were wedged in against too much jouncing by our kits and bundles already there. I looked among those and in the sling behind his seat for the weapon he had had. But the arm slings were all empty, and if he carried any such, they were hidden.

We all snapped on dark goggles as we crawled deeper into the knife-ridged land under the baking of the sun, which was reflected from the congealed flows. There was a crunched trail ahead twisting and turning upon itself, seeking the best passage. I thought that Lugard must have been this way many times before, though this was the first time he had taken us farther than past the first barriers of the forbidding territory.

Scrapes along outcrops suggested that some of those trips had been made in vehicles larger than the troop carrier in which we now rode or the excavator he had first put into working order, and I wondered what other types of machines he had brought into use. His determination suggested that, though he made his reports in an either-or manner, saying he thought he could find again his ice cave but was not entirely sure, he inwardly was more certain and was set upon proving it.

Now he took us along this very rough road at a pace that was the best a man might dare to hold in such broken terrain, as if there were a set hour for our arrival at the diggings and that it was important we not be late.

As he had earlier explained, and we knew, the lava caves were tubes that one could enter only through the collapse of some roof section. We passed now more than one promising hole. Twice we crossed a "bridge" spanning such a drop. There were bright lichens and a fringing of moss here and there. We had made so many turns in our trail that, had there not been a compass on board, I could not have truly said that the Butte now lay either behind or before us, for there was a deceptiveness to this land that I had never experienced before in the wilds of Beltane—as if the many frozen flows, cones, craters, and the like had been deliberately formed to confuse the eye and sense of direction.

Time was also difficult to judge. Under the heat of the sun in this hot bowl country, it seemed very long since we had left the Butte. Yet when I looked at my watch, I discovered that we had been on our way less than an hour. We had seen no signs of life, but then the constant crunch-crunch made by our own progress would warn away any animals that chose such a waste for their homes or hunting grounds.

We rounded at last a broken cone, which had the height of a steep-sided hill, and saw that the tracks led straight to a gap, above which was the skeleton frame of a derrick. Lugard pulled up beside that opening.

He had a small platform to lower into the hole and suggested that I go down with Thad as the first to embark, while he worked the lift.

I was not a speleologist and took my place somewhat gingerly on that unsteady surface, Thad facing me, our fingers interlaced on the safety cords, a pile of kits and one of Lugard's bundles between our feet. We spun down, and it was a sensation I was glad lasted no longer than it did. The light was dim and not dark; yet the murk arose to engulf us as if we were being swallowed up by some great beast.

It was cooler, a welcome relief from the parching of the sun without. I remembered that air movement underground was slow, and within a few feet of the entrance of any cave the temperature falls to that of the walls. Lugard had suggested we bring overtunics for that very reason, and now, shivering, I could see why.

The platform made several trips, bringing two passengers and kits and supplies on each descent. I wondered at the number of boxes and bundles Lugard sent down, since there were not only those from the troop carrier, but also some from a pile waiting at the mouth of the cave.

At last he swung over and down by himself, not drawing up the platform but using a rope with such ease as showed he had done the same before, while the platform remained on the floor of the cave. I suspected he wanted it so as a means of protection. He had not mentioned any return of the refugee-ship people, but he might be taking precautions against surprise. However, I was also certain he would not have brought the children here had he believed there was any real danger. Only, what is danger? We were to learn the degrees of that without warning.

Once below, Lugard switched on a beamer to reveal the road for us. Caves acted as cold traps in winter. Air settled to the lowest levels there to leave unending frost upon rock surfaces. Lugard was searching for an ice cave, and our path grew colder as we drew away from the entrance.

We had gone only a few paces in when Lugard shot the beamer ray toward the roof. Untidy masses were plastered there against the walls only a handbreadth from the ceiling. We saw restless movement.

"Westerlings!" cried Gytha.

Long-billed avian heads swayed or bobbed up and down. Westerlings they were, in nests of bits of withered stuff and mud. They were night flyers, mainly noted for the action that gave them their name—their flocks flew almost always from east to west when aroused from feeding.

But their nest colony was set close to the door into the open, and we were soon past them in the long bore that was the cave. This descended, not abruptly but at an angle, which did not make walking too difficult. I looked around for some signs that Lugard's machines had been at work here. But there were no tread marks on the floor, no scrapes on the walls.

At his asking we made use of the only aid he seemed to have imported into this stone tunnel—a small, treaded traveling cart, loading it with all the bundles he had brought down. But our packs we backed ourselves. Again I wondered at the reason for the pile of supplies, if supplies these were.

We had journeyed for perhaps an hour when Lugard halted and suggested a rest. He himself pulled the bundles from the cart, piled them against the wall, and turned to face back as if it was now in his mind to return for those we had left. But he never had a chance.

There was a wave of vibration through the walls of the cave, in the solidified layer of lava under our boots, giving one the sickening sensation that the world one had always accepted as solid and secure was that no longer. I heard a shrill scream and saw in the glow of the beamer wide frightened eyes and mouths opening on more cries of alarm. A small body lurched against me, and I instinctively threw out my arm to draw Ifors closer, while his fists balled wads of my coverall and he clung to me as if I were his only hope of protection.

A second shock came, even worse than the first. Lava chunks broke loose, rattling and banging. I cowered, deafened by the sound, while dust arose about us in choking clouds.

"Out—" I saw Annet staggering for the way down which we had come. She pushed before her one of the children and dragged another. A taller figure, which was Lugard, tried to intercept her, but, intentionally or not, she eluded him and wavered on. "Out! This way, children!"

"Get her!" Lugard rounded on me with that order just as a third shock wave hit with force enough to send me crashing against one of the walls, Ifors still clutching me in a hold that could not be easily broken. I saw Lugard go down, while the beamer he must have put on the floor went into a weird dance as if the surface under it were rising and falling in quick, panting breaths. There were more falling chunks, some of them striking the supplies he had just unloaded.

With one hand I fumbled with the buckles of my pack and managed to jerk at it until I was free of its burden. I saw Thad sitting down, a stunned expression on his face.

"After her," Lugard panted. "The entrance—loose rocks—it may cave in—" He was struggling to get to his feet, but the last tremor had caused the bundles to land on top of him, and his lameness was to his disadvantage.

I pried Ifors' hold from my coverall, and the fabric tore as I tried to loose the shocked boy. "Thad! Take Ifors!" With a last rip I held him away from me and pushed him toward Thad, who was getting dazedly to his feet. The others were all there, Gytha, on her knees by the beamer, setting it steady again, Pritha in a small ball beside her, Emrys shaking his head and pawing at his eyes with both hands, Sabian—Only the twins and Annet were gone.

To be caught in a collapse of the roof! I could share Annet's fear, but if she were running straight into danger—and Lugard knew the ways of these burrows best—I could not run, not over this rough flooring, but using my belt torch, I went at the best pace I could manage, back along the trail, calling Annet's name as I hurried.

She had not gone so far that I could not overtake her. But what had halted her was a fall of rock that almost closed the tunnel. Far above we could see a small patch of sky. As I reached her side, she was pressed against the wall, looking up at the freedom out of her reach, the twins in her arms, their faces hidden against her.

"Back! Lugard says it is dangerous here—the roof may come down!" I took a good grip on her arm. She tried to twist away, but my strength was greater than hers, though I could not drag her more than a pace or two back. And I feared a second collapse might crush us before we were beyond that danger point.

"Out—" She tried to pull in the opposite direction, even though the way was blocked. "We have to get the children out!"

"Not that way." I pinned her to the wall with my shoulder, my face only inches from hers as I summoned her to reasoned thinking again. "Lugard says it is dangerous. He knows these caves, and there are other ways in and out—"

However, I wondered at that. If the tackle for the platform had fallen—and surely such shocks had unseated it—then how could we get out, even if the fall choking the tunnel was loose and easy to clear? Someone would have to climb that shaft and see about the lowering ropes. And I knew who, though the thought of it made me sick, as my head for climbing was not good. Best get back to Lugard now and discover if there was another exit, one less demanding.

"Lugard!" Annet almost spat the name at me. "He had no right to bring us here—to endanger the children!"

"I suppose he could foresee this quake?" I demanded. "But we must get back. It is deeper and so safer back there." But that was another bit of reasoning of which I was not sure.

Reluctantly, she started back. I picked up Dagny, whose small body was convulsed with shudders. She was not crying but breathing in gasps, her eyes wide in her small face, clearly so deep in fear that she was hardly conscious of her surroundings. Annet half supported, half led her brother.

We had not yet reached the others when there came another series of tremors. We crouched against the wall, the two children between us, sheltered by our bodies as much as possible. Rocks rolled, not only from overhead, but also down the slope of the cave. It was a miracle that none of them struck us. After a last jar there was again a period of quiet, and a new fear stirred in my mind. Once this had been volcanic country. Could such shocks as the earth had just suffered open some fissure on inner fires and set the cones to blazing again? Annet was so right in her instinctive flight for the surface, and the quicker we *were* out the better.

"Vere! Annet!" Our names echoed hollowly up the corridor of the cave, the sound distorted and booming.

I got cautiously to my feet, almost fearing that that small movement could bring a return of the tremors, so unsteady had our world suddenly become. "Here!" I answered, my voice hoarse from the dust drying my mouth and throat.

Under my urging Annet got up also. I once more held Dagny while she led the boy, and we took one cautious step after another on the down slope. Thus, we gained the halting place. Lugard sat on the cart, his right leg stretched out before him as he rubbed at it with both hands, working with a grim purpose and determination. He looked up as we came, and I saw a flash of relief in his eyes.

"Aid kit." He did not leave off rubbing his leg to point to where that lay in the tossed bundles and abandoned kits, but rather indicated it with his chin. "Give each of them one of the green tablets—they're in shock."

He must have already so aided the others who needed it, for Ifors sat relaxed with his back against a bale and Pritha drank quietly from a canteen, while Thad was at work straightening out the mess of tangled boxes, Emrys helping him and Sabian standing by. Gytha knelt by Lugard, holding another canteen ready for his use.

Annet crossed to stand directly before him. "How do we get out of here?" she demanded. "The children—"

"Are probably safer right here than on the surface now—" he told her.

"In here?" she shot back incredulously. "With rocks coming down on their heads?"

"It's safer farther on. We'll move now," he said.

"A quake—or quakes such as these—" I knelt beside him to ask my own question in a whisper. "What about renewed volcanic action?"

"Quakes?" Lugard repeated. Then his mouth tightened in a

grimace that might have been caused by pain in the limb he nursed. "You poor—" He checked himself and began again. "Those were not quakes."

"No?" Annet squatted on her heels, finding it too difficult to see eye to eye with Lugard since he did not rise. "Then what were they?"

"Distributors."

For a moment I groped in the dark, and I do not think that Annet understood at all. Then the years-old meaning of the term struck home, and I think I gasped. I could have shuddered as deeply as Dagny was still doing against my shoulder.

Distributors—an innocuous name for death and such destruction as Beltane had never seen, though such had made deserts of worlds as peaceful as this one.

"The refugees?" My mind leaped to the only explanation.

"Just so." Lugard paused in his rubbing. Now he flexed his knee slowly and carefully, and he could not conceal a catch of breath when he set foot to floor.

"What do you mean?" Annet's voice rose, and Gytha drew closer. That stopped the work of his labor gang, and they all listened. "Distributors?"

"Bombs." Thad answered before Lugard could. I think that at that moment Lugard was angry with himself for revealing the truth, though it was indeed best that at least we older ones knew who and what we now faced.

"Bombs!" Annet was entirely incredulous now. "Bombs—here on Beltane? Why? Who would do such a thing?"

"The refugees," I told her. "What chance—?" I wanted to ask the rest of that badly but knew better than to blurt it out, though at least Thad, as I could read the expression on his face, was already close behind me in thought. No, it was best not to think now of what might be happening up there and to whom. This was the time to concentrate on those locked in with me and the responsibility I had to the group I had so trustingly led into peril.

I said directly to Lugard, "You knew—or suspected?"

Slowly, he nodded. "I suspected from the first. I was sure last night."

"The com link?"

Again he nodded. And the arm I held about Dagny tightened until she stirred and gave a soft cry, which was part moan. If

Lugard had had warning of attack, then he had deliberately brought us here because—

He might have been reading my thoughts. "Because this is the safest place on Beltane—or in Beltane—here and now. I told you we opened passages for shelters here before the war. I've been reopening those. If I had had more time, if those poor benighted fools of the Committee had only believed me—we could all have been unharmed. As it is, *we* are safe—"

"No!" Annet's hands were at her mouth, smearing the dust across her chin and cheeks. "I don't believe it! Why would they do such a thing? We gave them a home—"

"They may have only wanted a base," Lugard replied. There was a weariness in his voice, as if he had been driving himself to this point and that now, when his worst fears had been realized, he could no longer hold to such determined energy. "Also—perhaps the vote went against the two new ships, and those refugees were prepared to take what was not given."

"Where do we go now?" I broke the silence that followed.

"On." Lugard nodded toward the passage. "There's a shelter base down there."

I expected Annet to protest, but she did not, only got slowly to her feet and went for the aid kit. Lugard held out his hand.

"Give me a boost," he ordered. "We can use the cart for quite a while yet. Then we'll have to pack in."

"These are supplies?"

"Yes."

I helped him up, and he leaned against me for a long second or two before he tried to put his weight on his leg. Apparently, he could do that, and he took a limping step or two onward. But that it cost him more than just effort I deduced by a jerk of muscle beside his mouth on the untreated side of his face.

While Annet tended the twins, we all set about loading the cart, though I thought that before long we would have to dump some of it and let Lugard, and perhaps the twins, ride.

Thad and I shared the pull rope, and Gytha moved forward quickly and took up Lugard's hand to settle it on her shoulder, providing him with a crutch of willing flesh and bone and redoubtable spirit. Annet carried Dagny, who lay against her shoulder with closed eyes as the sedative worked, while Emrys and Sabian

between them guided Dinan along, and Ifors stumbled beside the
cart, one hand on the lashings that fastened its cargo.

We proceeded with many halts, and at last I persuaded Annet
to lay Dagny on the cart. But in turn she took one of the bundles
from the top. She did not try to argue any more. However, I
thought that she still did not believe Lugard, and she must be
raging inside to be out of the caves to prove him wrong.

Twice we crossed mouths of other caves splitting from the road
we had chosen, as if the long lava floods had divided. But Lugard
always nodded to the main tunnel. He was sweating, the trickles
of moisture down his face washing runnels through the dust. Now
and then he breathed shallowly through his mouth. But it was I
who called the halts, and he never made any complaint when we
trudged on again.

My watch told me we had been two hours underground when
we made a more lengthy pause and ate. I saw Annet stare down
at the food she unwrapped and guessed at her thoughts. High
among them must be disbelief that *this* could be happening, had
happened since this morning, when she had set together those
rounds of bread with a preserve of irkle fruit—fruit she had
stewed herself and stored in the cupboard at Kynvet.

Did Kynvet exist now?

Lugard made only a pretense of eating, though the children
were hungry and wolfed down all we gave them. I wondered if
we should hold back a portion. How long must we stay in these
caverns? Lugard had brought supplies—food, water—but—

And if we went out, what would we face? Suppose the refugees
had finished off—though my mind shied from that, and I had to
force myself to face a very grim guess—the sector people? Would
we fare any better were we to turn up after the initial massacre?
Yet Lugard must believe we had a chance for survival or he would
never have labored so.

He was fumbling in the front of his tunic, having set aside most
of his food untouched. Now he brought out his pipe. Beside me
Annet moved and quickly checked. Perhaps she had been about
to protest. But if so, she thought better of it.

So in the depths of that cave, with our world reft from us,
Lugard played. And the magic he wove settled into us as a reassuring flood of promise. I could feel myself relaxing; my whirling
thoughts began to still, and I believed again. In just what I could

not have said, but I did believe in the rightness of right and that a man could hope and find in hope truth.

I shall always remember that hour, though I cannot now draw back into mind the song Lugard played. The feeling it left in me I do know, and regret I shall not have it to warm me again, for of all we lost on that day, we had still to face the greatest blow from what men call fate.

It began when Lugard put down his pipe and we awoke out of the spell he had woven to soothe us. There was another sound, and it had nothing to do with music.

Lugard's head went up and he cried out, "Back against the walls!"

We moved as if his shout had been a blaster aimed at us. I hurled Annet, Dinan with her, back and swept up Gytha and Emrys to join them, while across I saw Thad, jerking Ifors and Pritha, stumble toward the opposite wall.

"Dagny!" Annet screamed.

She had been lying asleep on the roll of blankets by the cart, and now she was out of reach—out of ours, but not Lugard's. I saw him lurch forward and his arm crook about the little girl. He swept her back and away from himself. But when he would have followed, his leg gave way under him, and he sprawled on his face, while the glow of the beamer made it all clear. There was a rushing rock slide down the core of the cave, not directly from overhead. And before I could move to pull him free, that slide swept over and about him as might the flood of a river in high spate.

SIX

✳

The same river of rock had knocked out the beamer, and we were choking in the dark, coughing and hacking in the dust. For a moment I could do no more than lean against the wall and try to ease my tortured lungs. Then somehow I got my belt light on. In the place of the wide rays of the beamer, it was only a small thrust against the dark. And what it showed made me want to switch it off again.

Our cart, which had been left in the middle, must have acted in part as a dam, though the force of the sweep had carried it on. And in the debris that had piled up behind it—Lugard—he must be caught in that!

"Gytha! Dinan! Thad!" Annet's voice, so husky that the names could barely be distinguished, rang out from beside me. She was calling the roll.

One by one they answered. But I was already at the pile of rocks and Thad not long in joining me. We had to work with what seemed painful slowness since the stuff moved and we were afraid of starting a second slip. Then Gytha joined us, also lighting her belt torch, and Emrys. Lights flashed on, giving us a good sight. Annet took from me the stones I freed to put to one side, and I saw each of us had such a coworker.

We made no sounds except the coughs that hurt the throat, and I knew that all were doing as I did, listening with both fear and hope gnawing at them. We had to go slowly when there was such a need for speed.

It was part of the cargo of the cart that had protected him from an instant crushing death we discovered when we had him free. By some chance, two of the bundles had fallen on either side of his body, providing a part defense.

I hardly dared to move him from where he lay face down. He made no sound, and I was certain he was gone, but we cleared a space about him, and Annet quickly unrolled blankets, spreading them out as long as his dust-covered body. Somehow we got him over, face up, on that small easing.

His eyes were closed, and there was a dark trickle from the corner of his mouth. I am no medico, my knowledge being only enough to provide first aid in an accident. He had broken bones and, I was sure, internal injuries. Annet had the kit open. Luckily it lay close to the wall against which Lugard would have been safe had he not returned for Dagny. But there was little in that save what might alleviate pain for a short time. And to move him, even onto the cart, could kill him, but it could be our only chance to save him.

"Get the cart free," I ordered Thad. "Then strip it down."

He nodded and shooed the other boys before him to that task. Annet spilled some water to sponge Lugard's face from her canteen onto a strip of cloth she tore from an inner garment, and under her touch his eyes opened. I had hoped he would remain unconscious. Such hurts as he had taken must keep him in agony.

I saw his lips move and leaned over him. "Don't try to talk—"

"No—" He got that out as a whisper. "Map—inner seal pocket— get on—to safe quarters." Then his face went oddly slack, and his mouth fell loose, while the trickle from it became a dark froth, which Annet wiped away.

My hand felt for the pulse at his throat; I feared to try to touch his chest to hunt for heart beat. He was not gone—not yet.

Only I did not believe he could stand even lifting to the cart, and to carry him in a blanket would be worse. There were supplies ahead—he had mentioned that earlier. Suppose there were medical ones among those? Lugard had had all the stores of the Butte to plunder. In such there might be something—though one part of my mind told me that anything less than quick hospitalization at the port would not save him.

But you cannot sit and wait for death, not when there is the slimmest of fighting chances. Annet must have agreed with that, for she looked across to me.

"Take the map, go on. There may be things there—"

But to leave the rest—Again she read my indecision.

"It is the best. We cannot move him now. There may be a stretcher there—other things—"

"And if there is another rock fall?" I demanded.

"We can pull the blankets over there." She nodded to the side, her hands still busy with that patient washing away of the ever-gathering blood foam. "We shall have to do that much. And we shall stay there. We can't leave him here, and we can't wait forever. There has to be *something*—perhaps a better cart. You must try it, Vere."

We pulled Lugard a few inches at a time over to the wall. As gently as I could, I unsealed his stained tunic and took out a folded piece of plasta-mat. The lines on it caught fire from our lamps, and I saw it was drawn with cor-ink for use in limited light. But the branching passages on it were many, and it took me a moment's study to locate the tunnel that held us. Once I had traced that from our entrance point, I could see the path ahead running reasonably straight. And perhaps Lugard's secure place was not too far beyond.

Thad had found the beamer and set it up. It had been made for hard usage in the field, and after he had tightened a loose connection, it flashed on again. I took up one of the canteens, longing to drink but prudence warned me to endure the thirst as long as I could and conserve water, the more so as we found that the tank of liquid on the cart was leaking. Annet moved quickly to add what she could of its contents to all our canteens and began hunting around for other possible containers.

I stood for a long moment over Lugard before I left. He was still breathing, and as long as a man lives, there is hope. I clung to that as I went.

The beamer provided a beacon behind me for a space, but I did not turn to look at it. Then I came to one of those divisions of ways, and this time my fire-drawn map said not to stay on the main course but to take a new. Within moments I was in the dark and flashed on my belt torch.

Caves have their inhabitants, which vary with the depth,

moisture, content, and the like. I had seen in the labs some blind creatures taken out of this eternal dark. Beltane had once had a small biospeleology department, but when Yain Takuat had died, there had been no replacement for his specialty.

Only the creatures I had seen had come from the moist water-formed caves, while this was different country. I swept my light from side to side, hunting for any hint that this was not just dead rock. I would have welcomed a single slime trail, a single flatworm clinging to the roof overhead.

What my light did pick up was a curl of skin and bones rolled against the wall. I took a step closer. My first aversion was not justified—these were no human remains but the dried remnants of a wart-horn, one larger than I had seen before. But those lived in swamps. What was such doing here? Unless there was some outlet in the maze, leading to water, and the thing wandered in and became lost. That was reassuring in its way with the promise of water.

It was only a little way beyond that I came to where Lugard had said we could not take the cart, for here the floor of the tunnel, which had been sloping gradually all the way since we had left the surface, now gave way. There were a series of ledges—a giant staircase—to descend. I looked at it in despair. We could never get Lugard down unless we could find some aid—

I thought of a stretcher, even a section of crate or box. Could he be lashed tightly to that and lowered? When one is desperate, one can always improvise. Now I swung from one ledge to the next, my belt torch showing a wild scene of fallen rubble and bad footing below.

The air here was colder, far more so with every ledge I passed. I found it hard to lay hand to the surfaces of the rock, for there was frost on some of them. Then I reached the bottom and picked a way among heaps of fallen scree. There was a path here. Heavy objects had been dragged along, leaving a road. I wondered at the energy Lugard had expended. Or were these signs left by those who had once thought to make an underground war retreat before Butte Hole had been closed?

This lower cave widened out from the narrow end where I entered. Then my light picked out what was there, and I was startled into a full stop. There were structures, three of them, though my light could barely reach the end of the farthest one.

Between them were stockpiles of boxes and crates. Lugard certainly could not have done all this. It was the remains of the plan never carried through.

Each of the buildings was walled with cor-blocks, which had probably been fused together on the spot. They each possessed a single door in one wall but no other openings. And the roofs were half arcs made of sheets of cor that had been welded into solid masses.

If they had been locked, Lugard must have opened them. Perhaps the same master key that controlled the Butte door also worked here. The first I explored must have been intended for a headquarters, perhaps also a com center. The divisions in it did not reach the ceiling but arose about seven feet from the floor to make three rooms of the structure. One had two desks, a rank of files, and the board of a small computer. The next had banks of com boards almost as elaborate as those in the Butte. I tried to activate one. I do not know what I hoped for—perhaps to reach some answer on the surface—but here all was dead. The third and last "room" had four bunks and very simple living arrangements—by the look never put to use.

The next building held more bunks in one large room and at its end a smaller compartment with a cooking unit and water taps. I turned one, and there was a thin trickle from it, dripping down into a cor-basin. Water, anyway.

In the third building was a bewildering array of control boards, not coms I was sure. Perhaps they were meant to aim and fire missiles or destructs—weapons that might never have been installed on the surface at all, or if they were, had been dismantled when the last of the Security forces were ordered into space.

I went back to the bunkhouse. One of the light metal cot frames there was the only possible stretcher I could find. It took me some time to loosen it from the support stanchions. I looked at my watch. It must be well after nightfall now—not that day or night had any meaning here. At least the buildings had been insulated against the cold and could be made warmer if we could use the heating units. We had a far safer refuge here than I had hoped for.

The bunk frame made an awkward burden to pack, and I had found no rope we could use for making Lugard fast to it or for lowering it back down the cliff. Perhaps we could cut blankets into strips to serve. The climb up the ledges pulling the frame with me was a struggle that left me panting and ready to take a long rest when I at last reached the top. Only there was no time for that now.

At last I dragged it behind me, changing hands time and time again as my fingers cramped about the end rod. It scraped and banged along the rock, making enough din to give one an aching head. I had to stop again and again to flex my fingers free of cramp lest I lose the use of my hands. It was just too heavy to carry along and too large to drag well. Also it caught now and then on rough bits of rock, and I had to halt to free it, until the whole world shrank to my struggle with the stubborn thing and I could have gladly smashed it to bits with my bare hands.

I came out of the side tunnel and saw the light of the beamer. A black shadow ran toward me, and Thad came into the light of my own torch. He stared for a moment then hurried up to lay hands on the frame. I unhooked my fingers one by one and let him take it, and I staggered a little as I went.

"What's it like?" Thad asked.

"Good." I rasped hoarsely. "Lugard?"

"Still alive."

I had not dared to hope that would be the answer. But if he continued to hold to life and we could get him down to the lower cave—I had not hunted for medical supplies, but surely there would be some.

It was all I could do to make the gathering by the cart. I went to my knees there, breathing heavily, while Thad thumped the bunk frame flat on the rock.

Annet had covered Lugard, all but his face. She no longer wiped the dribble from his lips. That had stopped, and I could not guess whether that was a good or bad sign.

"Tie him on that." I made my idea as simple as I could. "Take him on the cart. But we will have to lower him to another cave. They had a Security base down there—even houses—"

"Houses?" she echoed. She held out to me an E-ration can from which she had just twisted the self-heating top. The smell of it was so good that I stretched out my hands, but my fingers were so numb that I would have dropped it had her grasp not continued. She held it to my lips, and I drank the rich contents, their warmth and refreshment bringing me out of the fog of fatigue.

"Installations in them," I said between gulps. "But there is a bunkhouse. We can camp out there."

Annet glanced down at Lugard. "He is unconscious—"

"Better so." It was the truth. We must handle him to get him on the bunk frame and to secure him there. I did not want to think what that might do to his broken body. Only I—we—had no choice. To go on gave him a slim chance; to stay, that was to do nothing but wait for the inevitable end. And there might be a second rock fall, though Annet assured me that nothing had threatened while I was gone.

We worked as best we could, lifting Lugard in the blanket, settling him on the bed frame, then winding about it all the strips Gytha and Pritha cut from our blankets, rendering him as immovable as possible.

The supplies, except for our own kits, we stacked to one side of the cave, but our packs we took with us. The frame we had slung on blanket straps that went about my shoulders and Thad's so we could lift him to the cart.

So we transported him at a slow pace, Annet and the children at the sides, the cart, with Thad and me to steady it, down the center. Gytha, with the beamer, was our fore-scout, and with such light it was easy to avoid the roughest bits. Yet all our straining could not make it really smooth going.

I was ridden by the need for haste; yet that we dared not attempt. The framework that held Lugard was balanced precariously on the cart, and the least shift, in spite of our efforts to steady it, might send it crashing to the rock.

We turned into the side that led to the lower cave. Annet came once to look into Lugard's face. There had been no sign he was conscious. I hoped he was not.

"We must get out. He needs help—Dr. Symonz at the port."

If there was still a Dr. Symonz and the port, I thought. But either she continued to hold stubbornly to the idea that Lugard was wrong in his story of bombing, or else she wanted to preserve hope for the children. I had no intention of trying to find out which. I was too busy trying to plan for that drop down the ledges.

"Look!" Emrys pointed to the withered carcass of the wart-horn. "What's that?"

"A wart-horn, silly," Gytha answered. "Probably got in here and was lost. But then he must have come from water—"

She made the same deduction I had.

"There's water below," I returned, "but it's piped in." But those pipes came from somewhere. And water could be a guide to the outer world.

We came at last to the drop, and Gytha swung the beamer down the slope to pick up in bright light and dark shadow all the roughness of that descent. I heard an exclamation from Annet.

"Down there! But we'll never be able to lower him—"

"We have to. I didn't have any luck finding ropes, though." I stared dully down that stairway of ledges, and threatening slope of scree at its foot. To go down and return—I did not know whether I had the strength. But Thad had the answer.

"Emrys, Sabian, uncoil what we found!"

At his order the two younger boys began to pull lengths from beneath their tunics. What they had when they spread it on the floor was no conventional rope that could be trimmed or broken, but strands of tungfors—the same alloy that was used to coat rocket tubes. These had been fashioned as chains, and there were hooks of the same durable metal at either end.

"Found 'em in the supplies we had to dump," Thad reported. "They what we need now?"

I could not have done better had I been able to pick and choose from a variety of equipment, and I said so as we laid them straight. They would reach from one ledge to the next, but whether we could take the strain of Lugard's weight for lowering I did not know.

"You go ahead with the children," I told Annet. "Thad, Emrys, Sabian, and I, we'll try to manage it. But I want you all safely down and out of the way first."

I could foresee that a single slip might rake us all from our feet and send us crashing, not only to our own peril, but also to that of anyone ahead. She might have protested, but then she looked at Dagny, whom she had carried most of that weary way.

"How? Yes, the pack harness!" She laid the little girl on the floor and began to shuck her own burden.

"I don't believe that—"

"I can do it!" She turned on me with some of the same fierceness she had shown when she tried to reach the surface after the bombing. And I could not deny her the effort. What strength I had left I must use for Lugard.

So we watched as they went over one by one—Gytha first, having shored up the beamer on the lip of the cliff to give light, taking Pritha's hand, cautioning her not to look down but only immediately before her; then Ifors; and last and very slowly, with Dinan between her and Ifors, Annet, Dagny made fast to her in the pack harness. Luckily, the ledges made a fairly easy descent, but the treacherous pile below troubled me more. I shivered with far more than the outer cold of that place as I watched them win, shelf by shelf, to the floor below.

Gytha was down, then the others—all but Annet, who moved slower and slower. By my own experiences in dragging the bunk frame, I could understand what wearied her. She rested for what seemed to me a very long time before she made the final drop into the scree.

Then they were all crawling through that. Emrys moved to loose the beamer. I shook my head.

"Leave that! We shall need all the light we can get."

"How do we go now?" Thad wanted to know.

I could see only one way—perhaps not the best, but the only one visible to me.

"Hook these, one end up here." I picked up one of the chains. "Other on the stretcher. One of us gets down to the ledge to steady it. I lower one line—you two the other."

Thad nodded. "Sabian to do the steadying."

Sabian was the smallest. We would need our major strength on the lowering. I looked to him.

"Think you can do it?"

"I don't know," he answered honestly. "Can't tell till I try, can I?" With that he slipped over to reach the surface of the first ledge and stood there, looking up, his eyes large and dark in a face that seemed unusually pallid by the beamer's glare.

We set the hooks in the frame at either end and tested their hold. The others we pounded into the rock beyond the lip and again tested. Then we slid the frame and its silent burden toward the lip and began what were the worst hours of my life.

It took us more than two hours to make that slow crawl down

since we paused on each ledge to test, to rest the strain in our shoulders and arms, to bend over Lugard and hear those painful bubbling breaths and know that we still dealt with the living and not the dead. I lost all measure of time as I had known it in a sane and normal world. This was time as some evil being might have conceived it as a special torture. During the last part I moved in a kind of thick fog, so that when we came to stable footing I collapsed, unable to do more than breathe shallowly. Nor were the other boys any better. Emrys lay limp at the side of the frame; Thad hunched at its other end. I heard a shuffle and then a thin cry of welcome.

"Annet!"

Something was pushed into my hands and, when I could not hold it, held then to my mouth. Again I sucked feebly, rather than drank, a hot mouthful of ration. I knew that such emergency food was laced with restoratives, but whether that could get me on my feet again now, I doubted.

In the end we staggered along while Annet, Gytha, Pritha, and Ifors made use of the blanket shoulder straps and carried the frame and Lugard ahead of us. I roused enough to put an arm about Emrys' shoulders and pull him up and to give some support to Thad. My shoulders and arms had gone numb. Now they began to ache, first dully and then with increasing pain.

We slipped and slid, though we never did quite fall, until we were past that treacherous pile and in the wider part of the cave. There was a blaze of light streaming from the door of the barracks, and to that we were drawn. I remember crossing its threshold, looking dully at the room—for the rest nothing at all.

When I awoke, I was lying on the floor, under me a pad that I had stripped from the bunk I had earlier dismantled. And I ached—how I ached!—as if my arms had been pulled from shoulder sockets, the bones of my spine put to such strain as no man could be expected to take.

Perhaps I made some sound. Even turning my head required painful effort. Annet's face hung over me, a face drawn with dark shadows beneath the eyes and a set to the lips I had never seen before.

"So, you're awake—" Her voice was sharp, and something in the tone brought the immediate past into focus.

I tried to sit up and found it an effort. She made no gesture to aid but sat back on her heels watching me with a kind of impatience in her tense position, as if she had been waiting too long for me to move.

I rubbed my hands across my face, felt the grit of rock dust between palm and cheek, and blinked.

"Lugard?"

"Is dead." She answered me flatly.

I think my first reaction was a kind of anger that all our struggle had been for nothing, almost anger at Griss that he should have slipped away when we had done what we could to keep him with us. And after that another thought grew. With Lugard gone, who did we have to turn to? As long as I had had the problem of getting him to this shelter, I had never looked beyond. There had been a kind of completion when we reached the foot of the cliff, as if our greatest struggle now lay behind. But that was not the truth.

Somehow I wobbled to my feet. Thad lay in a bunk to my left; beyond him, sharing another, were the two others who had aided in our ordeal on the ledges. From the back room where the cooking unit was installed, I heard the murmur of voices.

"Vere, you're awake!" I turned my head slowly. There was a feeling that if I tried any swift movement, I might fall apart. Gytha came out of the mess room.

She caught me by the arm. "Come on—supper is ready. You slept most of the day."

I yielded to her pull. Annet was on her feet, too, and when I staggered, she suddenly put out her hand to steady me.

"There is plenty of food, anyway," she said, as much to reassure herself, I thought, as me. "And the cook unit runs."

Perhaps the smells were not as enticing as the ones back in a Kynvet kitchen, but they seemed to me to be so at that moment.

SEVEN

I had to prop both elbows on the narrow table to steady my hands in order to raise a mug of steaming caff to my lips. As its warmth flowed down my throat, I awakened out of the daze of fatigue and not caring that had fallen on me at the bottom of the cliff. Annet sat down opposite me, her hands resting on the table top—lying I should have said, not resting, for there was such an aura of tension about her that her unease flowed across the surface dividing us.

"He was mad—he must have been—" she said flatly.

"You felt the tremors." I would not let her build vain hopes. I had seen the two refugees at the Butte, and I could and did believe that Lugard had overheard something on the com, enough to let him think we were fleeing actual danger. Far from being mad, I had come to suspect he had been perhaps the sanest man on Beltane when it came to foreseeing and assessing the future. But now—

"Did he regain consciousness before he—went?" I asked. If there were only something I—we—could use as a guide!

She shook her head. "He was breathing heavily. Then—all at once—that stopped. Vere, what are we going to do—if we can't get back the way we came?"

I put down the mug to bring out the map. Now I spread it flat on the table. In the steady light of the barracks, I was not so fully aware of the phosphorescence of its markings but they remained plain without that addition. From the entrance Lugard had found, I traced with a forefinger the path to our present camp, the huge lower cave. From that three passages spread. Two of them seemed to lead to surface outlets. But I remembered Lugard's saying that this whole section had been sealed by Security in the days before Butte Hold was closed. He had opened this way with hard labor—but he had not had time, I believed, to so deal with the others, even if he had wanted to.

There was no use in expecting the worst before it was proven, as I now said to Annet. She wanted us all to go as soon as we could. But I argued against further disappointment and perhaps shock for the younger children. Finally, it was agreed that I could try by the map both those passages.

But before I left, there was one more duty, and it was a hard one, perhaps more so for some of us than others. Ideally, one does not bear resentment for the dead, but I think Annet looked upon Lugard as a madman whose twisted fears had involved us in disaster. She would not have wished him dead, but she had no tears for him now. However, she shared with me the covering of his body by a plasta-sheet out of the stores. While we did so, something slipped from the blanket strips that had kept him secure during that dark journey I did not want to remember.

It crunched under my boot, and I picked up a shard of the pipe with which he had wrought his magic. It must have broken when he took his hurt. Now I searched and gathered up all the bits from the rock and tucked them carefully back under the edge of his tunic.

"Not Dagny," Annet said abruptly when we had it done. "Nor Pritha, nor—"

"Yes, Pritha." She spoke for herself. "And all of us, Annet, yes!" So in the end, Thad and I carried the stretcher back into the rubble by the descent. And the rest of them, save Dagny who still slept under sedatives, followed.

We could not dig in the rock, but we fitted the frame into a crevice and with our hands covered it, first with gravel we scooped up, and then with rocks, until we had built a recognizable mound. I wished for a laser so that I could mark the wall beyond. But, in spite of all that had been left here, we had found no weapons. We had only the stunners worn by Annet, Thad, and me.

Gytha dragged one last rock up and, with an effort, set it atop. I saw the shine of tear tracks on her cheek. "I wish—I wish we could have played the pipe. He—he was a gentle man, Vere."

Gentle was not an adjective I myself would have applied to Griss Lugard, but I remembered his ways with the children and knew that she saw him aright from her point of view. Suddenly, I was glad that this could be remembered of him, along with his courage and his belief that he must do what was to be done. That he did believe he had saved us, I had not the smallest doubt, let Annet think as she would.

Yet she, too, could not leave him so. She clasped one hand with Gytha, held the other to me, while I took one of Thad's, and he Emrys'—and we made a linked circle about that grave of a starman who would never see the stars again. And she began to chant the "Go with Good Will," we picking up the words after her until the song arose and awoke eerie echoes. We cared not for those but sang on to the end.

I decided it was best to wait for morning before I set out on my exploration of the other ways, though night, day, morning, noon, and evening were all relative here, marked only by the hours of my watch. Meanwhile, we opened more of the stock-piled supplies, finding blankets to replace those we had cut apart, food in concentrated rations—enough to last for a long time—and some digging equipment. However, there were no weapons, and the coms in the headquarters structure remained obstinately silent, though we tried them at intervals. Perhaps Lugard had activated only part of the installations here. We had heat in the barracks and a workable cook unit—which was a blessing, since the chill of the cave was biting.

There was some additional clothing, all Security uniform issue, so too large for any of us save Annet and me. There were several beamers, all in working order, and more of the climbing ropes such as Thad had found in the other supplies.

The children worked eagerly sorting out what we could use. But as I was dragging along a box of concentrated fruit paste, I saw Thad standing apart at the door of the structure I thought might be a missile control. I dumped the box by the workers and went to him.

"What is it?"

He started at the sound of my question and turned his head a little. He did not meet me eye to eye, his attitude evasive.

"This is a weapons control, isn't it, Vere?"

"I think so."

"Then, if one could use it, one might blow those—those devils right off Beltane—"

"You believe then that Griss Lugard was right?" I counter-questioned. Having been faced so long with Annet's stubborn contention that we were victims of one man's obsession, I was almost surprised to hear this acceptance.

"Yes. Vere, could we activate this?"

"No. The missiles it was meant to fire are either long dismounted or missing. When this base was closed down, it was stripped of arms, and they wouldn't leave the most important behind. Also, even if it were activated and ready, we could not just use it blindly."

"I suppose so. But, Vere, what if we get out to find they have taken over? Then what do we do?"

He brought into the open the question that had been plaguing me. Lugard, judging by the preparations he had made, must have planned a stay here for some time. But I knew that Annet, unless it was proved to her that there was greater danger on the surface, was not going to agree to any such thing. She had will and determination enough that if I did not try to find a way out, she would leave on her own. But if we went, I was also determined to make every move slowly and not run blindly into the very danger Lugard had died to save us from.

"We can scout. I don't think anyone will be interested in the wastelands," I began and then wondered. The rumor of Forerunner treasure, would that attract the attention of the refugees if they were now in command up there?

However, the waste might have been designed for hiding. And if we were up with a clear road of retreat back to this base, then—

"Guerrilla warfare?" Thad demanded.

"Warfare? With the Rovers? Be sensible, Thad. We can hide out if need be, for years. We'll just take it slowly until we can find out what happened."

He was not satisfied as I could see, but for the present I would not have to fear any rash action on his part. And of that I made doubly sure by appealing to his sense of responsibility and putting him in charge during my absence.

We slept away the rest of the period marked by the watches as "night." It was about eight o'clock the following morning, our third underground by such reckoning, that I set off on my exploration. I wished that I had a hand com with which to keep in touch with the base, but all such devices were as lacking as weapons. In fact, there were odd gaps in the supplies, and I wondered whether Lugard was responsible for the selection. Were coms missing so we could not attempt to signal the surface and so attract the very attention we had the most to fear by his belief?

I copied the map on a sheet of plasta, leaving that with Annet. Also I made her promise not to stir until my return and told Thad privately to make sure of that. Then, with a light pack, I walked resolutely away from the spot of light that was the camp. I glanced back once to see them lined up as dark shadows against that light. Someone, I thought by the size Gytha, raised a hand in salute, which I answered with a wave.

The left-hand passage was my first choice since it appeared to be the larger of the two possibles, though it was only a tunnel compared to the cave behind. I was heartened into believing I had chosen right when the rays of my belt torch picked up scrapings on the wall showing this way had been enlarged. It did not slope downward, as had the original one we had followed, but ran on a fairly level line. But within an hour I came to the cork that had painstakingly been put into it.

Someone had used a laser to good purpose. I could make out in the stiff mass that sealed the tunnel the half-melted bulk of work machines, mingled with rock that must have gone molten under the rays. They had driven their construction vehicles in here, piled rock about them, and used a high-voltage laser to convert the mass into a plug we had no hope of shifting.

That Lugard had done this was not possible. It had been a Security operation. I was puzzled. Why had they worked so to close off this underground retreat, as if they had some treasure to hide? Unless, of course, it was that control building—And if they *had* been forced to leave missiles in place here—

I considered that. Thad might have the right of it after all. We could hold under our hands an answer to any attempt to take over Beltane. Only I had not the least idea how we could put such a system to work, nor dared we try any experiments without knowing what was going on on the surface. No, that was out of the question. Only it was plain that great efforts had gone into the concealing of this base in the past.

If Lugard had known, then perhaps he had intended eventually to put it to our defense. Just another of the secrets he had not shared with us, and now it was too late.

I examined that congealed mass section by section, hoping to uncover some weak point, perhaps near the ceiling where the lava caves were the easiest to force. But there was no hope of that here. So I turned back, to seek the other passage on the map. When I came from the mouth of the first tunnel, I looked toward the camp. They had closed the door of the barracks. There was no longer any light since the huts lacked windows. Should I report my first failure? But that was a waste of time. Better be sure of the second now.

The second tunnel wound on and on, and there were no marks on its walls to suggest it had been in use until my torch picked out, canted to one side, its roll tread caught in a fall of rock, another of those carts like the one Lugard had used. Somehow it gave the impression that those who had left it so had been in haste—to get out? Was there an opening just ahead?

My deliberate pace quickened to a trot, always allowing for the rough footing, as I pushed past the derelict. The tunnel-cave was angling to the right even more and sloping down, which was a disappointment, though good sense told me that no opening formed by a lava flow could have gone up. So I came to the second disappointment, a fall of rock, again fused into an impassable wall. But there was something different about this one. I was not sure—I could not be—only I thought it was not ten years old but only days. Had this been done by Lugard?

It seemed less cold here. There was no frost pattern on the walls. Then I caught the gleam of metal and went down on one knee by a weapon—the very one, or its twin, that I had seen beside the door of the Butte when Lugard had faced the refugees. It was as new as it had looked then. I did not think it had lain here for long.

I picked it up with a rush of excitement and pointed it at the top of that fused pile with some idea of burning through. But when I pressed the firing button, there was no answer. The charge it had carried must have been exhausted in the making of the barrier. Now I was sure Lugard had closed this door.

But why? Why had he wanted to seal us in? The preparations for a long siege and now this—What had he so feared might lie upon the surface that he took such drastic precautions? Was it only to save our lives, or was there some secret here that must be guarded—so his move would serve two purposes?

I sat down on the floor, holding the laser, and tried to think. Not that any guess of mine might even come near the fringe of fact. All I could light upon was that I might find some clue back at the camp—either left by Lugard or those who had first built and then left that base. For our own protection, we should have as much of the truth as we could uncover.

There was the third passage, the one I had not believed worth exploring. Should I attempt that before I returned—or get back for a more intensive search of the headquarters structure or the silent missile control? In the end, I decided in favor of return, and I took Lugard's discarded weapon with me. There was a small chance that I might discover a charge for it and could then use it to burn us through one of those plugs.

It was past noon, and I was hungry, so I ate before I began my retreat up the tunnel. And it was as I was idly surveying the walls about me that I saw, in the smooth dust of the floor by one, a line of prints.

Much as I knew of the creatures of the Reserves, this was no track I had seen before. The prints were as long as my hand, which certainly argued for a creature of some size, and they were marked by three long toe lines, so thin as to suggest a foot near to skeleton. Had some other thing been lost like the wart-horn, to drag its starving body along?

And these had been made since Lugard had set this barrier! I had not noted them coming down the tunnel, and there had been no places along it where any large thing could hide. More than ever now I wished that the biospeleology lab had not closed and that I had some reference to what lived naturally in these underground regions. Of course, life that sought out the lava caves for a refuge would not be like that found in the moisture dripping, water-cut caves.

I hunched forward to measure my hand to the print. The fine sand and grit gave no impression of depth, so that one could not guess at the weight of the creature. But I did not like the looks of it in the least. And the three-toed structure was that, I believed, of some reptilian form of life.

It had, I decided, after closer study, come down the cave tunnel on one side, been stopped by the barrier, and crossed over to retrace its way up the other. Apparently, it had an affinity for walls, since the marks kept close to them.

I stowed away my empty ration tube and arose, playing the torch down on the tracks that led back toward the big cave. They could have been made an hour before I came this way—or a day or a week—whenever Lugard had put that seal here. But I disliked the thought that an unknown thing might be lurking near the base camp.

If it were carnivorous and starving—why, it might charge anyone in sight. A stunner will act quickly on any warm-blooded creature, but its effect, unless on high beam, was much slower for a reptile, and we kept our weapons on low beam.

So I scrambled along the tunnel at a faster pace than I had so far used that day. When I came to the cart, the prints moved out from the wall and were lost in the central rock. As I played my torch closer over the transport, I saw a ragged tear in one of the treads. Such clean-cut edges could not have come from rocks. They looked far more to me like rents left by claws. And claws able to break the tough substance of those treads were—I clutched tighter the weapon I had found. If I could only discover a fresh charge for that, we would have no worries. A laser with power enough to melt a rock plug would stop even a bear-bison, the most dangerous beast I knew—one never approached by a Ranger unless it was first stunned.

I came back into the large cave. There the prints turned sharply to my left, again along the wall. And for that I was thankful, for if the thing did not like open space, it would have to face crossing a wide stretch of it in order to reach our camp, while the shelters had been built sturdily enough to withstand any clawed attack. We would merely have to be alert when outside their walls.

I continued to follow the tracks until they vanished into a crevice, which, after a moment's comparison with my map, I thought must be the entrance to the third passage. There in the dust were several lines of three toes coming and going, which looked suspiciously as if this third way was a regular route for the thing. Also, from the mouth of that ragged opening came such a chill that I was astounded. If the thing was reptilian, then how could it face that cold? While reptiles could not take direct sun or baking heat, chill made them torpid and forced some into a state approaching hibernation. It had been the study of such animals, along with other creatures, that had first given my species the "cold sleep" that, before the discovery of hyperjump, had carried cargoes of mankind in coffin-like boxes across the vast distances between one solar system and another.

Here was a thing that left a reptilian track, yet seemed deliberately to choose a passage even colder than the chill cave. The latest prints, which overlaid the others, led into and not out, and I was content not to trail any farther.

Instead, I went to the camp. The door of the missile control was half ajar, the interior dark, and the com-headquarters building the same. On impulse, I did not go directly to the barracks. After all, I had set no time limit on my return, and I wanted, very badly indeed, a charge for Lugard's laser. Such might be found in headquarters. Had it been in the barracks or among the supplies, I would already have known it.

I stood in the stark office room. As I closed the door behind me, the light went on as it did in the barracks. It had not in the missile station. Could I deduce from that small fact that Lugard had reason to activate part of the equipment here? We knew that the com did not work, but what else was there?

I crossed to the files. They had security locks set to fingerprint release. But when I touched the first, it came open easily enough—to show an empty interior. There were sections for micro-tape and reading tape but no rolls. Thus it was with every one of them. Then I began to search the surface of the walls, looking for a slight depression that could mark another finger lock. I found four such. But if they held any secrets, they continued to guard them well. No pressure of my fingertip freed them. Perhaps they had been set to Lugard's pattern, or even my father's, if they had not been opened since the war began.

I sat down behind the desk, laying the weapon on it. There were three drawers, all as empty as the files. Then I noted a fourth, which was a very narrow slit set in the edge of the desk top. It would be seen only when the belt torch I had neglected to switch off flashed across it endwise as I moved.

There appeared to be no way of opening it, no releasing catch or button. I brought out the long iridium hunting knife that rode in my boot top and picked, with its unbreakable point, at that faint join line. It required a lot of patience, that struggle between knife point and the desk, but finally the less hard substance of the latter chipped, and I pried out a very shallow drawer.

It was so shallow that it held only a single sheet of the same plasta as my map, and it was also a map. I spread it out on the desk to compare it with the one Lugard had given me. A section of it was the same, but reduced to a miniature, so that the old only formed about a quarter of my new find. Again I saw a spread of passages ahead. In each case, beyond the stoppers I had come against, were sections that extended beyond dots indicating passage walls, as if there were rooms or installations of some sort built into and outward through those.

Missile pits? Or their equivalents? There were numbers so small that I found them difficult to read, which I thought were code. But since those ways were now sealed to us, it did not greatly matter what lay there. It was the chill third passage I wanted to trace. On Lugard's map it was only slightly indicated; here it was in far greater detail.

It led, according to this map, to a cave, which might be as large as the one we were now in, or perhaps two caves with a wide entrance between them. And the far side was left open as if it had not been fully explored by the map maker, so he did not know the exact perimeter. Also this space was given an added significance with a shading in print that glistened with the lettering of code.

I remembered Lugard's story of the ice cave where he had found the alien remains. The cold coming from the crevice could mean ice. And the special marking on this map suggested importance. But nowhere was there any sign of an exit to the surface. The fact remained that two were sealed, and we might have to return the way we came.

Doing that, we must clear the fall Annet had encountered. And beyond—I flinched from visualizing the climb back if the crane no longer worked.

I folded the new map with the old and stowed both in my tunic. A survey of the com room, and then of the stark living quarters, brought me nothing more. But I took the weapon with me when I left, determined to search carefully through all the supply boxes before giving up hope of finding a fresh charge for it. I wanted that fiercely. We needed it.

It was when I came out of the door of headquarters that I heard the calling.

"Dagny! Dinan!" A shout and the echoes of it rolled around the walls. "Dagny! Dinan!"

The door of the barracks stood open, the light streaming out. Annet was at the narrow tip of its radiance, calling. I saw a figure that could only be Thad moving farther out into the shadows, and one that was perhaps Gytha heading in the other direction, back toward the ledges. And I ran—remembering those three-toed tracks and fearing a scattering of our party that might lead to danger yet unknown.

"What is it?" I came up beside Annet as she voiced another of those echoing shouts.

She swung around, her both hands out, to clutch me by the upper arms.

"Vere, the children—they've gone!" Then she turned her head, still holding onto me, to call, "Dagny, Dagny! Dinan!"

Someone to my other side flashed a light ahead from one of the beamers. That reached to the wall of the cave, and the edge of it touched the crevice down which those sinister tracks had led.

"Home—" Under the echoes of Annet's call, I heard that other word and looked at Pritha. Meeting my gaze, she nodded as if to emphasize what she would say.

"Dagny wanted her mother; she wanted to go home. She didn't understand what happened. When Annet went to get her some food—she was asleep we thought—she ran away. And Dinan—he would never let her go alone."

That was true. Where one of the twins went, the other followed, though Dinan was usually the leader of the pair. He would not have allowed his sister to go into the dark alone.

But the tracks were so to the fore of my mind, I twisted up my hand and caught Annet's wrist.

"Be quiet!" I put into that order what force I could. "Get them back—all of them!"

She stared at me, but she did not call again.

"We may not be alone here." I gave her the best explanation

I had ready. "All of you—get in there and stay, and put your stunners on high."

Thad came running out of the dark. "They left a trail," he reported and then interrupted himself. "Vere! Is there a way—"

I shook my head. "There is no way out. And where are those tracks?" I had hoped against hope, but my fears were realized when he waved to the cold crevice.

"Annet, Thad, get the rest of the children in—and keep them so! And here—" I thrust the useless laser at Thad. "Scout through the supplies and see if you can find a charge for this. Shoot at anything that does not signal with a torch."

He nodded, asking no questions. Annet might have, but I gave her a push. "Get them in!"

"Where are you going?"

"After them—" I was already two strides nearer to the crevice. "And," I added a last caution, "keep that beamer on—pointed this way."

Light might not be any deterrent to a menace, but if it were a creature of the dark, it could help.

EIGHT

I found the tracks Thad had seen. There was no mistaking the small boot-pack prints. And they lay over mine where I had halted to study that other trail. Seeing that, I winced. Had I returned at once to the barracks instead of going to search the headquarters, I might have prevented this. But there was no time to waste on might-have-beens.

For a moment or two, I debated the wisdom of using my belt torch. While the light was needed, it could also attract unwelcome attention, but the advantages outweighed the disadvantages. I would not call as they had been doing, though.

The cold grew worse. The walls of this tunnel were covered with frost crystals, which sparkled in the light. What had drawn the children into taking such a forbidding way, I could not understand—unless, knowing I was exploring the other two outlets, they had determined to avoid me.

That was not like the twins. And I could only believe that the shock that had gripped Dagny had unsettled her usual rather timid nature. She had seemed half dazed when she had not been sleeping.

As I went, I listened for sounds of the children, for they could not be too far ahead, and, I will freely admit, with a pumping heart, for anything else that would suggest alien life in this hole.

Once again, after passing the rough entrance, I saw signs that this had been a used way. Projections had been lasered off; there were scrapes along the wall and a few marks of crawl treads, all signifying that not only men but perhaps one of the carts had traveled here. It was sloping down again as the cold grew. All I heard was the soft pad of my own boot soles. I saw nothing within range of the torch beam. I went with my stunner in my hand. And, as I had warned the others to do, I had turned it to the highest force, although to use that long would exhaust the charge. I tried now to remember how many extra charges I had. There were two in my belt loops, some in my pack—but those I had left behind. How many did the others have? I should have checked that last night when we were examining the other supplies, though at that time food and water had seemed all important.

I glanced at my watch. Four—in the afternoon where the sun still shone and it was day. But here such reckoning had no meaning. The children could not be very far ahead. Yet I dared not risk too quick a pace over rough surfaces. A twisted ankle could mean disaster for us all. If they could see my torch, would that make them hurry on? Or would they have had enough of the cold and dark and be ready to turn back? I longed to call, but the memory of the tracks kept me quiet.

It was now a smaller replica of the road we had traveled before, for the cave passage again ended in a drop, a rough one descending not by ledges this time but by handholds. I was surprised that the twins had gone down—but they must have, or I would have overtaken them.

I heard it then, muffled but still audible, a desolate crying, coming from down there. And I saw a faint glow that could only be a belt torch. Heartened, I swung over, into a cold so intense my fingers flinched from the stone. How *had* they come here?

Luckily, the descent was not as great as the place of ledges. Part way down, I let go, to drop, lest the cold destroy all feeling in my hands, my feet plowing into loose gravel, which was a sharp way to cushion any fall. But I was up again, having suffered only minor scraping.

"Dagny—Dinan?" I dared to call now.

There was no halt to that minor plaint, which somehow hurt the ears and made one's mind flinch. But I was answered; only the voice did not come from where the light glowed.

"Vere, please—Vere, come and get us—" That was Dinan.

"Where?" I still looked toward the torch, unable to believe that did not mark my quarry.

"Here!"

Here was farther to the left and higher, if the echoes did not utterly mislead me. I waded through the scree in that direction.

"Vere—" Dinan again, his voice very thin and weak. "Look out—for the thing. It went away when I threw the light. But it bit the torch and jumped on it—and maybe it will come back. Vere, get us out of here!"

I shone my own torch in the general direction of the voice, and there they were. It was a ledge of sorts but a shallow one. Dagny was crowded to the back, Dinan before her as if to serve as a buffer. She was crying, her eyes staring straight before her, no tears running from them, only the moaning from a mouth that hung loose, a dribble of saliva issuing from one corner to cover her chin. Her lack of expression frightened me, for all I could think of was that she had retreated into idiocy from which we could perhaps never draw her again.

There was fear in Dinan's face also, but it was a fear that was turned outward, not bottled within him. He reached down his hand to me, grasping my fingers in his cold small ones, in that moment giving a vast sigh as if an intolerable burden had rolled from his shoulders when he was able to touch me.

The perch on which they were crowded was too small for me to join them. And getting Dagny down, unless she became more aware of her surroundings and able to help somewhat, presented a problem.

"Dagny." I pulled myself up on a pile of rubble until I was able to take both her hands in mine. They lay limp in my grasp, as if she was not conscious of my touch. She continued to stare straight ahead, and that moaning never ceased.

In cases of hysteria, I knew, sometimes a sharp slap might bring the victim out of such a state. But that this was worse than any hysteria I was now certain.

"How long has she been like this?" I asked Dinan. Surely, she had not made all this journey down the icy tunnel in this state.

"Since—since the thing tried to get us." His voice quavered. "She—she won't listen to me, Vere. She just cries and cries. Vere, can you make her listen to us?"

"I don't know, Dinan. Can you get down and let me reach her?"

He edged along obediently and swung down, giving me room to put an arm around his sister. Again she showed no sign that she knew of my presence. I feared she had entered an enclosure for which none of us had the key. Like Lugard, she needed professional help, which could only be found on the world we were far from reaching.

Somehow I got her off the shelf; then she lay limp across my shoulder, still moaning and drooling. And I must get her back up that climb—

"Vere! Listen!"

I had been hearing only Dagny's moaning. But when Dinan pulled at my arm, I did listen. And there was another sound—a rattle, which could come from a stone dislodged to click against another. The direction was deceiving, though, because of the echoes. I thought it did not come from above but from the space beyond.

"Vere—the *thing*!"

"What is it?" Best be prepared with at least a partial description of what I might have to face.

"It's big—as big as you—and it walks on its hind legs. But it's worse than a wart-horn—all scaly and bad, bad!" Dinan's voice grew shriller with every word, as if he could no longer control his fear.

"All right. Now. Listen, Dinan. You said it came for your torch—"

"I don't know—Vere, it hasn't any eyes—any eyes at all!" Again terror spoke through him. "But it didn't like the light. I threw the torch at it, and then it didn't follow us. It jumped on the torch and bit it and threw it—and then—it went away."

Attracted by heat radiation I wondered? Perhaps this stalker in the dark had no need for eyes, but heat it could sense. Yes, small patches of knowledge came back to me. That was how the minute creatures found in the water caves tracked their prey, by sensors that picked up an awareness of body heat. Some of them, it was said, could be drawn from the crevices in which they dwelt by the warmth of one's skin if you set your bare hand against the rock near their holes. If this creature hunted by heat, then it would be drawn first to the torch—and it could now be attracted by the one on my own belt.

So perhaps I could use that as Dinan had luckily done with his were we caught in a tight place, though I feared trying to make the climb back without light and the helpless girl.

Dinan's torch still blazed, though now it flickered. These were stoutly made, and the beating he said it had taken might have battered it but had not extinguished its rays. Also, the sounds we heard now were from that direction.

I saw no way of getting Dagny up that climb without rendering myself almost defenseless under attack. That I dared not risk. There was one other choice—lure the beast into the open and stun it. And I could not be sure of that either, even with the stunner set on high.

Now I examined Dagny's belt as she lay against me, her face turned to the rocky wall, her eyes wide and seeing nothing. Yes, she still had her torch. I unhooked it, she limp and passive under my handling as if she were a toy.

"Listen, Dinan." So much depended now on what we could do. If I were to face this thing, I must do it on ground I could pick, well away from the children. I turned my torch up the wall we must go. Well above my head was the widest of the rest places I had found during my descent, one as good if not better than that on which the children had earlier taken refuge. "This is what we must do. I cannot risk climbing with Dagny while she is—ill—not with that thing able to attack. So, I am going to get you both up there. Then I will leave you this torch. Keep it safe. I'll come down here again and set up my belt torch as bait. When the thing comes at it—"

"But you don't have a blaster or a laser!" His voice trembled, but he was thinking clearly.

"No. But my stunner is on full ray. If I am careful—and I will be—that ought to work. It is just that we cannot climb when there is the threat of that overtaking us."

I saw him nod, and his hands closed so tightly about the torch from Dagny's belt that his knuckles were sharp knobs peaked in his cold-blued skin. The torch he had thrown away was flickering faster, weakly, on and off. I listened, but the sounds had ceased, and I could only hope that did not mean the creature was using some natural cunning to creep through a terrain native to it.

The struggle to get Dagny to the ledge I had selected for a temporary refuge confirmed my belief that it would be a long, hard pull to the top and one I dared not take with a threat of attack from behind. I must settle Dinan's "thing" before I took the road back.

Once I had Dagny wedged with her back to the cliff wall, Dinan before her to keep her there, I rested a moment, giving the boy my last orders.

"I'll go down near that torch you threw. And I'll switch mine on and wedge it between the rocks. I'll still be between you and the thing. Don't switch on your light. That is very important. If it does hunt by heat, it will be drawn to my torch first, and that radiance may block out the emanations from our bodies."

"Yes, Vere."

I handed him my canteen and supplies.

"Give Dagny some water if you can get her to drink. And there are E-bars in this bag. See if she will eat. She and you both need energy to combat this cold. Now, if you don't hear anything for a while, Dinan, don't worry. It may be that we shall have to wait."

But not too long, I hoped silently as I swung over and down. The cold here was such that the children certainly could not resist it for long. And my own reflexes were so stiff that I feared to depend too much on any agility in battle.

The periods of dark between light as the other torch flickered on and off grew longer. Its glow when on was quite feeble. I worked my way near it with all the care of one on a hunting stalk, though I was not prepared here to use the terrain to the same advantage as I could have on the surface. The continued quiet bothered me, for my imagination painted a picture of Dinan's thing crouched in some crevice, very well aware of my every movement, ready at any second to charge before I could bring my perhaps useless weapon to bear.

I wedged my torch between two rocks, switched it on, and hunkered down to wait. The cold crept upon me, dulling my senses, or I feared that it did. And I had to move now and then or I would have cramped, unable to move at all. The watch on my wrist I could no longer see, and time became a long stretch of discomfort and tension.

There was no sound to herald its coming—it was suddenly *there!* It stood, with its head a little to one side, its snout pointed at the torch, its shoulders hunched, while above frond-like strips of skin fluttered and then stiffened, pointing to the light—or perhaps to me behind that beacon.

It was a dead gray-white, and Dinan was right. There were two small swellings on the head that might mark the place of eyes it had surrendered for lack of use eons back in evolutionary time. How so great a creature could find enough here to sustain life I could not guess. My understanding had always been that cave life tended to be minute, the largest being the blind fish. But this thing was as tall as I as it stood on its hind legs. In addition, it was apparent that the bipedal form of locomotion was normal to it, for the front limbs were much shorter and weaker seeming, and it carried them curled close to its belly.

Skeleton proportions added to its eerie appearance. All four limbs looked to be only scaled skin stretched tightly over angular bones. The head was a skull hardly clothed with flesh, except for its antennae, and its body as lean as if it were in the last stages of starvation. Yet it moved alertly with no sign of weakness, so that the excessive leanness must have been its natural state.

As a biped, it was somehow more alarming than if it had run on four feet. We are conditioned to associate an upright stance with intelligence, though that can be far from the truth. I had the impression that I was confronted by no mindless beast but rather by something that ruled this dark underground world as much as my kind ruled the surface over its head.

But there was little time for such impressions. The blind head moved in sharp jerks right and left, always centering in a point at the torch. It was a long, narrow skull with a small mouth, which was surrounded by the only excess flesh on the creature, a puckered protuberance, as if the thing got most of its nourishment by sucking rather than biting and chewing. All in all, it was something out of a nightmare.

Now, without any warning, it charged. I was a second or two late in my reaction. Perhaps I had been so startled by its alien appearance that I had gone off guard. It was to cost me dear. I did swing up the stunner and press the button, aiming for its head, long since known to be the most vulnerable point of contact for that weapon.

Though known to be for most living things, it would seem that now I dealt with one not to be so judged. I did not even see how it altered course in the middle of a spring. But now it headed not for the lamp but directly at me. And those arms, which had looked weak when compared to the most powerful legs, snapped up and out, the clawed paws making ready to take me.

I beamed again at the head, but the ray did not slow it. Then it gave a leap that raised it to the top of the rocks behind which I crouched, and it aimed a blow at me in return. Its blindness did not appear to limit its capacity to know where I was.

The raking claws tore, but not across my head by the one scrap of fortune I had. Instead, those claws peeled tunic and coverall from my shoulder halfway across my chest on the left side, leaving bleeding gashes. All that saved me was that its rock perch moved under its weight, and it had to balance.

I threw myself to the right and rolled behind a rock, but now it was between me and the children. And, having made sure of me with a second blow or a third, it could take them at its leisure. So I must keep its attention and try to pull it away from the ledge, though how long I could continue such a desperate game I did not want to think.

It would seem that the stunner was useless. Two full head shots it had taken—which should have been enough to addle any brains it had. But they had not even seemed to slow it. My roll brought me closer to the lamp, and I surrendered a precious moment to loosen that for a lure. Not that I needed one now. It was thoroughly aroused, wanting nothing more than to get claws on me. But still the direct rays of the lamp appeared to bother it. To my relief it did not try another of those lightning charges but gave me a small breathing space in which to pull myself together, while it squatted on the top of the unsteady rock, its head turned at a sharp angle on its narrow shoulders to follow the light it could not see but sensed in some other fashion.

I wondered if it were a creature of the extreme cold so that even the limited radiance of the light was both an attraction and a source of discomfort to it. If so—if I only had a laser! But I might as well wish for a distributor to make entirely sure of it.

However, as I worked myself back, away from the cliff and the children, it leaped from the rock and followed, much as if I were piping it with Lugard's pipe. Only it came warily.

So tailed by the hunter, I came into a strange place. There were stalagmites of ice, like huge teeth, awakening in frozen glory and glitter when the lamp touched them. Parts of the floor were coated with transparent sheets of ice made up of hexagonal prisms standing vertically, their honey-combed divisions clearly visible on the surface. And, on the one portion of wall we passed where my light reached, I saw more, greater crystals with well-developed facets. At another time the wonder of it would have amazed me. Now I only tensed and feared, lest my boots slip on one of those patches and bring me down, easy meat for the stalker.

The creature showed no discomfort from the cold, and I believed that this was its native habitat, though it went against all we knew of such life. My shoulder and chest were bleeding, and the chill struck through the rags it had made of my clothing. If I let it herd me in too far, then the cold might be its aid in our final battle. I raised the stunner for the third time and fired, this time not at its head but at its middle section—with surprising results!

It shivered in the light of the lamp and threw up its head. Then from that puckered mouth burst an odd quaver of sound, which was answered—from behind me!

I swerved in my horror, brought up against one of those ice pillars, and fell, skidding across the floor. The stunner was gone, but somehow I clung to the lamp. My body whirled around, so that I hit with my good shoulder against a broken surface. And I was looking—looking straight at objects that were certainly not native to that place.

They must have been deeply encased in ice earlier, but something or someone had begun the process of melting them free. I could see shadows, shapes, all ice-covered. But what was directly before me was a rod projecting from a chest or container in which lay others like it. I seized upon that as my only hope of a weapon, though to swing it one-handed might be more than I could do.

That sucking hoot was louder. I did not waste time getting to my feet, rather pulled myself around on my knees and swung up the rod. There were depressions on the surface I gripped, into which my fingers sank as I tightened hold.

From the tip of the rod shot a coruscating ray of light. It struck one of the ice pillars. There was a hissing, a clouding of steam. Heat beat back at me; water boiled away. Again I swung the rod, this time with intent, pressing my fingers, and that thing that wobbled toward me across the floor was headless. But still it kept its feet! And it came on! Until I blasted it past its chest, it came.

Out from between the forest of ice pillars came another. But at the sight, or sensing of light, it became more wary, circling, moving with a speed that frightened me, for my own reactions were so hindered by the cold and my wounds that I could not match it. At last I simply did not aim the rod but whipped it about, unleashing it in a sweep across the whole sector where the monster bounded.

It went down, but so did other things. Pillars crashed in great knife splinters of ice, and there was a giving beyond those. It was as if the wall melted. A black hole opened there, and from it issued a rushing, roaring sound.

For a time I lay where I was, unable to find the strength to get to my feet. At last, upending that miraculous rod and using it as a support, I managed to stand up. Halting and wavering, I came to the black hole the ray had cut and shone my lamp through. The light was reflected from the surface of water, a river of it, moving from dark to dark again.

I began slow progress back to the cliff, shining my lamp ahead so that Dinan would know it was I who came.

"Vere! Vere!" Again I heard his call and leaned against a rock to consider what must be done. I had pressed the rags of my clothing as tightly against my wounds as I could. But blood still welled there. And the cold had eaten me, too. I dared not make that climb carrying Dagny with no more help than Dinan could give. Nor could I leave the girl and go for help.

"Dinan—"

"Yes, Vere?" he responded eagerly.

"Do you think you can climb to the top and get back to the camp?" It was a lot I was asking of him. Had the two monsters I had killed in the ice been the only representatives of their kind hereabouts? And would he be able to walk the distance unaided now?

"I can try, Vere."

"It will have to be better than try, Dinan." I dared not show concern; my firmness might be the one prod that would give him the will and grit to keep moving. "Now listen. I have here a weapon. I don't know what it is—I found it back there. You point it, you press your fingers in places in its surface, and it shoots a very hot ray. I am going to give this to you. If you meet one of those things, fire at the middle of its body—understand?"

"Yes, Vere." His voice sounded steadier. Was it because I could put into his hands some defense? One of our species always feels more secure with a weapon to hand, which may be why we have clung to such for all these generations, turning first to might of body rather than might of mind as those on Beltane argued should be done.

But to disarm myself—I faced around, pulling along by hand holds on the rocks about me, very unsure at that moment whether I could make the trip I must for the small margin of safety for Dagny and me.

"Wait, Dinan. I must get another weapon." I lurched forward, fearing to pause lest I fall and be unable to get to my feet again. The claw wounds burned with a fiery agony. I thought of poison and then pushed that thought resolutely from me, concentrating only on reaching the ice-bound storehouse and another of the rods.

I crept past the charred remains of a monster, and my torch picked out the half-thawed wall and the box projecting, its lid thrown back.

Now I stooped and picked a second rod from the chest. There were two more there. But these, my lamp told me, were different. The one I had just taken up was a steely blue, like the first I had found, the last two dull silver. I pointed the one I now held at an ice pillar and fired. Again the swift melting, the backwash of heat.

Only that one chest was free. I was able to see dimly behind it massive boxes, shadows I could not be sure of. Was this Lugard's alien treasure? If so, who had left it here and how long ago? And Lugard, had it been his efforts that had freed the one chest from the grip of the ice?

A momentary dizziness nearly sent me reeling. My shin rapped painfully against the edge of the chest as I strove to retain my balance, and my torch swung close to its surface. It bore a pattern, not incised deeply, but lines to be seen under the direct light. A head formed out of those lines. The monster! No, this one had eyes, but the general shape of the skull was the same, if not so emaciated. Could—could the hunter and its companion have been left here, too, eons ago? No space traveling man says aught is impossible. We have seen too much on too many worlds that we cannot explain satisfactorily. But that picture was allied to the monsters—there was no doubt in my mind.

I had no time for speculation or exploration now. I must start Dinan on his way for help. Holding tightly to the remnants of my strength, I staggered back to the cliff face.

NINE

As Dinan climbed, I squatted on the small ledge, my arm around Dagny. Her moans had grown fainter. Her eyes were half closed; beneath those drooping lids no pupils showed, only white arcs. The second rod I had taken from the cache lay across my lap, but I pressed my free hand against the still seeping wounds on my chest. The chill was bad. We should keep moving to stimulate circulation. But Dagny was a dead weight, and I was too weak. Also, I had killed two of the monsters, but that was not to say that more were not lurking among the ice pillars.

My thinking slowed, grew muddled. I was sleepy now—so sleepy. Yet some small spark within me sounded alarm. No sleep—that was the way to extinction. I fought to rouse, to listen. It seemed to me I could hear even from here the sound of the buried river.

River—water had to flow somewhere. Suppose we could trust to that stream for a road out? I knew of no major river in the lava lands. But that section of Beltane had never been fully explored. In latter days when men had been so few, and the majority of those engrossed in the labs, there had been little curiosity as to what lay outside the settlements. Only the Reserves of the animals had been patrolled to any extent. I believed that we had been the first to come this way since Butte Hold was closed.

So for all the evidence we had one way or another, the river

99

could be our way out. And if we discovered no other, it would
have to be.

Dagny's weight against my good shoulder became heavier as
time passed. I had forgotten to mark the hour when Dinan had
left and had called from the crest that he was safely up and over.
So looking at my watch told me nothing. The road back was
straight—if he did not meet another blind prowler!

But he was a small boy, chilled, tired. I could not reckon his
speed by the same effort I would put into that journey. I fumbled
one-handedly with the ration bag and brought out a stick of
Sustain. In the light I saw Dagny's face was smeared with traces
of the same food. Dinan must have tried to feed her. But when
I attempted the same thing, she allowed the nourishment to slip
from her slack mouth, and I saw it was no use.

I sucked away. The stuff had a strong, unpleasant taste, but it
had been meant to fortify a man through physical effort, and I
forced myself to finish the bar. Still Dagny moaned. And time
crawled with no real passing at all. A man could believe endless
day-night drifted by.

The need for being alert was a constant spur. Finally, I learned
to press tightly against the claw wounds. The pain from that
touch broke through the haze in my mind. Yet as time went on
and on and I heard nothing from above, though I warned myself
that it was still far too soon for a rescue party to arrive, I lost
heart. Would Dinan see that they would come with the right
equipment? Why had I not made plain our needs before he left?
I should have given him definite orders, outlining our needs. I
could not trust to Dinan to know—

In that, though, I was wrong, for when they did come, I found
that he had wrought better than I expected. They had the climbing
ropes we had used to bring Lugard down the ledges. And Thad
came down to adjust a sling about Dagny, climbing beside her
inert body as those above drew her aloft.

When I tried to move, I found I was so stiff and giddy that
I could not help myself much, so I had to huddle where I was
until Thad made the return journey and slipped the same looping
over me. That pressed against my wounds, and I cried out until,
with pushing and tugging, we got the support lower.

What I could do to aid myself, I did, but that seemed little
enough, and I progressed so slowly that I thought they must find

me as much of a burden as Lugard had been. At last I was over
the lip and lying face down, which was agony against the wounds
until somehow I managed to roll over.

They had brought one of the large beamers with them, and the
wash of light from that was all about me, harsh and blinding in
my eyes. So I closed them while hands searched out my wounds,
pulling from them the rags I had used to stop the bleeding. I felt
coolness, a blessed soothing on those painful cuts, and knew that
they used plasta-heal from an aid kit. The relief was so great that
it left me weak and shaking, but I opened my eyes to look at
Annet and Thad. A little beyond, Gytha sat on the floor, Dagny
lying across her lap, while Pritha wiped that loose, drooling mouth
and tried to dribble water between the uncontrolled lips.

"Can you walk?" Annet asked slowly, spacing her words as if
she had need to reach the understanding of someone not quite
of her world.

It was not a matter of what I could do, I thought, but rather
what I must. To burden them with my weight even on a level
surface was impossible. Time was of the essence for Dagny. And,
since they had tended my wounds, a certain amount of strength
flowed back into my misused body.

With Thad and Annet steadying me, I got to my feet, though
that was difficult. Once up again I found I could walk, waveringly,
but I was sure I could make it.

"Take her"—I nodded to Dagny—"on. She needs attention."

Annet gathered the little girl out of her sister's hold. That even
her loving care could do anything for Dagny now I doubted, but
she would have the best Annet could give her I knew. Perhaps
that and time would heal—unless we might get top-world to
the real attention she needed, again always supposing that the
port and its people still existed. Would the enemy war against a
child—a sick child?

I found Gytha by my side. As she had done once for Lugard,
she raised my good hand and put it on her shoulder, offering a
support I did need. Of the rest of that journey I have only scanty
memory until once more I awoke in the barracks.

This time the bunks around me were occupied with sleepers.
Someone moaned, another muttered, both sounds born out of
dreams. I felt cautiously across my body. My tunic was gone.
My fingers slipped over the covering that healed and protected

my wounds, and that light pressure raised no tingle of pain. We could thank such fortune as still smiled on us that medical supplies were at hand. I knew that under that coating I was well on the way to healthy scarring.

However, I was hungry, and that hunger moved me, so I crawled to hands and knees, eased up to my feet, and reached the mess section, leaving my blankets behind. There was a dusk here. The hut had been darkened for sleeping, but it was not the complete black of the caves. I could see the cook unit and the cans of ration and other supplies ranged on a shelf against the wall. I crossed to those.

Opening a ration tube bothered me. Though my wounds were better, I was still almost one-handed. So I twisted off the cap with my teeth and waited for the heat to be released in the contents. The stuff smelled so good that my mouth watered, and I did not wait for full heating but sucked it avidly.

"You—"

I turned at that exclamation and saw Annet in the doorway, a blanket draped around her shoulders. Her eyes looked puffy and her face haggard, and she was no longer a girl but a woman who had hard days and perhaps worse nights behind her.

"Dagny?"

She shook her head and came into the room, closing the door carefully behind her. Then, as one doing one thing but thinking about another, she swept one hand over a plate in the wall and the light became brighter.

"There's caff—on the unit," she said in a tired voice. "Press the button."

I put down the empty tube and did that, then picked up two mugs and set them on the table. She made no move to help me but sat down, putting both elbows on the table and resting her head on her hands.

"Perhaps—at the port—they can do something—" But she sounded very doubtful. "What about the passages, Vere?"

One-handed, I poured the caff into the mugs, surveyed her critically, and added to each two heaping spoonfuls of sweet cane crystals. And I stirred hers well before I put it down to deal with my own.

"Both stoppered. We haven't the equipment, or at least I haven't seen any yet, to open them."

She stared unseeingly before her, not noticing the mug or me.

I felt a stir of concern. Her expression at that moment was far too near Dagny's withdrawal.

"I found something else, in the ice cave—"

"I know—the rod. Dinan showed it to us."

"It controls a force like a laser. Perhaps we can cut through. There is a river, also—"

"River," she repeated dully, and then with a spark of interest. "River?"

I sat down opposite her, grateful for having broken through her preoccupation. Between sips of caff, I told her of the fall of rock wall in the cave and the finding of the river.

"But with the rods you can burn a passage through one of the other tunnels," she observed, dropping her hand to the mug. "That's better than trying to follow a stream that leads you don't know where. And if you brought down the wall of the cave with that one, it ought to work in the passages as well."

I had to admit her logic was sound. Yet somehow my thoughts kept returning to that waterway, though I agreed to try the alien weapon or tool to burn our way out.

I did try, but to no purpose, for I discovered that, as with the laser we had found, it was a matter of power lack. I must have used all that remained in the ancient charge when I fought the monster in the ice cavern. When I tried it on the sealing of what seemed the better of the two blocked tunnels, it flared for several moments and then vanished. And all my working of its simple controls could not produce another spark, while the second one I had taken from the chest answered with only one quick burst. I made the trip back to the cache and brought out the other two, but neither responded in the least.

Whatever else was hidden behind that murky wall of ice was as well kept from us as if we had an ir-wall between. We could chip at the ice, and we tried. But the chill and the slowness of that labor showed us that was a task requiring more time than we had—for Dagny's sake.

With infinite care and effort, Annet managed to get enough food and water into the child to keep her alive. But beyond that she could do nothing. At last she agreed to try the river, since a return up the way we had come proved that at least one more cave-in had closed that path also.

By testing we discovered that the stream behind the wall was about waist deep, but the chill of the water, plus the fact it had a swift current, argued against wading. Under our beamers the liquid was so clear that you might step into it by mistake, thinking that some stone on its bottom was above the surface and not below it.

We drew on the supplies and set about constructing a raft that would ride high enough above the water to protect us and the packs we must take. In addition, we could make use of some pieces hacked free from the installations in the "missile" hut to serve as poles for guiding and for braking against too swift a forward sweep, while the climbing cords could provide anchors.

Of course there was always the dark chance that we might come to passages ahead completely water-filled. For that we had an answer in a roll of water-resistant plasta-cover, though whether it would make the raft and its passengers waterproof when carried under a surface, I could not be sure until we tried.

During our labors we lost all count of time. We ate, slept, and worked when we were hungry, tired, and refreshed. I forgot to check my watch, and the number of days we had been underground we could now only guess at. In fact, the very mention of that subject was apt to cause arguments, until, by Annet's suggestion, it was forbidden.

But at last we had the raft ready, which was as secure a method of transportation as all suggestions could make it, and we loaded it with supplies we would need for the trails above, if we were ever fated to reach the surface of Beltane again.

I counted heads in the bunks on our last night in the base. One was missing. Once more I made that silent roll call, this time using my forefinger to number each.

Gytha! But where—?

I had my bedroll by the door, but I had visited Annet in her curtained cubby to see if she needed aught for Dagny. Her sister could have slipped out then. Where? Surely after the adventure of the twins she was not trying exploration on her own!

No calling yet. No need to rouse the camp until I did some searching on my own. I slipped out to look about. It took a moment for my eyes to adjust to the dark, and then I caught the faint glow of a belt torch as if radiating from some place among the rocks at the foot of the ledged cliff. With irritation at her recklessness, for we could never be sure, though we had found no more traces, that there were no more monsters in the caverns, I started after.

I planned to speak my mind sharply when I caught up with her, but as I saw where she stood, I paused. The shadows thrown by the debris were thick there until she went to work, for Gytha held in her hands one of the rods from the cache, its point to the cliff wall. From the point came a series of flashes, feeble indeed when compared to the blaze it had produced in my fight with the monster.

"Gytha!"

She turned her head, but she did not drop the rod. And there was a stubborn determination in her face, which at that moment clearly showed her kinship with Annet.

"You said these were no good for what you wanted," she returned defiantly, ready to justify her action. "But they'll work for this."

She was using the two rods, first one and then the other, to incise letters on the rock. Reading tapes have for so long been in use that manual writing had been almost forgotten. But on Beltane the lack of supplies had revived some of the ancient forms of record keeping, and Gytha had taken with enthusiasm to such learning.

"'Griss Lugard.'" She read what she had already set there. "'Friend'—It is true; he was our friend. He did the best for us that he knew. And I think he would like that said of him more than to list his rank or tell other things."

I took the rod from her, and why I did it, I cannot tell to this day, but below the rather shaky letters of her "Friend" I nursed every spark from that rod and the other to add five other letters.

Gytha read them one at a time as I set them into the rock.

"P—i—p—e—r—Piper. Oh, he would have liked that to linger in memory, too. It is just right, Vere! I couldn't go away and leave him without any marker at all!"

Romance learned from story tapes, some would have said. But I knew she was right, that this was what must be done. And I was glad she had thought of it. As a fitting finish I thrust both of the now exhausted rods into crevices of the pile so they stood upright, staffs without pennons, markers that perhaps no living creature would see again but that we would remember down the years.

As none had marked our going, so none witnessed our return. Nor did we mention it again, even to each other, but went directly to bed.

In the "morning," if morning it was above the layers of rock and soil between us and the open, we made a last check of our kits. We had drawn on the supplies Lugard and the earlier sojourners here had left. I now wore a Service tunic from which I had stripped rank badges that had no meaning. The one that fitted me best had carried a captain's shooting star, and I wondered who had left it here and what had happened to him on or between other worlds.

We made the descent into the ice cavern easily enough, having done with Dagny as we did earlier with Lugard, immobilized her in blankets and an outside wrapping of plasta that would protect her once we were afloat.

We had left the raft by the broken wall, and on it were already lashed the heavier of our packs. It cost effort to launch it and then hold it steady for embarkation. When I got aboard and loosed one of the hooked lines while Thad threw off the other, I had a moment of faint-heartedness and apprehension concerning the unknown that might lie ahead, wondering if we had chosen the best solution after all. Yet I also knew that we dared waste no more time if we would save Dagny.

Luckily, the current was not as swift as I thought, just strong enough to carry us along. One of the big beamers had been mounted on the prow (if a raft can be said to have a prow) so we would have a warning of dangers ahead. And Thad and I took the poles on either side to ward off any swing against the walls. The air remained cold, but as we were pulled away from the ice cave, it grew less frosty and finally became more like the temperature of the camp cave.

I turned to my watch again as a check upon our passage. We had left at twelve, but whether that marked midnight or noon I had no idea. By fifteen hours we were still in passage, and while once or twice the roof had closed over us so that we had to lie on the raft's surface, we had not had any real trouble.

We were ten hours on that voyage, and I had no way of figuring how far the waters took us. But suddenly Emrys cried out and pointed up, his hand outlined against the back rays of the beamer—

"A star!"

At the same moment the beamer showed us a bush that certainly could not have grown underground, though we still passed
between rock walls. We were aware then of fresher air to fill our
lungs, not conscious of the underground taint of what we had
been breathing until it was gone. So we were out of the caves,
but since it was night, we had no idea of where we were.

I crawled forward and loosed the beamer so that I could swing it
a little from right to left. Bushes, but they were small and stunted-
looking. Rocks, among them pieces of drift that argued that at
times the river must run higher here than it did at present.

Then the canyon, or whatever it was in which we floated, widened out, and a long spit of sand ran out into the water. The raft
made one of its half turns, since Thad was alone at the pole, and
grounded against that sand bar with a thump that rocked us all.
I swept the beamer to pick up a sandy beach with tufts of coarse
grass growing farther up. A good-enough refuge to hold us until
daylight. I said as much, and the rest agreed.

We were stiff and cramped from the voyage. Thad and I fared
the best because of our employment at the poles. We tumbled
out onto the sand bar, and then all turned to drag our craft out
of the pull of the current until we could be sure that it would
not be tugged away, leaving us marooned.

So we made camp, and then I looked at the compass that had
been among the supplies. The second map showed nothing of the
river. That must have been hidden from the mapper. But according to the compass, we had come southwest—which meant we
must be over the mountains, in the general direction of the large
Reserves. This was all wilderness if I was right. But there were
the Ranger stations, and if I could sight some known landmarks
in the morning, I thought we might find one of those. Even to
be out under the stars gave me such a feeling of relief that I suddenly had no doubts that all would go better from now on.

We ate and unrolled our beds. Fatigue settled down as might
another blanket. I put Thad at one end of the camp, with his
stunner to hand, while I took the other. I did not think that
either of us was in shape to play sentry, but we must do the
best we could.

Sound woke me. A loud squawk was repeated. I opened my
eyes to sunlight, blinked, and saw a bird walk into water and the

river close over its head. A guskaw! We might have alarmed it
by our presence here, but the fact that I saw it at all meant we
were in the wilderness. I sat up to look around.

None of the other blanketed bundles stirred. It was quite early
morning, the light grayish, and we were in a canyon. I looked
back the way we had come and saw my landmark, one large
enough indeed. Whitecone, a former volcano that now wore a
perpetual tip of snow. So we had come over the mountains by
underground ways.

With Whitecone in that direction, this must be the Redwater,
though the clear stream lapping the sand only a couple of arms'
lengths away had none of the characteristic crimson tinge it wore
in the Reserve. I knew of no other body of water as large in this
direction, and since my ambition had been to be a Ranger here,
I had pored over aerial survey maps of this area.

If this was the Redwater, and I was sure it was, we need only
continue our voyage and we would reach the bridge on the Reserve
road. Then Anlav headquarters was only a short distance north
from the bridge. I gave a sigh of relief. It was good—almost as
good as sighting the com tower of Kynvet.

I set about getting breakfast, using the portable cook unit.
Warm food would mark our triumph over the dark and the
caves. One by one the others roused, as eager to press on as I
now was. There would be a flitter at the station. If we could not
all crowd into that, why Annet could take Dagny and as many
others as possible, and the rest of us could wait on a second trip.
My plans spun ahead, and then I remembered. We might have
come out of darkness into light, but what had been happening
here? It could be that we were no safer really than we had been
at the cave camp.

So I warned them that we must move warily still. I did not
think they all agreed with me, however, and I made it plain by
an order, though whether I could enforce that I did not know.

"We do not know what has happened. For our own safety
we must be sure just who or what we face. There is a chance
that any trouble at the port or the settlements would not have
reached here. I hope we can get help at the Anlav headquarters.
There will be a com there, and with it we can learn more. But
we must go carefully."

Some of them nodded. I had expected a protest from Annet,

but that did not come. Then she gave the ghost of a smile and said, "Well enough. To that I agree. But the sooner we do find out, the better."

I had wondered at her change of position. Had she at last, to herself, admitted that Lugard had been telling the truth and that we returned to danger and not to aid and comfort? But I had no opportunity to ask her.

Once more we floated the raft and repacked it. But here the current was not enough, and Thad and I stood and poled until we grew too tired to push. Then Annet handed Dagny to Pritha, and she and Gytha took my place, Emrys and Sabian, Thad's. In spite of doing the best that we could, dark came and we still had not reached the bridge. The river, now running between banks of red soil, had taken on the color that made it a proper landmark.

Once more we camped, rose with the dawn, and bent to the poles. It was midmorning when the bridge came into sight. We forced the raft ashore, made a cache of most of its cargo, and took only trail supplies. Gytha, Annet, Dagny, Ifors, Dinan, and Pritha settled into hiding at the end of the bridge where there was a good cover of brush, and three of us went on, Sabian taking sentry go at the other end of the span.

There were no marks of any recent traffic on the road. Ground cars were in general use here. Hoppers too often frightened the animals. And there had been a recent storm, which had left patches of red mud drying and cracking under the hot midday sun. No marks across that, save here and there a paw or hoof print where some creature had gone.

That unmarked road was disturbing, and I found myself drawing my stunner—the one that had been Annet's—looking from right to left and back again as if I feared sudden attack from the walls of brush.

TEN

"This is the largest Reserve, isn't it?" Thad moved closer, his voice low, as if he shared my uneasiness and feared being overheard, while Emrys kept to the middle of the road a little behind.

"Yes. Anlav." I did not believe we need fear the animals. They kept mainly to the wildest parts of the Reserve, though I did not know about the mutants that had been housed here.

Anlav had once had top priority among the mutation labs. But that had been some years ago. The curtailing of such work had made them center on the Pilav Reserve for a time.

We rounded a curve to see the Ranger station. Like all such posts, it had been deliberately fashioned to blend in with the natural scenery. Its walls did not run straight but were made of rough stone unsmoothed. The roof had sod and vines planted on it, growing as if their support were a natural hillock, and the vehicle park was concealed by a brush wall.

I cupped my hand trumpet-fashion about my lips and gave the recognition call. But though we eyed the patch of dark that must be the door with growing impatience, there was no response. Now there was nothing but to cross the open.

If the force field was up, we would know it soon enough. Warning the boys, I took the lead, my hand outstretched as a warn-off. Animals coming against that screen suffered, I had been told, a mild shock. What effect it might have on a human I did not know.

But my hand met no barrier, and I came to the door, which stood a quarter open. The distrust of all about me grew with every step I took. Anlav was of such importance that the Ranger station should be manned at all times. What had happened here?

The door swung in at once under my touch. I crossed the threshold warily, coming into the main room. It followed the general pattern of such places, consisting of three rooms, the largest running the full length, a combination living-office space with a cook unit at the far end. To the back would lie a bunk room and, flanking it, a small lab and storage space.

I almost fell, for my eyes were bothered by the contrast between the light outside and this interior gloom. There was something on the floor to trip me. I switched on my belt torch and glanced down at a sheet of plasta, the kind generally used for storage protection. As I swept the light on around the room, I saw other signs of disorder. A chair had been pushed back so hurriedly that it had fallen on its back, and legs pointing at me like stunner barrels. There were dishes on the table with dried bits of food. And on the desk a com-ticker had gone on spewing forth report tape, which curled to the floor until the machine had finally run down.

The wall rack on which large-duty stunners usually rested was empty. There was a rustling as I approached the desk. A furred thing, moving too fast for me to get good sight of it, darted out from under that piece of furniture and scurried on through the door into the storeroom. The post had not only been left suddenly, but also some time ago.

I saw the control plate for the lights and passed my hand across it twice for the brightest beam.

Thad asked from the doorway, "No one here?"

I tried the bunk room. Small personal items were still on the hanging shelves there, and all four bunks were neatly made. Whatever had called the staff away, they had not packed. I made sure of this by trying the wall cupboards, peering at changes of uniform and underclothing.

The lab-storage was neat, but there were some signs of rummaging at floor level—gnawed containers, rations spilled and half eaten out of them. I heard a warning snarl from behind one overturned box.

"They're gone," I answered Thad's question as I backed out of that room, not wanting to turn away from whatever might be hidden there. There are some small creatures that do not look menacing to the uninformed but are formidable if you underrate them.

There might be one possible answer. I crossed to the desk where the duty tape had twisted into coils on the floor. Though I could not judge the amount of use such a machine had in Anlav, I thought that more than one day, or perhaps two, had elapsed while the machine ground out unread reports. And there was no way of telling how long it had been since it ran down entirely.

The loops of tape were in code, but it was a simple one, for condensation only. I read it without trouble—all routine dictation from Eye-Spies set up on feeding grounds and on game trails, reports of animal movements. There were two alarms about predators in grazing grounds, which would ordinarily have sent the Rangers on field duty out with a stunner.

"Com—" Thad pointed to the other installation.

One stride brought me to it. When I picked up the hand mike, I could hear the unmistakable thrum-thrum of an open connection. But there was no other sound carrying through. I levered the visa-plate, but that remained blank. The broadcast did not come through.

"Call in!" Thad was beside me.

"Not yet." I put the mike down and fingered the button that broke the relay. "Not until we know more of who may be there—"

For a moment it seemed he might question my decision, and then he nodded.

"Might be alerting those we wouldn't want to know—"

"Just so. Let's look for a flitter."

What we found in the vehicle park were a ground car and a hopper. The former had its engine box open, and tools lay in disarray as if the one working on it had been hastily summoned elsewhere. Thad went to look at it.

"Putting in a new pick-up unit—just needs the tri-hookup, but it's based."

Emrys had gone to the hopper, climbed in, and was gunning for a take-off before I could stop him. But there was no purr of answer. Perhaps both vehicles had been abandoned because they were useless for those in a hurry.

"Get out!" I snapped at Emrys. "Remember what we agreed—go slow. We take a hopper, and we can be picked up on an income screen. If we use any transportation, it must be the ground car—that has a distort shield."

"And," I added as he came out, his look sullen rather than contrite, "if you need action, get back to the bridge and bring the others in. It's going to rain and soon."

The brightness of the morning was gone. Clouds rolled dark and heavy, and one could almost drink the gathering moisture from the air. As he went, I turned to Thad and the land car. He was right. About two-thirds of the work on it had been done. It needed only the final connections. And if that was the only repair needed, once we had completed that we would have a mode of transportation far better suited to our purpose now than any far-ranging hopper or flitter. Though it traveled only at ground level, it was equipped with screens that distorted the vision of those without so that it was, for all purposes, invisible. It could not travel fast, but it would be able to move without detection, though a radar could pick up some hint of it. Meant to get close to the animals on the open grazing ranges, it would be a type of transport unknown to the refugees, if they were now our enemies.

"Close it up now," I told Thad. "We can't do anything until the rain is over. Let's hurry the rest along."

We did not beat the rain, for we were all wet through when we at last dodged into the post. I laid Dagny down on one of the inner bunks, and Thad quickly switched on the heat-dry unit. When we closed the door to the storm, we were well sheltered, even better than at the cave base.

"What happened here?" Annet looked at the dishes, the chair none of us had bothered to right, and the tangle of tape on the floor.

"The staff must have left in a hurry—I don't know how long ago. Meanwhile, let's make sure we have no uninvited guests." Stunner in hand, I went into the lab-storage. I warned the others to keep outside and turned my weapon from maximum to low, since what I hunted was small enough to take refuge behind a box only knee high.

I gave a swift cross spray of the deadening ray and then pulled crates and boxes around until I discovered my quarry, lying limp, its sharply pointed nose turned up as it slept, if not peacefully, well.

It was an inflax, always a camp raider when it could get a chance, but not as harmless as it looked, for this was a male with the hollowed fangs for the irritating poison. I picked it up and laid it on a box top, while I searched for any other visitors. But this seemed to be alone. I carried it out and pointed to its armament in warning, then set it outside the door under an outcrop of the wall that would keep the worst of the storm from it. The outer air and the added whip of water would speedily awaken it.

Annet had found the com and changed the dial to the range of the port. I had just time to grab the mike from her hand.

"What do you—" she began fiercely.

"We agreed—no rash steps until we were sure!" I reminded her.

"We haven't time to poke and pry!" She tried to force the mike from me. "We have to get Dagny to the medico and as quickly as possible. If we call, they could send a flitter."

"First, try the incall." I thought that the fact I had not been able to pick up any broadcast might impress her. "Feeholme is the only settlement this side of the mountains. Try that!"

I gave the mike to her and clicked on the proper relays. If there was any broadcasting, we could pick up the chatter, even if our wave was not narrowed to either call or reception. Again we could hear the thrum of an open beam but no whisper along it. Once more I dialed for receive, taking a chance to do so much, my hand ready to break connection instantly were we to attract the sort of attention we did not want. But the sound of the system was all that came to me.

Annet stared at the mike in her hand and stooped to read the symbol above the switch I had activated.

"I don't understand. They should be on the air. At this hour there would not just be an open circuit and no broadcast."

"Unless there was no one there—"

She shook her head violently, not only in denial of my suggestion, I thought, but also against her own fears.

"But the com is *never* untended. Try the distress call—"

"No. Listen, Annet. If Lugard was right, we could trigger worse than what we have now. We agreed not to rush blindly. There is a ground car here. They were repairing it when they left, but

I can finish off their job as soon as the weather clears a little. Ground cars may be slow, but they have protection which may be of benefit to us. I promise you, as soon as we can use it, we'll take off for Feeholme. And from there a lift over the mountains is nothing. But tell me, does this suggest to you that a normal state of affairs exists?" I indicated the room. "And when they left, they took all the armament this station had."

"All right. But as soon as we can—"

"We'll go," I promised her.

She moved away from the com and stooped to pick up the chair to set it straight again. Then she was at the cook unit, opening the supply cupboard above it, while I went to search the desk for any hint of what had happened here. There was nothing but routine record tapes. The tape from the floor, though I gave it more detailed study now, also held nothing but reports from the Reserve.

The force of the storm lessened by midafternoon. As soon as we could venture out, Thad and I were back at the ground car. He proved knowledgeable and was the kind of co-worker one could wish for. But since neither of us was trained as a tech, we were not as swift about it as we might have been. We had no more than made the last connection and slammed down the cover, than a second storm was upon us, driving us to shelter in the post.

That was a wild night. Perhaps our sojourn underground made it seem twice as bad as it might have otherwise. I had a sudden idea to fit another tape in the general report and click it on, centering its attention to details of what might be happening on the road between us and Feeholme.

It clicked away steadily, grinding out code for downed trees, overflow of some streams, animals fleeing before the lash of wind and rain. And as the worst of these possible delays were noted, I marked them in turn on a map from the desk so that we would have preparation for trouble the next day.

We started shortly after dawn. It was a wet world that faced us, but the violence of yesterday was passed. The ground car had been intended to carry equipment throughout the Reserve, and by stripping it of all but the seats, we had room for the whole party within it. I did not yet activate the distort, since I must save that for the approach to Feeholme.

The road was gullied and puddled, but the treads of the car were meant to take worse than that smoothly. We ground on at a steady pace. Twice we had to detour around fallen trees, and once there were a few anxious moments when we forded a stream and the storm-swollen waters lashed around the sturdy body of the vehicle as high as the seats within, sending a few trickles about the doors to wet our feet. But I went at a slant, more with the current than directly across, and the treads bit and pulled us up on comparatively dry land.

We caught sight of animals but always at a distance. At noon we pulled into the lee of a high rock spur that was capped with a pickup rod, one of the link of supervisory contacts across the Reserve. There was no sign anyone had been there, though one of the guidelines for the pickup had broken and whacked against the rod in the pull of the wind.

Annet, however, had no eyes for what was around us in the wilderness, for she had at last won a small response from Dagny, who asked for water. Not that she seemed aware of those around her, but as we ate, she sucked from an E-tube, and it was not necessary to squeeze it into her mouth and then try to get her to swallow.

I thought we might make it by dark and began to prepare Annet now for the further precautions I wanted to take when we reached there. When I spoke of halting the car, leaving them in it in distort while I scouted, she seemed amiable, but it was as if she humored me, not that she believed it necessary.

Feeholme I had seen only once, and then it had been an in-and-out visit, a point of departure and change from the flitter that had brought me with two other Ranger candidates from the port to the hopper that carried us into the Reserve. It was larger than Kynvet because it was the only settlement this side of the mountains. But it was no more than a village probably when compared to towns off-world. It was the headquarters for Rangers.

We crawled on, and I kept an anxious eye on the gauges. The worry over the reason for the half-repaired engine was always at the back of my mind. If transportation failed us here, it might be grave. But so far there were no signs of trouble.

Twilight came early as clouds were massing again, and I put on what speed I could to race another storm. We came to the foot of a rise, and there I turned off the road, creeping into a small copse of trees and through that to the ravine they guarded. There were rocks here to form a natural wall, and I backed the car against that. If the others kept inside, they would have the best protection I could find from any gale.

I did not take anything with me save the stunner, and it was my hope that somehow, somewhere, I would find a replacement for that, a weapon of greater power. I made Annet promise to keep the lights off while I was gone, while Thad took my seat at the controls with orders to switch on the distort as soon as I was out of range.

Then I moved up the rise. When I turned to look back, it was as if the car had vanished, and I knew a small lift of relief. They were safe as long as they stayed inside that.

There was no reason to return to the road. I cut across country, where there was more cover. Below now I could see the dark blot of Feeholme, a very dark blot for not a single light showed, and that was an immediate warning of trouble.

The country around the settlement had been cleared of the thicker growth of trees and underbrush, leaving only enough to please the eye and give shade. Here the houses and the head-quarters buildings were not set off by themselves but around an oval, the center point of which was a landing place for flitters and hoppers. I did not know the exact population, but I thought that those dark buildings should shelter at least two hundred. In addition to the Reserve headquarters, there was a shopping center, which had once sold off-world products but now served as an exchange for the output of various other labs and settlements—for there was a small trade in specialties from different sectors. Each of the settlements was practically self-sufficient, however—a reason for the dwindling interest in off-world trade, which had not, after the first ten years of pioneering, ever supplied more than luxuries and exotics.

I came now to cultivated fields, drawing back to leap the safe-current—until I saw that there was no thin blue radiance string-ing from post to post. A branch pushed forward to where the current should run did not shrivel. The protection for the crops, already near harvesting, had not been activated. I saw a small herd of verken taking advantage of that. Judging by the extent of trampled and eaten plants, I guessed that this had not been their first visit here.

They snorted, snuffled, and scattered at my coming, but they did not pursue their loping run far, facing about to see if I would give chase. When I did not, they shuffled back for such a feast as they had probably never known before.

Dark houses, inactive field protection—it added up in a way I did not like. Then I came upon a hopper, well off the road, its nose slammed into a wall until the front was crumpled. I flashed my torch into the cabin, then flicked it off and tried to erase from my mind what that instant of light had shown me. But having seen it, I came directly into the open. *That* would not have been there had there been anyone left in Feeholme to care.

So I tried the first house and again found—No, a single glance was enough to send me out faster than I had entered. But there was still the headquarters, and perhaps I could discover something there, if only a hint on a message tape. There were others who had died in the open. And there were scavengers from the Reserve come to feast. I avoided what I could. But I had to step over part of a skeleton to enter the building I sought. There I found men who must have died at their posts in the com room and elsewhere, but nowhere any sign of what had come so suddenly to end a settlement almost a hundred planet years old.

I made myself examine some of the dead. There were no wounds or laser burns. It would seem that these had simply fallen at their duties and died, perhaps in a matter of seconds.

Gas? But what of those in the open? Or had they been the stronger and managed to crawl as far before collapse came? I could not account for such wholesale slaughter by any weapon that I knew.

The off-worlders might have such. We had heard rumors of all types of things developed for the exploitation of enemy planets, things that would remove a population and leave their world empty. Had the refugees put into service such a one here—perhaps trying it out before they turned pirate as Lugard had foretold some of the remnants of the tattered fleets would do? But why such wanton slaughter?

I stood in the com room. The circuits were still open as they had been when a dead or dying hand slipped from the control board. I saw the steady light of clear channel on the board. Stepping closer, I read the symbol for Haychax over the mountains.

But all that came through the amplifier was the same thrum-thrum we had picked up at the Ranger station.

At any rate, this town could give us no aid. And I was not about to lead our party into what lay here. But I did search for weapons. In the end, I found three more stunners and one long-shot laser meant for ground clearing, but that was too bulky to transport, and when I turned it on, the glow was so reduced that I knew it near extinction. The fact that in a settlement that supplied three Reserves these were all to be found in the way of arms was another disturbing point. It would seem there had been other searchers before me. When I came into the store place, I found evidence of that.

I faced wild confusion. Boxes and containers had been ripped open and much of their content wastefully spilled and trampled. The tracks in some of the wastage were signature enough to tell me that no Beltane settler had done this, for two or three boot prints were so clearly marked that there could be no mistaking—space boots. The looters must have been from the refugee camp. Had they also caused the death of the town? I went down on hands and knees and tested with fingertip the leakage of a broken canister and decided it had begun perhaps only a day earlier, while the town had met its fate long before that—perhaps even on the same day we had gone underground, or shortly thereafter.

Now I foraged in what was left, finding a drop bag meant to be parachuted to Rangers in the Reserve where there was no landing place. Into that I packed small cans and ration tubes. We had brought little enough out of the caves, and if we had to stay away from settlements, we would need all we could find.

It was too heavy to shoulder when I left, so I had to drag it after me, but it had been made for hard usage, and I did not worry. I had come out of another door into the landing place of the settlement. Here again was a scene of wanton destruction. I dared to use my torch, though only in quick flashes. What I saw were burned flitters, at least two of them. Half a dozen hoppers had been worked over with lasers until they were masses of half-melted metal. There was not one remaining unwrecked transport.

I had seen enough of Feeholme—the tomb that Feeholme had become. There were two other Ranger stations on this side of the mountains, but I doubted whether we could find help at either.

And if we returned to Kynvet, it would only be by taking the car as far as we could run it, then hiking over the mountains on our feet. But perhaps there was no reason for such a return—

Dragging my pack of supplies, I went back across the fields. I was in the shadow of a copse of trees when I saw a spark in the sky. It was well away from Feeholme, but it was no star—rather the light of a flitter. Its course was erratic, moving up and down, side to side, as if whatever hand lay on the controls was either inexperienced or under some difficulty. I headed to where I had left the car, and I hoped that those I had left there would not strive to signal the pilot. What I had seen here made me more determined than ever that we must keep our guard.

Rain broke then, cold and heavy, and I found the bag a greater weight as I struggled up the rise. I could no longer see the light of the flitter. There was a roll of thunder and clashes of violet lightning, which made me flinch involuntarily and try to run.

ELEVEN

I lay belly down under the very dubious shelter of a bush, my head pointing downslope toward the car I could not see as long as the distort shield was up. The rain water ran down my back, gathered in the hollow of my belt when I moved, and then, in sudden icy jerks, trickled down over hips and thighs. Though it was summer and the days were warm enough, this stormy night held the threat of coming autumn, and I wanted nothing so much as to be under cover. Yet the sign of that flitter had made me doubly cautious. Any signal I gave those waiting below might betray us.

Cupping my hands about my torch, I made a funnel so the ray I needed would be hidden to anything above, though no flyer with a grain of sense would keep a light-bodied flitter aloft amid such tossing winds.

Now I pressed the button on, off, on, off. As far as I could see they ought to be able to pick up those flashes easily. But when nothing moved below, uneasiness boiled in me, and I was ready to go charging down with a stunner. My ever-present fear was that they had attempted to signal the flitter with the car com, and if they had been successful, who knew now what we might have to face.

There was a flickering below, and then the dark bulk of the car came into view. No lights on in it—so my warnings had taken

123

root to that extent! I got to my feet and went down, dragging my heavy bag.

"Vere?" Annet's voice in anxious inquiry.

"Yes!" I scrambled to the door. "Let me in—quick!"

I thrust myself in as I might have charged an enemy-occupied room. There were startled protests as I forced a place for my wet self.

"That flitter—you did not com it?" I leaned across Annet to thumb up the distort once again, only breathing easily when that defense was on.

"No," Thad answered. "You said—"

"Why shouldn't we?" Annet's demand overrode his answer. "He held the mike where I couldn't reach it, or I would have. Why—what has happened, Vere?"

I was so tired I could no longer fence. After all, they were going to find out sooner or later, and they should have been bright enough to guess for themselves with all the clues we had had.

"I found a dead town," I replied flatly.

"You mean everyone gone?" She sounded more startled—disbelieving. "But where did they go—to the port, over the mountains?"

"I said dead, not deserted. A town of the dead—"

I felt her stir beside me, as if she cringed away to the extent anyone could move on the overcrowded seat.

"But how—killed?"

"Those I—I looked at showed no signs of laser or blaster. They had apparently just dropped at their duty posts. But the town is dead. And its store has been looted at a later time. I brought two stunners—the rest of the weapons are gone."

"Then Lugard was right!" Thad cut in. "The refugees attacked—but why kill everyone?"

"No!" Annet was shivering. "No! It can't be true! Vere, we've got to get back to Kynvet. Take a flitter—there must be flitters at Feeholme."

"There were flitters. Someone systematically destroyed them. Lasers had been used on those—on hoppers, too. There is no workable transportation left."

"Then—then what are we going to do? Dagny—"

"We have this car, and I brought all the supplies I could that were light and yet highly sustaining. Our best move now is to head back into the Reserve—cross the mountains—"

"That flitter—" Thad asked. "Do you suppose it was the looters?"

"It could be our people, hunting survivors," Annet said. "If it was and we didn't com them—" Her tone was accusing.

"Did you ever see a normal flitter following such a flight pattern?" Thad asked for me. "There was something wrong with the machine or the pilot. Do we go back the way we came, Vere?"

It was a temptation. There was the Ranger headquarters where we could find shelter, perhaps use it for a base while we scouted a possible route over the mountains again. However, it might well be that any structure would serve as a magnet for looters. There were maps in plenty; they could have found one in Feeholme that located every station in the Reserves.

"I think not. We strike due southeast from here, into the hill country. There is a reception point for mutants at Gur Horn. We can head for that—perhaps pick up more supplies there."

We would go nowhere this night, however, uncomfortable as it would be; rather we would try to shelter and rest in the car. I was in no mind to switch on driving lights, which would be beacons in the dark. Rough cross-country travel was impossible, and to seek the roads was to ask for discovery. I thought Annet would raise opposition to this decision, but she did not. Instead, she set about reorganizing our seating so as to give maximum comfort in our minimum of space. Some of the food was shared out.

We slept, I think out of sheer fatigue. Twice I was awakened by cries from the sleeping children and knew that they dreamed. But I did not, and for that I was thankful. Annet was quick to soothe and comfort. The last time, when Pritha whimpered herself half awake, Annet reached out her hand as if seeking support, and I grasped it. There was no other sound from Pritha, but Annet turned her face nearer mine and whispered, "Vere, *can* we get over the mountains?"

"If we take one step at a time, we can. This is summer; the Reserve pass will be open. If we use that, we shall come out not too far from Butte Hold." Then I hesitated, remembering those visitors Lugard had faced down with a far more formidable weapon than any we possessed. If a hint of treasure had drawn them to the Butte, they might be there now, hunting for Lugard's rumored find.

"Vere—" Her whisper was now such a thin thread of sound I could hardly hear it. "There was something—"

"What?" I prompted when she did not continue.

"You know, at Yetholme, they did controlled experiments for the forces." I could hear her swallow as if the words were being forced out of her.

"That was years back, and didn't they close down entirely?"

"Everyone said so. Dr. Corfu—you know what he did."

"Took a double cold-sleep pill and never came out of it."

"He—he wouldn't go ahead with their last experiment, and they pressured him terribly. I heard Mother—she had seen the initial steps. They were working on a mutated virus. Vere, it would kill off intelligent beings—it affected the brain—but it left a world intact, to be taken over later by jump troops. It had no affect on animals unless they were specially sensitized to it. Vere, what if—?"

Again I remembered one of Lugard's warnings. There might be secrets here which would-be raiders would welcome as part of their armament for future attacks. A virus with such properties, seeded in secret across an unsuspecting city, even a continent, or a world, a period of waiting—then easy picking for the seeders. But a virus—my hand caught at the latch of the car door—if such a thing had been loosed in Feeholme, then I could now be a carrier, already a dead man myself! Perhaps it was too late for all of us. I had spent the night here, in close quarters, breathed the same air, touched them. They could all be dead because of me!

Those in the town had died so quickly and at their posts that my guess had been some type of gas loosed off to blanket the settlement. Would a plague have worked in that manner?

"I might have—"

"No. You said they had been dead for some time." Her whisper was ragged.

"Yes."

"What they worked on at Yetholme was a forty-eight-hour strike. Then the virus died, unless someone came too soon. And there were immune shots. If we could find records, we would know. But you can't take this car up to the pass, can you?"

"No. But we shall use it as far as we can. Gur Horn first. If I remember rightly, there was never more than a small staff there. It was a mutant introduction point, and all they did was watch over the high types. They may have been summoned just as the other Rangers were. We can get more supplies there, shelter. It is the highest of the permanent Reserve bases."

"What mutants were there?"

"I don't know. The time we visited Anlav, we didn't go there. They simply informed us as to what it was when we sighted it from the flitter."

"Would the staff have transportation?"

"A hopper maybe, a ground car certainly. They had to be ready to transport injured animals for treatment. There was always the danger of a mutant being attacked by a control. And in order to study them properly, they couldn't keep them penned or caged."

A hopper, yes, we might just find a hopper there. And that would lighten our mountain journey by about half. I found myself impatient to set out for Gur Horn.

The storm blew itself out by dawn. And as soon as we had light enough to see before us, I put the car on steady power, though that was drained by the energy to keep up the distort, which was never intended to run steadily. These cars were meant for very rough usage, but I had no idea how long or how far their unit charges would take them. We might be put afoot before we reached our goal, though I tried to make the best time possible.

Luckily, the southeastern way took us mainly across open country. It was rolling, though, with an up-and-down hillock route, which, before noon, forced us twice to pause when Pritha and Ifors became ill from the motion. Dagny lay inert, wedged in with blanket rolls. She ate and drank, but she lay with her eyes closed, and Annet could not tell whether she slept or was in a stupor.

We nooned beside a small stream, eating E-rations rather than trying to heat any food. The sun was hot outside the car, and it bore down on one's head and burned any exposed portion of skin. We did not tarry long, and I filled all our canteens before we pulled out. I had no notion of water supply in the hills to which we were pointed.

Those grew higher about us, and I had to find a twisting path among them instead of taking an upgrade and downgrade route

as I had before. It seemed I was right about the lack of water, for
the terrain grew more and more desert. Storm waters had torn
through gullies, leaving drift behind, and our progress grew slower
and slower. Then we hit upon a cleared trail that could only be
that to Gur Horn, and recklessly I turned into it, determined we
must make speed.

Distances as seen from the air and the ground vary a great
deal. When we had flown this route on the instruction trip, it had
seemed that the mutant station was a very short space removed
from Ranger headquarters and that both were about within shouting distance of Feeholme. Now I wondered if I had mistaken the
way and missed Gur Horn, to travel lost into the hills.

We moved down an alley between high-growing spiggan bushes.
Since it was fruiting time for those, the branches were so loaded
with their purple burden that they bent far ground-ward, and our
road was crowded. Insects, from small ones to those large Zand
moths that I could not cover with my hand, wore their brilliant
wings outspread as they clung to the overripe and rotting berries
already fallen in a mucky carpet across ground and road. There were
birds in plenty, and here and there small animals that had glutted
themselves into a drunken stupor and lay, some on their backs,
their limp paws pointed skyward as they slept off their indulgence.
I knew it was good we drove enclosed, for the odor of the too ripe
fruit was nothing anyone would want to smell twice.

We were away from the far end of this feasting place when
I stopped, for the creature standing in the middle of the way
facing us had not fed here, and its stance now could only be
explained by the fact that it not only saw us (though how could
that be with the distort on?) but also that it wanted to halt us
purposefully.

"An ystroben!" Gytha leaned forward until her head was level
with my shoulder. "Vere, it's an ystroben!"

At first sight I would have agreed with her. It had the thick
red fur, the rounded head, the fan-shaped, fur-edged ears, the
rounded muzzle, the black paws, and the stub tail. Yet there
were differences, and the longer one stared at the animal, the
more apparent those differences became. In the first place, the
head—it had a higher and wider dome of skull. Also, it was
larger than any ystroben I had ever seen. And it was far from
timid. Also—it saw us!

"Vere, it wants us to do something—see!"

Had I not watched what happened, I would not have believed, for the beast arose from its plump haunches, came a little farther toward us, and deliberately raised a forepaw to beckon. There was no mistaking that gesture—it *had* beckoned.

"A mutant!"

"It wants us to do something," Gytha repeated, emphasizing that with a firm grip on my shoulder.

"But"—Annet's hand went out to touch the lever among the controls—"the distort is on. How can it see us?"

"If it is a mutant," Gytha retorted, "it can do all sorts of things. Vere, we must see what it wants."

But I had no mind to play games with animals. And mutants could be untrustworthy. Who knows what could be roaming about now, freed from some lab control by the failure of a dead man's hand to touch the right buttons?

I activated one of the safety devices of the car. And, while we felt nothing at all, the things feeding on the berries seemed to go mad. Those that flew and could still depend upon their wings and their equilibration arose in the air, some so sharply that they collided. And the four-footed ones still conscious rolled on the ground or ran as fast as their legs could carry them, scattering from the vicinity of the car as if that had exploded.

The ystroben shuddered and strove to stay where it was, making a visibly great effort to do so. Then, its mouth opened in what must have been a shriek, though whether of rage or pain we could not hear within our soundproof cocoon. And it fell to its four feet, to weave drunkenly off the center, staggering into the wall of bushes.

"What did you do?" Thad asked.

"Sonics—used to ward off animal attack."

Gytha's hand on my shoulder became a fist, which she brought down with bruising impact on my flesh.

"You didn't have to do that!" she cried. "It wasn't going to hurt us. It wanted us to do something—"

I closed my ears to her protest and stepped up the speed of the car, wanting to be out of the overpopulated bush as quickly as we could. We came into an open space where there was more luxuriant growth than we had seen for hours. The reason for that was plain, for a fountain played on a level space, and from it flowed a stream, to reach a little hollow, puddle into a pond, and again seek a way on a pebbled bed until it was swallowed up by reeds and water-loving vegetation.

Beyond the fountain was another of the artfully constructed houses blended with care into the landscape. Behind that soared the unusual formation of rock that gave it its name—Gur Horn, for that towering spear of stone was indeed shaped to the fashion of a gur horn, even having the spiraled markings one sees on the adult male of the species.

We had come so suddenly into the open that I had no time for any hide and scout precautions I wanted to take. But there was no sign of life, and the parking space to the side of the house housed not even a ground car.

I pushed off the distort, and instantly the world was alive with the noise it had cloaked. Noise it was—a mournful lowering, a moaning, and now and then a scream or rumble or growl, all of which seemed to come from the house.

"What—?" Annet had her stunner ready.

I had been about to open the door; now I hesitated. The amount of that sound and its plaint suggested trouble, bad trouble. Yet I could see nothing moving.

"Vere, the ystroben—" Gytha demanded my attention, pulling at the arm she had bruised minutes earlier. I turned my head in the direction she pointed. The animal that had tried to withstand the sonic, or its close twin, staggered out of the berry-walled lane. Its eyes were half closed; it shook its head from side to side as if it had been deafened. But doggedly it kept on its feet and passed us, heading for the house. Now it was uttering sounds, too, a kind of rumbling, and the other cries began to subside.

"Vere, look! It's asking you again!"

It had reached the level of the fountain and was standing there, its flanks heaving, its mouth hanging a little open as if the effort that had brought it so far was exhausting. Now it did indeed balance its weight on three paws, raise the fourth, a fore one, to make a clumsy beckoning gesture.

There was no denying its urgency. And somehow I could not. But as I slid through the door with stunner in hand, I gave orders sharply.

"No one follow. Close this after me, and wait for an all-clear sign. If I don't show again promptly, take off—"

I did not give them time to protest but slammed the door and started warily toward the fountain. The ystroben, seeing that I was on my way, seemed satisfied. It turned and made, not for the house which I first thought its goal, but to the right. And I hurried after it.

There I found the beginning of tragedy. There must have been a shipment of mutants from some lab just before whatever devastated our world struck. They had been housed in pen cages for eventual release into the Reserve and then, apparently, forgotten. No food, no water, and there were some pitiful bodies on the ground that testified that, for some, release would now come too late. The ystroben hunkered down, its nose against the wire of an end cage. And there within was another of its species lying on its side. It tried to raise its head at the coming of its comrade and failed.

One look told me there was no danger here for us but much to be done. I hailed those in the car, and soon we were all busy opening cages, carrying food from the containers in view, which must have been an added torment to the animals, and water in pails from the fountain.

Some of those already lying prostrate were still alive, and we worked over them. Those first to recover went down the hill into the wilds of the Reserve. For the others we left cage doors wedged open and plenty of food and water, to let them recover at their own rate of speed. Five were dead.

The house was deserted, with the same signs of haste the Ranger headquarters had shown. To have gone with caged animals on the premises was so foreign to all training that I knew the need must have been great. Had some message gathered in all the outlying personnel to Feeholme where they could be conveniently disposed of? That was the only explanation I could see as logical.

But this was not a house claimed by the dead, so we settled into it thankfully, though it had been intended only for a staff of two, and we found it crowded. What pleased me most was the discovery of a recharging unit on the wall abutting the parking space. We could spend a day, or a part of a day here, making sure that the power in the car was fully restored. I hoped we could continue to drive well into the heights.

"Vere"—Gytha came up as I was studying the charge dials and trying to remember the necessary steps for a full hookup—"these animals, they're all mutants, aren't they?"

"I think so."

"How smart are they?"

I shrugged. Without lab reports how could anyone estimate? The ystroben had certainly displayed intelligence in its struggle to win our aid for the caged ones. We had all heard tales, of course, of the beast teams—mixed collections of animals working with and under the director of a trained human leader. There had been some exciting stories of those out of the war. Survey and exploration were using, or had used, animal aides on newly discovered planets, the men depending on the keener senses of the animals. But not all mutants were successful telepaths, which was necessary in both beast team and survey work.

There had been twenty beasts in those cages, of fifteen different species, some of which were totally new to me. Five were dead—among them two of the unknowns. They would all be loose here now, but the tests they had been sent here to make would never be set up. I wished them well but thought they were no longer our problem.

"I don't know—maybe no one did," I said in answer to Gytha's question. "They could have been sent here for just that reason—to discover what they could do," I told her as I began uncoiling the hookup wires.

"Were—are any of them dangerous?"

"No. They should all be conditioned. They will protect themselves, but they should not be aggressive. The normal wild ones, though, are not adjusted to man. There are some parts of the Reserves you never visit without distorts and sonics."

"That wart-horn—"

For a moment I did not know what she was talking about, it was so long past.

"What wart-horn?"

"The one we saw on the Butte com. Vere, was that a mutant?"

"Couldn't have been. There was no work done with native animals that I ever heard of."

"But there could have been and not reported?"

"Anything is possible—"

She was nodding vigorously. "You know, after the commandant left, when everyone said they were through working on war projects, a lot of the labs never reported to Center any more."

That was right. But why did the wart-horn bother her now I asked.

"I don't know. But Pritha keeps mentioning it. She said it was watching us, that it didn't like us—"

"Even if that were so, which I don't believe," I replied, "that thing was over the mountains to the north and a long way from any place where there is any settlement now. It could be no danger to us."

"But, Vere, if everybody—" She hesitated and then went on. "If everybody except us is dead, then the mutants—they could be people, or like people in time, couldn't they?"

It was possible, but it was not a thought to dwell on.

"We cannot be sure all are dead," I told her firmly. "Tomorrow we shall do some scouting. As soon as we can map out the best trail up and over, we'll take it. You'll be back home before you know it."

"I don't want to be, Vere. Not if Kynvet is like Feeholme."

"Winter is coming; we must get home before the passes close," I continued as if I did not hear her, for I did not know any answer to an observation that matched my own feelings. It would be better to shelter at the Butte, or in a Reserve cabin, rather than return to a dead Kynvet. I knew that I could not take the children into a place of ghosts and expect them to stay. Not all parents had been so remote with their offspring as the Ahrens, and those who had had a closer family relationship must not be allowed to see what had happened if the fate of Feeholme had also been visited on Kynvet.

"Vere, look up there—" She caught my hand and brought me half around to face the Gur Horn.

It had been put to good use by the Rangers, for the spur had been turned into a lookout to give a wide view of the surrounding country. Thad had climbed there at my suggestion not long before, and now he was waving vigorously, pointing north. I signaled to him to come down, hurrying to the foot of the climb pole to meet him.

"A flitter, crashed over on the hill due north—" he gasped. "And it's afire!"

The one that had passed over us the night before? Crashed and afire—there would be little hope for her crew.

"Sabian, the aid kit." Annet had come up behind us. "Thad, can we reach it by car?"

He shook his head doubtfully. "I don't know; it's pretty steep. But you might climb up—"

"Where do you think you're going?" I demanded.

"To the people on board!" She looked at me as if I had grown wart-horns. "They are probably badly injured. We had better hurry."

And I could see that at that moment there was no argument I could raise that might move her.

TWELVE

"Thad, you stay—take guard duty here." There was no detaching Annet from what she believed was a duty, but we could not just go off without some order.

I almost expected him to protest, but there was no longer any trace of sullenness in him when I gave orders, as there had been in the days before we entered the caves. He nodded, and I handed over one of the extra stunners.

"Stay under cover. You know what to do." I paid him the compliment of not amplifying and again he nodded.

Annet and I only. She had shouldered the aid kit and was already striding off in the direction Thad had indicated. I had to hurry to catch up. But we needed no real guide. In the twilight the fire was a beacon no one could miss.

She set a punishing pace over rough ground, and I did not try to deter her. She slowed of her own accord quickly enough and stood panting on a rise before she could take breath to go on. I pulled up beside her. The scene of the wreck was plain. The flitter had met a cliff head on, and the blazing tangle was a crumpled wad at its foot, as if caught in some giant fist and squeezed into a lump.

"There are no survivors of that," I told her.

Her deep breaths were close to sobs. I pressed the point.

"Go back—"

"And you?" She did not look at me; her eyes were still on the wreck as if something in her did not allow her to look away.

"I'll look—" But privately I thought a journey to that pile of mangled metal was useless.

"All—all right—"

Annet was shaken as I had not seen her since the cave passage when she had come upon the fall-in and realized we were sealed from the surface. Beltane life had been so unmarked by violence and tragedy that we had not faced death often. She had seen Lugard die, but she had not seen Feeholme, and no amount of description from me could make that real to her. This carried the impact of a blow.

I watched her turn back. She did not once look at me; rather her head was bent as if she forced her eyes only on the ground under her feet. I again centered my attention on the wreck.

It had fallen in one of the barren places, and for that I was glad, since the fire could not start any grass blaze. Of course the storms of the past two days had thoroughly soaked the vegetation, but there was always a chance that a smoldering could start up again, given wind to fan it. And of all the dangers to be feared on a Reserve, fire was the worst.

There was probably no reason for me to go closer. I could not approach the wreck to identify it and whatever—whoever—had been in it. But there was always the slim chance I could pick up a hint of what had happened to Beltane, so I went.

I was right. The heat reflected from the rocks kept me well away from the general proximity of the burning machine. But as I tried to trace the lines of the flyer, I was suddenly sure this was not a ship from any settlement. Even crumpled and broken as it was, it had an unfamiliar look.

Then I found on the ground, thrown well away from the crash as if the cabin had burst wide open and scattered cargo, a blaster. It was regulation Service issue, though meeting with a rock had split it past repair. I had not seen one of those on Beltane since the forces had left. I did not try to touch it. Annet's virus story was too much in my mind. If the flitter—or whatever it was—had been piloted by men dead or dying (which could account for its erratic flight), then contagion might still lurk in their possessions.

But the victims I had found in Feeholme had been settlers.

Had the plague spread to the refugees? Had they been too greedy, raided some settlement before the "safe" period? A man could guess and guess and piece together a logical surmise, but that did not necessarily mean his guesses were correct.

So I did not touch the blaster and stepped carefully over and around other bits and pieces of debris. There was enough remaining to make me sure my conjecture concerning this ship had been correct—that it was not a regulation flitter and its origin was off-world.

The fire was dying down, having consumed most of what fed it. There was no reason for me to linger.

When I returned to the station, I discovered that Annet and Thad had moved our belongings in. Dagny lay in one of the bunks, and the girls' bedrolls were in that room, while Emrys and Sabian had spread ours in the main portion. Annet had the cook unit on and was heating food, which smelled so good that I could believe it would draw us as Lugard's pipe had done.

"Anything?" Thad asked as I entered. I noted with approval that he had stationed himself by one of the window slits from which he could see the approach to the cabin and that he had one stunner in hand and the extra one lying beside him. With the cabin backed against the wide base of the Gur Horn, we had only that front sweep to defend.

"No. Except I don't think it was a flitter. Perhaps a ship's scout flyer. But there's not enough left to make sure. And—we stay away from there."

Annet caught my eye. "Yes," she agreed quickly, "yes!"

We ate, and I set up a program of watches. Annet was to be immune from that duty since Dagny was her special charge. But Gytha, Thad, Emrys, Sabian, and I would split the time. What I expected might come on us out of the night, I could not have said, but it seemed wise to make sure we could not be surprised.

I took a torch and made the rounds of the mutant pens. Already the majority of the creatures had gone. The ystroben that had hailed us was inside the cage beside its fellow. It was pushing food to the weak one's mouth, while that one ate feebly, seemingly yet unable to get to its feet.

Seeing an empty water pail, I brought more, set it close to the enfeebled animal, and cupped my hands full of the liquid for its lapping. Its companion moved aside with not so much as a warning growl. The other drank and drank again, but the fourth time I offered water, it turned its head to one side and nosed at the feed with more vigor than it had shown before.

It was a female, and I thought it was in cub. The other must be its mate. I did not know much of ystrobens. They were off-world imports and quite rare. That they had been only so recently brought to the Reserve made me wonder if they had not been part of some long-time experiment just concluded. And if they had been lab-housed, perhaps during the whole of their lifetimes, how would they manage turned loose to forage in the wild with no Rangers for their protection? They were omnivorous, of course. No animal was ever sent to the mutant stations for release unless its feeding habits had been adapted to the range. But—However, I could not worry about these unhappy wayfarers now.

I brought still more food and water. The male followed me to where the containers of food were piled. He stood on his hind feet and pawed at the top of one as yet unopened, looking at me meanwhile with some of the same entreaty he had exhibited in the berry-walled lane. I used a rip bar on the top of that box and stood back to see what he would do.

He bent his head to give a long sniff, but he took nothing—rather went to four feet again and padded back to his mate, apparently satisfied that the food was there if they needed it.

I spent a little time in looking over the remaining animals, hoping they would leave soon on their own, for I did not believe that we ourselves should linger too long here. Again I was tempted to make this our headquarters, though it was less roomy and not as good a base as the Ranger headquarters.

I had no idea how long it might take us to get over the mountains, and sometimes storms hit the heights in late summer to close the pass. If the Butte was unoccupied, it was a far better camp for us than anything this side of the range.

I had selected the last watch of all, so I took to my bedroll as soon as I returned to the cabin, knowing that Thad would wake me when the time came. Again I slept heavily, the exertions of the past few days acting, once I had relaxed, as a drug, but I roused quickly enough in the dark when Thad shook my shoulder.

"Nothing—" His lips near my ear carried a thread of whisper. "Some of the mutants came back for food, but nothing near the door."

"Well enough." I took up the duties. So much time at one of the slit windows, cross over, and an equal time at the other. But there was nothing to see under the light of the full green moon, one of Beltane's natural wonders.

I had left the car hooked up for recharge, and that would run without tending until it reached repletion. How much longer we could use that transportation was the question. Though Annet assured me she saw an improvement in Dagny's condition, it came very slowly indeed, and I thought she would have to be carried once we left the car, which meant we must also limit the supplies we could pack. E-rations were best, designed to supply bulk of energy with minimum of substance, but at the same time we needed water and clothing for the cold of the heights—for even in summer snow powdered the pass at times. We could strip down what we carried now, but there were things we dared not leave behind. I listed those in my mind as I kept watch.

Against the wall at the far end of the room was the com that had linked this station with Feeholme. We had tried the night before with faint hope, quickly extinguished. I had decided to set the com in the car on the widest band, though that would necessitate some extra wiring in the morning. Suddenly, it was needful to hear a voice, any voice, even if it were that of a potential enemy, to let us know that we were not alone on Beltane.

What if we were? One must be prepared for the worst. Then there was the port SOS, which could be set on automatic to continue to beam a distress signal into space. Any ship passing within range of that must answer, unless it was a warn-off signaling some contagious plague. In that case, the answering ship must relay that call to the nearest Patrol center.

Patrol center? For centuries of planet time the Patrol had policed the star lanes and such planets where trouble had broken out endangering life. But if Lugard's dismal prognosis was right, did the Patrol still exist hereabouts? Or had the remnants of it been pulled back, closer to the wealthy inner planets where civilization might continue to exist for a while?

I had heard dire stories of worlds where law and order vanished overnight, sometimes as a result of natural disasters, sometimes because of war or plague. The settlers of Beltane had used the war-ravaged ones as horrible examples for their pacific arguments.

What if we faced both here, or rather their aftermath—war and plague? And if there came no answer from space?

Technology had begun to fail already. It would regress faster under the circumstances. Thad and I knew enough of mechanics to keep a hopper, a ground car, or even a flitter working. But once there were no more spare parts, nor charges, nor—There were draft animals at some of the settlements, kept for experimental study. There were plantations of food under cultivation by robos. And how long would those continue to carry out their implanted orders to sow, reap, store? I had a sudden vision of a plantation where the robos kept on, laying up foods for men who never came—until the storage bins burst with rot, never halting until their inner workings wore out.

Ten of us and a whole world—but that could *not* be! Somewhere there were—there must be—others! And in me the need to find them grew stronger until my impatience was such I longed to wake the company, to set out at once on the search.

I throttled down that impatience, and when morning came and the rest were astir, I made preparations with all the care I could summon. We sorted supplies, those from the ground car, those I had brought from Feeholme, and those we had found here, setting aside those easiest to transport but high in energy. Our old trail kits, which had come all the way from the Butte, were turned out. All that was not absolutely necessary in them was thrown out, and they were repacked with what we must use once we left the car.

A hunt through the tapes and records of the station uncovered another map giving the western face of the mountains and the approach to the pass. There was a marked trail that might serve the car.

Once our kits were stowed, we turned to the packing of the storage space in the car, putting in all the food and water we could. We then went over our clothes, substituting parts of the uniforms in the cabin for those garments too worn or torn. Annet, Pritha, and Gytha worked with seam-seal to fit them better to the smaller members of the group. Such preparations took us all day.

In midafternoon Ifors reported that the two ystrobens had at last left the cage and were going downstream. At his summons we gathered at the door to watch them go. The male padded ahead, very plainly on watch, his mate moving unsteadily with

frequent halts, during which her head hung low and her breathing was labored.

Gytha waved, though neither turned to look at us as they left.
It was as if all their energy and determination was centered now
on the need for getting into the bush. "I hope they can find a
nice den," she said.

"Vere"—Pritha looked at me—"there will be a lot of mutant
animals left loose now, won't there?"

"I suppose so. But most of them are already free on the Reserves.
Remember, the Committee suggested that some months ago. It
was too hard to get special lab foods for some of them since the
off-world ships haven't come."

"But will there be others left in cages with no food, no
water?"

"I don't think so. There was only one big mutant lab left—at
Kibthrow. These came from there. I see the markings on the food
boxes. They were probably getting rid of them all."

"Kibthrow," she repeated, as if that made an impression. "That's
over the mountains, north of the port, isn't it?"

"Yes."

"Then, Vere, when we get over the mountains, could—could
someone go there—just to be sure?"

"Yes, I promise you we shall!" I did not mean that lightly.
I might not have been ready to yield to the entreaties of the
ystroben in the lane, but what I had found here made me sure
that wherever we went in search of survivors from now on, we
would also make sure that no animal had been left to die because
a man did not release it.

"In the morning." Annet smoothed the last jacket they had cut
down and fastened together with seam-seal for the small frame
of Dinan Norkot.

"Yes," I agreed to her unasked question. In the morning we
would be on our way.

Though we had seen nothing during the day to suggest that
we might be in any danger, we kept guard for the second
night. It was clear, and the moonlight very bright. The last of
the living mutants had left the pens. But I spread all that was
left of their food along the side of the brook so that, if they
returned, it would keep them away from the house. Not that
any of them had shown any interest in us once their wants

were satisfied and they were free to go—It was almost as if we had a distort about us.

I wondered, as I took my sentry turn, about what Gytha had said. Suppose with mankind on Beltane reduced to a handful (I refused yet to believe there could be only *us*), what then would happen to the mutants? Some of the experimenters had made high claims for the intelligence of those they had bred and trained. The continent was wide and mostly wilderness, and those that might withdraw beyond the nebulous boundaries could continue hidden for a long time. Could another intelligence race ("men" as we must judge alien men) arise here, unknowing its original seed? But that was supposing we would vanish—

We had our last meal in the camp and packed into the car. For the first time Dagny appeared awake and really aware of her surroundings. She sat in the curve of Annet's arm, pressed tightly against her, looking about as if she saw the land and us, though she said very little. Annet confided that she was sure coming from the caves and the fact that we had had no more alarms, but traveled through a peaceful countryside, had wrought some healing. We warned the others against mentioning in Dagny's hearing anything of the past or what might face us. If her still cloudy mind accepted that we were on a camping trip such as we had taken before, then all the better.

Our path led by the cliff face where the flyer had come to grief, but I made as wide a detour around that as I could. There was still a small sullen plume of smoke ascending from the wreckage, but the frame was so tangled and melted that I could not identify it.

We came upon a wash leading up into the mountain country, and according to the map this was the best way, as long as no more storms could push a flood upon us. The flotsam from the last was still caught among the rocks to serve as a reminder that this desert did not always lack water.

On we crunched and crawled, our pace such that a man walking briskly could have left us behind. I kept off the distort since we moved mainly in the shadow of rising canyon walls and there were few beasts that came here that were formidable enough to fear.

Midmorning we came upon a galophi—rounding a curve to front it. As a specimen of its species, it was a fine example, one of the few creatures native to Beltane to attain any noticeable size. Its back scales were coarse and thick, as wide and long as fingers, and each edge where it fitted over another displayed fringe that resembled bristly fur but was really a fleshy growth. The same made a frill about its throat and a kind of mane stretching from between its large faceted eyes back to become a spine ridge ending only at tail tip. The front paws were clawed and the back feet wide and flat for swift travel over sandy soil. When really disturbed, it would inflate its mane and ridge hair into a spiny bush, flick out its forked tongue, and run two-legged.

This one was not about to run, and I knew why a second or two after our surprise meeting. It was of the dull green shade of a female that had recently laid the yearly clutch of eggs. Somewhere in the rocks around us must be the nest site, and we were facing now a truly formidable opponent, some six feet long and able, if it were really provoked, to tear open the ground car.

I brought my fist down on the sonic as the galophi reared, not to turn tail but to charge us, and saw its tongue slap back and forth as if a laser beam had touched it. A galophi hears through that appendage, having no ears as we rate them, and that eerie blast must be torment for it.

It writhed and twisted and finally lost its balance altogether, falling behind the rocks from which it had been about to leap. I gave the car extra energy as we grated by.

Emrys, wedged in at the rear, gave us a report. "There's its head! It's still waving its tongue around, but it isn't following, Vere. No, now it's lying down with its back to a crevice."

"Nest," I replied briefly. I silenced the sonic. We were far enough away so I did not think the galophi would follow. Instinct would keep it close to that nest until the young hatched, and it could not be drawn from that vicinity. But the episode had been a warning not to accept the country at its bland face value but to be better prepared.

"Dagny!" I glanced at her. Would such a happening throw her back into that twilight state where she had lain so long?

Annet shook her head at me in both warning and reassurance. Dagny leaned against her, and her eyes were closed. "Sleeping."

We scouted our noon stop well before we left the car to eat. Though the sun was high, it was cool here. We had come well up into the heights, and by studying the map, I thought that we would have to leave the car not too far ahead. So I suggested that when we reached that point, we should spend the night in its shelter, even if some hours of daylight remained, beginning our foot travel with the new day.

At last we ground to a halt on a ledge. To reach it, I had taken some risk in forcing the car. When I got out, I worked with the boys to wedge rocks under the wheel treads for safety. It was chill here, though the sun was still up. I sealed my outer tunic and said I would scout the trail for at least an hour but that we would camp here for the night.

The going was rough, but it had been marked by blaster cuttings and some smoothing over bad stretches. So I was on course, and the pass lay beyond. If we started at dawn in the morning and climbed well, we should be through that gap and part down the other side before dark. And on the down side was, or had been, a trail shelter.

I found an outcrop and perched on it, lying full length to use the distance lenses back over the country through which we had come. There was no sign of movement there, save for a lazy winged flying thing or two. Indications were that the weather was in our favor.

Annet sheltered a portable cook unit behind some stones, and when I returned, she had a steaming mug of caff for me. That was one of the small comforts we would have to leave behind, and I applauded her wisdom in giving us a heated meal and drink. We would be having nothing more save E-rations until we reached the Butte. I hoped we could make that in two days, though thought of the lava country worried me.

We stood sentry again this night, Annet taking a turn, so we cut each period shorter. However, the sleeping quarters in the car were so poor, I think only the smallest rested easily enough to sleep well. I know my long legs were cramped, and I had an aching back when I crawled out to face the dawn.

Once more Annet heated caff and rations before we stored the unit and the rest of the extras back in the car. Then all of us, save Dagny, shouldered packs and took up two canteens apiece. I was pleased to see Dagny was on her feet, seeming even nearer to her old self than she had been the day before. She was to march with Annet, Pritha immediately behind them to lend a hand if needed.

I took the van, then Gytha, Emrys, Sabian, Annet and the two girls and Dinan, Ifors and Thad bringing up the rear. We would trade positions, except the lead would remain mine. Thad and I both carried the hooked metal ropes, which had served us so well and which might be needed as life lines aloft.

Thus, just as the first rays of the sun appeared, we set off on the pass trail. And I do not think any of us looked back.

THIRTEEN

We took the climb at a slower pace than I would have journeyed had I been alone, but this was a case of conserving strength. The longer Dagny could walk, the better it was for the rest of us. It was cold, as cold as it had been—almost—in the ice cave. And there were winds to search out the thin parts in one's clothing.

No more trees, only patches of grass here and there, and scrubby wind-trimmed bush were to be seen. A pacca sat on a rock unafraid, watching our passing with round eyes, the wind ruffling its long blue fur, though it kept its tail tight folded about its toes. Its cheeks were puffed far out from early morning gleaning, which it was taking back to a burrow, for this was its harvest period when it laid up food for winter.

From every level place where we paused for a breather, I turned to sweep the lenses over our back trail. I did not really know what I expected to see. Surely no one had survived the wreck. Yet there was always the possibility of a bailout before the final moment of crash.

Now and then I would pick up a dot that must be one of the larger animals from the Reserve, but nothing on the path we had taken, nothing near the car we had left with its wheels braced by stones.

Though no rain fell, the sky was overcast, and that was enough hint of bad weather to keep us going. So far Dagny was doing better than I had hoped, keeping pace with Annet and Pritha. She even noticed the pacca and commented on it, which was heartening.

We came to where nothing save lichens grew. There were pockets of snow in the shadows of some rocks, hollows as deep as cups into which the sun must seldom penetrate. The wind made us tuck our chins into tunic collars and pull tighter the hoods that usually flapped as small capes on our shoulders. It was here that Dagny faltered, but we could go no slower—we must get through the pass and down as soon as possible.

There was a crevice between two pinnacles of rock, and we huddled in that shelter, bringing out E-rations. I looked at the map from the mutant station. There was no fear of losing the road; the marks left by those who pioneered it were easy to see. I tried to measure the distance to the cabin on the other side of the pass.

"How far?" Annet asked. Dagny was on her lap, the child's head resting against the older girl's shoulder, her eyes closed. I thought she breathed overfast, though all of us did in the rarefied air of these heights.

"Through the pass, then perhaps a little more than the distance from where we left the car on this side." I gave her the truth. This was no time to coat it with hoping.

"She cannot do it, not walking." Annet was definite, and I knew it was a fact.

I unbuckled my pack and squirmed out into the open to unwrap it. We had pared and pared its contents. But we had also foreseen that we might have to pare again because of just such an emergency.

I began to divide up what we could not do without. The extra charges for the stunners I stowed away in the front of my overtunic. E-rations could be shared—most might be eaten soon anyway—while the blankets—

Thad laid hand on one. "I'll take this. You'll need the other to put around her. And this"—he selected the largest of the remaining necessary items, one of the beamers—"I can strap to my belt."

So when we set out again, I carried Dagny in a webbing of ropes on my back. She had not roused but rested with her head against my shoulder, once more in a condition approaching coma.

Luckily, the rocky path was not one to require exertion, and I blessed over and over again the Security men who had cut this road. It was not as smooth as a plains trail but better than I had dared hope for.

The pass was a deep notch between two peaks, each almost as spectacular as the Gur Horn. It was twilight dark in that cut, and the wind thrust through it with full blast force, so that we hugged one wall or the other, keeping hand holds, going one wary step at a time. Dagny's weight was greater than the pack, so I had to be doubly careful I did not overbalance under the push of that blast.

Beyond, the way sloped down. We would come out at a lower level than we had entered. That I welcomed. We could no longer talk—it would require a shout to better the moan of the wind—but communicated by sign when there was need. Once a tongue of snow licked out from a crevice, and we crunched through it. But at the end of that cut, we ran into real trouble.

Still in the lead, I came to a crosswise break in the rock that slashed the trail as neatly as if some giant hunting knife had been used to bisect the puny efforts of my species to make a road. Whether it had originally baffled the surveyors of the pass, I did not know. At least it was not marked on the map. But it was too wide to leap, and I did not see how we could bridge it.

We drew back into what small shelter we could find in that place, huddling together. There were the ropes with hooks. Employing those, it might be possible to lower ourselves into the crevice and use that for a road, hoping that either of its ends would give access to the surface on the other side.

I left Dagny with Annet, ordering the others to gather the blankets around them for warmth. Thad made fast the ropes and oversaw my descent into the cut. There was unsteady footing at its bottom, for rubble had long rolled into it. The right-hand way was of no use, for it soon narrowed into too slim a slit.

The left was more promising. I picked my way along and finally found a wall that could be climbed with the aid of the ropes. It took us much effort and time to cross, and the last haul up the other side was exhausting. Thad went ahead a little, to return with a lightly encouraging report that he had found again trail markings, plus the fact he had been able to sight what he believed to be the roof of the shelter. But that still lay a goodly distance ahead.

Night was coming. We ate and conferred. Annet was opposed to spending the night in the open. She was worried not only for Dagny but also for the rest of us in these heights, and I was inclined to agree with her. We had our torches, though to use them could draw the kind of attention we were better without.

"That is only a possible danger," Annet pointed out when I voiced that as a warning. "A night here is a more probable one. One light carefully used—"

"Shielded," I mused, "bent only on the trail. To travel so will be slow—"

"But better than staying here."

"Thad," I said, "you take scout." Carrying Dagny, I could not be properly alert and unencumbered. "Emrys will serve at the rear."

I was putting a burden on the younger boy that I had not yet done. But he had marched well, and he was level-headed. Annet could drop behind near him. We must, however, keep close together and not string out in a place where a misstep in the dark could mean trouble.

Through those hours of deepening dusk, I did not consult my watch, so I have no idea how long that down-mountain crawl lasted, for crawl it was. What might have seemed not too difficult a trail for the rested and unburdened was harsh going for those carrying packs and already weary. We had Thad's torch, and he used it well, shining it back to guide us all when he struck a particularly bad section.

The night was cloudy, but I thanked Providence, whenever I had time to think of more than just my footing, not stormy. Then I noticed we were in scrubby bush and that the wind no longer tore so relentlessly at us. Once more there was the suggestion of a cleared trail. But this had been much overgrown, and I saw the rise and fall of Thad's arm and realized he had out his long-bladed hunting knife and was cutting free our path.

Some time, what seemed a *long* time later, we came out into a clearing where tough mountain grass grew tall enough to wreath around our boots, and Thad's light illuminated the front of the shelter.

It was not as substantial or as well constructed a building as the Reserve cabins had been. Its door hung on one hinge, while drifts of leaves and earth had blown over the threshold. In a way, I welcomed those signs of abandonment, for they meant safety to us in the here and now.

We stumbled in and collapsed almost as one on the gritty leaf-strewn floor. Thad swung the light from side to side to show us the poverty of our refuge. There were bunk frames along one wall, mere empty shelves. But there was nothing else to show occupancy—no other furniture, no cook unit, nothing at all. A tangle of dried grass and leaves in one corner and in it the gray-white of small, well-gnawed bones said that, after man had left, it had offered a lair to some animal. But the bones were old and the bedding of last season, or perhaps the season before that, so even that use was no longer made of this place.

Annet unhooked her pack, got our blankets, and spread them hastily on one of the bunks, taking Dagny from me to rest there. I wanted nothing more than a hot drink, which there was no chance of my having. Those who had no bunk room rolled up on the floor. I leaned against the door frame, my stunner unholstered. Tired as we all were, there was still a need for a sentry, perhaps more so this side of the mountains.

The wind that had been with us in the pass and on the mountainside died away. As I sat there, I was so tired of body that it was a great effort to move, but I was not sleepy. It was as if I had passed some point where sleep normally waited. I could hear the heavy breathing of the rest. There were no moans, no signs of nightmare tonight, only the deep rest of exhaustion.

Once there was a rustling, and my hand was ready on stunner grip, though my reactions were woefully, almost frighteningly, slow. But that sound had come from without, and whatever made it did not seek to enter.

How far we might now be from Butte Hold I did not know. Perhaps the map could have told me, but I could not consult it tonight. And whether we would have to cross, on foot, the devilish waste of the lava country was another point on which I had no briefing. If that were so, it might be well not to try to return to the Butte—in spite of the fact that we had left a hopper there and that we would have a wealth of supplies.

I was too tired to think clearly, yet thoughts marched, countermarched, milled about in my overactive brain. In so much was I ready to follow what Annet had urged from the first, a scouting expedition into the settlement lands. Going on foot would make that a longer and slower journey, one the whole party could not take. Therefore, we must find a base from which to operate. And such a safe base I could not see, save the Butte.

"Vere—"

I turned my head away from the door to the dark shadow that crept across the floor as I recognized Thad's whisper of my name.

"I'll take guard—"

I wanted nothing more than to relinquish even this small portion of my responsibility, but I knew sleep was beyond me.

"I can't sleep," I told him as he crept closer until his shoulder nudged mine. "I'll stay on—"

"Vere"—he did not accept my unspoken suggestion to return to his blankets—"where do we go now?"

"Butte Hold, if we can."

"You mean, we may not get over the lava fields?" He must have already considered that himself.

"That—and the fact it may be occupied." In a few quick whispers I told for the first time of that meeting between Lugard and the refugees.

"So you think they may hunt the treasure, that stuff we saw in the ice cave?"

"It would draw them, yes."

"Then what do we do?"

"The best we can. In the morning we'll look over the maps, see if there is a back way to the Butte, one that will give us any advantage of approach. If there is and the Butte is clear, we move in. It has defenses."

"But Lugard knew them; we don't."

"Then we'll have to learn, by trial and error if need be," I retorted. The exchange with Thad was, oddly enough, quieting my nerves, as if I needed only this stating of near and far objectives to drain the tension. All at once sleep assaulted me so I could not keep my eyes open.

"Take over, Thad," I found the energy to say. I remember faintly starting to crawl to the pile of blankets he had just left, and then nothing.

I awoke with the sun hot across my face. It was a good heat, one my body welcomed. I heard stirring sounds, whispered talk. When I sat up, rubbing my hands across my eyes, I saw that some pretense of order had come into the shelter.

The leaves, the mess of the old lair, much of the drifted grit and sand, had been swept away. Blankets were neatly piled on the bunk, save for where I now lay. Annet sat in my old place by the door. A stunner was near to hand, but she was occupied with hulling berries, which she dropped onto a wide leaf. Pritha was similarly busy, and Dagny sat between them, now and then reaching out to take a berry and eat it. Of the rest there was no sign. Pritha glanced up, saw me watching, and smiled.

"Vere's awake, Annet."

"It's about time! You can sleep sounder than anyone I ever knew!" Her words might have been an accusation in another tone, but she was smiling. Now she got to her feet. "Go wash up. There's a spring out there. Then get some breakfast—you'll need that as much as you needed sleep."

"Now that you mention it, yes." I was aware of a vast empty space somewhere in my middle, but I still blinked. There was a different atmosphere. Annet almost might be on one of our old camping trips, certain that we would return to the home we had always known. Was it because we were now back on the fringe of familiar territory? Did she think we would find all the same when (or if) we returned to Kynvet? At any rate, I was not going to break the spell; I was too grateful for the easing of the tension that had ridden us all since the closing of the caves.

A small spring had been channeled into a basin of rock, and I made good use of it. To be able to wash added to my feelings of well-being. The clearing was largely overgrown, and the berry bushes where Annet had done her harvesting were a major part of that encroachment.

I was still on my knees by the water as Thad pushed through. Seeing me, he headed quickly in my direction to report abruptly.

"I looked at the map this morning. We have lava land between us and the Butte. But"—he was frowning—"I went up to the highest point for a look-see. There's something—I didn't tell the rest, not yet. I wanted you to know first."

"All right." I wiped my hands on a tuft of long grass. "Where?"

"Vere, are you ready? Breakfast—" Annet called.

Thad's frown grew.

"Something which"—I nodded to where the girls waited—"is better not spoken of yet?"

He nodded. "Gytha saw it, but she'll keep quiet. It—it won't go away. You might as well eat, or they'll wonder."

"Vere"—Gytha came through the bushes in turn—"there's a—"

Thad made an emphatic gesture, and for a second she looked mutinously indignant; then comprehension dawned.

So I did not enjoy my breakfast as much as I might have done, but I swallowed E-ration, which no longer tasted like a guesting banquet, and praised the berry pickers for their addition. I could guess that both Thad and Gytha were curbing their impatience better than I would have believed they could. At last I was able to give the excuse of inspecting the lookout and leave. For the first time Annet did not ask when we were moving on, and I was eager to get away before she did, as I had no answer for her.

Thad led the way to an improvised ladder leaned against a wind-twisted borgar tree. The ladder was a fensal topped in some storm and thrown until its branches had become entwined with the borgar. Its weathered red trunk, now missing most of the aromatic bark, was sharp in color against the borgar, which had lost its early season leaves to produce the pale blue flowers of the second stage.

With Thad perched on a neighboring limb of the borgar to direct me, I used my lenses. What came into clear view as I adjusted the distances was a hopper. As far as I could see, it was in no state of disrepair. Clearly, it had been landed on a strip of level, unwooded land, not smashed in a crash.

"Take us to the Butte without trouble," Thad commented.

Which was perfectly true, but the mere fact it was sitting there within perhaps an hour or two hours downhill walking did not mean it was usable.

And I think Thad also had doubts, for he added, "Don't know what's inside. But we've watched it, Gytha and I, turn-about, for most of the morning. No sight of anyone around. Could be bait in a trap—"

Good thinking, but he might be going too far with it.

"If it is bait, not for us," I said. "We could hardly have been

tracked here without our knowing it. There's only been that one
flyer, and that cracked up. On the other hand—"

Gytha hung halfway up the fensal. "You think there's someone
dead in there, just as they were at Feeholme—"

There was no reason to deny the shrewdness of her guess.

"It's very possible."

"But if they died of the virus, it won't hurt us now, will it?
And we do need the hopper—"

"What do you know about the virus?" But I might have guessed.
We had been in close quarters in the ground car, Annet and I,
when she had told me of her fears.

"We heard. Thad and I know, and Emrys and Sabian. But we
didn't tell the others. Pritha believes her mother's waiting for her.
And Ifors, he talks all the time about his father. They mustn't
know until they have to. But, Vere"—she returned to her main
question—"couldn't we use the hopper if we didn't have to worry
about getting sick?"

"I suppose so. Only we can't be sure that what has struck or
did strike at Feeholme was that virus."

"You aren't sick, Vere, and you went in there. You brought back
food. We ate it, and none of us are sick—except Dagny—and that
isn't from any virus." Gytha hammered home her logic point by
point.

"True enough. All right. You stay here. Thad, I turn command
over to you. I'll go down and scout. If it can be used, I'll lift it
up here." I snapped the compass from my belt and took a bearing, then marked what guiding landmarks I could. "If I start right
now, I might be able to return before dark. Tell the others I am
scouting a trail down."

"Will do." Thad waited for me to leave before he swung down
after. Gytha was already on the ground to face me.

"I want to go too, Vere."

"No."

"But, Vere, suppose it is a trap. I'm good with a stunner, and
I won't go up to the machine. I can cover you while you look
at it."

"No." Then I lightened that with an argument that I hoped
would satisfy her. "It is because you *are* good with a stunner,
Gytha, that I want you here. One person alone can slip around
and get away. And believe me I shall take every precaution. But

if a trap *was* set for us, if we *have* been trailed in some way, then they may be up here. I want everyone in the shelter, ready with lookouts—understand?"

The threat was remote, but it was there; in that much I did not stretch the truth any. She still had a mutinous expression about her mouth, but she turned toward the clearing with no more protest.

"If I'm not back by dark," I told Thad, "take cover. I still think the Butte is the best place to go—if it is empty. But—"

I was at a loss. How could I foresee all that might happen to me, to them? And why burden them with suggestions that might not be right if I did not return and the situation altered?

"Use your best judgment." That seemed a weak ending but the only one I could give.

"Yes. And Vere—"

I glanced around, for I was already two strides on my way.

"See you take care," he said almost angrily. "We can't afford to lose you."

So far had we come from the feeling I had had—was it only days earlier?—that Thad was waiting to challenge my authority. It struck me that, as I had looked to Lugard at the beginning of this fated venture, so now Thad was looking to me. And that I did not like, for it pushed me into a role I shrank from. I raised my hand for an answer and pushed into the brush.

Thus far we had not planned much into the future. I had speculated, as must all of the older members of the group, that something very wrong had happened. But to look beyond tomorrow had not been done.

What if the worst had happened and we were the only humans? Go to the port; set the distress beam. But there was no promise that that would be answered for years—or ever. Then what? I shied from such forecasting. It was safer all around for me, perhaps all of us, if we looked no farther than the duty immediately to hand. And mine was now to investigate the hopper.

If it had been abandoned or if it housed only the dead, then it was a gift from fortune. We need not fear the trek through the lava lands. Having seen that country, I shrank from attempting such a journey on foot, with limited supplies, no guide, no detailed map.

In order to follow my present compass bearings, I had to leave the old trail and strike off to the left. This was a forested country, though the trees at the timberline were not the giants one might discover farther down. I took frequent bearings, intent on not getting lost. The knowledge that had made me a Ranger cadet was all I had now to depend upon.

The trees grew taller, the ways under them more shadowed. I paused now and then to listen. But never did I hear more than the usual woodland sounds. Then there arose a screen of brush, and beyond it was the clear space in which stood the hopper.

I kept to cover, working my way along to where some of the bushes thrust forward. The door of the vehicle, which I could now see, hung open a little.

And when I saw what held that door open, I got to my feet, in spite of the churning of my stomach, and walked out to face what I would rather have shrunk from.

FOURTEEN

There had been four passengers and one of those unwilling. He was in the pilot's seat and wore the coveralls of a settler, while the one behind him had the semi-uniform of the refugees with a laser close to hand. It was easy to deduce that he had been holding that on the pilot when the end came. The other two were also in uniform.

I do not want to recall the next hour. I had nothing with me for digging. The best I could do was heap loose earth over them. In the end, that was done, and I had a hopper that was in running order.

Where they had been bound I could only speculate. Perhaps over the mountains, perhaps even to Butte Hold, for there was no other camp or settlement in this direction. But they had all been dead for some time.

At last I was able to lift back to the shelter on the mountain-side. This machine had been well kept, even better, I thought, as I relaxed at its quick response to controls, than those at Kynvet. Since it had been left on manual and not a journey tape, I could not tell from whence it had come any more than its destination.

It was twilight when I set down in the small clearing. And I was glad to see that none of the children was in evidence as I climbed out of the cabin.

"Home!" Annet ran her hand almost caressingly along the side of the hopper. "Now we can go home!"

"Not yet."

"What do you mean?" she demanded fiercely. "We have to get back to Kynvet, learned what has happened."

"I know what happened, a little of it," I told her and all of them, for the sooner they knew the need for caution, the better. "There was a prisoner and guards in here. And the prisoner was a settlement man, the guards from the refugees."

"Who—?" Annet asked.

I shook my head. "I don't know."

To my relief she let that subject drop, but instead asked, "Where, if not home?"

"To Butte Hold. Remember the com room?" That was all the bait I had to offer to win her compliance. Would she argue in exchange that the coms elsewhere had done us no good? And if she insisted upon going to Kynvet, would my authority be strong enough to deny her? We had never reached a point of absolute contradiction, and it was the last thing that must happen now.

"The Butte," she repeated, and was silent as if thinking it over.

"It is the strongest refuge I know of. And we don't know all its resources. Lugard said it had defenses nothing on this world could crack."

"Defenses against what?" she asked bitterly. "So far we have found no menace to us—here. And we must know—"

"Yes—"

She must have caught my thought and the significance of the swift glance at those about us, for she looked startled for an instant, and then, perhaps because she felt guilty, she surrendered.

"The Butte then. Do we go tonight?"

"In the early morning." I had no mind to land in a nest of Zarvna vipers. And if the Butte was occupied by treasure seekers, it could prove just that for us.

So we spent a second night in the bare shelter. But we were this much favored by fortune—we had transportation and need not face a perilous trek across the lava country.

I tried the com of the hopper. It was open and working, answering with the thrum of a waiting channel. But I did not try to send, only pick up any hint there was still life in the valley. Nothing came.

In the morning, at dawn, we loaded into the cabin. As with the ground car, it proved a tight fit, but we were happy. To have again the familiar about us was heartening—to a point. I set a course I thought would be a direct line to the Butte.

As we passed over the lava lands, I was thankful we were not making that journey on foot. The desolation of which we had had a taste on our way to the cave entrance had been modified by the fact we used a road Lugard had already pioneered. Looking at this tortured, twisted land, I could see we might have been lost forever in its hold.

We raised the Butte before noon. Annet, seated beside me, had manned the snooper scope. The skies were clear of any flyers; not the faintest beep gave warning. And now, as she turned it groundward, she reported the landing space also clear.

That surprised me. "The hopper we took in—" When? How many days ago? I could not have numbered them due to our sojourn underground.

"Yes!" That struck her, too. "Where is that?"

Picked up by prowlers who came after us? And Lugard had locked the big door when we had gone. If he had left all guards up, we were now deprived of what I wanted most for us, a secure base. I thought of my folly in not making sure, back in the cave, that I had the metal plate that unlocked all for Lugard.

Then Annet reported the main door open, so one small barrier did not exist. However, I did not land the hopper there, but rather maneuvered with all the skill I had to set down on the roof. If there was some trap within that door, we might so escape it.

As soon as I had magna-locked the wheels on that surface, I dropped out, stunner ready. There was the faint wailing of the wind among the weirdly sculptured rocks, the heat of the sun pouring full force on my head and shoulders, making me instantly aware that the clothing meant for the mountains was not for the lava lands—nothing else.

I made for the door of the watchtower. Annet took my place at the controls, and I had her promise to lift should there be any trouble, whether I could make it back or not.

It was an eerie business, this step-by-step descent into the deadly quiet of the Butte, for it was thus that the silence impressed me—with a perilous promise, as if each forward press of an unwary foot could plunge one into disaster.

I stopped frequently to listen, but there was nothing to hear. Inside these walls even the sound of the wind was lost. Down and down I went until at last I was in the main hall from which opened the com room, the grav lift, and the mess hall where we had eaten so long ago. I had met no challenge save that raised by my own unease.

In the mess hall I found the first proof that the Butte had been visited. As in the raided storehouse of Feeholme, there were signs of hasty pillaging, though there was not the wanton breakage I had seen. Whatever they had taken still did not greatly deplete the supplies.

The com room was my next objective. There was no disorder here, so I could not tell whether or not it had been in use. I did not try to activate its installations. I ran to the open door and saw that it had been forced by laser, so that that could not be closed again. That was something of a blow to my hopes for defense, but we could see to that later.

However, the place was now clean. At my signal the rest disembarked, and we moved into the Butte.

For two days we worked to make it the fortress I believed we might need. I expected Annet to object to this as a waste of time. But to my surprise she did not, though she spent time in the com room. I did not doubt that she tried to pick up some broadcast to reassure her.

The grav lift still worked, though I did not trust it too far, but we discovered a second opening into the underground depot. I hunted for this since I knew the machines Lugard had used had not been brought up via the lift. This opened directly into one of the narrow lava ridges.

We experimented with the machines until we found one like that which must have been used to seal off the cave camp. It mounted a laser and could be pulled, by a great deal of effort, around to the front of the Butte.

Into the burned-out door space we then packed material as tightly as we could and melted it all into a solid stopper with the laser until where there had once been an opening was now a lump as unbreakable as the walls it joined. We now had no ground entrance—only that via the roof and the one in the lava cut. I thought it would take a massive attack to break in.

There were piles of supplies in the depot, and we need not want for sustenance for a long time. On the night of our third day within those walls, I lay on my bedroll, tired to the point of exhaustion, but with a feeling of real security such as I had not known since this whole adventure had begun, but I was not left to enjoy that long, for Annet came to stand over me.

"Kynvet." She said only that one word but with such determination that it was both promise and threat. Then she added, "I can pick up nothing—we must know."

She was right of course. Only something in me, now that we were so close to the final revelation, wanted to delay it.

Then, perhaps seeing that reluctance mirrored in my face, she said, "If you do not go, I do—even if alone."

And that, too, was a promise I knew she was determined to keep.

"I'll go." My sense of security fled. It had been such a short time of well-being. It was as if I stooped to pick up again a shoulder-bruising burden I had only set aside.

"If—if the worst has happened," she continued (now she did not look at me, but rather beyond as if she did not want me to see what lay in her eyes), "there is the port and the signal."

"You know, Annet, that the signal—"

"May go unanswered for years, yes!" She caught me up with some of her old fierceness. "But that is a chance we shall have to take. Kynvet and—and then, if necessary, the port. But, Vere, not this time alone."

"Not you," I countered.

"Not me," she agreed at once to my relief. "Only we must be sure, of Kynvet, of the port signal. Two are better than one. Thad—"

"But—"

"Oh, I know. You look upon him as the eldest in line, the one to step into your shoes. Certainly he is not Vere Collis, just as you are not Griss Lugard. But you must take him for the very reasons you wish to leave him here. He is the next to you, the best we have."

Thinking it over, I could see she was right, though I did not want to admit it. Thad did have the qualities that would enable him to carry on the needed tasks if anything happened to me.

And the very fact that Annet foresaw such a possibility suggested that she no longer cherished the hopes that had made her so stubbornly set on coming over the mountains. But I did not question her, for that all was better unsaid now.

I took one more day, though I knew Annet begrudged it to me, to make sure I would leave the Butte in the best possible shape to withstand trouble. Then we left on foot, for that was one thing in which I did not yield to Annet. The hopper must remain as a final possible means of escape for those in the Butte.

It was also my argument that we could move better under cover, even if it took us longer. And the ability to keep out of sight might be our best protection.

The trail out from the Butte was largely overgrown. For ten years it had been left to nature, and all recent traffic had been by hopper or flitter. But enough traces remained to guide us. We took only very light packs and stunners with extra charges. I had searched and researched the supplies for a more formidable weapon. But, as in the cave base, they must all have been taken when the forces left. My final act at the Butte had been to dismount the laser we had used to seal the door, get it by painful effort to the roof, and there affix it as a defense. I did not think that Annet looked upon it with any favor, though, and I was not sure she would use it, even in extremity—though no one knows what he will do facing death.

We might have been moving through wilderness as little tamed as that of the Reserves, but at noon we came upon the first of the far farms. There we found another kind of tragedy. As at the mutant station, animals had been penned here, and they had, for the most part, died in captivity. We freed two of the burden beasts still alive—they had eaten to stubble the grass of their paddocks—and fed and watered them, turning them loose to go as they willed, though I had the thought that if we could find them upon our return, it might be well to lead them back with us. But for the smaller creatures—the gleex with their fleece for garments, the obor birds, and two pidocks—there was nothing to be done.

The house was empty, and we found no sign of what had become of the owner and his family. No raiders had been here, but it was a dark beginning to what, I am sure, had no light ending, nor could have.

We pushed on, keeping to the road as a guide where we could. I think we needed that road for our spirits, as it was a link not only with what civilization Beltane had possessed, but also with the secure past. But we did not talk much until Thad suddenly burst out, "You think everything—everybody's gone, don't you, Vere?"

"That is a possibility."

"The refugees, too?"

"Those in the hopper were dead. They may have loosed something they did not know how to control."

Thad stopped and looked at me directly. "Is it better—really—to know?"

"We have to."

Thad's position at Kynvet was not far different from mine, or had been. His parents died as a result of a lab experiment gone wrong, and he had been taken in by the Drax family, who were relatives of his father. So he had no close kin to miss. Yet it did not follow that he could be as detached as I had always felt. After all, he was not of a Service family and so not set apart from the rest of the community.

"I suppose so," he said reluctantly. "And what do we do, Vere, if it is true—that we're now alone here? Oh, I know we set up the port call. But who knows if that will ever be picked up."

"Boat law," I said briefly.

"Boat law?" he repeated. Then understanding came. "Oh, you mean the space regulations. We start a colony because we are marooned. Only we aren't survivors of a shipwreck."

"Near enough to follow the law. And we shall be starting with more than many such survivors ever had. We have all that is left here. Always supposing that it *is* ours now without dispute."

"The machines won't run forever. A lot of them need more servicing now than we can give. And when everything stops running—"

"Yes, we'll be on our own. We'll have to do all we can to establish ourselves before all the machines stop."

But that meant planning for years ahead, and I still shrank from that—until I had to. I think that perhaps Thad liked such thoughts no better because he was quiet. What we said for the remainder of the day was limited to matters of our traveling.

We made a cold camp that night in a small copse beside a

stream. We shared watches through the dark hours, ate E-rations in the morning, and went on.

It was past midday when we came into familiar fields. Animals had been loosed here and wandered aimlessly. Some trailed us, making plaintive sounds as if they wanted our company, but we eluded them when we could, not wanting to call attention to our passing.

So we came to Kynvet, or where Kynvet had been. We had seen tapes of wartime destruction on other worlds, but I did not believe they meant much more to us than those of fiction or history tapes, displaying events far out of our range of direct feeling. And the force of this was now like a blow in the face.

There was churned earth of sickly yellow, bits of material that might once have marked homes and labs we had known all our lives. But not one landmark remained to say that once a settlement had been here. It was as if a giant fist had crushed and blotted out all men had done.

"No—" Thad's denial was half moan. He did not move out into the area of disaster in any search for what had once been, but he looked to me, his face stricken.

"What—"

"This is what we must have heard in the caves."

"Why?"

"We may never know."

"I'll—I'll—" He swung up his stunner as if it were a blaster and he had the perpetrators of this within its sights.

"Hold your fire—until it is needed."

That got through to him, that promise of retribution.

"Where do we go now?"

"The port." But I had little hope we would find better there.

We had meant to camp at Kynvet, but we did not want to stay anywhere near. Instead, we pushed on at a swifter pace than we had followed all day, striving to put between us and that scar as much space as possible. And it was well into dark before we halted—for we felt as those fleeing a disaster—in a shed meant to store harvest on the edge of another line of fields. Between Kynvet and the port the land was largely under tillage.

Those crops were very near harvest. In fact, it must have begun because we had passed some fields with only stubble left, though there had been no bagged grain, no reaping robos in sight. It might well be that once we were—sure—we should see to that harvesting. Though the yield would be far more than would be needed for our small band, yet letting it rot in the fields sat ill with me. We had been so trained to thrift and economy since the wartime breakdown of interworld commerce.

The next morning we crossed the edge of Yetholme land. Perhaps the settlement had not been treated as Kynvet, but in the caves we had felt the shock of more than one bombing. At any rate, on the way back we could detour to pass both Yetholme and Haychax, but now the port mattered most. I had the idea that if any life remained, it would center about there anyway.

We covered ground at the steady trot, rest, trot that was a part of Ranger training and that they had, in turn, learned from the Security men. It was as speedy as any foot travel, and across fields one could keep it steadily. But we were still outside the port when we saw those two tall pillars of metal, sky pointed.

"Ships!" Thad cried aloud.

"Easy!" I caught his arm and pulled him back with me into a screen of brush that had been set out to fence field from field. With those in sight, we must use all the caution and cunning we had.

They were certainly not government ships, nor did they have the round-bellied, cargo-carrying look of Free Traders—though such might have planeted only to be captured.

"Patrol?" That was no identification but a question from Thad.

We crept now, flitting from one piece of cover to the next. Perhaps we were wrong; the settlers might have set an off-world call, and these come in answer. If so, we were safe. But I accepted nothing untested.

There were signs of disorder and fighting among the buildings around the port gate. Seared marks and melted patches told of laser beaming. We passed broken hoppers and a flitter crashed into the roof of a house, its wreckage still hanging there. But there was no sound, no sign anyone had been there for days.

At last we reached the gates and crouched behind an upended and partly lasered hopper. I got out my lenses, determined to make sure before we advanced.

The ships had been a long time in space—that was certain from the scouring of their sides. The nearer would not rise again.

Its tubes were badly eroded. I wondered at the skill of the pilot who had brought her in, three points down, on those. Perhaps he himself had been left speechless at such fortune.

There was insignia on both, half effaced. It was of some old force, I was sure. The refugee ship had not landed here—but maybe these were the two who had followed her and demanded similar privileges.

Their hatches were open, the landing ramps out, but about them nothing stirred. I focused on the ramp of the far one, looking for a long moment, then got to my feet.

"What is it, Vere?"

"There's a dead man on the ramp. I don't think we need fear the ships. Let's go to headquarters."

We did not approach the ships but were emboldened enough to walk across the open end of the field to the headquarters. Our soft-soled wood boots made no sound in the halls where the magnetic plates of space boots had once sounded a welcome clatter. The signs of neglect had been here even before the disaster—doors long closed, sections of hall and concourses where nothing waited to be shipped, no off-world passengers gathered, nor had they for long years. It was like a monument—not to a dead hero, but to a dead way of life. And I found, in spite of the stuffy warmth, I was shivering.

The com room was our first objective, and it was in wild confusion. There had been a fight here. Rays had seared and wrecked installations, and there were splotches of dried blood on the floor. Also there had been some attempt at repairs. Tools lay about one board, which had been loosened and laid back to display fused wiring. It was, I believed, that meant to signal ships in orbit.

But the repairs had hardly been begun, and what remained was beyond my knowledge to continue if I had wished. However, what we sought was still farther in the small room opening off this. Avoiding bits of wreckage, we crossed to that.

The door resisted our pushing until we both put our shoulders to it with all our strength. Then it grated harshly as it moved. Within, on a central base, was the beacon—or had been the beacon! What stood there now was a melted mass of metal with no possible use for us or anyone on Beltane.

"No beacon," Thad said after a long moment. "They were fighting here, too."

"Someone may have tried to set it and was caught—"

Though I had never really believed in any help from space, yet now I felt a sense of loss, of closing in, as if the room about us grew darker even as we looked at the failure of the last link with the world of the past. I turned away, and when Thad did not at once follow me, for he was still staring at that melted lump, I put my hand on his shoulder.

"Come on. It's past use now."

There was one other place in this building that I must visit. Not that I could get any aid, except an answer, perhaps, to a question, but answers I wanted.

The headquarters must—should—hold some clue as to what had happened. Report tapes from all the sectors came in here daily, were sorted and stored by the memory banks of the computer. If that unit had not also been destroyed, we could find the final reports and glean from them information. I said as much to Thad and we left the wreckage of the com center, padding down the hall in search of the memory banks of Beltane.

FIFTEEN

I fully expected to find that the computer banks had also been damaged or destroyed, but that was not so. Either the fight had never reached this point, or no one had been interested in the records. I went to the control seat in the center of the room and studied the buttons on its board. The wall ahead was a vast visa-screen, meant to give visual as well as audible answers to questions. And built into the walls were the relays to carry not only the full history of the colony since First Ship landing, but also all data from the research labs. Most of that was classified, though, to be released only in codes I did not know.

Now I hesitated, not knowing just what combination would give us an account of what had happened in the last days. And for want of a better key word I decided upon "refugee," for it would seem this had all been triggered by the arrival of the first ship. Therefore, I set up that simple pattern.

"On the fourth day, sixth month, year 105 PL—"

The voice of the recording rang startlingly loud through the chamber, and I hastened to cut the volume. The bare facts continued—that the refugee ship had asked for landing, had been granted such to the north, and had planeted there. Then were added some facts concerning the new settlement.

From this the recording went on to the coming of the next ships, the appeal for the second landing, a meeting between representatives from the ships and the Committee—plus the voting of the settlements. That brought us to the end of what we already knew. I leaned forward eagerly to hear what would follow.

"On Twelfth Day, seventh month, year 105 PL, it was decided in open meeting to ratify a second treaty, admitting the second ships, on the understanding there would be no more. This was voted in general meeting 1,200 to 600—"

The voice was silent. It would seem that was the end of the refugee problem as far as the memory banks were concerned. There was one other place we could perhaps find out more—Once more I punched a code and waited.

What came in answer was code, a series of numbers and allusions intelligible only to those who set it up. So it ran on and on, and I wondered what good those reports on experiments and sector progress would ever be now. Then—

"Sector 4-5. Refugee party came early this morning. Wanted medical aid—took Dr. Rehmers by force. Left men on guard behind—killed Lofyens and Mattox—looted the Rytox lab. Have most of our personnel now under guard. Warning: they took the old records—" Once more the voice fell from that stark report into code. But I marked the numbers in my mind, signaling to Thad. He nodded, and I saw his lips move, so I knew he was also striving to memorize. The voice ended abruptly, and we heard the snick, snick of unfinished tape.

"6-c-r-t-tex-ruh-903," I repeated from memory.

"Yes," Thad agreed.

Now it remained to be seen—or heard—whether the information answering to that was also in code beyond our translating. I set up the call numbers and activated the banks.

"Classified, classified—" chanted the voice. And on the board a red light flashed. I knew an alarm had gone to the quarters once occupied by the commandant. But there was no one to alert now, nor would any guard come pounding down the hall to investigate.

Having given its warning, though, the machine was ready to oblige with the rest filed under that heading. Most of it was formula that meant nothing to us, but finally it shifted into understandable speech.

"Highly volatile and unstabilized, not to be recommended. Results as follows. Plague possibilities: will kill within forty-eight hours. No symptoms except slight headache. Produces cerebral hemorrhage. Contagious as long as subject is living, but cannot be communicated except from living to living. Will destroy only intelligent life to the—" Another rush of code, then: "Classified, fifth level, double code. We shall destroy all but master formula, which shall be coded in lock-files—"

Again an end. Thad moved forward to stare down at the keys that had brought us that report.

"They must have found that formula. But why—?"

"Lugard had fears of this." I told him what the veteran said concerning a pirate fleet using biological weapons known to researchers here. It seemed, though, that this weapon had gotten out of hand.

"Then they used it, and everyone just—died—" Even though he had seen the port and Kynvet, I do not think that before this moment Thad had really believed in the end of Beltane.

"We'll probably never know exactly what happened," I said. I was setting the code again for daily reports. There were two more, one from Haychax, the second from Kynvet, and that was broken off in mid-word, though neither had held any hint of danger.

"That's that." Perhaps sometime we could return here, experiment to break codes, or find a way to open fully the secrets of the memory banks. But we had no time for that now. I rose slowly from my seat, glancing from one wall to the other. There was a wealth of knowledge locked in here, but it was largely too specialized, with little to help us now. But there was something—I had been here several times on errands, and I knew what I wanted and where it was stored.

I crossed the room to the far wall and punched a request pattern. There was a clicking of relays, and two rolls of Zexro tape fell into the open trough below. I picked them up and was about to leave when there came another and louder click.

"Sign, please. All requisitions for tape must be signed for."

I heard a choking sound from Thad, half laughter, half something else, which warned of his state of mind. But I turned and set my thumb into the sign block, repeating my name and the fact I was from Kynvet on official business.

"Stop it!" I caught the boy's shoulder and gave him a hard shake.

"Sign—" he repeated. "Sign—as if nothing's happened and you just came in for supplies!"

"Yes." It had struck me, too, that indifference to all but a patterned programming. A world might be dead or dying, but the machine demanded a signature to release two rolls of tape. To us, it brought home with a rush all the wastage and horror about us.

We turned and ran, out of that room of unfinished, or perhaps now, finished history, down the corridors beyond, out of that building, and into the field where the silent, dead ships stood pointing to the stars from which we were now perhaps forever exiled.

But once out in the open, some of the feeling that had set us fleeing the headquarters vanished. Under the unchanging sun, with fresh wind about us, we could be sure we were alive. Though our principal reason for coming to the port was a failure and hope of rescue was gone, there were others things here that could be of service to us. I decided to do some exploring for what we could eventually transport to Butte.

Also, if we could find a flitter in working order, we would be even more fortunate. It would have been easier to split up and do our searching alone with an appointed meeting place, but neither of us wanted that. To roam a town of the dead alone was at that moment beyond our courage.

However, what we needed could be only in a few places—the park where all the in-use vehicles could be, the warehouse for off-world shipping (though that must be near empty), the machine shop where repairs were made on transports and machines still running, and the supply depot. I listed them, and Thad agreed. We needed more than what remained of this one day to search, and we decided to risk a stay in town overnight, camping out in the warehouse. Neither of us cared to enter a dwelling.

The vehicle park was a disappointment. Like that of Feeholme, the majority of the flitters and hoppers had been systematically destroyed. The one or two that had escaped were near the repair center and needed work. Given time and a chance with the instruction tapes, though, I thought we might put at least one into service again.

What bothered us most was the silence. Oh, the wind blew, and we heard the calls of birds (too many birds for a place where men lived), and now and then the sound of some four-footed scavenger. But this place made one look uneasily over one's shoulder and glance about sharply now and then. There was an odd feeling that someone had just left each room we entered or that someone had vanished around a corner only a second or so before we came into view. And that tension grew until Thad put it into words.

"They *are* here!" He made it a statement rather than a question.

"No—at least we have seen nothing." But my feeling of being watched made me so modify that negative. Was it because we knew this was a place of the dead that we were so haunted by what we could not see?

After the park we searched the warehouse. I could dimly remember coming here with my father when I was small. Then it had been a busy place. Why, there had been four or five ships out on the pad at once, discharging cargo, taking on the exotic side results of lab experiments, while this building had been crammed with cargo.

Now it was largely empty. There were a few bales at the far end, and we walked toward those. It was dim in here. The lights must have shifted to "low" long ago. And even the soft pad-pad of our boots sounded too loud.

"Looters—" Thad said abruptly.

He was right. The remnants of those off-world supplies had been looted. We saw broken boxes, torn bales, and again wanton destruction of what the raiders had not wanted. A careful search might reveal something worth carrying away, but since we had no transport save our legs, we were not going to add to our packs any except very exceptional finds.

"Supply depot—" I took the next on my list.

"It'll just be another write-off," Thad replied. "Food is what we'll need most—"

He was right. When I thought of it, breakfast was a long while back. We went into the office where the customs and the cargo masters had once dealt together and looked about. The room had two doors, one giving on the vast emptiness of the warehouse, the other on the outer street. I opened that to look out—into silence. When I closed it again, I set the thumb lock. Why, I could not have told, save that with the door locked against the silence and the coming dark, I felt safer.

There was a small heating unit in the cupboard, probably

intended for the brewing of caff. And a moment later Thad, peering into a drawer, found half a jar of that and an array of mugs. They must have been for official visitors, for on each was the insignia of one of the settlements.

I noted that when he picked out two, he did not take those with names on them we knew well, but rather set out a pair marked for over the mountains. I measured caff into the brew-master and set it on the unit. Small tasks to keep the hands busy were good. When we sat down to wait the heating on either side of the desk, which served us for a table, we tried not to look at each other.

"What do we do now?" Thad broke the silence first.

"Go back to the Butte."

"You think that we—we are alone here?"

"There may be someone left in the north, but I doubt it. They would have come into the port, too."

"And the refugees?"

"Would also be here—with those ships—if they still lived."

"I suppose so." He glanced over his shoulder to the door into the warehouse, which we had left a little ajar. "I can't help feeling that there *must* be someone, some place. And"—his voice became more rapid—"I don't want to meet—whoever it is!" He picked up the mug of caff, sipping, but as if he still listened. And I knew what he meant.

We put our blankets on the floor—hard beds, but they suited us that night, for in this office there was no hint of "ghosts." There might have been far softer rests in the port, but this night they were not for us.

Though we had seen nothing to make us think a guard was needed, we agreed to share sentry goes. Thad took the first, and I rolled into my blankets. We had turned off the light in the office, preferring the dark with the subdued light from the warehouse. I thought I would not sleep, but I did—until I awoke to Thad's shaking. His other hand was over my mouth, impressing me with the need for silence.

As my sleep-dimmed wits cleared, I heard it. There was the rap of footsteps on the warehouse floor, and only one kind of boot made such a clatter—a spacer's. One man—no, I thought I could make out the sound of at least two.

Thad's mouth was close to my ear. I felt his breath on my

cheek as he whispered, "They came in from the field. I heard a flitter set down there."

Together we crept to the door and peered into the warehouse. There was the glow of a beamer at the far end where the looted cargo was. And we could see two figures moving around there. So we were not alone—

Once more Thad whispered, "Do you think they were watching us? That they know we are here?"

"No—or they would have attacked," I answered. "They have the superior weapons; no need to worry about jumping us."

From what we could see, they were searching through the already tumbled containers, a kind of haste in their movements that suggested they were pressed for time or were frightened men.

If the virus was already seeded in them, then they were walking dead and must know it, having witnessed the fate of other victims. Also, they were more menace to us just living than if they hunted us with laser beams crackling through the air.

"Pack and out," I murmured to Thad. "Leave nothing to let them know we have been here."

We moved cautiously, assembling our packs. Thad collected the mugs and restored them to the drawer, while I snapped shut the door of the cupboard with the heating unit. We dared not turn on the light to check, but I thought that should anyone glance in, it would appear untouched. Then I loosed the lock on the outer door, and we slipped into the street.

It was just when I was sure we had made it safely that we heard a shout behind. We were a block away from the warehouse, needing to skirt the landing field to reach the open beyond the town.

"Lasers!" I warned Thad, and we jumped to cover in a deep doorway. The door gave inward, and we half fell into a hall. I had the door slammed again in an instant. They could burn in easily, but even the small portion of time needed for that would give us a fraction of head start.

Thad stumbled over something in the dark and nearly went down. He uttered a wild, gasping cry and shrank from what had tripped him, breaking past me down the hall. I dared flash on my belt torch for an instant, saw—and followed him as precipitously.

The hall ended in a grav shaft, but I took the first room to my left, pulling Thad with me. I was rewarded for my choice by a large window. This was open to the night, and it took us only a second to drop through, landing in a garden, almost in a garden pond.

The space was walled with a lattice vine, so thickly entwined that nothing short of a laser beam could cut through it. But the strength of our fear and revulsion was such that, in spite of the cuts the thorns made, we went over it, hardly aware that we climbed until we dropped on the far side, once more in a street.

We still heard a distant shouting, sounding at intervals as if the shouters were not giving an alarm but calling questioningly. Did the hunters believe we were of their own band? And if so, why would we run—unless all men had become very wary of each other since the plague hit.

For some moments I was confused as to which way we should head. To get away from the port and into the open country would, I was sure, give us the advantage. And I said as much to Thad.

"Where then—back to the Butte?"

"No. We dare not let them trail us." Though we had tried to make the defenses as strong as possible there, I had seen too much here at the port to believe we could hold out if they brought their strongest weapons against us.

We ran down the street, using every pool of shadow to cover us. There was a flash of beamer, centering on Thad for an instant, before he threw himself flat and rolled.

"Hellloooo—"

Not the searing rays we had expected, but rather a call. Were we wrong after all and those who chased us were not the enemy but our own people? But I was too certain of the click of space boots in the warehouse.

"Wait—!" Again a hail instead of fire.

But wait we did not. I hauled Thad to his feet with a quick jerk, and we slipped between two buildings, striving to put the rows of structures between us and pursuit.

"Flitter—" Thad gasped.

There was no mistaking the beating sound of a low-flying flitter. We ducked instinctively, hoping to melt so well into the shadows around us that we did not register for the pilot. It skimmed the roof near us and went down in the street we had just quitted, perhaps to pick up those on foot there or to join them.

"Come on!"

We used every trick we could think of, and enough of them worked to take us out of the port. A backward glance was startling. Lights had flashed on there. It was such a blaze as I could remember from my childhood—a reckless burning of lately hoarded energy. They must believe us holed up somewhere in there.

"They didn't fire," Thad observed. "Why?"

"They could have enough of killing," I said bleakly. "Or else we were out of their reach before they discovered we were not their own kind."

"Could they have been ours?"

"Not wearing space boots—and I heard space boots in the warehouse."

"What do we do now?"

"Circle north. If they try to trail us—"

"How can they? If they are off-worlders, they have no tracking experience."

"They don't need any. All they need is an infra-scope. And those are to hand. That's why we stay as far from the Butte as possible as long as we know they are after us—or even casting about in search."

Infra-scope—another thing meant for a good purpose, which could now be used to put an end to us, unless we could get out of range. There were plenty of those at the port. The Rangers used them regularly for tracking animals. And they could easily be adjusted to human warmth broadcast—since they had also located men lost in the Reserves.

So we headed north, in direct opposition to the path that had brought us to the port. I tried to think of some way we could baffle the scopes. Underground—yes. We must keep away from the lava country, lest a pickup from the Butte betray what we wanted most to guard. But there were other caves in the hill country. Our supplies were low, and I had had no chance to replenish them from storage.

By dawn we were well out in the wild, but a flitter could run us down with ease. We needed rest, so we chose a thick copse and settled down. Thad slept first while I mounted guard.

It was cool under the low-hanging branches of the trees. I was sure that even hovering overhead a flitter could not sight us. But they would not need to actually see us. If the scope told them where we were, they need only train a laser in our general direction, and that was that.

I heard a flitter coming from the south. The woods were thick here, and if we separated for a short space, that might give them two targets, spoiling their aim. I shook Thad into wakefulness.

"What—?"

"Move!" I shoved him a little to the right. "We go north—but not quite together."

"Yes." He shouldered his pack, and we veered from one another. The flitter sounded as if it hovered just over us. I waited tensely for a burning lash to strike about me. Instead, I heard the booming voice of a throw-com, hollow and ghostly in the night.

"We know you are there. Come out! You have nothing to fear—" The speech was in Basic, the off-world trade vernacular.

"Come out! We mean you no harm!" It blared away.

Did they think us so stupid? Why stop to talk? It was plain they had not wasted talk on the settlements.

Yet they did not fire, though by the sound the flitter still hung there. I could hear Thad moving through the brush, keeping pace with me but some distance away. Had our split-up, which seemed such a desperately futile precaution, really baffled our trackers? Or was there some reason why they were reluctant to loose death now?

We had seen their dead as well as ours. Could it be that they were reduced to as small a company as we were and that they now thought that those who had worked in the labs here might have some counter to the plague? My imagination supplied such an answer. I would probably never know whether or not it was the truth.

"We could cook you," the broadcast shrilled, "you know that, beam you right where you stand. But we haven't. Come out. We're all the same now—we die, you die. Only you'll die the quicker unless you come out!"

Pleading and then threats, but manifest reluctance to carry those out. They wanted us in their hands, not dead, which meant they had a pressing use for us.

In the end, the land saved us by a route we could not have foreseen. This section must have been one of those once included in a small Reserve for study purposes. We came to where the tops of the trees met to veil a narrow ditch, a hidden observation walk.

I found it by tumbling in and seconds later heard Thad crash after me. That it was artificial was proven by its pavement. When I stood, the edges just topped my head. I whistled the call of a tree lizard and was answered by Thad who moved to join me.

We felt our way in the dark, buffeted and torn by briers, tough roots, all the impediments protruding from the sides of the cut, unable to use our torches. To my surprise I heard the flitter swing away, no longer hanging directly overhead, and I wondered why, unable to believe that its crew had simply given up the chase.

If they did not want us dead, they must be baffled as long as we stayed in thick cover. It might mean they were now seeking a place to set down from which they could move in on foot. If so, the advantage would be ours.

"I think they are setting down," Thad said.

If they were considering a landing, they had chosen wrongly for their purposes, for the sound moved far from us. We continued through the cut, which must end somewhere ahead.

SIXTEEN

The cut grew shallower, though the thickness of the brush about it did not thin. Twice we came to spaces that must have been intended for observation posts, with seats before shelves on which snoopers or scopes could once have been bolted, but from the growth and uncleared condition of the runway, I thought it had been a long time since these had been used for such a purpose.

What lay to the north of the port was unfamiliar to me. This had always been the less populous section of the continent, with only a fringe of settled land, backed against wilderness, where only a few Security posts had been garrisoned by rotation. The projects once set up here had been the first abandoned.

Somewhere ahead were the hills that eventually joined the mountains across which we had come. I thought if we could reach that stretch of country, we would have a curtain from the flitter, for the infra-scope was notably erratic in broken country.

We came to the end of the slit when I struck my shin painfully against an obstruction. With searching hands I discovered a set of steps, so narrow as to hold but one foot at a time. There had been no sound of the flitter for some time. If they had come to earth, we now had the advantage, since we were trained to this, and they must be surer in space than planetside. Now was the time to put as much distance between us as possible. I said so.

"Can we get back—to the Butte, I mean—if we go north all the way?" Thad asked.

"Not soon. We shall have to circle west."

"There are no trails there."

"No. If we get far enough out, there are the Security posts."

Those posts, they must all be in ruins now. I remembered the one we had picked up by chance on the com. The warthorn, sitting in the chair as one with a right, staring back at us. Somehow that memory now sent a small shiver coursing down my back.

We issued from the slit into what had clearly once been a road.

"Where are we?" Thad moved closer. "We—we are in woods, aren't we?"

His uncertainty was well founded. Visibility was almost nil. I explored gingerly, and my hands encountered a springy wall of brush. By following that up as high as I could reach, I discovered they bent, or had been trained, inward, to meet in a thick mat overhead. I recognized this as one of the blind ways used in a mutant Reserve for the coming and going of observers.

But a mutant Reserve to the north? All I had ever heard of were over the mountains. However, general knowledge on Beltane was limited. There had been so many Security projects begun in the early years—and many of them abandoned later—that a hundred such could have had being in remote portions of the continent, unknown to settlers not directly concerned.

Now I dared to use my torch, knowing of old how well constructed and secret such ways were. We looked both ways down a tunnel formed from growing brush. This had been trained over a mesh of ro-steel, which resisted all assaults of weathering for years, and its matting made as thick a wall as one of the settlement structures. We had a choice, right or left, and the compass said left. No flitter could spot us from overhead. If this followed a pattern set on other Reserves, a number of low grade distort patterns had been installed in that mesh that would interfere with an infra-scope. Luck had brought us into a safe way—for as long as it lasted.

It continued to puzzle me that so elaborate an observation installation had been so near to the port and yet unknown, for while I had not explored possible informative tapes with the same fervor Gytha applied to such research, I had prided myself on knowing as much as the next about the Reserves.

"What—where is this?" Thad drew closer. Though we went single file here, he was near to treading on my heels.

"A mutant observation run, as far as I can tell. As to where—no Reserve listed now. Ah—" We had come to what was apparently a dead end of brush, but this I knew how to deal with. I had Thad hold the torch while I hunted among tendrils of vine and twig ends for the release that must be there. Only, after I had found it, I had a struggle to force it open, proving that this way had not been used for a term of years. Branches parted and vines tore as we united our strength to break through.

Before us was what I wanted least to see, open ground—and not only open ground, but also boggy territory. Clumps of vas reeds were almost as tall as the trees we had left. They still wore their wide summer crowns as fans to catch even the smallest breath of wind, so they were always in motion, striking one against its neighbor with click-clicks of stiff fronds, dislodging with every blow some of the fruit developed at the end of those fronds.

In addition to the vas reeds, there were grotesque humps of hortal, a fungi growing in weird lumps, to die quickly, riddled by flying things and animals for homes. They were unsafe to touch simply because they were so occupied that one never knew what kind of stinging or biting inhabitant might be decanted in a fury.

Straight into the bog led a pathway of rocks, now overgrown and discolored by algae and mosses, while above the muck, the slime-ringed pools, and all the other traps for the unwary danced or stood, like evil greenish candles, the swamp fires. This was as foreign to the Beltane I had always known as if, in coming through the tunnel, we had crossed space to another world.

"Do we go through there?" Thad wanted to know.

Someone once had and often enough to need the road but I had little inclination to follow. We could retrace our steps and explore the other end of the covered way, though it ran directly opposite from where we wanted to go.

The effluvia of the swamp reached our noses as the vas reeds rattled loudly under a rising wind. This way was risky even by day I decided. I was about to turn back when I heard a shout from the trail we had followed. It must be that our hunters had fallen into the slit and so were still on our track. If we retreated, we would come face to face with them.

I studied that broken stone road with closer attention than I had earlier given it. As far as I could see, it must follow some ridge of high land. None of it disappeared in a scummed pool, nor was it matted by reeds. Then, startled, I realized that in spite of the dark of the night, I was able to see those stones, that they appeared to be coated with some phosphorescence, which made them clear to sight. Thus, this path must have been meant to be traced in darkness. Were what the observers wished to spy on nocturnal?

"We'll have to go this way," I decided. And I took the first step.

I believed that those who followed after, wearing metallic plated boots, might have trouble, for the stones seemed coated with some slippery substance, but our soft-soled forest gear planted us firmly as long as we did not hurry. For a time we went straight out into the bog, the odors of its foulness rising about us. The vas reeds now grew thicker, and when the road curved to the left, they curtained off the back trail.

Since our eyes were well adjusted to the dark, the glow of the stones was enough to lead us on. I did not try to use a torch. We were well into that dismal land when we came to an island rising so much higher above the general level of the bog that five of the stones had been set in the slope of the hillock to make a stair to its surface.

The top of the hill-island had been smoothed, though bushes and matted grass proclaimed that it had gone unvisited for years. In its center were a series of pens resembling those we had seen at the mutant station—a place where mutants had been kept before release into an environment attractive to them?

This could also be the dead end of the road, and I began to think my choice had been stupid. I wasted no time in crossing to the other side of the hill. Here again steps, but these only brought us down to what had manifestly been a landing place for flitter or hopper.

That was walled in with the glowing stones, others of which had been set around as markers to be seen from the air. Why had it been necessary to deliver cargoes here by night? All this suggested nothing else.

We paced along the wall of the space on three sides. There was no break in it anywhere to say that the road led on, but finally I dared to use belt torch, beaming beyond the wall, hunting some possible foothold on through the swamp.

What it brought into view was a ridge of higher ground, much the same as the one that had supported our road in, save there was no pavement of stones on this. If it were a continuation of the road, then it could support us, but to use it was a gamble.

We climbed back to the place of cages. For the first time I saw a small structure, no larger than the cages but with walls of mesh covered, as had been the tunnel, with living growth.

Its door was open, but the vines of the wall had laced across that, barring entrance until we cut our way. This had been, I thought, as I flashed the torch cautiously about, fashioned for the same blending-with-the-landscape concealment as the stations on the Reserves. And it was never meant for more than a temporary shelter.

Like the mountain lodge, it was bare of any furnishing, save for two bunks built into the walls, now covered with a layer of evil-appearing fungi. It smelt vilely of damp.

Thad gave a quick exclamation, and I saw the flicker of stunner beam shoot to my right. Then his torch caught and held a thing that lay kicking very slowly until the full effect of the ray took and it was still, its belly upturned, its tearing claw starkly revealed.

A koth crab—nasty enough when it leaped before one could bring it down. And behind it a web of its fashioning with some swirling movements in it—

"Out!" I backed, Thad with me. Not just one crab, but a nest of them!

What other unpleasant dwellers this hillock might have I did not know, but I had no desire to discover. We would have to turn back now—only when we reached the end of the hill, we heard that sound, saw the wedge of a beamer aimed from above—the flitter had trailed us!

I grabbed the torch from the fore of my belt and thrust it back into the hut, having set it to give the appearance of someone inside.

"Come on!"

We hurried to the lower landing space, over its wall, to that ridge of hard ground that might or might not run to the other side of the bog. If they were hunting by sight now and not by scope—but we dared not hope for such a favor from fortune. At least, seeing the light, they might delay by the hillock.

Now we had to move by the feel of the ground under us, and that was a treacherous guide. After we had gone a short way, though, the surface under my boots felt as solid as the stone had been. I slashed with my woods knife and cut off a length of vas reed. With this in hand, I tapped the way ahead, testing for any change in the surface or for a turn we could not see, though the eerie marsh lights played here and there, giving a faint light.

The unmistakable sound of a flitter settling came from behind, and for that I gave a sigh of relief. They had caught a glimpse of the landing stage and set down there, perhaps beaconed in by the torch left in the hut, which meant they no longer hunted by scope—or they would have known that for a decoy.

Suddenly, under my rod there was no surface. In panic I quested to right and left, hoping that loss meant a change in direction and not an end to our narrow margin of safety. It did, for slightly to the left once more there was firm meeting of reed and ground.

From then on it was a matter of nerves. We fought tension, for the path no longer ran straight but wavered right and left, then right again. Each time it changed made us fear we had reached its end.

I began to think that this ridge was not natural but had been thrown up for some purpose, though it was not paved. It wove back and forth too much to be normal high ground. Now the marsh lights were fewer and behind us. We still moved through the stink of stagnant pools, and things slid, slipped, and splashed away from our coming. We expected at any moment that which might not flee but stand to dispute our passage.

At last the ridge skirted the edge of a small lake. I heard Thad gasp and might have echoed his exclamation of astonishment.

What we saw were lights—not the marsh fires, nor any torches such as those the flitter might have used, but pale living bars of a chill glimmer that had much in common with the earlier road stones.

Of the stones! It did come from stones! They had been set in rough pillars, not in any regular pattern, but here and there. Between those pillars, which rose out of the surface of the dark

water, were rough mounds plastered together above the surface
with mud and reeds in rude masses.

"Wart-horns!" Thad cried in a half whisper.

Wart-horns, yes. But never had I seen a whole village of them
so gathered. Wart-horns were generally solitary creatures, a small
family perhaps in a single pond. Yet here I counted some twenty
of the mud and reed mounds with the pillars between them.

Nothing troubled the water's surface, and as I saw from one
of the nearer mounds (there was a hole in it a little above the
water level), they might be abandoned. Yet it was something so
far out of the normal for that species that it was worrying, and
one learned early on Beltane that it was best never to let the
extraordinary pass without note.

We edged along the narrow path and so passed very close to
one of the pillars. I saw that it was indeed a makeshift structure,
the stone having been plastered together with the same mud and
reed mixture as formed the sides of the domes. Wart-horn doing?
But why? Wart-horns were not intelligent enough to work out
such a system of lighting.

The stones were uniform, exactly like the blocks that had
formed the roadway to the island. I suddenly went down on one
knee and ran my hand over the ground. So doing, one could feel
indentations, though they were seasons old and much worn away.
The pillars had been built of road stones!

Watching those domes warily, we felt our way along. There
was this to hearten us. While the wart-horns liked water to base
their dwellings, they did not live entirely within the swamps, for
they needed certain foods that grew on higher land, so they must
here be near the edge of the bog.

With the graying of the dawn sky, we were again on solid land,
the swamp well behind us, and we had not heard the flitter again.
The road that had guided us through the morass ended abruptly
at a second park for transportation. I searched the ground ahead
for some sign of a cave or like shelter. We were lagging, and we
could go little farther without rest.

"Vere!"

I turned my head. Thad was pointing eagerly at the cliff wall
a little ahead.

"Eeopoe, Vere!"

I saw it, too, the turn of broad-billed head, the flash of brilliant orange and white. It soared high and then shot down and seemed to disappear directly into the rock of the cliff. We started for that point. The eeopoe is a cave dweller, liking to set its nest, a plaster of feathers and moss and a secretion of fluids from its mouth, directly on the side of some opening. It nests in the dark but comes forth to hunt insects. Thus, our fortune had held that we saw it at all.

Had it not been for the bird, we would never have found the cave, for there was a towering rock to mask the entrance. One had to squeeze through a narrow slit between that and the parent cliff in order to enter at all. We found ourselves in a twilight, sandy-floored space.

This was not lava formation, and I had no intention of going too far in—just enough to deaden any scope the hunters might have on us. But we were free now to light the remaining torch.

The narrow inlet was like the neck of a bottle and, through that, was a strange place indeed. Though our travels through the lava caves had been good practice in underground oddities, the light showed us something new.

From the cave floor sprang a dense growth of pure white vegetation about knee high. It had rooted from seeds dropped by the eeopoes, whose murmuring calls sounded in strange, echoing moans over our heads. Some of the sprouts had already withered and died; others still fought for a doomed life. Thad lifted the rays from that ghostly growth, and it shown in the eyes of the birds on the nests until they stirred restlessly.

There was another sound at floor level, a scurrying. Thad flashed his light downward to catch a furry rump and puff tail—a weaverbrod. That tail whisked out of sight into a huge topple of nest, made partly of withered fronds from the ghost garden, partly of debris brought from without. The whole mass was almost waist high where it was packed against the far wall and must have been gathered by more than one generation of brods. The characteristic weaving of grass lengths was broken and crumbling in places, but it was clear the nest was still very much inhabited.

We avoided the ghost garden and the brod nest, also those portions under the eeopoe nests where there were showers of an unpleasant nature marked on the walls and fouling the ground sand. That left us a narrow strip on which to hunker down, the torch burning to the continual worriment of the birds, while we ate sparingly of our supplies. Then I brought out the map to try to plan ahead.

Sentry watch we took by turns. Twice more we ate. The eeopoes became accustomed to our company when we turned off the torch and would make their swift flights out and back. Timing by my watch told us we spent a day and a half in that hiding. This would, I hoped, baffle our pursuers into giving up. Yet I could not risk staying too long for fear they might cast southward and pick up the Butte.

The folly of our com calls was now apparent. Should Annet try again during our absence, she might beam in their destruction. The last hours spent in the cave were hard; we wanted so much to be on the move.

At last we followed the eeopoes out at dusk. There was no sign we had been trailed this far. Now we had to aim directly by compass, south and west once more. This was not easy country in which to follow any straight bearing, for it was rough, foothill land.

We skirted the swamp for the first night's journey. But we had the moon, sometimes entirely too much of it. There was no need to feel out every step, and we moved at a faster pace. I kept watching for a wart-horn trail. Such a group of them as suggested by the village in the lake would certainly leave a very noticeable regular swamp exit.

When we finally came upon that "road," I was startled, in spite of my anticipation, by the width and depth of the paw-pounded expanse. It was wide enough to accommodate a ground car, and it was worn below the surface of the surrounding soil as if it had been a main thoroughfare for generations of the creatures.

I had certainly no curiosity as to where it led. Having seen traces it was still in use, I wanted only to leave it behind. Wart-horns were not formidable creatures alone, but a pack (unknown heretofore) might be prudently avoided.

We hurried on until the swamp veered to the south, and we took a path more to the west. Meanwhile, we listened for the flitter, but when we were able to make such good time without hearing or seeing anything that suggested we were still the object of a search, we relaxed somewhat, but not enough to walk into the trap they had set.

I had no scope, but I did have something that anyone with

even limited Ranger training developed speedily or else was no aid to such service at all—a sixth sense of warning. I stopped short as we came to where we must round an abutting pillar of rock, throwing out my arm as a barrier to halt Thad also.

Instead of advancing, I inched back, pushing Thad. I listened, tried to sniff any alien odor (though scent is the least of all warning for my species). There was no sign of danger ahead—except that I *knew* something waited for us there.

With a last rush I threw myself back into a pocket behind the rock, carrying Thad, half under me, to the ground. We lay there for a long moment, listening.

I do not know how they knew their trap had failed. Perhaps they had the scope at their service to tell them we were near. They were hard driven, so hard driven that they tried now openly what they had failed to accomplish with their ambush.

"We know you are there."

The voice boomed among the rocks as it had in the air near the port. "We mean you no harm. We need your help—truce oath."

Truce oath? Yes, once there had been such promises, and men had kept them. But for what had happened here on Beltane—after what we had seen—there was no trust in the "honor" of those we faced.

"You need us, we need you—" the voice continued, and there was a note of desperation in it.

"Look, we'll disarm. See—"

Out into the moonlight beyond the rock spun weapons, four of them. They clanged down on the stone and gravel and lay with the light shimmering on them; a blaster, two lasers, and another piece I could not identify but had no doubts was just as deadly as the other two—perhaps more so.

"We're coming out now—empty hands—truce oath—"

I could see their shadows before I saw them. I readied my stunner and saw Thad do likewise.

There were three of them, and we did not see their faces plain, for they had their backs to the light. They moved slowly, as if each step was an effort. Though they held their hands high, palms out, I saw one come to a halt and touch his forehead with his right hand. I remembered the disease symptoms, and I froze in fear.

"Now," I whispered to Thad, "give them full beam!"

SEVENTEEN

They went down, crumpling to earth as if they were indeed made of clay that dissolved under a stream of well-directed water. They were not dead, but we had no fears of them for a time.

"Thad, stay away!" I ordered sharply, for he was moving toward the flaccid bodies. I did not know how to look for signs of the plague, or even if it had visible signs, but that these men had so pressed after us was a warning. I believed I could guess only one reason for that—they knew us to be of Beltane and thought we might have an answer to the demon that had been released.

"Contagion from the living," I reminded Thad when he looked at me. "Take their weapons, get away before they come to—"

He nodded and scooped up the nearest laser and blaster, while I gathered up the other two arms. We made a careful detour to avoid the men themselves.

"The flitter—" Thad said.

"Yes."

If we could find their transport and make it ours, we would not only leave them afoot and unable to trail us south, but we could hurry our own return to the Butte. We had not heard the flitter in passage, but that did not mean that they were not grounded somewhere nearby, so we began to search for it.

I had no idea how long the stunner would render them unconscious. That varied with individuals. But with all the weapons now in our hands, we were in control of the situation. They had only one arm, though that was a formidable one if they realized it—they need only pass the infection to us and we would be dead men, though we still walked, talked, seemed alive.

Together we scrambled to the top of the cliff along which we had been traveling. From that height I made a careful survey of the surrounding territory, to spot what we sought in a small meadow strip around the point of the cliff.

I focused on the flitter with the lenses. The door of the cabin was open—and, in the trampled grass there, a man lay prone. He might have fallen from the cabin or collapsed while he stood sentry duty by the doorway. But he lay very still, and not from any stunner. I was sure of my foreboding—the party carried the plague with them. But the flitter—dared we take it? It would mean so much to have such a means of transportation to hand. And to leave it where any of the enemy continuing to live would have it at their service—A questing flight south could bring them to the Butte. It only remained whether the machine was infected.

"He's dead, isn't he?" Thad sighted on the flitter. "Plague?"

"I'd say so. If we dare take the flitter—"

We had no idea of the size of the hunting party. There might be others, dead or dying, inside.

Thad, watching the flitter, tensed so visibly that I was aware of his surprise.

"What is it?"

"Look at the tail—beside that stand of red grass."

The growth he named was vivid, its blood-scarlet stems and narrow blades doubly visible because it was flanked with drab zik leaves. For a long second or two I made out nothing, so well did the lurker blend into the background with the natural camouflage of its species. Then it moved, and I was instantly able to trace the ugly, horn-snouted head lifted to peer at the motionless body.

"Wart-horn?" I wondered, for its present actions were those of no wart-horn I had ever heard of.

Normally wart-horns were not dangerous, though their ugliness was apt to repulse. They were amphibian, a well-grown specimen standing some ten hands high at its humped shoulders. Their wide faces with gaping slits of mouth and the three warty growths, one mid-section where a human would have a nose, the other two above pop eyes, were exceedingly ugly by our standards. They also had the faculty of being able to alter their skin shading to blend with their surroundings. Mainly, they were timid creatures, preferring their mud sinks, fleeing when disturbed, though the males had fangs, which at certain times of the year exuded poison. Their method of fighting was to leap from behind on their prey, grasping tightly with sucker-padded paws, tearing for the throat with their fangs.

This one was larger than any I had seen recorded. Its head, held at a strained angle above those hunched shoulders as it struggled to see better, was out of shape, having a wider and higher expanse.

It moved now with one of its characteristic hops, a tremendous effort that brought it from the tail of the flitter to thud to earth beside the body. Then it bent forward, its face very low above the man, head swinging from side to side, either inspecting or sniffing.

Apparently satisfied, it suddenly reached out with its front paws, planting one on either side of the door, drawing up in a very awkward and visible effort, to put its head inside. Again it remained so, its warted back presented to my lenses, as if it were carefully surveying the interior of the cabin.

Dropping back to the ground, it turned its attention once more to the man, putting out a forepaw to fumble over the body.

"Vere! Look what it's doing!"

I had seen that, too. The creature from the boglands now had in its paws a long bush knife. Light flickered along the metal blade. It was holding up that find, studying it with bulbous eyes. Everything in its movements suggested this was no longer an animal but a thing with intelligence who had found something it could put to future use.

"Vere, why—?"

"Mutant." I gave the only possible explanation. What I had just seen, coupled with the village in the pond, meant—So there had been mutant experiments with the native animals as well as with imported ones! But for what purpose?

Once more the wart-horn bent to survey or sniff the man it had despoiled. Then it turned again to the flitter and made a futile effort to climb into the cabin—so extraordinary a departure from the norm as to keep me breathlessly waiting. But the squat body prevented that feat, though it strove with determination and effort. At last it left in two great bounds that carried it in the direction of the swamp. The knife had gone with it, carried in its slit mouth.

It had done one thing for us. Its actions at the flitter had made plain that there were no passengers in the cabin who need trouble us. And we needed that machine.

Shouldering our small packs, we climbed down from the crag. We did not hurry. And we scouted the strip of meadow before we moved into the open in a quick zigzag run.

We avoided the body as we had the stunned men, though I noted in passing he wore what had once been a space uniform. What alliance he had once owed, we would never know.

While Thad stood on guard, I followed the wart-horn's lead and looked inside. It was a six seater, one of the large ones from the port. Behind the passenger section was a muddle of boxes, as if those who had brought it here had been looting. I swung up and in and went to the pilot's seat. As I thought, the controls were not set on a journey tape but on manual.

"All right." I summoned Thad.

He obeyed with no waste motions, slammed the cabin door behind him, and settled in the co-pilot's place. I triggered the controls, hoping it would fly. The charge dial wavered near low. Since I had no time to waste going for a recharge at the port, I could only hope it would get us as far as the Butte.

I had never pretended to be expert with a flitter, and I had not had much practice with such a machine. Hoppers were left to the less expert at this period on Beltane. However, I got us airborne with only a jerk or two. Then I sent it south and west at the best speed I could reach, which was better than a hopper's best. I picked a course not too near the port, having no wish to alert any remainders of the enemy force that could possibly be there.

"Vere"—Thad broke the silence—"those wart-horn mutants—"

"Yes?"

"There was never a public report of an experiment such as that."

"No." And how many other such secrets were now to come to light? Perhaps experiments had gone on that had never been reported at all—even in code to the memory banks.

"What if there are other things, Vere?"

"I think we can almost count on some more surprises."

"But we can't get any help from off-world now. And—"

"And we may have to share Beltane with mutants, unchecked?" I finished. "Just so—something to consider."

"The Butte, it's out in the wastelands, far from any Reserve. Vere, do you suppose we could open up the caves again. The base would make a safe place—"

"Always supposing some of the wild life wasn't indigenous there. Remember the ice caves?" I reminded him. He was right in that, though. Lugard and those before him had thought to make it a final refuge.

"Vere, look—over there!" It was Thad who spotted the movement, for I had been concentrating on the controls.

What he had sighted might, under other circumstances, have been a very common occurrence at this time of year. There were harvest robos at work in a field below, gleaning, threshing, spitting out at the end of every three rows a bag of grain. But who had programmed them? There were two more fields beyond, now only stubble. So they had been busy at least a day, maybe two.

The refugees? Had they any survivors who had had the foresight to set the robos going to save the crops, even as I had speculated on doing earlier? Robos had to be programmed carefully, since our fields of food stuffs were not too large, and a robo was apt to go on working through fences, even into heavy brush, unless it was supervised. These could not have been running long, and the fields had been correctly harvested. Yet no one with control in hand was in sight. Nor was there any near farmhouse. And—

"Gusset oats!" My identification of the crop brought my hand to the controls in an almost involuntary gesture and sent the flitter off course to circle the field. That was no food for human beings! This coarse grain the robos now bagged normally went to the Reserves, where it was kept to supply some of the wild life in a bad winter season. Why would anyone activate robos to harvest gusset oats now?

The robo working below us came to the end of the field. I fully expected to see it crash on, into the fence. There was always the chance that some half-delirious dying man had activated the machine without knowing just what he was doing.

But it came to a dead stop inside the boundary. I made another circuit of the fields, noted the row of bags waiting to be carted away, the now quiet robo. The fields had certainly been recently cut, not more than a day or so earlier. But the bags that should have represented the harvest were not all there. Only three beside one fence remained. The rest were gone.

"Someone's alive!" Thad cried. "Let's look for him. Vere, we must!"

There was a lane leading from the field. But a spurt along over that did not bring us to a farm or to any small settlement, only to a warehouse meant for storage. And no one moved there.

In spite of the pressing need to return to the Butte, I could not pass up the chance that some settler might be alive, so I set down in the open where cargo carriers had parked.

The doors of the warehouse were wide open. And inside, nothing—no bags. We called, and when I saw a com mike on the wall, I tried to raise an answer from it. But there was not even the thrum of an open line.

It was when we returned to the flitter that I saw the marks in the dust. They had not been left by a hopper or a ground car, nor were they the tracks of forest boots or space footgear.

Hoofprints, and ones I knew. Very recently, since the last vehicle or men had troubled this dust, more than one Sirian centaur had stamped this way. Gusset oats and centaurs made a neat pattern. But the robo harvester—who—or what—had guided that? Suddenly, I thought I did not want to know, I wanted to be back at the Butte, among my own kind and a wasteland where the unbelievable might not have been set free to roam.

"Vere, look—these dragging marks—" Thad pointed to lines. Manifestly, something of some weight had been dragged. Feed bags or—? I wanted no more of a place that now seemed alien. It was as if we had lingered too long where we were not wanted. Not that I had any feeling that we were being watched, or that any scouts of a nonhuman kind lay hidden out there, their attention on us. It was rather as if we had returned to a deserted house where no one of our race would live again.

Telling myself to curb an imagination that was only too ready to visacast pictures one should see only with the aid of one of the most fantastical amusement tapes, I settled in the flitter. As we lifted with all the speed I could safely muster, I determined not to be pulled off course again.

We did swoop over other fields awaiting harvest. What grew down there was for the filling of human stomachs. Nowhere were robos busy. Another month, even three weeks or so, might be too late to save these crops. The feeling grew in me that this was something we of the Butte must seriously consider. We should keep the supplies for emergencies and live off the land where we could. A margin for safety must be maintained.

It was necessary to detour around the port, and thus we crossed two small settlements—Riveholme and Peakchax. Neither had been bombed, but they were clearly tombs for their inhabitants.

By twilight we headed into the wastelands that cradled the Butte. On a chance that Annet might still be manning the com as she had continued to do from time to time, I channeled the instrument on the flitter to the port call, which, I thought, would not give away our true destination, and rapped out in our own code: "Vere here, Vere here—come in, Griss—" Trusting she would catch my meaning, though I did not really expect any answer, I set the broadcast on repeat and allowed those clicks to continue until they were drowned out by a strident series of louder clicks.

I read them aloud as I translated: "Condition red, condition red."

I flipped my own button and tapped out a demand: "What happens?"

"Mutant force, mutant force. Under siege by mutant force—stay off!"

She must believe us still afoot and vulnerable. But a *mutant* force—what could that mean? The wart-horn that searched a dead man for a knife, those centaur tracks and robo harvesters that might have served no human master—what had been loosed on Beltane now?

In the past I had not discounted the rumors of unusual experimentation with mutants. The beast teams sent off-world during the war were matters of certified record. But always those and the survey teams had been animals of intelligence linked with man, a human commander of a scaled, furred, or winged force, amenable to human control and discipline.

What if there had been rogues among such adaptations—or what might be considered rogues by the lab people, mutes unwilling to acknowledge human rule? The safe answer would have been to destroy such mutineers, make sure the strain was not used in breeding. Only, with all curbs on experiments removed in the past few years, there were scientists so immersed in their own work they could have deliberately chosen to raise intelligence and pay no attention to any aberration that accompanied it, as long as the specimens were safely housed and so, they would believe, not dangerous.

"Mutants," I rapped out. "What kind?"

"More than one—cannot tell. Stay off—" came her answer. And it was Annet who replied, for I recognized her touch in the tapping, there being as much individuality in such as in a man's thumb seal.

"We have a flitter." Since it was not a refugee force that threatened, I dared be plain. "Is there room for a roof landing?"

"No! They have ungers with them—"

Thad gave a low whistle, which I could well have echoed. Among the things native to Beltane were these giant hunting birds of the open plains. An unger was large enough, and brainless enough, to not only attack a flitter, but also to damage it. An attack by more than one at a time could knock us out of the sky. But to try to land and reach the Butte on foot, through a force of mixed mutants, especially with the ground level sealed against us, I could see no sense to that.

I glanced at the weapons we had taken from the refugees. Two lasers—

"I'm going to set on steady flight," I told Thad. "You take that window, I this. Use the lasers—if you have to. We'll cut our way through."

He pulled the nearest laser across his knees and inspected the firing mechanism as I did the other. It was simple enough, no more complex than the stunners we were accustomed to. There were sights and a butt button. One aimed and then fired by pressing that.

"We have weapons," I told Annet. "We are coming in."

Go in we did, even as the dusk closed about us. I saw a beamer ray pointing up into the sky as a beacon. Back and forth through that column of light flapped ungers, seeming to patrol the air above the Butte. There was no sight of our people on the roof, but the hopper we had left there was now drawn well to one side. The beamer had been broken from its stand and battered, but its light did not fail.

"Going in!" I warned Thad. The sound of our motor must have alerted the flying guard. One wheeled and came straight for us. I waited until I was sure it was well within range and used the laser. The flame caught the unger in mid-body, and it was over in an instant, the charred carcass falling heavily.

I saw the tracer of another ray catch the wing of a second unger and shear that off and knew Thad was alert. We took out six before they left us alone, beating up into the streaked sky from which the sun had gone but not all color faded. I left Thad to the defense and loosed us from the set course. Now came the tricky part, to set the flitter down on the roof. I was not sure I had skill enough, but that was our only possible landing place.

Three times I made a circle in, all but the final swoop. And on the fourth, sure that I would never have a better approach and that I must do it this time or utterly lose my nerve, I buttoned for a landing.

I was not sure we had made it safely until I sat a whole moment in the now stationary flitter and knew that we were down. I cut the motor and unlatched the cabin door, slipping out, laser ready to repel another attack from overhead.

There was a barrier at the door at the foot of the tower. I slammed at it impatiently with the butt of the laser, then swung around as I heard a whistling cry from the sky. Thad ran across the roof, turned halfway, went to one knee, and fired. I saw the dark mass of the unger glide on and knew he had missed, but a second later I did not.

Then came a pattering sound, and something struck the roof, first not far from the flitter, then closer to a point between Thad and me. He stumbled on, to where I was by the blocked door. Once beside me, he switched on his belt torch, and I saw what caused the pattering—darts of some silvery material, with an ominous stain about their points. They came from below, beyond the walls of the Butte. They continued to fall, moving ever closer to where we stood. We could not return to the flitter save through that rain, and I had a strong suspicion they were even more dangerous than they looked.

"Lasers—" I said to Thad. "Burn me a path. Aim into the air and get them as they fall!"

He did that, leaving me scant space to dart under his beam, the hot breath of it scorching. I laid hands on a smoking carcass of unger and dragged it back to shelter us. Now, if those below were only alert enough to loosen what they had built up to secure the roof, we had a chance, always providing they did know we were here and worked fast to tear down the barricade.

The darts continued to fall. Thad wanted to burn them, but I thought caution was indicated. We might need all the charges the laser carried before we were through. We could only wait and hope.

"What kind of mutants—" Thad said. "Wart-horns? Centaurs?"

"They could be anything. There were lots of imports." Yes, my mind added, plenty of imports and no one among us now with the knowledge of just what part of the memory banks to explore to learn the nature of this unexpected enemy.

We heard a sound from behind the tower door.

"Vere?"

"Here!" I shouted.

It seemed a long, long time up there on the roof until they pulled aside enough of their barrier to let us in, only to have Emrys, Gytha, Sabian, and Annet, with hardly a glance at us, return to its rebuilding. Annet looked at me over her shoulder as she rammed a box back into a cranny.

"They made an assault on the roof not three hours ago. We were about to seal it forever."

"Good you did not." I helped her at the building. "Who—or what?"

"We don't know, Vere, we don't know! They came so suddenly. Some we recognize, some we don't. Animals that aren't animals. Vere, has the world gone mad?"

"No more so than the men responsible," I told her. "We stand alone now."

She caught my meaning, and her face aged as I watched.

"All dead—"

"Or dying." I thought of the refugees.

"And how do we—we make peace with those?" She flung out one hand at the wall of the Butte and what lay beyond.

How indeed? I had no answer for her, nor had anyone in that hour.

EIGHTEEN

The mutant band had arrived out of nowhere as far as they could tell us. Of their number, or even of all the species that comprised that company, we gained but little idea during the siege—for siege it was, to hold us within the walls. Finally, I took the flitter aloft again, in desperation flying low over the ground where they lay in hiding, while Thad and Emrys sprayed from the cabin windows with stun beams. After that one fight with the ungers, we did not use lasers again.

For a long day after that stunning, we saw no movement among brush and rocks. On the second dawn, being on lookout in the tower, I witnessed the withdrawal of that strange force, fading back and away toward the mountains. For three more days we dared not believe they were really gone, or at least had not left a holding force behind.

The reason for their attack we did not know, unless, having at last been freed from human control, they were not minded to come under it again. How they had known we were in the Butte was a mystery. Gytha suggested that one of those we had loosed at the station in the Reserve had followed us through the pass. Only that spoke of some organization already existing among them. To weld such diversified specimens into an army was so complex an action that I found it difficult to believe the mutants could rise to it.

For some time we speculated as to whether they could have been under some human commander—if some survivor of a Ranger patrol, perhaps crazed by what had happened, had sent them against us thinking we were the enemy. But Annet said that until the arrival of the ungers, they had all repeatedly shown themselves on the roof of the Butte, so that any human watcher would have recognized another human.

At any rate, that attack and its conclusion was to remain unsolved—just as we shall never know exactly what happened to set off the attack on Kynvet and the loosing of the plague.

We knew that with the withdrawal of the mutant force, we were in perhaps the strongest position we could now find on Beltane for the preservation of our kind. Perhaps the fact that we had to face such harsh reality was the saving of us, for there was so much to be done that we labored from dawn to dusk, and exhaustion gave us dreamless sleep.

The flitter was our salvation. We dared not try to get through the country at ground level. Although we did not see any mutants, nor were we again attacked by any, yet we could never be sure that they were not lurking to pick off any straggler.

Thad and I never took the same trip out, lest a pilot be lost. He became as competent as I had ever been, then better than I at the flying and maintenance of our precious machine. We went out alternately on scouting trips, though never again did we see any traces of refugees or of any survivors of our own people. The machine shop at the port was Thad's principal point for visiting, and he took Emrys with him as a guard while he loaded with tools and supplies, transporting back to the Butte enough of both, he assured me, to keep the flitter and hopper running for years, barring accident.

Gytha, Sabian, and I made two visits to farms and activated the robo harvesters, leaving them to work during the night, for night or day meant nothing to those, returning at dawn to ferry back as much of the harvest as we could carry during the days, loading warily under guard every time we touched down at the edge of the fields.

We saw other robos in action and were sure the mutants had put them to such tasks. But these were busied by day and the harvest collected at night. So the mutants had reversed that order, probably because some were nocturnal.

Then came signs that their organization, if there had been one in truth, was coming apart in a bloody fashion. We went into an orchard of hyborian apples to discover we were not the first there. The ground was cut by the sharp hoofs of centaurs, and there were, in addition, paw marks of a type I had not seen before except in the dust around the Butte. There were also patches of blood still congealing, though no bodies.

My small hopes for us arose after seeing that. If our enemies of the four-footed kind now broke the truce kept among themselves, we were in less danger. They would be more occupied with their own quarrels than with us.

Three times I returned to the port and tried to make some sense of the records. I could pick out bits and pieces, but only scraps. Gytha, whom I took because of her long acquaintance with tapes, did little better. But we did dismantle a small reader, which ran on neutro power. This with all the tapes Gytha chose in searches of the central library files, we brought back to the Butte and installed with a hookup to the large com screen. What knowledge was within our grasp (too much of it was highly specialized and so of little use) we tried to gather.

It was at that time I began this record of the immediate past so that it could be added to Beltane history. Yet I feared there were so many gaps that we were losing or overlooking information we could need sorely in days to come.

We could bring medical supplies to the Butte and the information tapes from the medical library. But none of us had training to use the complex diagnostic or surgical techniques, so we lost much of the health protection known for centuries.

The lower rooms of the Butte became crammed with a vast miscellany of material from the port and from some of the settlements where, emboldened by no more attacks, we sought for what we could find. As yet we did not try to sort it all, merely brought whatever seemed worth carrying and was small enough to pack into the flitter.

The fall rains began, pouring their floods even across the waste of the lava country that was usually desert. Their fury was such that we staked down flitter and hopper and covered them with sheets of plasta, which had protected the machines in the underground depot. Then we turned to picking over what we had brought, sorting out items of immediate use and putting aside others to be stored.

There were some brisk exchanges of high words when classifications did not agree and tempers wore thin. But with so much that was interesting and needful to be seen and handled—for our foraging teams had made widely varying choices—we soon forgot disputes.

At last, since our badly organized sorting had led to greater confusion than ever, we held a council, and it was determined to draw up a list and reduce our rummaging to plan. Thereafter, though we worked as hard, we did so to more purpose.

I had wanted to try to reenter Lugard's caves. Not only were the supplies in the base cave there, but we would also have a refuge if need arose. In addition, there was the cache of ancient things in the ice cave, which might hold even greater wonders than the rod that had accounted for the monster. But to work out in the wastes to open the caves, even under guard, was folly.

Along with our search lists, we also drew up study programs, putting on each one the need to learn all he could of some specialty, as well as such general information as was needed for survival.

It was then that we became strongly aware (when I say "we," I mean Annet and I) that these were the children of people who had for generations been specialists and workers by mind more than body. The first settlers of Beltane had been picked for their knowledge, and while these descendants of theirs lacked the advanced schooling their parents had known off-world, they had inherited the inquiring turn of mind that sent them seeking information.

Thad chose technical learning and pursued it doggedly, with Emrys trailing him as lieutenant. They would descend to the depot beneath the Butte and take out manual repair tapes for the machines there, disembowel the motor sections of such as we thought we would not use and reassemble them to the best of their ability. I thought that there could be no more useful training for us now.

Annet's bent was biology. She gathered and read all the tapes I thought might explain the mutants, and was buried in them whenever she had a spare moment, while Gytha, always more interested in general rather than specific information, became our librarian and record keeper.

To my surprise, Pritha took up medicine, coming into that

field through an interest in healing herbs, which she had always had. Sabian had been fascinated by the robos and their field work during our quick harvest season. Now he wanted all we could feed him on agriculture.

Ifors showed no special bent, but I found him often with the reader. The tapes he had chosen covered so wide a range of general material that I thought he was following Gytha's path. Dinan, too, made no choice as yet but studied stolidly whatever we put before him.

I have made no late mention of Dagny, for that was our first sorrow and a lingering one. During the fall the improvement that had come by slow steps after we left the caves continued. Pritha and Annet spent hours with her, but there were so many regressions, less patient tutors might have given up in despair.

Gytha played simple story tapes over and over, and we were all joyful when she responded to such tales. But it was as if some important function in her mind worked now by erratic jumps. We would be encouraged over what seemed a significant gain, dashed when she slipped back into her old withdrawal.

I do not think she was ever completely aware of what had happened, nor why life was now lived behind the thick walls of the Butte and not at her home. She showed no curiosity—which seemed to Annet the most ominous of symptoms.

As the rainy fall progressed, she took cold often and spent much time in bed, coughing, falling into sleep. Her appetite was poor. There were times when she must be fed spoonful by spoonful and then would turn her head stubbornly away before Annet or Pritha had gotten more than half a cup of soup down her.

Though there was a heating unit in every room of the Butte and Thad and I worked on the relays, using every manual we could find to aid us, we could not keep the hold warm on the days when our autumn rains turned to sleet and then to snow. Dagny spent all her time in bed now, and I noticed that those periods when she sat up with pillows behind her grew shorter and fewer each day.

What tore at us most was the fact that had we had the knowledge, we might have saved her—or at least knowing what the medics had done in the past, we believed that. As it was, all we could give her was comfort and loving care until the end.

That came before Midwinter Day. She roused one morning

much her old self. Dinan spent a long time with her but finally came to Annet much disturbed and demanded to know what he should tell Dagny, for she wanted to go home and kept asking where their parents were. With wisdom beyond his years, her twin had said they were visiting another settlement on lab business, and Dagny had been satisfied for a time. But now she was very restless and wanted to go to them.

Dinan, remembering how she had taken him into the ice cave during a similar search, was frightened by her insistence. Annet found her sitting on the edge of her bunk, pulling a blanket around her shoulders, ready to set out. Annet's coming calmed her, and she consented to rest in bed, sharing a special ration treat with Dinan.

From that overexertion she slipped into a deep sleep, from which she did not wake. We laid her to rest as we had Lugard, since the ground was ice-bound. This time I used a laser beam and cut the name and dates, though we had lost track of time and moved now by seasons and not set days, for we were never sure how long we had been in the caves.

Thus, we lost the second of our company. And so small a band were we that, though Dagny had not really been one of us for months, there was now a gap we could not fill. Annet, Thad, Gytha, and I worked hard to keep the young ones busy.

We had a celebration on Midwinter Day, checking the date as best we could. We hoped that the children would not contrast it with the feasts of a year ago. Annet made us a fine dinner, using off-world supplies, which she now hoarded jealously. When we had done, Gytha rose in her seat and came to me, her hands holding a slender package.

What she had was a pipe—not such a one as Lugard had carried, certainly lacking the magic that had clung to his. But she put it eagerly into my grasp, and I saw them all look to me expectantly.

So I, who had once made small music on hollow reeds during our carefree days but had never done so since I had heard Lugard, raised it to my lips, doubtfully at first, because the making of music had long been lost to me. But then I recalled note by note one of the trail songs.

It came jerkily and then with greater ease. Straightway, Annet began to sing, the others following her, until their lusty voices drowned out my piping—which was perhaps all for the best.

When the song was finished, Gytha said, "No song now, please, Vere—just music."

That put me on my mettle, so I dared try one of those rippling series of notes such as I had once made at campfires when we had been the Rovers and not survivors in a dead world. I played it through to the end, noting they listened with an intensity, as if the music I drew from that rod was a key to better days.

After Midwinter Day the cold increased. We shivered and tinkered with the heating units, not often stirring out of the Butte, though there were days of bright sun on the dazzling banks of snow.

Though the Butte meant safety, yet I was troubled now and then by the thought that another season should mean a move for us. I had not too much liking to return to any settlement. Memories clung there. But a settlement of our own nearer the port might be prudent to consider. I had no hope of repairing the off-world signal. On the other hand, if the chaos following the war was not so great or lasting as Lugard had foreseen and someone seeking contact with Beltane did come, it was at the port such a ship would planet.

If they found that in ruins and searched some of the nearer settlements without result, they would probably not penetrate this far into the wastes hunting survivors.

Finally, I mentioned this at one of our weekly councils. None of the port buildings could, without labor we could not undertake, be made as secure as the Butte. If we tried, it would entail more than one season's work. Also we must plant, Sabian insisted with more force than I had ever heard him use before. Though we could not put under cultivation, even by robo help, all the fields that had been utilized before, we must do our best to keep in growth the most essential foodstuffs.

Those fields lay nearer to the port than to the Butte. Once the robos had been programmed, they could take over the bulk of the field labor. We had not forgotten the mutants. While the only evidence we had of their continued interest in us were tracks in the snow encircling the Butte (and we could not even be sure those were made by mutants and not wandering animals), we did not want to be cut off from our fortress in need.

Thus, it was decided that I was to fly into the port and make a general survey of the prospects for adapting one of the smaller buildings to our need. Emrys would go with me to keep the flitter aloft while I scouted, so there would be no danger of losing our most precious possession.

We set out in the very early morning of a day that promised to be clear. For the past two days there had been warmer winds. The snow in drifts around the lava ridges was beginning to melt. I wondered if I would ever be able to return to the caves—perhaps not for years to come.

The quickest route to the port took us cross-country, where the snow could not disguise the arable fields. We winged over the site of Kynvet, now all hidden from view.

At the port, one of the refugee ships still stood pointing to the stars, but the one with the eroded tubes had crashed, its nose having beaten a hole in the wall of the warehouse. There were no tracks marring the white surface of the field or the silent streets.

We circled once, and I decided on a small house to the far side of the field, where the commandant of the port had lived in the good days. It had been built when the port was laid out, solidly constructed of poured plus-stone, almost as durable as the Butte.

I swung out of the cabin, and Emrys immediately took the flitter up to cruise the surrounding area while I searched the dwelling.

It might do, I decided. Luckily, it had been unoccupied since the leaving of the last commandant, so death had not been here. We could do as we had at the Butte, block up the lower doors and windows and then we could rig a movable outside stair to an upper room. It would be difficult work, and perhaps we would take all year for it.

Emrys winged back at the appointed time, and he was highly excited.

"To the north, Vere—a town!"

A town! The refugees? Or settlers who had fled earlier homes?

"Show me!" I demanded. Obediently, he pressed the course button.

A town it was, if a collection of straggling huts could be given that title, though on Beltane now, I supposed, it could. The town had inhabitants we could see pouring out of those makeshift shelters as we winged down for a better look, Emrys switching on to hover.

"Up and out!"

His answer to my order was, luckily, instantaneous. I had seen enough to know that we might have done as ill as the man who plants a stick in a hor-wasp hole and turns it to incite the dwellers therein.

"Those—those were mutants!" Emrys said a little dazedly as the flitter leaped up and away. "But they had houses!"

What *had* gone on in those experimental labs? I had, even in those few moments when we had hovered over the untidy mixture of huts, counted at least three species—all of herbivorous types to be sure—but *three* living together apparently on good terms. If this could be true of the herbivorous, what of the carnivorous or the omnivorous species? How many such haphazardly organized "villages" were there scattered around?

At least, though I was sure the centaurs had put the robos to work last summer, they were still not able to use, perhaps because of their body structure, mechanical transportation and so could not follow us.

But to discover such a settlement close to the port negated our plans for moving there. We could only leave some message that would make sure we would not be overlooked if a relief expedition ever came. And this I determined to do—not because I had any even faint hopes of such an arrival, but because it would satisfy our need to believe in life beyond Beltane, life of our own kind.

So now we live in a fortress, and we go armed when we venture forth. We preserve what small remnants of human civilization we can by treasuring our knowledge and striving to enlarge our learning. We tend machines with care, knowing only too well that they will not last even our lifetimes. We realize that those of our small colony coming after us will slip farther and farther down the ladder of civilization, perhaps, in time, to meet those others climbing up.

It is now three years since we followed that Dark Piper, Griss Lugard, into the safety of his caves. Two years ago Annet and I stood up before our small company and took the vows of life companionship. This spring, while the snows still lay, our son

Griss was born, the first of a generation who shall never know the stars, unless some miracle occurs.

We have lost no more of our company, though at last harvest Sabian and Emrys held off an attack of mutants—this time an all-one-species pack of carnivorae remotely of canine breed.

Gytha has hopes that someday we may be able to deal with at least a few of the species on a more tolerant level. She cites our freeing of those left to die in the station pens as a beginning and has wanted to return over the mountains to try to contact the ystrobens. But we dare not do this—we are too few. One more member lost might endanger the whole colony.

The mutant settlement near the port has been a success. They ran the robos in several fields for two harvests; then these broke down. At Annet's and Gytha's urging, as a gesture of friendliness toward those most likely to accept us, Thad and I flew in by night and repaired the machines, setting those going at dawn. But though we left also some food as a gesture of peace, notably blocks of salt, they have made no return.

They still spy on us, and we only go out in pairs, though we do not kill, using stunners only.

Thad and I spent long days at the port, hooking up alarms and tapes. We hope our makeshift installations will work if any ship comes. The ship that fell is rusting, and that left standing is now canted to one side. Had we been trained, we might have taken off in that—but where?

It would seem that Lugard's prophecy of the end of a star-wide civilization is coming true. No one has visited Beltane since the refugee ships. I do not believe anyone will soon, maybe not until the beginning of another era, when somewhere, on another planet, a race will crawl once more out of barbarism, relearn old arts, and take to space.

If such rediscover Beltane, we hope they will find this record and the others we shall continue to tape as long as we have Zexro reels, for as we finish each tape, we set it with the permanent records at the port. Thus, they will learn how one world ended for us and another began.

This is the end of my part of the story. It is agreed that Gytha will carry on the recording. Tomorrow I shall lift to the port and place this one in the custody of the memory banks.

It is harvest time again. We shall watch the fields of the mutants, give them what assistance we can, always hoping that someday there will be a breakthrough and our species will face one another in friendship. If it is otherwise, our future is as dark as the caves we traveled through. Then we found again the open world and light. Now we ask each day that that may prove again.

DREAD
COMPANION

ONE

✺

But a few days ago (I shall never trust the divisions of time again and say with any certainty, "This is a day; that is a week; we face a year!") I was shown some very ancient tapes, copied, I was assured, from ones that had been made originally on fabled Terra. And some aspects of the information they stored were so like my own experiences that I could only believe that those who had first recorded them, back in a mist of time so great that I could not count the planet years—any more than one can truly give sum to the number of stars—had followed a trail like that which chance and my own stubbornness set me.

Had I not invincible proof of what had happened to me and several others, I might be judged now to be spinning some comet-hair tale for the astonishment of the credulous. But this much is true, and records prove it. I was born on Chalox in the planet and space-time year of 2405 After Flight. I was between sixteen and seventeen years old, planet age, when I left Chalox to land on Dylan. I am still no more than a year older—yet the year is now 2483!

Time! Sometimes, when I look squarely at those dates and think how those years fled for me, it brings back such fears that I must busy myself feverishly about some task, putting all my strength and thoughts into it, until the surge of panic that chokes me lessens. Were it not for Jorth, whom I can reach out

217

and touch, who shares my burden, I might— But of that I shall not think at all—now or ever!

As I say, I was born on Chalox. My father was Rhyn Halcrow, a Survey scout. He was of Talgrinnian stock, which means Second Wave, Terran outspread. My mother was a Forsmanian, of a trading family. They were human, too, but of the First Wave outspread, and had mutated from what is believed to be the original Terran.

Their marriage was a planet one as is usual for a man in the services, and it lasted three Chalox years. After the ceremonial break-bond, my father was assigned to a new outwave exploratory pattern. He left my mother with the excellent life pension of a planet wife and her freedom to contract another tie if she wished—or if her father wished, for the Forsmanians are strictly family oriented, with the eldest male making the major decisions for the clan.

Within a matter of months, my mother did take another husband, one of her cousins, thus keeping her first grant-for-marriage dowry strictly within the clan, in what her people considered a very practical and equitable arrangement.

As for me, I was already established in the crèche for Service children at Lattmah. The break was complete. I never saw either of my parents again. That I was a girl presented a minor problem, since the majority of such cross-births are male and the offspring trained from childhood for government service.

Unfortunately, I inherited my mother's sex but my father's spirit and interests. I would have been supremely happy as a scout, a seeker-out of far places and strange sights. My favored reading among the tapes were the accounts of exploration, trading on primitive planets, and the like. Perhaps I might have fitted in with the free traders. But among them women are so few and those so guarded and cherished that I might have been even more straitly prisoned on one of their spaceports, seeing my mate only at long intervals, bound by their law to remarry again if his ship was reported missing for more than a stated time.

As it was, I did what I could to prepare myself for a possible escape from Chalox. I became a keeper of records, adept in several techniques, including that of implanted recall. And I had my name down—Kilda c'Rhyn—on every possible off-planet listing as soon as the authorities allowed me to register.

That no opportunity presented itself began to worry me. I was less than a year from the time when I could no longer stay at the crèche but would arbitrarily be fitted into any niche those in charge might select. They might even return me to my mother's clan, and such was not for me. So, in desperation, I appealed, at last, to the one among my teachers whom I thought the most sympathetic.

Lazk Volk was a mutant crossbreed. The mixing of races in his case had resulted in certain deformities of body that even the most advanced plasta-surgery could not correct. But his mind showed such a potential for learning and teaching that he had never left the crèche. Through his vast tape library and the visits of scouts and other far travelers to his quarters, he had gained knowledge far outstripping any local memory bank except the government one.

Because in some small ways we were alike, each yearning for what was denied us, Lazk Volk and I became friends. I had served for four years as recorder and librarian for him when I voiced my fear of being without a future, save one not of my choosing. I was hoping that he might answer with an offer of steady employment. Though that would be no true solution to my desire to travel, I would have, in his wealth of knowledge, the second best.

He stretched out his thin double arms in a gesture habitual to him, wiggling his boneless fingers above the keyboard that produced anything he might wish—from the complete history of the planet Firedrake to a dinner-of-first-ceremony. With most of his misshapen figure muffled in a robe of Bora rainbow cloth, rippling rich color at his slightest movement, he was like a thick bolster perched on one end. Only his four arms and his conical head showed he was a living being.

For the second time he flicked his wiggling fingers back and forth. Then his slit of a mouth opened.

"No."

"No? Why?" I was startled enough to use a demanding tone that I would never have tried with him ordinarily.

"No—I do not take you into my service. That is the easy way, Kilda. And you are not meant to walk easy roads." He pressed one of those many buttons now, and my chair spun about so that I no longer faced him, but rather the wall on which was a projection screen, now like a huge mirror.

"What do you see?" he asked.

"Myself."

"Describe!" His tone was such that we might be in one of the training booths where he had begun to shape my mind for the retention and collection of knowledge.

"I am a woman. My hair—it is—" I hesitated. Those living in the crèche were so varied from crossbreeding that we had no norm of either good looks or downright ugliness. I knew that certain kinds of faces, coloring, forms gave me pleasure to look upon. But I had no vanity, nor any idea as to whether I could be deemed even passable in appearance. "My hair," I began again resolutely, "is of the color dark brown. I have two eyes—which are blue-green—one nose, a mouth. My skin is also brown, but lighter in shade than my hair. For the rest—my body is humanoid, and it is healthy. What is it that you wish me to see—other than this?"

"You have youth. And though you list your attributes so baldly, Kilda, you will discover, once you walk beyond these walls, that you will be considered above the ordinary in the sight of most. And, as you note, you have an adequate and healthy body. Therefore, you shall not waste this by crawling into shadows and turning your back upon the world."

"It is better," I protested, "to stay where I am happy than to be returned to a Forsmanian clan house or to be a clerk in some government hive until I become as dull-witted as the walls about me."

"Perhaps so." He nodded. I was surprised at winning my point so easily. Then he went on. "But you cite only two of the possibilities before you. There are others—"

"Trade marriage?" I ventured the third I had considered.

"As a means of escape? I think not. The traders are too careful of their women, having so few of them. You might find such an alliance even more stultifying than your first two suggestions. There is this—"

He must have pressed another of his buttons, for there flashed on the screen, obliterating my own image, a government announcement. It was one of those general offers to emigrants, a fulsome and probably much overstated listing of all the glowing opportunities awaiting the properly qualified on a frontier planet.

"You forget"—though I did not see how he could—"that I am not hand-promised, nor am I medically trained, nor—"

"You are in a very negative mood." But he did not sound impatient. "This is the official listing. There are other possible ways of joining such a company, namely as a house aide for someone with children of a teachable age. You have given assistance in the classes here. And certainly your training is above that of such aides. The position would be temporary, of course, but it gives you a chance for emigration. And on a new world there will be more opportunities. There is a tendency—unless the emigration group is that of some close-knit religious sect—to be less rule-bound on a frontier world. You might well have such a position there as is barred to your sex on these inner planets."

What he said made good sense. There was only one flaw.

"They may think me too young."

"Your recommendations will be of the highest." He said that with such confidence that I had to believe he had thought the whole matter over and only my consent was needed.

"Then—then—I'll do it!" I had always imagined that if I were offered any chance to leave Chalox and lift into the unknown of the far stars, I would do it without a moment's hesitation. Yet now that I said I would go, I found an uneasy stirring within me. It was as if, now that the door stood open, I was far more conscious of the safety of the room it guarded.

"Well done!" He brought my chair around to face him again. "But remember, Kilda, I only provide the means for your first steps; the march beyond is up to you. This much will I do for you. I shall appoint you one of my off-world reporters. You shall keep your skill sharp by taping for me anything that you think may add to this library."

I felt some easing of that tension within me. Now a spark of excitement lit in my mind. There was probably little enough I could add to the great wealth of material from a thousand—a hundred thousand—worlds that Lazk Volk stored. But were even a few sentences of mine thought fit to be included, I would be honored indeed.

"So it is decided." He spoke briskly. "The rest you will leave to me. Now—I want a run-through of the Ruhkarv report in comparison with the tridees from Xcothal."

I busied myself in producing the two tapes of archaeological mysteries for his viewing. With one thing and another, three days went by filled with work. In fact, I was so busy tracing down buried facts—which had not been called for for years—that on the third night, as I returned to my room to kick off my toe slippers with a sigh, I had the suspicion that Lazk Volk was keeping me running from one end of the archives to the other for some purpose of his own.

On the fourth morning when I reported for work, I found him not barricaded by rows of tape containers, but sipping a cup of caff and staring at his projection screen as if it bore lines of formulae. He looked at me sharply as I came in and then used his lower right hand to indicate a box of some size on the corner of his desk.

"Take that and put on its contents. You have an interview at the tenth hour with Gentlefem Guska Zobak. She is staying at the Double Star."

"Put what on—"

"Clothing—proper clothing, girl! You go out in the city in that"—he nodded to my crèche dress, a one-piece garment planned for service and for neither fit nor show—"and you will be the center of attention, which, I assume, you would not care for."

To that I agreed and took the box into the storeroom beyond. But I was a little surprised at the contents. I did have one utilitarian robe, which I wore into the city on the few errands that took me there. It was as plain as the uniform and, like it, shouted that it was institutional wear. But these brilliant lengths of silky material were very different. I had seen such worn—but only by the daughters of landed families.

There was a pair of loose trousers of a darkly rich plum shade. Over those went a tunic of the same color, but a different material, for it was thick and had a texture like fur. This had long sleeves coming to the knuckles, and it was latched from belt to throat with a series of silver buckles. A belt of the same metal drew in the waist tightly.

My hair was much shorter than that of any woman outside the crèche. But there was a long veil of silvery net, with the eyeholes ringed with glitter, to cover my head, dropping to my hips in the back, to the waist in front. In such clothing I was disguised, and certainly none of my fellow students would know me.

When I went back to Lazk Volk and caught sight of my reflection on the mirror screen, I was so astounded as to let out a small gasp. He nodded, and at the same time he pushed a transportation plaque to me.

"Very good." He approved my masquerade, for such I felt this clothing to be. "Gentlefem Zobak is bound for the planet of Dylan. She has two children, a son and a daughter, both quite young. Not being in robust health, she has applied for a house aide. Her husband is only temporarily stationed on Dylan—for about two years planet-time, I believe. I do not think the Zobaks will stay longer. But they have the power to ask for extra service, and if you please them, they might open other doors for you. Now, you had better go. It would never do to keep the Gentlefem waiting."

It might not do for me to keep my prospective employer waiting, but it was plain when I reached the Double Star that the situation was not the same for her. I was shown into an outer reception room, where I found others before me. There were two women seated there, with the look of those having waited perhaps already too long. Since we all followed the custom of keeping our veils down with strangers, all I saw of them was their clothes, much like those I wore, but differing in color and material. I spent some of the tedious time in trying to place my fellow employment seekers.

One wore rusty brown. I noted two mended slits in her veil. And the hands that showed (her sleeves were significantly shorter than mine) were red and roughened as if she had done hard work with them. I gained an impression of harassed middle age. The other, sitting across from me, wore blue, but there was something cheap about the too extreme cut of the tunic (with sleeves that touched the fingertips in an arrogant boast of the gentility of a wearer who did not have to worry about using her hands). And not only were the eyeholes in her veil edged in glitter (those of her neighbor being bound in plain material), but they were also of a width to bedazzle the viewer.

The work-worn woman was summoned first and did not reappear; then my companion of the over-glitter, who did not return either. I guessed there must be another door for leaving. Finally, the servo robot jerked a beckoning prong in my direction.

The room I entered was a standard luxury one of a caravansary. But its present occupant had introduced other elements. She lay in the bed, its back elevated to give her support, the surface before her strewn with a variety of objects either dedicated to amusement or to the care of her person.

I politely threw back my veil to meet her eyes. She was small and very delicate in appearance. Her hair had been fashionably bleached and retinted to a very brilliant green, striking against the pallor of her skin. She represented the height of fashion as I had seen it on telcasts.

Though there were two easirests waiting to comfort occupants, she waved me to a backless stool-cushion near the bed and stared at me without speaking for a long moment. She had a fretful look about her mouth, and her hands were seldom still, rummaging among the things that lay on the bed before her, though she never looked down at what she picked up, nor, indeed, held it long.

"You are Kilda c'Rhyn." She did not make a question of that, rather a statement, such as one would use in naming an object—as if, were I *not* Kilda, she would make me so. I wondered if such was meant to unsettle one, a tone she always applied to prospective employees.

"It is so, Gentlefem." I treated her statement as a question and gave answer.

"At least you're young." She continued to stare at me. "The data said you are well grounded in teaching. You're from the crèche—" There was a note of curiosity now, as if my background gave her a measure of interest. "You understand this employment is only temporary. We have to go to this awful frontier world for a year, maybe two, because my husband is stationed there. Are you a good spacer?"

As to that, how could I tell, never having lifted on any ship. But I do not think that she was really interested in me, for she swept on.

"I am not, not in the least. I go into voyage sleep at once, just as soon as we take off. But Bartare and Oomark cannot do that for the entire trip—they are too young. You'll have to take care of them during wake periods. I don't know—you're young—" What appeared to have faintly pleased her earlier now seemed to provide a question. "Bartare is quite difficult, very difficult. She has to have guidance. Her learning level is near eight and will increase, they tell us. You must provide mental stimulation that will induce that increase. But then, you're crèche-trained, so you ought to know all about that. And I haven't time or strength to interview a lot more dreary females—or unsuitable ones. You'll have to do."

That she considered *her* choice the final settlement of the matter was plain. And though I had read into her outpouring some hints of a demanding and exasperating future, I knew that Lazk Volk had been right. This was probably the only door that would open for me, and in this way I could have a different future.

She hardly listened to my assent. Instead, she issued a series of instructions as to where I must meet them. And I learned then that I could have only two days before leaving. This I did not like, but before I could protest, she gave a last order.

"The servo will show you to the children's room. You should meet them, and they must see you. That way, and remember—at the eleventh hour on Seven Night Day."

I did not get a chance to finish the farewell-of-ceremony before the servo ushered me out of the room and into a hallway. There it paused before another door and sent in an announce-call, though it did not wait for permission to enter. It would seem that Gentlefem Zobak treated her children with no more ceremony than she did her employees. I was sent to view and be viewed, and that was that.

It was true that I had taught children at the crèche. But the situation there had always been one of restraint and discipline. Crèche children were most carefully screened. Those with problems of personality or temperament were early given professional treatment elsewhere. The children I had taught had been good and willing scholars, already set in the patterns of applied study. I was used to bright children who wanted to use their brains to a purpose. So my employer's comments about urging her daughter to best efforts made sense and were familiar to me. But some instinct warned me, even as I entered the room, that this was not going to be like my almost casual schoolroom supervision in the crèche.

The room was as luxurious as the one their mother occupied, but it was purely a sitting room. Strewn over a table under a lamp was a muddle of odds and ends such as had littered their mother's bed. But one item seemed of such interest now that neither child looked up.

Bartare was small, fine-boned, and delicate-looking, like her mother. But she had no languor. Instead, there was such a tension

of concentration about her small, thin body as reminded me
disturbingly of that I had seen Lazk Volk display on occasion.
Her hair was twisted back from her face, which came to a point
with a small, sharp chin, with silver cords that gleamed the more
because the hair they confined was dead black. She had very
well-marked brows, which met over her nose, so they formed a
solid bar across her face. And her eyelashes were unusually thick
about eyes, almost as deeply sable as her hair. In contrast, her
skin was pale, having no trace of color in the cheeks and only
a faint tinting of lips.

Her dress was dark green, an odd color for a child, yet one
I would always thereafter associate with Bartare. With a strip of
material of the same color, she was now wrapping one of the
small carven images the country folk set up in their kitchens for
protection against the powers of darkness, only this one, crude in
its beginning, had several refinements. Metallic wires had been
twisted around the head to form a crown—for one.

Watching his sister robe the image was Oomark. Though he
was the younger in years, he was perhaps a finger's breadth the
taller, big-framed and solid-looking. His face had still a babyish
roundness, and now it wore an odd expression, almost as if he
were both fascinated and alarmed by what his sister was doing,
too unusual a look to accompany the dressing of a doll.

He glanced up at me. Then he leaned over and touched his
sister on the arm, almost diffidently, suggesting he was in awe of
her and yet knew he must attract her attention.

"Look, Bartare—" He pointed one finger at me.

Bartare raised her head. Her stare was deep, measuring, and
somehow very disturbing. I felt almost as shaken as if I had
encountered, behind the outer shell of a small girl-child, something old, authoritative, and faintly malicious. But that was gone
in a flash. Bartare laid down her doll with the care of one putting aside an important piece of handiwork and came away from
the table to sketch one of those curtsies used by children of her
class as a polite greeting.

"I'm Bartare, and this is Oomark." Her voice was clear and
pleasant. It was only when she shot a sudden glance at me from
beneath that eyebrow bar that I was a little chilled.

"I'm Kilda c'Rhyn," I answered. "Your mother asked me—"

"To see us and let us see you. I know." She nodded. "That

means you're the one going to go to Dylan with us. I think—"
She hesitated a moment and then used an expression that was
rather odd. "I think we may suit." But was there or was there
not a stress on the word "may" that hinted at reservations and
could be a warning?

I cannot remember now much of what we spoke about at that
first meeting. After his recognition of my being in the room,
Oomark never spoke at all. However, his sister displayed not only
excellent manners but also the fact that she was a child of superior
intelligence and poise. She—well, I could have said nothing but
good of her. Yet I had reservations, an uneasiness all the time
we were together, as if we were both acting parts.

Once I saw a tape from Lazk Volk's files portraying a theatrical
production on another world. The actors and actresses carried
elaborate ceremonial masks mounted on sticks. Each had several
of these, fastened by fine chains to their girdles. In time for their
speeches, they chose one or another of these masks and held them
before, but not directly against their faces, as they recited their
lines. This came to my mind now, for it seemed to me that both
Bartare and I were holding masks and that what was behind our
masks and our stilted, polite conversation was very different.

Yet I was not so disturbed that I would refuse to take the position. In fact, once I had subdued that initial sense of unease, I
was intrigued by Bartare, and I thought that I might find the next
year or so interesting for both of us. I also judged that Oomark
was too much in his sister's shadow, and he might well benefit
by special attention.

In any event, I returned to the crèche well enough pleased with
the bargain Lazk Volk had aided me to, prepared to cut ties with
my old life and lift off-world to a new.

TWO

✵

I was not long in saying good-bys at the crèche. Save for Lazk Volk, my close ties there now were few. By his influence I had stayed a year longer than others of my age group, being, as I have said, perilously near to the time when I would have been forced to leave whether or no. My leaving fees were paid to me, half in clothing suitable for my future on Dylan, the rest in a small number of credits that I clung to, knowing them to be my barrier against misfortune.

My last hours I spent with Lazk Volk, accepting from him the recorder he was empowered to give me under a reportship. I was not a badge-wearing representative. The authorities would not agree to that. But whatever I returned to Volk's storehouse that was countersigned by him as useful would add to my rating and, perhaps, might lead to more employment.

Yet he warned me not to squander the supplies he was giving me on anything but the most important. And I realized that I must make a little cover much. The baggage of a space traveler was very strictly limited, and I could expect no further supply of tapes should I misuse those I carried with me—at least not unless I had returned one with such useful notage on it as to warrant sending me another.

He asked me what I thought of my charges, and I hedged somewhat. That Bartare was a promising student, I was almost

229

sure. Oomark would be less troublesome. But "troublesome" was
the term I applied to his sister. I know that Lazk Volk noted my
reserve, though he did not comment.

I did not join the Zobak family until we met in the entry place
for the ship. The Gentlefem was wrapped in the thick folds of a
journey cape, but Bartare had pushed back the hood of her outer
garment to stare up at the starship as if that presented some
problem. Oomark turned excitedly from side to side, his interest
all for the coming and going of the crewmen.

As I came up, Gentlefem Guska turned to me, though I could
not see her face under her veil. Her voice was even more fretful
than I had remembered it.

"You are late. We are about to go on board—"

"I am sorry," I answered. I had schooled myself, having taken
her measure at our first meeting, to supply no excuses or explanations. She was of those, I decided, who accepted only one
answer—that being their own. And to combat such was like trying to erect a firm tower out of dry sand. Better not to attempt
it in the first place.

"I expect promptness," she was beginning when a load cage
swung down a few paces from us and the ship's steward, standing
within it to direct traffic, beckoned us forward.

"I hate this whirling about!" She clasped my arm so tightly
that I supported her into the cage, the children moving with us.
And she kept that painful grip as we were swung up, to slide
into the hatch. I must admit that that swaying trip gave me little
pleasure either.

Once inside, they ticked us off on their entry records, and Guska
went away, still leaning heavily, but now on a stewardess, to be
put into deep voyage sleep. The children and I were escorted to
a small transport cabin and only part suspension.

I earned whatever funds Gentlefem Zobak was depositing to
my account, and I earned them well during that voyage, for in
the wake periods both children were my sole responsibility. I
tried to establish a good relationship with them, and I thought
that with Oomark I succeeded. He was plainly not as brilliant as
his sister and far more biddable. Bartare did not disobey me. In
fact, she was politely cooperative, all that one might ask for in a
child. It was only that the impression was now firmly rooted in
my mind that she moved behind a mask and played a part, so

that I waited continually for some revelation of what lay behind her words and actions. This feeling fretted me, so that I had to subdue inner impatience and irritation.

I went into the final suspension period before break-through and the landing on Dylan with the problem of Bartare remaining as baffling as ever. But now I had accepted it as a challenge, though I knew that I must go very slowly and not try to push the girl into any disclosure.

Though my knowledge of other planets through Lazk Volk's library was extensive, probably beyond that of most general travelers, Dylan was the first new world I had ever visited myself. And I was excited as we were swung down to the landing strip.

The familiar skies of Chalox had carried a green tinge, so that one believed that was the only natural color for any sky to be. But here the arch over us was blue, cut by masses of white clouds. Together with the children, I had pored over the information tapes supplied by the ship's library.

Dylan had been located some one hundred years earlier, oddly enough, because of a distress call set on automatic, though the ship that had sent it had never been found. It was Arth type. And there were some very unexplainable remains that suggested it might once have either had native inhabitants or been a colony of one of the Forerunner races. In fact, it was to gather information about one of these that Guska Zobak's husband had been sent here. He was not an archaeologist but a government man empowered to declare the diggings protected if experts thought it necessary.

There were two cities on Dylan. Tamlin was the port where we disembarked; the other was Toward, on the other side of the planet providing an alternate landing site. Neither was large. Dylan was mainly an agricultural world. The western continent was one of open plains. And since the native wildlife was very sparse, these plains provided grazing for imported herds and flocks. The eastern continent, of which Tamlin was the center, was planted heavily with vor vines and husard fruit—both of which were luxury items off-world.

But such planting was spotty since both products required special types of soil and drainage, so that the settlements had stretches of wilderness between them. Such distances meant nothing, though, with all plantations and villages linked by air flitter travel.

The buildings of Tamlin did not resemble those of the long-settled worlds. They were all very like, having been constructed to plans worked out off-world, their blocks placed by robo workers. Any difference between them came from the planting about their walls. Here were not only native growths pleasing to the eye, but also exotic aliens imported and flourishing.

As we disembarked from the landing stage, a number of people moved forward to greet the new arrivals. But the man who came to Gentlefem Guska certainly bore no resemblance to the tridee the children had of their father. He was a much older man, wearing the uniform of a port official.

"Where is Konroy?" Guska demanded of him. "Surely his duty does not demand that he not be here to greet us!"

"My dear Guska!" The officer caught both her hands in his. "You know Konroy would be here if he could. It is that—"

"He is dead!" Bartare's words might have been a war alert the way they froze us all for a second that seemed to stretch far longer than that.

She took a step forward and stood looking up at the officer.

"That is the truth," she continued. "Why not say that he is dead?"

I saw one kind of astonishment replace another in his expression, and I knew that Bartare *was* speaking the truth.

"But how—" he began with a bewildered protest in his voice.

"Dead!" Guska gave a shriek that was echoed by a lesser cry from Oomark. She sagged forward into the arms of the officer, and I moved, one hand going to Oomark, who turned and threw his arms about me, burrowing his face into my traveling cloak. But Bartare shrugged off my touch on her shoulder and stood quietly, no expression at all now on her small pale face.

There was a flurry about us. Guska, unconscious, was taken in the officer's arms to a waiting ground car, while we were ushered by two young spaceport police into another. Oomark continued to hold on to me with a desperate grip, but Bartare was as aloof as if she were only a spectator and a faintly contemptuous one. I felt alienated from her at that moment, as baffled as if I were confronting an unknown life-form that must be handled with supreme caution.

We were given quarters in one of the government rest houses, and I persuaded Oomark to loose me long enough to try to find someone to tell me what had happened. But when I returned to the children, Oomark was fronting his sister, his tear-streaked face twisted with anger.

"You—you knew about it! You don't care!" He accused her shrilly.

I halted where I was, just outside the door. Perhaps he would get an answer she would not give in my presence.

"She told me. His time was finished. And—he is not necessary to us—not any more."

"She's bad!" Oomark's red face was thrust close to his sister's pale one. "You listen to her tell you bad things! Bad—bad—"

For the first time, then, I saw Bartare's composure break. She slapped her brother hard enough to rock his head, leaving a hand print on his cheek.

"Be quiet!" Her voice was not controlled and even now. "You don't know what you are saying. You can make things worse than even you think just by saying things like that. Be quiet, you fool!"

She turned away from him, and he stood where he was, cowed and shaking, big tears streaking down his face, making no move to wipe them away. When I went in, he came to me in a rush, again burying his face against me, demanding comfort by action rather than words. But Bartare stood at a window, her back to us. And there was something about her stance that gave me the queer feeling she was listening intently, but not to any sound audible to me.

I thought it best to let her be by herself for a time. That scrap of conversation I had overheard gnawed within my mind. Who was the She to whom they had both referred? To my very certain knowledge, the children had been with me continually on board the ship and during the very short time on landing before the officer had come to us. I had not given such news to Bartare, and most certainly her mother had not. Therefore, how had she learned it—and from whom?

And the phrasing of that comment about her father, "His time was finished. And he is not necessary to us any more."

I longed to be able to discuss what I had heard with someone, to ask advice. I had thought myself so well armed and self-sufficient as a result of the crèche training. Yet here I was suddenly as helpless as an infant entering the first class, the more so because there was no instructor for me to turn to with questions.

We were not left alone long, for the same official who had taken Guska away came to see us. He brought with him his wife, a pleasant-faced woman, who swooped upon the children while he drew me to one side with information.

I learned that Konroy Zobak had been killed in an accident when his flitter had been caught in a freak storm a day earlier. There could not be an immediate return to Chalox for his family, though that was what Guska had demanded upon regaining consciousness, for the liner that had brought us was outward bound on a system-wide swing that would not bring them back to our home world for several years. As a result, we must remain on Dylan until other transportation might be arranged—and when that might occur, my informant, Commandant Piscov, had no way of telling.

He offered us quarters in his own home, but told me that Guska had insisted upon going to the one prepared by her husband. He did not like the situation, but had to agree to it. He wished me to keep in touch and call on him for any needful services.

I could not understand why Guska wanted to be alone since she was the type of person I would have believed would lean both physically and emotionally on the nearest support in any time of trouble. But the commandant said he was sending a nurse to be with her for a time. And I was relieved to know that I need not be responsible for her as well as the children.

After he had told me this, the commandant turned such a measuring look on me that I felt uncomfortable, even though I knew I had done nothing to merit such regard.

"Did you tell the little girl about her father's death?" he demanded.

"How could I? I did not know it myself. Did you send a message to the ship before landing?"

He shook his head, his frown deeper. "No, it is true—how could you have known? The matter was only reported to me this morning after the flitter was found. Only a few knew it. But how did *she* know? Is she esper?"

His suggestion was logical, though I had never known so young an esper to be able to hide such power.

"I was not told so, nor does it appear on her chart."

"There are cases of sudden breakthrough," he said thought-fully. "Shocks have activated dormant gifts. I shall speak to the parapsychologist. He will get in touch with you."

I nodded with relief. What better aide could I have than that of a well-qualified parapsychologist? And, of course, the commandant had hit upon the reason for the strange knowledge, perhaps even the unease Bartare had awakened in me. If she was a latent esper, then one might in periods of heightened tension sense this, just as her power could be released by a shock.

Only, as I followed the children and the commandant's wife out to the ground car, I began to perceive holes in that theory. First, Bartare had not been on this world when her father had died, nor had she ever given any indication of mind-linkage that would end in shock at his death. And what of the She both children had discussed? Their conversation had given me the firm impression that it was a third person to whom they referred, one whom Bartare accepted as a friend and Oomark met with a mixture of fear and dread. Who was She? All I could swear to was that she had not been one of our visible company that morning.

Visible company? Why had my thoughts supplied that par-ticular word—as if we could have invisible company among us! I gave myself a kind of mental shake. As Lazk Volk had often commented, I was too prone to allow my imagination play. One must hold to the evidence. Only in this case the evidence went beyond sense.

The house Konroy Zobak had prepared for his family lay on the outskirts of town. It was set in a district mostly used by administrative officers and visitors of rank. Still, the houses were very much of a pattern, one story, built around an open inner court into which all the rooms opened.

That court was centered by a pool and had, in addition, well-kept beds of flowers or decorative shrubs, each guarded by a low wall. The pavement was patterned in colored stones and blocks of crystal formation. I suddenly noted, as we walked behind a servo balancing our luggage on its flat top, that Bartare was crossing that pattern in an odd skip-hop, managing each time to touch her foot, as it came to the ground, on a crystal piece. She stared down at the pattern with such absorption that one could believe she was engaged in an operation on which much depended.

Then she jerked up her head and looked about quickly as if to assure herself that she had not been seen. Our eyes met and held for less than an instant. She turned her head and walked normally, paying no attention to what lay under her feet. But I knew she had seen me watching. Again I felt uneasy, wanting very much to discuss this with someone who knew more than I.

The three rooms made ready for the children and me were at the rear of the courtyard. Those intended for Guska, when she would arrive with the nurse, lay to the right. The four at the left as we entered comprised the library and office of Konroy Zobak, a dining room with hall servos for cooking, and a storeroom.

Each bedroom had a small fresher opening off it. To someone used to inner-planet luxury, it might seem a bare and rather starkly planned house, but I thought it pleasant. And the open courtyard provided an attractive place to sit. I thought it far better than the crowded quarters I had been used to all my life.

I had enough soon to keep me busy, settling the children in their new quarters and then lending assistance to the nurse who accompanied Guska. They had given her a sedative so that she moved in a dreamy haze and obeyed the nurse's suggestions languidly. But the nurse confided to me that she had become so distraught when they had suggested she stay with the commandant's family that the doctor thought it better to allow her her own way and to hope that the quiet of this house would help her.

She passed into a deep sleep once we got her in bed. And since nothing then seemed to disturb her, the nurse and I moved about unpacking and putting her things in place.

We dialed the servo for a meal and found the food good. Oomark ate heartily, and I noticed that today Bartare, who was inclined to pick at her food and dawdle over her plate, showed an appetite almost as good as his. It had been mid-afternoon when we landed. Now it was growing dark, and I suggested bed for the children.

Again I was agreeably surprised when neither of them rebelled but seemed willing. And I was even more astonished when, as I tucked Oomark in, he caught my hand and held it tightly, looking up into my face as if he needed reassurance.

"You won't go? You will be here?"

"In this room, Oomark? Do you want me to stay with you until you go to sleep?"

Neither child had before shown any such feeling. And I was

heartened to think that Oomark had so turned to me, though I regretted the reason for it.

For a moment I thought that he would accept my offer. But then he released my hand and shook his head. "Just here—in the house." He raised himself on one elbow. "Bartare says—She doesn't like you."

"Bartare doesn't like me?" I countered, though I had a suspicion that the She of his speech was not his sister.

"Bartare won't like you if She doesn't," he said. "Bartare—"

"You want me, brother?"

Bartare stood in the doorway. She had her nightrobe pulled about her. And her hair, freed from its daytime cords, was loose on her shoulders.

"No." He turned his head away sharply as if the last thing he wanted was to see his sister. "I'm sleepy. Go away! I want to sleep."

I knew better than to try to press him then, so I pulled the covers smooth and wished him good night. As I went to the door, his sister retreated before me. But I found her waiting outside.

"Oomark's just a little boy, you know," she said, as if a long range of years separated her from her brother.

"A frightened little boy."

"*He* has nothing to be afraid of here." A simple sentence, but the intonation of the word "he," the look she sent in my direction from under her bar of eyebrows, was revealing. She was delivering a warning. And there was such vast effrontery in it that I was astounded because in that moment, if only for a second or two, our roles appeared reversed. I was subject to her control, not she to my responsibility.

I think she was quick to sense she had made a mistake, gone a little too far, for the other something that she wrapped around her as a cloak vanished, and she was a little girl again.

"It is strange—" She glanced away from me, around the courtyard, as if she were trying to suggest that she, too, was a little fearful of this alien world. Only her change of mood was too late and too false—though I kept myself under control and did not reveal any knowledge of her mistake.

"But a pleasant planet from what we have seen of it."

"It killed my father, you know."

"An accident." I could not understand her, and perhaps I was no match for her either.

"Yes, an accident," she agreed. And again, though perhaps I was overly suspicious, I read a warning in her words.

"Do you want to go to bed now? I thought you said you were tired—"

"I am," she agreed, and there was almost a note of relief in her voice, as if she were thankful for my suggestion.

And she was all little girl again as I settled her in bed as I had Oomark.

"You are going to bed now, too?" she asked as I was about to leave her.

"In a little while—"

"But you are not going far away?"

"I'll be in the courtyard." But I did not believe that she needed any reassurance of mine. It was rather a desire to know where I would be to satisfy some purpose of her own.

I sat down where I could see the doors to both of the children's chambers. Before I had so settled, I set the servo-alarm at the courtyard gate. Nothing could come in or out now without alerting a guard robo and sounding an alarm. Why I had taken that step I did not really know, but I felt safe when it was done.

In the light of the very large and yellow moon that served Dylan by night, those crystal patches in the pavement fluoresced and glowed, almost as if each had a small lamp beneath the block. I could see the night light burning in Guska's room and knew that the nurse planned to sit up with her for part of the night.

But though I tried to think coherently and purposefully of all that had happened since we had landed, I found myself growing more and more drowsy, until I stumbled out of my chair toward my own bedroom.

I had come into the room with my head slightly turned, so that I saw a flicker of movement from the corners of my eyes. But when, aroused a little, I jerked around to face that straightly, I saw nothing there save a mirror. And I imagined it had been my own reflection that had momentarily startled me.

That alarm had shaken me more awake, and I set about preparing for bed more briskly. It was not until I sat down before the mirror, combing my hair, that it happened.

My brown skin, the hair above it, my green eyes—they showed very large and more green in this mirror than I had ever seen them. I examined what I saw closely, remembering Lazk Volk's words concerning my looks and wondering if he had spoken the truth, that I had some small claim to a pleasing appearance—a thought that will intrigue any woman.

Then, my reflection vanished, as if a flick of the comb through a tight curl had winked it out of existence. And I saw—

The bare bones of it, maybe, were like unto mine, but what leered and postured there was not me. Horror held me dumb and still, though in me grew a need to scream. The smooth brown skin I had seen was sere, wrinkled, freckled with dark patches. The teeth were gone, so my mouth was shrunken into a wrinkled opening, and my chin and nose drew together. My hair was white and thin, hanging in limp, sparse strands over a seamed and corrugated forehead. The eyes were only dark and empty pits—yet I could see!

I heard a choked cry and saw that horror in the mirror shake and reel, even as I swayed back and forth before it. The comb fell from my hand and clattered on the dressing table. And that slight noise broke the illusion. It was gone, and I stared wild-eyed, with a heart beating so fast and heavily that it frightened me, at what I had always seen in any glass. The vision, nightmare, whatever it was, was gone. But as I sat there limp, shivering with a cold inside me, I knew I had seen it. *It?* What *had* I seen? And why?

THREE

Badly shaken, I crept into bed and lay there shivering, trying to make some sense of that illusion, for illusion I was sure it must be. Only no possible combination of light and shade in this room could have accounted for the hideous thing on the mirror's surface. And I had certainly not taken dream smoke or any of the hallucinatory drugs. As I drew the covers tighter around my body, feeling that I could never be warm again, I searched my memory for some hint of what must have really happened during those few moments.

There were numerous accounts of odd experiences on many worlds to be found in Volk's library. I had read enough to know well that what seemed "magic," totally unexplainable to one species or race, might be commonplace to another perhaps a quarter of the galaxy away. Even espers could achieve strange results to baffle their own race—

Espers! Had the commandant's guess concerning Bartare been correct, and was my experience some projection of her thoughts concerning me—forcing me to see myself as she wished me to be?

That idea was terrifying enough, but it was less weird than some of the other explanations that I resolutely thrust away. On impulse I got out of bed again and caught up a robe to wind about me. That thick drowsiness into which I had sunk earlier was dispelled. I was as far from the need of sleep now as I would have been at morning rising.

I thrust my feet into loose flap-slippers and went to look out into the courtyard, for the second time catching a flicker of movement. But this time as I faced it squarely, it did not disappear. There was a figure slipping along the inner wall from the shadow of one doorway to the next—a small figure.

My first impulse was to call out. But then I remembered the guard I had set at the outer door, and I wanted very much to see all that I could before I revealed myself. I moved as silently as I could along the same way, trying not to allow my slippers to flap against the pavement.

The one I followed had reached the final inner door, that of the library. And there it or she lingered so long that I wondered if that was the goal. Then, as if reassured that she was not being watched, the figure came out into the bright moonlight.

Bartare! Somehow I was not in the least surprised.

She no longer wore her nightrobe, but had on her favorite green dress, though her hair swung free as I had seen it last. She was carrying something in both hands as if, though the object seemed small and light, it was so precious that she must take good care of it. Holding it out, a little away from her body, she stood intently studying the pattern of the pavement.

Then, as if she had made some important choice, she set that which she carried on one of the crystal pieces, taking some care in that placing, as if she must be very sure of what she did.

Having so centered it to her liking, she withdrew a little, and her small hands moved in a series of gestures that wove for me a disturbing pattern. They must have a meaning, but to me the feeling was that of searching for some important word eluding the conscious mind.

I heard a murmur of sound, too far away, too low-pitched for me to distinguish any words, yet speech it was. And so speaking, perhaps to what she had put in place, perhaps only to the empty air, Bartare began a dance that led her feet from one crystal block to another, while she took great care not to tread on anything else.

Since the pattern was wide and those blocks well scattered, her round brought her slowly to where I stood in the shadow of the door of her father's study. Now I could distinguish separate word sounds, still without meaning. It was plain she chanted, the words strung together in a cadence of a ritual salutation or invocation.

Invocation! I fastened upon that. It could explain much, and while danger lay there for any imaginative child, yet it was normal enough. I could have quoted hundreds of cases where the young, especially girls entering into adolescence, had created for themselves imagined forces and played with the belief in powers unknown to others. If Bartare was esper without realizing the fact, this might well be the fashion in which her slowly expanding power would lead her.

She halted her dance not too far away and turned to face the thing set up in the full moonlight. Once more she gestured, as if she were grasping and pulling to her some emanation. Having so gathered the invisible, she rolled it between her palms as one takes wet clay and balls it to make a sphere. Then she threw what she did not really hold, aiming it at the door of her mother's bedroom.

Again she drew from the object, rolled and threw. This time that toss of nothing was for Oomark's doorway. When she began for the third time to collect invisibility, I had no doubt that it was meant for the room I did not occupy, and so it was.

After she made that last throw, she visibly relaxed. I read into her stance a feeling of security such as had been mine when I closed the courtyard entrance, as if she had now bolted some doors leaving her free to do as she would.

She went back to the object, still careful to step only on the crystal blocks, picked it up, and hugged it tightly to her. Then, still treading on crystal only, she went to the outer gate of the courtyard.

However much she believed in what she had done, she had not triumphed over the robo protector. The crackles of a force shield flashed warning before her, and the alert of an audible warning brought a small answering cry from her. She stopped, her right arm raised as if again hurling something at that which barred her leaving, but this time with no results. The shield held, the alarm purred, and I judged it time to show myself.

"Bartare!" I stepped out of the shadow.

She whirled, sliding her feet from the crystal block on which she had stood. Her eyes glistened as might those of a cornered and startled animal, just as her lips drew back against her teeth, showing small white tips bared to bite. She might have been expecting some physical attack.

Her move brought her away from the warning zone of the gate protection. Both the alert and the force field stopped. She did not move toward me, but waited for me to join her. Her arms tightened about what she held, as if that, above all, must be protected. And I saw it was the doll-image she had dressed in green.

"Bartare—" I was rather at a loss for words. And I was sure she would answer no questions I might ask now. Perhaps I would be on better terms with her, more able to win her confidence, if I did not push the matter. That this was a secret thing of her own, I did not doubt. "Bartare—it is time for sleeping—"

That sounded feeble as no one knew better than myself.

"Then sleep!" she returned. "They do—" That slight nod indicated the rooms of her mother and Oomark. "Why do you not?" It seemed to me that the fact I stood there was disconcerting for her, marked a failure.

"I don't know. Perhaps because this is my first night on a strange world. Who can say that one does not change a little when stepping on alien soil?" I spoke to her as I would to Lazk Volk.

"All worlds are strange—if you look."

I guessed that she was referring obliquely to what had occurred here, so I nodded.

"That is true, for no one can look through another's eyes and see exactly as she sees. What I call a flower—such as this"—and I reached down to touch a cup-shaped bloom in a nearby bed—"you may also call a flower and yet not see it as I do—" I halted, for the blossom I had touched was going through a frightening transformation.

It had been pale ivory. Now from the point where my fingers had so lightly touched it, a dark, unwholesome stain spread. The flower was withering, decaying, dead and dying, as if my touch polluted and killed.

Bartare laughed.

"I see a dead flower. What do you see, Kilda? Is it the same? Do you see death coming from your fingers?"

This might be hallucination, but how it had been produced I could not tell. It was certainly unnerving. My hold on logic was the hope that it might indeed be so fragile a bloom that any touch would harm it. There were sensitive plants, though I had never seen one so much so as this.

"Do you see death often, Kilda? As in mirrors?" She came closer to me, her glistening eyes on mine, trying to see into me, see the fear that had filled me when I had looked into the mirror. At that moment I could believe—I was *sure* that Bartare not only knew what had happened, but also why and how. And I could not hold back questions.

"Why, Bartare—and how?"

Again she laughed, shrilly, a little cruelly, as sometimes a child may when she is single-hearted and set on gaining her own desires.

"Why? Because you look, Kilda, and you listen, and you want to know too much. Do you want to look in other mirrors, Kilda, and see always what you would not like to? There are other things that can happen—worse than just a reflection."

Deliberately she turned a little from me to gaze out over the moonlit court. Then she spoke once more, but it was not to me. She addressed those words to the empty air.

"You see?" she demanded. "Kilda is no more than any of the others. There is no need to think twice of her."

She waited as if for an answer. Then she retreated a step or two, and the look of triumph vanished from her face. My own imagination supplied a rebuke that I could not hear but which had chastened the girl's self-esteem. If that was what had happened, she might be ready to vent her disappointment and anger on me, the more so because I was a witness.

But her discomfiture was that of a child. She lost the strange, disturbing maturity that had masked her. Instead, her features screwed up into a familiar pattern of frustrated anger as she shrilled at me, "I hate you! Spy on me again, and I'll make you sorry! I will! I will! You'll see!"

She turned and ran, paying no attention now to the blocks over which she fled, intent only upon reaching the door of her room. And an instant later that clicked firmly shut behind her.

I stood for a long moment looking across the courtyard, then stooped to examine more closely the flower I had touched. The courtyard was certainly empty. And the flower was a black ball of quick decay. Almost I had expected to find it intact. But that much was real, or looked real. I broke the stem of the flower and took it with me. But before I went again to my own room, I looked in upon Oomark.

He was sleeping heavily. Having seen him so, on impulse I visited Guska Zobak's room in turn. In the dim night light, the nurse huddled in an easirest, sleeping, too, while Guska lay inert but breathing in the bed. It was almost as if they had all taken a sedative.

I had a dead flower in my hand, I had a detailed memory of what I had seen in the courtyard, and I had above all now a pressing need to confer with someone. I decided then that if the commandant did not go forward with his suggestion to bring in a parapsychologist, I must instigate such a meeting myself.

With that thought in mind, I went back to bed. I thought that I was too wrought up to sleep, but that was not so, for my last memory was of stretching out and pulling up my covers.

Even now I have no way of explaining what happened in the morning. I awoke with a feeling that I had dreamed significantly—that was all. The memory of the night before and the help I needed had been lost. I had only a teasing half-recall, which bothered me during the day, the necessity to do something, see someone—yet I could not clarify it.

Gentlefem Piscov called on us before the morning was over, and I found hers a soothing presence. It was apparent she liked and understood children. And Oomark and Bartare both acted like ordinary children that day. She took us on a tour of the city. We had landed on the eve of a week of national celebration marking the landing of the colony's First Ship. And soon we were drawn into the festivities of the government circle.

I saw Oomark develop friendships with two boys near his own age, though Bartare, always polite and with manners that impressed adults if not her contemporaries, did not have such a social success.

Little by little, as one collects fragments of a dream to fit them together hazily, I did remember that scene in the courtyard. But oddly enough, it had no power now to alarm me or make me think it serious. I had come upon Bartare playing some highly imaginative game and allowed her actions to overcome my good sense. I would have more control over her in the future if I refused to consider such a performance more than a childish game. So can one be influenced without realizing the fact.

Bartare, showing no more desire for midnight wanderings or talking to the air, made it seem less and less important. Her present slightly antisocial attitude with other children did not alarm me, for she was much like what I had been myself at her age. And I do not think it right to force children into ways adults deem "normal" but which will irk and alienate the child.

Instead, I did find a common meeting ground with Bartare. She watched me unpack the recorder Lazk Volk had given me and seemed interested. I told her of Volk's galactic library and the fact that I had worked there, saying that now I hoped to be able to add something to it—providing I could find material here unusual enough to be worthy. But I explained that I must be highly selective as I was limited in the amount I could send.

I suppose her interest, as it was meant to do, disarmed me—one of the oldest ploys in the world—so that when she made her suggestion, I was pleased that I had found something through which to reach her and was really intrigued by the value of her comment, for it was her proposal that we visit the ruins her father had been inspecting before his fatal crash.

But that this could be done was dubious. In the first place, the site of the ruin was deep in the wilderness, quite a distance from Tamlin—meaning an overnight stay—and the accommodations there were limited to the staff at work. I explained this to Bartare, and while she seemed disappointed, she then suggested there might be other points of interest nearer to the city.

So well, far too well for any child, did she conceal her own wishes in the matter that I was quite convinced she merely wanted to see me in action as a recording expert. And I drifted along in a fog of complacency.

Guska Zobak also continued in a fog. But this was, or so it seemed at that time, a far more serious one. She was content to lie and drowse. Any attempt to rouse her brought on a return of hysteria. After two such battles, the medico reported complete bafflement. As long as she was left to her half-sleep (and this was no longer drug-induced), she was manageable. To attempt to shake her awake brought her to such a state that he actually feared for her sanity.

He finally admitted that her case was beyond his solving and that she needed expert off-world treatment. So, the fact that the first ship planeting here that could provide room for us would carry us back to Chalox was accepted. The trouble was that such a ship did not come into the port, though more than one freighter or outward-bound transport finned down as the days passed.

Oomark was happy with the boys. And he now went to the port school, where he fitted in well. It seemed to me that he was more at ease than I had ever seen him. He spent more time out of the house than in it, but I thought that very natural, that with masculine company of his own age he was secure and leading a more normal life than he ever had under Bartare's domination. Also a house in which quiet must be maintained for Guska's sake was not for a small and active boy.

Bartare objected so strongly to the port school that I took on her tutoring, knowing that Guska had intended this to be so. She had a quick and vigorous mind, one that was best served not by an imposed code of learning such as formal schooling demanded, but rather by guidance and sharing of discovery.

I could not grow fond of her as a person. There was always that feeling that she tolerated, sometimes impatiently, those about her. But I respected her abilities. And when she showed no more signs of imaginative play or action, I grew far more easy with her.

She did not forget her desire to find something for me to record for Volk's files and returned to the subject often, making many suggestions. At last, perhaps because I was weary and even a little ashamed of my constantly saying "no" to her eagerly advanced ideas, I agreed that we would spend a small portion of my tape on a visit to the Lugraans.

Dylan had been found oddly lacking in larger native life, and one Survey account tentatively suggested it had been deliberately denuded of such life at a remote time. Thus, there were a few things visitors were always escorted to. And one of those was a favorite picnic place for children—the Lugraan Valley.

The Lugraans themselves baffled the scientists who had studied them. In the first place, any attempt to transport one of the creatures from the valley resulted in its death, the body being left without any sign of what caused that death even under the minutest of autopsy examination. So now it was forbidden to approach them closely, though one could watch from rock ledges above their living place.

They had already been taped, of course, and I did not doubt that Volk had such tapes in his collection. But they were the only native things of any note, and I could try my hand at a few lengths of such recording, giving Bartare pleasure and, I did admit to myself, so continuing to hold her interest.

It seemed that luck favored us as Oomark's group of level mates at school were about to visit the Lugraans. And this outing included parents and other members of the family if so desired. Thus, Bartare had an excellent reason for pushing the expedition.

To Oomark, however, this was not pleasant at all. When I spoke of it, he looked, for the first time in days, like his old self. Much of the eager animation vanished from his face, his lower lip pushed forward in a pout, and he scowled at his sister.

"*You* want to go," he said to her rather than to me. And his tone made the words an accusation.

"Of course. Kilda is going to make a recording—"

"It isn't your kind of place!" He was openly hostile. "Don't let her come—" He turned to me. And the strain on his small face was out of all proportion to the situation. He might have been despairingly watching all he had won of friendship and freedom being threatened by a power he could not hope to combat.

I could not stand against that plea. If it meant so much to Oomark, I would not insist. We could go to the Lugraan Valley by ourselves. I said as much, and he showed a flash of relief, which vanished when he glanced at his sister.

My eyes followed his. The shadow I saw in her expression awoke a twinge of the old uneasiness. Somehow Oomark braced himself, as if with my support he was going to defeat Bartare this time.

"Do you want to go alone, not with us?" Bartare asked. She spaced those words a little, giving them more weight than such a simple question needed.

Oomark flushed and then paled. But he stood his ground.

"Yes—yes—"

Bartare smiled. "Let it be your choice then."

Oomark gasped, turned, and ran out of the courtyard as if he were already late for school and must get there—or away from us—as quickly as possible. Bartare looked to me, still smiling.

"He'll change his mind—you'll see. And you ought to tell Gentlehomo Largrace that we'll go."

"No, not this time. If Oomark wants to be alone with the other boys, it's better to let him."

She shook her head. "He'll want us—you'll see. Just wait and see."

Something about her certainty brought the first crack in the shell of comfortable acceptance that had encased me during the past few days. Memory stirred deep in me. There had been a mirror, and I had seen something in it—

Bartare's smile vanished. She looked concerned as her eyes met mine.

"It is of no matter, none at all," she said hurriedly. "Please, we were going to the Vorright to see the wind pictures—"

And she did what she seldom did, slipped her hand into mine. Bartare had a dislike for being touched that I learned early in our association and that I carefully respected. For her to deliberately seek physical contact was very rare indeed.

We went to the Vorright display hall, and apparently Bartare was absorbed in what we saw. She was playing her little girl role. But my awakening was proceeding, and I was on guard as I had been before that night in the courtyard. Whatever Bartare might be—and I was beginning to wonder if we could discover that—she was not a normal child. And now, remembering her performance in the courtyard, I found it so disturbing that I longed to be able to pour out all my doubts, surmises, and suspicions to someone such as Lazk Volk, who knew much of the universe and would be open-minded.

The parapsychologist—how or rather *why* had I forgotten my desire to call him? Why had the commandant never moved on his suggestion to do so? Did Bartare have some unknown, heretofore undiscovered esper power to lull thinking in those she wanted to influence?

I reached one answer for myself. But I did not know how she could do it. And until I was able to find out, it would be far better to play her own game of masks, to be the uncaring companion she wanted.

Nor did I doubt now that if she wanted badly to go to the Lugraan Valley, Oomark could not stand against her. But I very much sympathized with his desire to keep as far from his sister as he could. Perhaps, until the circumstances here on Dylan had made it possible, he had never had freedom from her control.

Once freed from whatever restraint had been placed upon me, my own imagination went to work. I had to exercise control over it, tell myself firmly that I would remain alert but that I must not believe Bartare could do much—not until I had concrete proof.

The proof came in such a way as to arouse all my foreboding, to alert all my personal warning signals.

We had returned from town, discussing what we had seen. But Oomark had reached the house before us. His usually round small boy's face appeared gaunt, just as his skin, lightly tanned by Dylan's sun, had now a sickly pallor.

I hurried to where he leaned against the wall, both of his hands pressed to his middle, beads of perspiration distinct on his forehead and upper lip. His mouth worked as if to control nausea.

Before I could reach him, he stood away from the support of the wall to face his sister.

"Take it back—take back what She did to Griffy!" His voice held the shrill of approaching hysteria, that same wild note I had heard in his mother's the two times the medico had tried to rouse her.

"I haven't done anything," Bartare returned.

"You don't have to—She did! You make her stop! Griffy—Griffy's good. He's—" Oomark's eyelids squeezed together, and tears came from between them. "All right, all right! You can come—you can go—anywhere you please. I'm—I'm going to be sick!"

He moaned then, and I caught him up, carrying him as fast as I could to the fresher. Nor did it matter at that moment what Bartare might say or do in answer to his outburst.

FOUR

✳

I washed Oomark's sweating face. He had been thoroughly and miserably ill. Now he sat on the edge of his bed, hunched together, staring down at the floor. He allowed me to tend him, and when I would have gone to return the washcloth to the fresher, he caught at my overtunic. So I sat down beside him, put my arm around those small shoulders, and drew him close. He turned his face against me.

"Can you tell me about it?" I asked. It was plain he had had a shock. And if Bartare was responsible for this—At that moment I was willing to be primitive enough to apply punishment with my own hands.

"She said I'd be sorry—" His words were muffled. "And I am. But not Griffy! They didn't have to do that to Griffy!" Again that hysterical note.

I was at a loss. Which would be better—to urge him to tell me just what had happened or to try to get him to forget it and ask the nurse for some sedation?

He decided for me, moving about so that he showed again his tear-streaked, pale face.

"Griffy—he lives with Randulf. He's a poohka—a real, live poohka, not just a stuffed one like I had when I was little. He goes everywhere with Randulf, even to school. Only he wouldn't ever come here 'cause he knew, you see—he knew!"

"Knew what?" A poohka was an alien life-form from off-world and created with its small, furry body the instant desire to cuddle—a perfect pet. But since they were fabulously expensive, I was surprised that any child this far from their planet of origin would have a poohka.

"He knew—" Oomark was emphatic. "He knew about her."

"Your sister?"

The boy shook his head. "Oh, maybe he knew about Bartare—'cause She and Bartare—they are always together. But She's the bad one! And She made Griffy be hurt! I know she did. He was hurt bad. And maybe even the medico can't help him. She wanted to make me sorry 'cause I didn't want to have Bartare go with us. But She didn't have to hurt Griffy—he never did anybody any harm, and he's the nicest fur person I ever, ever knew!" His small body began to shake, and I was frightened at the severity of this upset. I freed one arm and pressed the call for the servo. When that machine came trundling in, I taped a message for the nurse.

Together we got him soothed and to bed. Then I went in search of Bartare. I found her in the library, a tape reader going, listening with dutiful concentration to a history lesson. But I pushed the cutoff button and faced her.

"Oomark believes you have in some manner harmed his friend's poohka." I had come with the firm intention of asking searching questions, of demanding illuminating answers.

She looked at me blankly, as if completely surprised or startled. "How could I, Kilda? I have never even seen any poohka. And I have been with you all day."

"Oomark keeps talking about a She who is responsible through you—" I persisted, determined that this time I would not allow her to put me off.

"Oomark's just a baby," she answered. "I used to scare him when he was bad. I told him that a Green Lady was coming to get him and that she would do all I told her to. Now he thinks there really is a Green Lady and—"

"And you still play upon his fears to get your way?"

"Well—sometimes—"

Plausible enough given coincidences, which do happen. If I had not seen and overheard enough to make me suspicious, I might have believed her. What to do now—should I accept her explanation and wait for her to irretrievably betray herself? Or should I at once call the parapsychologist and arrange an interview?

"I wouldn't, you know." She held my eyes with a straight stare as she said that. There was a faint shadow of an unpleasant smile about her lips.

"But you see, Bartare, I am not a little boy you have managed to frighten by your tales. I do not believe in your Green Lady, nor shall Oomark any longer. It is apparent you both need more help than I can give you."

Her smile was broader. "Try it and see!" There was an exultation in that, far from any child's emotion. "Just try and see!"

To my horror, I found she was right. Try as I might, I could not reach the com when I went to call Commandant Piscov and ask for the help I was sure we needed. And, truly frightened by this check, I returned to Bartare, who was again listening to the tape, very much the schoolgirl absorbed in her lesson.

"You see"—she glanced up as I came in—"I told you that She won't let you do that."

I sat down on the chair facing this enigmatic charge of mine. "Suppose you tell me who She really is—your mother?" I made as wild a guess as possible, hoping to surprise some answer. The results were past my hopes.

Bartare was out of her seat, leaning over me, her whole face convulsed with some emotion I could not read.

"How did you—" Then that emotion was gone. She turned her head a trifle. Her attitude was so much that of one listening that I also looked in that direction. There was nothing—no one—there.

"Who is She?" I asked again.

Then she gave a pert answer. "That's for me to know, and it would be better for you not to find out, Kilda. Really it would. I like you—a little. But if you make trouble, then you'll find trouble. Don't worry about Oomark. And you can tell him Griffy's going to be all right—as long as he does what he's supposed to. You'll be the same, for the same reason. We are going to the valley. It is important."

With that she left me sitting there.

My first reaction was a flare of anger. Luckily my crèche training helped me to face facts. I was badly hit in both my self-confidence and my self-esteem. It would appear that Bartare had some power, undoubtedly esper, which could keep me from summoning aid. I had very little left to me in the way of a weapon. And when I faced that bald fact, I was almost as frightened as I had been by that vision in the mirror. Now I did not, in the least, doubt that that had been some product of Bartare's arranging also, that she had done it either as a warning or a threat. Was Guska Zobak aware of what she had produced in a daughter?

And was her present withdrawal based on a desire not to face the fact of Bartare without the support of her husband? Or was it also engineered by Bartare? She apparently was able to keep me from summoning help to deal with her.

My knowledge of espers and esper powers was only that of the average well-read layman, garnered from Volk's tapes. And it is difficult for one without such abilities to judge, or even believe, in the extent of what one so endowed can accomplish.

Esper or not, my nature rebelled against becoming, as Oomark had, one Bartare could dominate. Perhaps she did not believe, in her child's confidence, that forewarned is forearmed, and there were measures that could be taken to forestall take-over—I was startled to find my thoughts had ranged so far. To be controlled by a child only little more than half my age! It was impossible—or was it? That chill question hung over me as a constant mind-shadow.

I did not have the knowledge I needed, only scraps and bits of information. And from those bits I must build an inner armor and strengthen it until I could stand up to Bartare. How I longed for only an hour's access to Volk's library.

Outward compliance was my best cover for the present. I agreed to that bitter fact reluctantly. There were exercises against hallucination, and I would begin those. In the meantime—what better material could I supply to Volk than my own entanglement in this weird web? I had come a long distance in search of some wonder to add to his store of knowledge, and I had found what I sought—not on Dylan, but within myself.

I went back to my room and brought out Volk's recorder. Yes, there was a thought transcriber attachment. I had used one but only briefly, and I was not sure I had the training to completely record a report thus. But I believed now it was the only sure method, for I had no idea how far Bartare's esper powers penetrated or whether she could overhear an audible recording.

With the lock beam set on my door, I lay down on my bed and began to compose within my mind the clearest record I could of all that had happened to me since I had met Guska Zobak and her children. Twice I outlined events in my thoughts, edited and strove to make them as free as possible of my own reactions and guesses. It might be possible to add those at the end, but what I had to deliver first were facts, not my interpretation of them—though, as with any report, no matter how hard the compiler strives to make it impersonal, there would continue to exist traces of the maker.

Having done my best to assemble a coherent and meaningful sequence, I strapped on the forehead disk and began, giving my twice-edited account. I used the high speed so that much could be embodied on the smallest possible portion of the tape. And I found the whole process much more exhausting than any two regularly dictated accounts.

Then I spun the tape back so the spool looked unused. That I was taking the precautions of one being spied upon, I realized. But I would not make the mistake of underestimating Bartare.

Oomark spent the rest of the day in bed. Also, it was apparent that just as he had turned to me earlier for help, so now he shrank away. As far as I knew, Bartare had not visited him. But I could be sure of nothing now, and it was plain that he feared either me or what he had told me in his confusion. He did receive a call via visa-com from Griffy's owner and was reassured that the poohka seemed to be responding to treatment.

The next morning he went off eagerly when the school transport picked him up, though I noted he glanced several times with apprehension at his sister's door, she having made no appearance. Within the hour she did appear, wearing sturdy outdoor clothing, ready for the valley expedition.

I had changed into breeches, land boots, and a warm innerlined tunic—for which foresight I was to be very glad. And I packed a shoulder bag with trail rations, making sure that though we might go to the valley with the group escorting Oomark's class, we would not intrude upon their picnic lunch. The farther I was able to isolate Bartare at present, the better. To my relief she appeared to accept the idea of staying to ourselves quite as if that was the best thing to do, though perhaps she was as eager to keep me from contact with those outside our private field of struggle as I was to restrain her.

We reached the flitter park in good time and found our-selves assigned to a craft with two mothers and one aunt. At best, I found casual social contacts difficult because of my own background. And now, with my inner tension, it was an added burden. I seemed to preserve my outer shell so well, though, that they accepted my account of Guska, in answer to their inquiries and other small talk, as if I were acting my part well.

Bartare played the small girl correctly, responding politely to the suggestion of one of the mothers that she meet the other's daughter. She carried, as she insisted upon doing, the recorder, holding to it with purpose.

The trip was longer than I had supposed, for we swung out over the countryside, which was at first divided into sections and fields rich with nearly ripened crops, and then into unsettled land. It was here the fact that Dylan was a sparsely occupied frontier planet hit one squarely.

I had lived all my life on a congested planet where one's only sight of growing things was carefully tended, long-tamed, well-trained gardens. Though the art of making little seem much greater was assiduously practiced by their designers, they were only specks compared to this.

Here was the open as I had seen it only on visa-tapes. And it hit one with a hard impact. There was something frightening about those long stretches of open country over which we sped. The land here was not as rich as it was nearer Tamlin. There were few trees, and those more like bushes. Under us the level was rising. More and more rocky outcrops appeared, breaking through the soil. We winged over a basin in which steam arose from heated mineral-impregnated springs. It was a strange place, fascinating to look down upon. But I do not think I would have cared to cross it on foot.

Beyond this were jagged ridges. The sun shone bright on crystalline seams. The land must have once been torn by fierce volcanic action. And it was into the heart of this very inhospitable country that we were flying.

Bartare stared down so intently that her face was pressed against the plasta-shield of the window. Her attitude was that of one searching for a landmark that was very necessary to find. But I did not trust my reactions to Bartare. I was so much on the defensive with her that I knew it was very easy for me to read more into any action than might be there.

We landed at a much used parking strip, a plateau leveled to make an excellent flitter perch. There we were organized into parties by the rangers in charge and escorted to the upper ledges from which one could watch the activities of the Lugraans.

I admit I was taken off guard there—fatally as it proved. Bartare was beside me and Oomark wedged in some distance away, standing between his instructor and his good friend—Griffy's master. He had not so much as looked at us since the party had been counted out and marched to this stand. I was acutely aware of his avoidance, though perhaps others had not noticed it.

Bartare made no move to join her brother. When we reached the ledge, she handed me the recorder. And because I could not let her guess the service to which I had put it earlier, I went through the motions of training its visa-lens on the scene below us.

The Lugraans showed no interest in us. We might have been totally invisible as far as they were concerned. They were non-humanoid, though they did walk erect. Their plump bodies contrasted with long and thin upper limbs, short and thick lower ones, and a broad, fleshy tail, which, when they paused to face one another at intervals as if they were carrying on conversations, they thrust stiffly against the ground, forming with their legs a supporting tripod.

In color they were a dull red, a growth of stiff quill-like hair covering all over their bodies. Connected to those bodies, by necks so supple and long as to remind one of reptilian creatures, were heads provided with a heavy brightly yellow beak and with a crest of longer quills on top.

Their forepaws were equipped with handlike appendages, which they used well—judging by the huts made of stones piled together, all so well selected and fitted that they stood sturdily. They also carried on a type of agriculture represented by the cultivation of fungi and the keeping of some monstrous insects that were their equivalent of human food herds.

They were certainly unusual enough to rivet the attention—far too much so, as I realized suddenly when I looked around and saw that Bartare was missing. Nor was she anywhere in our party. And, in searching for her, I discovered that Oomark, too, was gone.

I edged toward the back, my first faint alarm becoming a certainty that the children must be found and quickly. But when I
wanted to speak to the ranger, the instructor, or even to one of
the other children, I discovered—to my mounting fear—that the
same inhibition that had kept me from calling for aid in handling
Bartare back in the city had returned. I could think what I must
do, but it was impossible to do it. However, there seemed to be
nothing preventing me from leaving the ledge. I went back along
the path. None of the others turned their heads to see me go or
ask questions, though I tried to will it to happen.

My discovery of Bartare's and Oomark's withdrawal must have
come sooner than the girl expected, for I caught sight of them
ahead, not on the path returning to the flitter park, but scrambling
over the rocks to the right, climbing up the height beyond. Unable
because of the inhibition forced on me to attract any attention,
it was left to me to follow them.

It was plain I must have both hands free for the climb, and I
must choose between the recorder and the bag of supplies. The
latter had a strong carrying strap, so I set down the recorder at
the turnoff where I must follow the children. I hoped it would
be a marker to the way we had gone.

Almost I feared that leaving that small signpost might be forbidden to me also by whatever had clamped down on my ability
to alarm or warn. But no, I could leave it so. I could even follow
the children without hindrance.

They had already vanished out of sight, and if I were not
to lose them somewhere in that mass of broken rock, I must
hurry. Though I had kept in good physical condition, thanks to
the regime of the crèche, I might never have climbed the first
pull, for it was harder than it looked from below, save for my
grim need. The slope was treacherous, with sliding stones, which
gathered others in cascades unless one was very careful. And I
concentrated entirely on what was immediately before me.

I reached the top of the rise and surveyed the way ahead, to
see that I had not utterly lost the children. They were already part
way up the next ridge beyond. Oomark was lagging, however, and
now and then Bartare paused to wait for him. What she said I
could not hear, but it was enough each time to bring him along
in a short spurt of renewed effort. I remained where I was until
I saw them reach the crown of that other rise, for I had a strong

suspicion that were Bartare to see me in such close pursuit, she would take steps to stop me. I could only follow some distance behind until we reached a countryside formed for easier travel.

Once they were over the crest, I made the best time I could down and up. Then I could look down on a long stretch of fairly level territory, save that here the rocky outcrops were numerous and the ground so uneven, with ruts scored in the rock and piles of windswept and worn large boulders, that it was the sort of place where one went slowly and carefully.

Oomark was definitely lagging. Even when Bartare turned and waited with whatever encouragement or lash she had, he trudged at a slow pace. His head hung, and he seemed never to raise his eyes from the ground immediately before him. But he did not stop, and probably Bartare had to be content with so much.

They crossed the open space and were gone. It took me longer to follow. When I reached the far side, I found a sharp and even longer drop. Almost immediately below me Bartare stood with her back to that wall of rock. Her hands rested on her hips, and her head turned rapidly from right to left and back again.

Oomark was still descending the wall. Then he slipped and fell. I gave a gasp when he did not rise again but lay at Bartare's feet. Her impatience was plain to see as she reached down and caught with both hands the material of his tunic where it crossed his shoulders, pulling him up, first to his knees, and then to his feet. Even though he stood again, she kept her hold on him, as if, were she to let go, he would fall.

The cliff was the wall of a wide open space that might once have held a river, long since dried up. Though there had been shall shrubs of a prickly kind standing here and there among the boulders behind, here not the faintest trace of lichen or moss showed.

Most of the large stones were dull gray-brown. But set here and there among them were others whose hue was so different that they were instantly noticeable. They were a dark red—rounded into crude balls. Some stood as high as the children's shoulders. Others might be picked up and held in both hands. And they were widely scattered, as if some giant had idly flung a handful of colorful pebbles down so they fell and rolled as they would.

Having once been sighted, they drew the eye. In some places they lay close together; in others they were widely apart. There was a medium-sized one, about waist tall to Bartare, not too far away.

Dragging Oomark with her, the girl came to that rock and picked up a small piece of stone. With that she struck the red boulder. The answer was a musical note, like the ring of a bell. Bartare listened until the faint echoes died away.

She took hold of Oomark's shoulders once more and gave him a sharp, hard shake. I could see her lips move, though I could not catch the murmur of her voice.

Whatever she said was effective enough. He stooped to pick up a fragment of rock and stationed himself by the boulder she had already struck, while his sister moved on to a larger red stone.

She waved. Oomark struck his boulder, she hitting at the same time the one she had selected. Two notes rang out—but they were markedly different.

Bartare shook her head and beckoned to Oomark. They went on to try a second pair. Nothing daunted by what she seemed to consider ill success, Bartare appeared ready to work their way so across the plain. When they were far enough away, I descended the cliff in turn.

It was my hope that Bartare was so deeply absorbed in what she was doing that she would not see me, though what I would do when I did catch up, I had not the slightest idea. I was sure only that my responsibility was to remain with the children.

I reached the floor of the valley, drummed along by the continued striking of musical rocks. Sometimes they approached the same note closely. And once Bartare signaled Oomark to try a certain one again. But whatever she sought continued to elude her.

They were well out across the middle section of that valley when I followed, weaving a course among the rocks. I slipped once and put out a hand to steady myself. My bare palm met one of the red balls, and I snatched it away. It was as if my skin and flesh had rested for an instant against a heated grill, perhaps not quite hot enough to burn, but warm enough to startle me.

Testingly I touched one of the ordinary gray boulders and found it no warmer than any sun-heated stone might be, far less than the red one. And I carefully avoided any contact with those again. Then I looked up to see Bartare staring back at me. She raised her right hand and made the motion of one hurling some object, and a spear of light seemed to strike me full in the face and eyes.

FIVE

How long that bedazzlement blinded me, I cannot say, for blinding it was. When sight returned to me again, the children were a long distance away, not at the opposite wall of the valley to which they had been heading, but moving to my left.

Blinking to clear the last of the fog from my sight, I saw that they were still pounding on the ball-boulders. I tried to go after them, but my feet might have been caught in some treacherous engulfing trap. I swayed but could not raise either foot from the ground.

I was afraid. Yet I struggled to go after the two pulling farther and farther away. There the rocks stood taller, masking the children's movements, and finally I could not see them at all.

Their disappearance was the key to unlock my bonds. I stumbled and began to walk, though the footing was so bad that I dared not hurry. There were too many small loose stones that rolled and slid under my feet with almost diabolical purpose. I had to creep where I wanted to run, to clutch at rocks to draw myself forward.

Somehow I reached that place of taller outcrops and pulled my way among them until, at last, a rolling stone was too much, and I fell, twisting my ankle sorely. I rubbed it cautiously, fearing a sprain. But when I got to my feet, I discovered I could still stumble along.

As if their purpose had been accomplished, the loose gravel and stones were less, the footing firmer. At length I stood between two rocks taller than my head, steadying myself with a hand against one, as I gazed into an open space where there were many of the red rocks, much larger than those at the fore of the valley. And there were the children.

Oomark dragged along as if he were exhausted. I could hear a distant murmur I took to be Bartare's voice, urging or exhorting him to greater efforts. Once he hurled away the piece of stone he carried and turned as if to retreat. But Bartare moved so quickly that she disappeared at one place and appeared at another, to bar his way. I saw Oomark's face. His cheeks were red and bore smeared tear tracks. It was plain he obeyed his sister against his will.

She pointed, and he picked up another stone. Something in the slump of his shoulders made me want to run to him and stand before him protectingly. He turned slowly and went to the nearest of those red spheres as if he did not really see the rock but sensed it was there.

Bartare made another lightning move, and I thought she was so engrossed in what she was doing that I could catch up.

There came a low singing note from the ball Bartare struck, and I heard her give a cry of triumph. She did not move on, but waved Oomark on to tap another.

He hit its surface, and she tapped hers again. The notes were close together but did not meet. It was when her brother went to the third ball that she had what she wanted. The two sounds blended to make a single note.

Bartare listened, her head a little to one side, her eyes fixed ahead as if she expected now to see something there. When, after a long pause, nothing happened, she signaled her brother to strike again.

Once more that long, throbbing sound rang through the air, and yet it was through my body, too. I have heard that sound can be vibration, but this sensation of being impaled on a singing note was daunting—so daunting that I knew I must stop what the children were doing. Knowingly or unknowingly, Bartare was evoking forces beyond the control of the world we knew.

I started forward, my ankle paining me. Oomark had thrown aside his banging stone for the second time and stood with his right arm up, crooked before his face, as if to shelter from a blow. And though I could hear Bartare railing at him, he did not move to obey her.

"Do it!" Bartare's cries reached me. "Do it, Oomark! Do you want me to point the power at *you*? Do it now!"

For a long moment I thought he was going to refuse. But either her threat or the fact she had dominated him so long won. He stooped and felt about for the stone, not looking. Rather he kept his eyes screwed shut as if the last thing he wanted to see was his sister.

"Strike!" she shrieked at him.

Again that double note sounded in a vibration I could feel as a physical assault. Once more whatever she expected in answer did not come. But her absorption was so great that I was sure I could get near enough to seize her. My attack would have to be from behind, or she might apply the very efficient counter she had used before.

It was Oomark who betrayed me. He faced the direction from which I limped, and some change in his expression must have warned Bartare. She swung her head a little, as if to view me from eye corner, and she shouted again:

"Strike!"

As if that order moved me also, I stumbled and fell against another of the red boulders. The supply bag I carried bumped against it, and three notes, not two, sounded together.

If I had felt the vibration as a physical sensation before, that was nothing to what engulfed me now. I have no words to describe what I felt. The best is to say that I swung out as if I were on a rope over some immeasurable abyss, that I so hung for a space beyond the reckoning of any time I knew, and then that all ended in total darkness and nonknowing.

But the period of unconsciousness came to an end, and I opened my eyes, to shut them quickly again as violent nausea racked me. What I had seen bore no point of reference to anything I had known, was so alien to all I did know as to make me doubt my sanity.

Yet though I lay on some smooth, hard surface, I knew also that I could not remain so forever. I must make an effort, no matter how limited. Trying to keep control and master the raging fear inside me, I looked again.

I stared straight up at first, dreading to see what lay to right
or left. There was no sun, no moon, only an existing grayness
like that of an early summer twilight. Only it did not soothe as
might that hour on a world normal to my kind.

Slowly, very slowly, I turned my head to the right. What I saw
were not rocks such as had ringed me before. Rather there were
geometric figures, some stationary, some moving. Of those that
moved, a few drifted, apparently without purpose, slowly. Others
jerked along zigzag paths. Their erratic pace, together with their
unearthly shapes, brought a return of nausea, so I had to close
my eyes and struggle for control.

Though the air about me was gray, these forms were in clash-
ing colors, some of them such as to sear the vision if one gazed
at them too long or strove to inspect them closely. Now I turned
my head without opening my eyes until I could see what lay left.
Then I looked.

There were more of the stationary triangles, oblongs, and a few
circles, with only one or two of the floating things, none moving
fast. I braced my hands against the surface on which I lay and
raised my body a little.

Though that action made my head whirl, I persisted, until the
vertigo passed and I dared make another move. I seemed to be
lying on a rock surface, cushioned here and there by drifts of
shining motes, which, when my fingers dug into them, felt like
the grit of very fine sand. Some of the glitter clung to my skin,
outlining fingertips and palms when I raised my hands.

I had been aware mainly of what I saw. Now I was alerted by
what I heard. Somewhere a child was crying, not in loud bursts
born of rage or disappointment, but with a pitiful whimpering, as
one who had been reduced past hope. And in the midst of this
weird world I could not be sure of the direction from which that
plaint came. But I guessed which one of my charges made it.

"Oomark—" I called, aware that perhaps sounds in this place
might also be dangerous. But I must answer that sobbing.

When I called his name the second time, there was a halt in his
gasps, and he answered questioningly, as if he could not believe
anyone was here, "Kilda? Please, are you Kilda?"

"Yes. Where are you?" I thought he must be to the left. And
I hoped I need not face shooting things to find him.

Somehow I got to my feet, and after an instant or two of

vertigo, I discovered I was able to shuffle on, my ankle still pain-ing, worse than before.

"Where are you?" I repeated when he did not answer.

Then his voice came, very low and fearful. "I—I don't know."

"Is Bartare with you?" At that moment I hoped not. I was in no shape to face a struggle of wills. I needed time to pull myself together.

"No—"

"Can you tell me where you are? What is it like around you?" I tried to get some bearing on those figures apparently rooted enough to serve as landmarks.

There was a dark crimson cone that had not moved since I first sighted it and, a little beyond, a vivid green triangle, and to the left of those a cylinder of burnt orange. It seemed to me that Oomark's voice came from that direction, and if he saw the same figures, I would have a guide.

"There's a big tree—and a bush with yellow berries—and some rocks—" His words were separated by sniffles.

But what he said was impossible!

"Are—are you sure, Oomark?"

"Yes! Yes! Oh, please, Kilda, come and get me! I don't like this place! I want to go home— Please, Kilda—come!"

Certainly his voice did come from just beyond the crimson cone. But I shuddered to a stop as a blue rod with two hex-agonal fins swooped past my head and skimmed the surface of the orange cylinder. When it was gone, I set out doggedly in its wake.

"I see you now, I do, Kilda!" Oomark called. A small figure came running. To my relief it was Oomark in his own proper human body, who caught and held to me tightly. I had half suspected that perhaps both of us might have been altered as much as the land about us. But apparently he, too, saw me as normal.

He clung so to me that I could not move. And I must confess that my return hold on him was a kind of anchorage. At last his sobs died away and his grasp was not so tight. I dared then to say more than the soothing sounds meant to comfort him.

"Oomark—"

He looked up. His face was dirty with dust and tears, but he was attending to what I said.

"Tell me—what is that?" I pointed to the orange cylinder.

"A bush—with berries—so many that the branches are bent way over," he answered promptly.

"And that?" The green triangle was my next choice.

"A tree."

"That?" The dark red cone came now.

"A big rough rock. But, Kilda, why do you want to know all that? You can see it—"

Slipping to my knees, I put my arm about him, to draw him close. I must be careful of what I said now, but I would have to tell him the truth.

"Oomark, now listen closely. I do not see them so at all—"

I paused, hardly knowing how to continue. That very admission might be enough to increase his fear. I knew he had turned to me as a safe anchor, and if I proved unstable, he might be lost.

"Fern seed—" was his amazing comment.

It was so unexpected that I thought he had taken leave of his senses. But he nodded almost briskly, as if my words were proof of something important.

"What is fern seed?" I asked, with cautious gentleness.

"She gave some to Bartare once. If you get it in your eyes or eat it—you see things different. Bartare must have put some on me. What do *you* see, Kilda?" He asked that as if genuinely interested.

"Fern seed," "She," all more bits of a puzzle I felt as if I might never solve.

"Your bush—to me it is an orange cylinder. The tree is a green triangle, and the rock a dark red cone."

His eyes followed my pointing finger. "Then you don't see right here, do you, Kilda?"

"Not as you do, Oomark. Now listen—you say that Bartare is gone, or at least she is not here. Where is she? Did you see her go?"

"I didn't see her, not after I got here," he said. "But I feel her—here!" He loosed his hold on me and raised his right hand to tap the middle of his forehead.

"Do you think you can find her?"

He shivered. "I don't want to, Kilda. She is—she is with her—the Lady."

"And who is the Lady, Oomark?"

He pulled away, turning away his head as if he did not want to meet my eyes.

"She—She is Bartare's friend. I don't like her."

"Where did Bartare meet her?"

"First in a dream, I think. One day Bartare said we must do some things—sing some queer words. She poured layre juice on the ground and crumbled sweetie cakes and tore up some of Mother's pretty feathers and mixed them all together. Then we sat down in the grass, and she told me to close my eyes and count to nine, then open them, and I would see something wonderful. Bartare did—but I never. The Lady, She told Bartare I didn't have the right kind of eyes or something. But She came often after that and taught Bartare things. Then Bartare didn't like me much any more, but she made me help her. But she didn't want to play with Mayra or Janta or any of the girls. She used to pretend to go to see them, but instead she would hide and talk to the Lady. And she said the Lady promised her that if she learned the right things and tried hard, she'd be able to go into the Lady's own world someday. And—" He looked about, his mouth quivered, and his eyes began to fill again. "I guess that's what's happened. Only we had to come along, too. And I don't want to stay here— Kilda, please, let's go home!"

There was nothing I wanted more myself, but how to achieve it I did not have the least idea. I was hesitating over my answer when, with a flash of shrewdness, Oomark guessed what I did not want to say.

"I guess we can't go back, not until Bartare and the Lady let us. But, Kilda, can—can they keep us here forever?"

"No." Perhaps I was too firm, but seeing him so shaken, I dared give no other reply. "But if we find Bartare and the Lady now, maybe we can ask them to let us go."

"I don't want to—I don't like the Lady. I don't like Bartare either, not any more. But I'll go to see them if you think they'll send us home."

There was one other question I must ask. "Oomark, you said Bartare has known the Lady for some time. Did she know her on Chalox?"

"Yes."

"But now we are on another planet a long way from Chalox—" If this wild maze was a part of Dylan—I had no way of being sure of that. "Did the Lady come with you on the ship? And was her home here all the time?" I was feeling my way. Certainly—unless this was a hallucination of such power only a long-trained adept could force it on us—this was no result of esper work. But if I set aside that explanation, what was left save a nightmare founded on nothing known in my time and space?

"She—" He frowned, as if I had presented him with a problem he had not considered before. "She was there, and She was here. And *this* is her world. She doesn't like our world. She's been trying for a long time to get Bartare to come to her because it is so hard for her to visit Bartare. But I don't know where this world is!" Once more tears were close.

"Never mind. Perhaps it doesn't really matter, Oomark." I gave him a quick hug. "What does matter is finding Bartare and the Lady and telling them that we must go home."

"Oh, yes!" As I got to my feet, he caught hold of my hand and drew me along.

To me, the alien landscape provided no road. However, it seemed that Oomark was confident he knew where we should go. Now and then he pointed to one of the brilliant shapes and said it was a tree, a bush, some natural feature of landscape. But to me there was no change in the alien country. The pain in my ankle increased until the best I could do was hobble. Also, I was both hungry and thirsty, and finally, as I sat down under a dull blue octagon Oomark informed me was a bush, he said wistfully, "I'm awfully hungry, Kilda. Those berries were good, but I didn't eat a lot of them—"

"Berries?" I pulled the supply bag across my knee to open it. "Which ones?"

"The yellow ones back there on the big bush. I landed in the bush when I came here, and they got smeared on my hands. I licked off the juice, and it tasted good, so I ate them. Oh, look here." He scrambled to his feet before I could put out a hand to stop him, to lunge at a triple-peaked blue cone a short distance away. Both of his hands disappeared to the wrist in it, and he pulled out a red circle into which he bit. I could hear a crisp crunch and spoke my warning too late.

"No, Oomark! You can't be sure of any strange fruit—"

But he had swallowed the last bite and was reaching into the cone, withdrawing another fruit. This he offered to me.

"Eat it, Kilda. It's good."

"No! Please throw it away, Oomark. You know space rules.

Things growing on other worlds can be deadly dangerous. Please throw it away. See here—I have some choc squares." I dug hastily into my bag and chose what I thought would attract him most, one of the sweets.

He set the circle on the ground and reached out for the square. But he did so with visible reluctance. Oomark loved sweets. It was not like him to be so slow.

As he unwrapped and raised it to his mouth, an odd look of distaste came over his face. He acted as if the smell of the confection of which he had always been so fond was now disgusting. Slowly he rewrapped it and held it out to me.

"It smells funny. Maybe it's spoiled or something. I don't want it, truly, Kilda."

I took it and opened the covering to sniff for myself. There was no odor save the familiar one of choc, so I suspected something in the native food he had eaten had affected him. I decided better not to urge the sweet on him now. When he was hungry enough, he would be willing to eat the rations I carried. Only there were so very few of those. I could not help but suspect that we were indeed on another planet, though the how and why of our transportation I could not explain. And the first rule of any explorer so situated is to use normal supplies and *not* to live off the country.

However, I did not argue now with Oomark as I allayed my own hunger with a concentrate wafer. And I put as tight a strapping as I could about my ankle before we started on.

The passing of time did not register. The twilight had in no way deepened into night or lightened into day. Only my fatigue argued that a good many minutes, or even hours, had passed since Bartare and I had dismounted from the flitter back at the Lugraan Valley.

"Is it far—to where Bartare and the Lady are?" I asked as I stopped to rest again, far too soon after we had left the place where we had eaten.

"I don't know. It's—it's funny here—" Oomark was assuredly trying to explain. "Things can be close sometimes. And then they—they kind of stretch so they are far again. If—if I think about any place, then it seems far off. But if I just walk along and think of Bartare—why, it is closer again. Please, Kilda, I don't know why that's so—really, I don't."

He was plainly distressed, and I did not press him, though his answer did not make sense. And my whole body now ached with the effort I must make to keep moving. On the other hand, since our pause and since he had eaten the fruit—if fruit it had been—Oomark was as brisk as if he were starting out in the morning after a good night's rest. When I had to stop a third time, he came back to me.

"Kilda, does your foot hurt a lot?"

"Some," I was forced to admit.

"Let's stay here for a while." He looked about. "I know you can't see it as I do, but this is a nice place. Over here"—he tugged gently to turn me to the left—"there's some tall grass, and it looks soft and nice to sit on. Please, Kilda. I can find Bartare any time. She can't hide from me. But if we get to her and the Lady when you're so tired, Kilda—Bartare and the Lady together—I'm afraid of them! And you should be, too, you really should!"

My aching body supported his argument. My will struggled against a vast cloud of fatigue, and my will lost. I stumbled and fell to my knees in the very spot to which he had guided me. Finding softer ground under me, I could not summon the resolution to rise. With a sigh I surrendered.

SIX

✵

I rewound my ankle wrapping. My eyes smarted and burned, as they might after exposure to a bright glare. This was a world never meant for our species. Yet Oomark saw it differently, as a normal one. Had Bartare in some manner prepared him?

As I squinted my eyes against that discomfort, I was far from sleep. Here I felt walked danger.

"Oomark, how long has Bartare known the Lady?"

When he did not answer, I opened my eyes wider. His head was turned. All I could see of hunched shoulder and averted head spelled a desire not to reply. Then he said in a harsh whisper, "I don't want to talk about her. She—She knows when I do!"

"Bartare?"

"No—the Lady! It's not good to talk about her—it makes her think of me." He was obviously disturbed. Much as I wanted and needed to learn more, I realized I must not push him too far.

"Have—have you ever been here before, Oomark?" Was that question also infringing on forbidden territory or would he answer it?"

"No. Back home—back on Chalox—there was no way to come. Bartare, she found out only a little while ago that there was a way here. She wanted to run off—just me and her—but it was too far to come. So she had to wait until there was a chance to get a ride."

"Was that why you didn't want her to come?"

He nodded. "She was always saying she had to go someplace. But—I didn't want to come 'cause I don't want to be here! I don't!"

"None of us do." I tried to suggest that it would only be a matter of time before we could return to safe Dylan.

"Bartare does. She wanted to come badly. She won't go away again. You'll see."

The trouble was that I might not see, but I could feel he was right. And I had no idea what I might be able to do once I did confront Bartare. It was up to me to think seriously about a confrontation.

I rubbed my smarting eyes. The burning sensation was a real source of pain.

"Oomark, tell me how it looks, right here, I mean."

"Well, there's a big bush, tall as a tree," he began, and then he paused so long that I opened my eyes. The boy was staring at a triangle of pink-yellow to our right. I averted my sight hurriedly, for its glowing color increased the burning.

"What is it?"

"I—I don't like it, Kilda. Please could we walk—just a little way, maybe. I don't want to stay here any more."

"Of course."

I got to my feet, and we started on. It was not my ankle nor my general fatigue that slowed us so much now, but rather my sight. I kept blinking tears out of my eyes.

We came to an open space where there were few of the rooted colorful shapes. The absence of glaring color aided my sight a little.

Oomark halted. Before us ran a wide zigzag. On its golden surface one could detect a shimmer of movement.

"A stream." Oomark gazed into the shimmer. "It looks deep, Kilda. And the water—it's thick. You can't see any bottom."

"Do we have to cross it?"

"Bartare's over there somewhere." He waved his hand across the zigzag.

"Maybe we can find a place where it narrows or grows more shallow," I suggested. "Shall we go up or down?"

"She's more that way." He waved his hand to the left.

"Then that way it is."

However, as we shambled along, the zigzag did not vary in width. Oomark continued to report that it was as forbidding as ever. Suddenly he paused again.

"We're going wrong now."

One of the turns had made a sharper than usual angle. If we continued along, we would be heading away. But before I could consider that difficulty, Oomark faced me.

"I don't want to go on, I don't!"

His vehemence was marked. He turned his head from right to left and back again, as if he were backed into a corner and must find a way out.

"Oomark, what is it?"

"I don't—I won't go! You can't make me—you can't!" Hysteria was shrill in his voice. "No—no!"

The boy lunged at me, and I gave a step or two, taken so off guard that I could not reach out a hand in time to catch at him. He brushed by and was gone, running into the grayness that curdled about and swallowed him from sight.

"Oomark! Oomark!" I was afraid I had already lost him. What had forced him into flight, I could not tell, unless those we followed were so discouraging pursuit.

I listened. He had not answered, and my only hope now was to pick up sounds in the haze. I did hear such and hobbled along, putting my ankle to painful strain.

Then there was utter silence, and I called, "Oomark! Oomark!"

I heard a whimpering such as that which had first guided me to him. And I tried to steer for its source. The space here was once more filled with blazing shapes. In fact, their strident coloring was worse and kept me rubbing at my tormented eyes.

At last I ran into a parallelogram of pulsating yellow. But though I saw thus, what scratched and tore at me were thorned branches. I staggered back, crying out, my hands streaming small trickles of blood. Falling to my knees, I looked down. All I saw was velvety gray. However, when I ran my hands across that surface, what I felt was the grit of earth and sand, the softness of moss or very short-stemmed grass.

The fact that touch and sight were no longer allied did not at the moment mean so much as that Oomark was gone and now I could not even hear the whimpering. I crouched and called, listening.

"Oomark! Oomark!"

My voice roused only a faint, distressing echo like a moan. Should I blunder on? But I could not be sure of direction.

"Oomark?"

This time there was an answer—a muffled cry, from the other side of the growth into which I had run. But how far on the other side? If he would just keep on answering—!

"Oomark!"

Answer he did, though I could not make out any words, only sound. I floundered on, taking care to avoid contact with any other shape, though they blazed about me until they reminded me of leaping flames.

"Oomark!"

I had been so sure my last answer had come from a distance that I was startled when he replied from close before me.

"I'm here."

He sat on the ground, and somehow he seemed to have taken on some of that gray hue, so that only when he moved was I able to see him. And as I dropped down, spent, not too far away, I blinked and blinked against the pain, against the tears, trying to see him better. Because there was something—

I was not mistaken about his blending so well with the gray. He must have taken several tumbles to cover himself with soil, for he *was* gray, all gray— Or was it my sight? Fearfully I rubbed at my eyes. No, I could still see the orange and yellow, crimson and scarlet. But Oomark was gray—and his drab hue was darkening!

"I'm not going back—you can't make me! Bartare and the Lady, they don't want me to! If I go, they'll do something—something bad! I won't go!"

"All right." I was too tired to try to talk reason into him now. "You don't have to."

"You'll try and make me. I know you will!" He was aggressively hostile, and I thought that at any moment he might take off again. If he did, I had a strong feeling I would never find him again.

"No." I tried to be as emphatic as I could. "I won't. I'm too tired now to go any farther."

"That's 'cause you wouldn't eat the fruit." There was a malicious note in his voice. "You don't want to change—"

"Want to change?" I repeated dully.

"Yes. You have to change, you know. This place doesn't like you if you don't. If you change—why, then everything will be all right. Truly it will, Kilda!" His voice softened. He stretched out a gray hand as if to touch mine, though he did not quite set fingertip to my flesh.

Change—perhaps it was not my eyes, then, that saw Oomark growing more and more the color of the ground on which he sat.

"Are you changed, Oomark?"

"I guess so. But, Kilda, if you don't change, then I can't stay with you. And if I'm not with you— I don't want to be alone! Please, Kilda, don't make me be alone! Please!" He reached out both hands as if he would clutch at me. Yet, I noted, he seemed unable to complete that gesture. He either could not or would not touch me.

When I put out my hand in return, he shrank back. Then he arose and moved slowly backward, his face turned to me, as if he were wary of some attempt on my part to seize him.

"You've got to change, Kilda, you've got to!"

He turned and ran to one of those flames. And so much was the color like a blazing torch that I cried out. But when he retreated from the haze of light, he had in his two hands a blob of quivering stuff. This he thrust at me.

"Eat it, Kilda. You've just got to eat it!"

What might have led to a struggle, for he was determined I saw, to force it on me, never happened, for from between two fiery columns sounded a strange noise.

It was choked, husky. It might have been a mumble of words in an unknown language. Oomark dropped the jelly blob. He looked over his shoulder to give a shriek of terror.

Then he ran, passing out of my reach. After him, touching first one point to the ground and then another, was a dark purple thing, which might have been two triangles welded together in the middle. From it emitted the gobbling noise, as if it struggled to call out in recognizable speech.

Awkward as it looked, it was swiftly following Oomark with purpose. I could not guess what it was, but Oomark's reaction suggested something terrible.

It bumped past me and was gone, crashing in the boy's wake. I tried to hit it with the supply bag as it passed. But either my aim was poor, or else no touch affected it. And it showed no interest in me.

Somehow I arose and started in the wake of hunted and hunter. It had all happened so quickly that at first I was moved perhaps by instinct alone. Then the full horror of that chase urged me on. That Oomark still ran and the purple thing trundled after him, I was assured by sounds.

I was not to be a part of that chase very long, for suddenly a long ripple of crimson writhed out just ahead of me. I couldn't avoid what twined between my feet and brought me crashing to earth in a fall hard enough to drive both breath and sense out of me.

Dark—it was very dark. There was some reason why I must move. That need prodded at me savagely. Now I crawled, dragging forward inches at a time. Still that need would not let me rest.

My hands, outstretched to pull me on, suddenly plunged into wetness. Liquid rippled about my wrists. Water! I craved that water more than anything I ever had in my life. I dragged on farther, to fall again, my face in the water. Then I drank and drank, as if I could never get my fill. It was so sweet and good. I must still have been drinking when I lapsed once more into darkness.

I awoke from a sleep so profound that I did not even know a stir of memory until I sat up and looked around in childish wonder.

There was no sunlight. A thought stirred—what was sun? Bright warmth should be overhead. I turned up my face to a sky that was silver-gray, through which mist arose in curls. There was no direct source of the light that I could detect.

I stirred uneasily as memory awoke. My eyes no longer hurt. Why—this was a normal, natural world in which there were no blazing shapes. I was beside a pool into which fed a miniature fall of water, from which trickled a small rill over which hung plants with tall fresh green leaves shaped like the blades of ancient swords. In the midst of each cluster of those blades, as if it were some treasure they were bared to defend, stood a stalk of darker green crowned with large white flowers, each petal tipped with a spot of silver glitter.

Farther away were bushes, each heavy with flowers, cream white or silver pale. Nowhere, as I turned my head slowly to view the hollow where I was, were there any colors save the shades of white and cream of the flowers, the silver gray of the rocks, the green of the foliage.

I cupped my hands and drank again. And I remembered everything.

Oomark? But that other world—I must somehow have returned to Dylan. Then what of the children? Were they back, too? Or were they still entrapped, over there—in there—however you might deem it. I must find them—or get help to find them.

"Oomark!"

As I got to my feet, my body was curiously light, restored. I felt no pain, no ache, no fatigue now. I was not hungry, only impatient.

"Oomark?"

Studying the disturbed moss and soil, I could see the track I had made crawling to the pool. Perhaps if I backtracked—

I had, indeed, left a well-marked trail, first through a break in the wall of flowering shrubs and then between trees. There was a strong fragrance from the flowers, and among them gently fluttered gauzy-winged creatures that were never still enough for me to be sure whether they were birds or very large insects. The trees had dark green leaves. And here and there among them were large, plate-flat flowers such as a small child might draw, a round center, each petal distinct. These were green also, but much lighter and brighter. And some had touches of blue at petal tip, while others showed a faint silvery dusting. Yet both kinds grew on the same tree.

Though I had an urgent need to hunt the children, yet I looked about me as I went, for it seemed I could see details more clearly than I ever had in my life before.

The marks I followed ended at last in a place where there were footprints instead. Seeing those, my belief that I had won free from the other world was shattered, for I read my own boot marks. And those followed and in some places overlaid earlier spoors, consisting of smaller prints overrun again by larger. The large ones were oddly shapeless, so I could not be sure what manner of creature had left them, save that they must be those of Oomark's pursuer.

So I followed that new trail. It led on, dodging among the trunks of the trees, as if Oomark had fled, intent only on out-distancing whatever followed him. My fear grew as I ran as fast as I could in the same direction.

Here the trees grew farther apart. I came out of the woods into open land, though mist limited my range of vision. When I glanced back, I could see fog closed in behind me.

Trees gave way to bushes, many of them hung with the perfumed flowers. Something swooped over my head and was gone. Some bird or flying thing must be coursing prey.

I had a growing sensation that I was under observation. Twice I stopped short and turned to look along my back trail. Though I sighted nothing moving there, yet the feeling that something had just scuttled into hiding was strong.

The trail I followed, which had been so clear to read in the muck of the woodland, was harder to discern here. I caught only a few faint impressions, and sometimes in an open patch the marks of Oomark's boots or the imprint of the shapeless foot of his hunter. Once I lost them altogether and had to circle back and forth until I found some smudged and beaten-down grass, which, I thought at first with a leap of fear, must mark Oomark's capture. Yet, to reassure me, there was beyond a boot mark.

He had made a sharp turn to the right. And I wondered if he had been trying to head back to the woods, away from the open, for there was no more cover here save grass. That was very thick and lush, brushing above my ankles as I moved.

The peculiar misty atmosphere hid the trees from which I had come. It enclosed me in a small bit of open, which moved with me, as if I were under some perambulating cover designed never to permit me to see very far. Now there pushed up through the grass, rocks, until I was among some towering as tall as trees. When I reached that point, I heard sobbing, alerting me to danger by its very hopelessness.

So warned, I crept on as softly as I could, taking care in the setting of my feet among the gravel and small stones thickly strewn among the rocks, until I came to a place where I could look down a slope.

Just within the wall of mist were those I sought. Oomark was wedged between two stones, as if he had fought his way into a very cramped pocket of safety. He was crying, though it was more a kind of bleating, a sound that might come from a human being who had been driven by fear into the escape of near-mindlessness. And he kept moving his hands feebly in a pushing motion, as if so to defend himself against some attacker.

Yet that which had hunted him was not close but rather kept a goodly distance away, pacing back and forth, as if some invisible wall stood between him and the boy. Him—it—that— I drew a breath of disbelief, but I was also sure that my eyes reported truly the form of what prowled there. Man-sized, humanoid in general shape, it was like no man nor alien I had ever seen. Its shoulders were thick and bowed, which made its too large head bob forward when it moved, rather than be held erect. Its arms were long, its legs thick, and it was covered with a mat of black hair, curly as an animal pelt. Yet it was no animal—for on and over that furry body were ragged remnants of clothing, twisted and tied together, as if, though the creature might have been far more comfortable to discard them, it clung to those as one might cling to a charm.

Now and again it stopped and turned toward Oomark, and I could hear the same unintelligible mumble it had voiced when on the chase. But Oomark did not answer, nor did he move, except to continue those pushing motions.

I wondered why the creature had not gone in and plucked the boy out of that poor refuge. Certainly its strength was infinitely more than that of the frightened child. Yet it was obvious that for some reason it could not carry through whatever purpose had led to the hunt.

And its indecision or inability gave me a chance at rescue. I shrugged the storage bag off my shoulder. Its present contents I stuffed into the front of my tunic. Then I began to search about me for stones of suitable size and weight.

SEVEN

With the weighted bag in my hand, I slipped along, using the rocks as a screen. That monstrous figure had gone back to pacing. The pacing was so ponderous and deliberate that I thought that its reactions might not be too quick. Yet one could not be sure. To undervalue your opponent may be disastrous.

I watched that prowl, judging the right moment for attack. Then I leaped, swinging the bag and bringing it down full force, aiming at the monster's head. But my improvised weapon was awkward, and the blow landed glancingly along the shoulder below.

However, it had hit hard enough to make the beast thing cry out. It reeled away and went to its knees. I passed it and reached the rocks where Oomark was. Once there, I whirled to meet any attack the thing might launch.

It was still on its knees, one paw at the shoulder I had struck. And it made a mewling sound, shaking its head. How long it would be so incapacitated I could not tell. I reached for Oomark, though he tried feebly to beat me off. Somehow I clawed him out of his crevice. He struggled, plainly too overwrought to know who I was, fighting for his freedom. I was bitten, scratched, but I held grimly, trying in the meantime to soothe him with my voiced assurances that he was no longer alone.

I do not know which form of reassurance finally reached him, or whether it was just that he was too tired to struggle longer. At last he collapsed in my hold, a limp weight. I groped for the bag with one hand, while I steadied him against me with the other.

The beast thing was still occupied with its hurt. Only, even as I dared to believe we might escape, that hairy head swung around to face us. There was little sign of nose, and the eyes were so deep-set in twin pits they could not be seen. The mouth was a slit, now well open as if the creature struggled for breath. And the fangs so revealed were such threatening armament as made my poor bag of stones a straw opposed to a laser.

"Oomark!" I tried to put command in my tone, to reach through the fear that made him captive. It was plain that I could not carry him and defend us, too. "Oomark! We must get away. Do you understand?"

I could feel the painful shuddering of the small body pressed to mine. He gasped, but he did answer me.

"Kilda?" It was as if he suddenly was aware I now stood between him and the source of his fear.

"Yes, I am Kilda!" There was no longer any time for lengthy soothing. We must be on the move before that thing fronted us again. I controlled my impatience as I added, "I have come, Oomark. But you must help me now. Can you walk if I hold your hand? I cannot carry you."

"Kilda—that thing!" His hold kept me from moving. "It'll get us!"

"Not if we go away." I kept my voice low. "I hit it, Oomark. It is hurt. But we must go before it can stop us."

The boy turned his head a little to look. And as Oomark did so, my own hand brushed the top of his head. I must have uttered a cry of surprise, for he tightened hold on me again.

However, it was no action of the beast that had startled me. It was what my hand had found on my charge's head, what I could see when I looked for them. Evenly spaced, one above each temple, Oomark had small protuberances. The lumps were too regular to be bumps gained during his flight. Nor did they seem sore, for he had not flinched when my touch crossed them.

I gave him closer study. It was true his skin was a curious gray. And along his small arms and legs, where his tunic and breeches were torn and showed skin, there was a soft fluff of fine hair growing. He was changed, changed into something far different from a small human boy!

For a moment I even forgot the hairy thing, our common enemy. But a sound louder than its heretofore mewling made me face it. The creature was on its feet, but it moved unsteadily. And I began to hope that, glancing as my blow had been, I had injured it somewhat.

It tottered a step or two in our direction. I had the cord of the bag tight in my hand, ready, and I swung it. I meant that to ready it for a blow. But the creature must have taken it as a warning. It stopped.

I saw its slit lips work and spittle in the corners of its mouth, as if it were engaged in some struggle. Then it lifted one paw and held it out, palm up and empty, in a gesture of appeal, while those writhing lips shaped two words, garbled and far from clear human speech, yet understandable.

"No—friend—"

That reaching hand went to its throat, grasping and tearing at the hairy skin there, as if it were so frustrated at its inability to make me understand that it would tear the words from its vocal cords.

After a long moment I began to move. Now it made plain, by the best way it knew, that it was opening a passage for us. How much this change in attitude could be trusted, I had no idea. However, it was true that it might have pulled Oomark from the rocks with very little effort, and it had not. I would have to take the chance—

While I so hesitated, it turned its back on us. Still holding hand to shoulder, it shuffled away. Nor did it turn to gaze in our direction again, but continued out of sight. Was this all a sham, and would it stalk us, lay some ambush among the rocks?

Staying here was no solution. I thought that, in spite of the mist, I might be able to get back to the woods, perhaps to the pool where I had awakened. Only—what would that avail me? The important thing was, I was convinced, to find Bartare and this mysterious Lady. A door opens two ways, and if one had brought us here, it should let us go again. It need only be that we find it. And the best way to do that was to discover who held the key.

"That thing is gone." Gently I took Oomark's head and turned it so that he could see for himself. "Now, while it is gone, we must go, too."

"Now—quick before it comes again!" His grip on my belt pulled me toward the open. But I had had my fill of wandering. We must go only with a goal in sight.

"Oomark, you want to get away from this place, this whole world, don't you?"

He did not raise his head to face me squarely, but shot a look at me in an odd, sidewise fashion. With a second shock I saw that his eyes were no longer a warm brown but hard and glinting gold, such as I had never seen in a human face before.

"Away from here—" he echoed. "Yes, please, Kilda! Before the thing comes back!"

"Oomark, do you still know where Bartare is?"

Another glance from those golden eyes. "I always know. She doesn't care—not any more."

"Why?"

"Because—because—" His small face screwed up in perplexity. "I guess because it doesn't matter now."

I wanted to know why it did not matter. But somehow I could not bring myself to ask. Instead, I inquired, "Can you find her now?"

He looked at me directly, with a long, searching, unchildlike stare. There was something cold, aloof, not of the Oomark that I knew in it.

Then he nodded. "Now I can. Come on!"

He grasped my hand and pulled me to the left and away from the rocks. At least, unless the creature had circled back once he was out of sight, we were heading away from where it had disappeared into the mist.

"I'm hungry," he announced a moment or so later.

His recovery from the abject terror and mindless state of a short time earlier seemed very rapid. I marveled at it a little, wondering whether it were natural or another manifestation of the change in him.

"Good enough. I have rations." I put my hand to the bulge of things I had stored in the front of my tunic.

He made a face. "Not that rubbish—real food."

"It's real enough," I assured him, "even if it is a little banged about. Let's find a place away from these stones, and we'll eat." Now that he mentioned food, I found I was also hungry.

The area of stones became stretches only of sand and gravel.

But this was the most colorful thing I had yet seen among the greens and whites, for many of the smaller pebbles were of deep, warm colors, reminding me a little of the brilliance through which we had earlier come.

Oomark released my hand and darted away, then stooped to root something out of the ground. He returned holding a fan-shaped growth that was dark purple—its fleshy leaves veined with green.

"Good!" He waved it before me, and a torn strip of his sleeve fluttered to show his arm where the growth of fine gray hair looked to be even thicker and longer than before. He carefully broke the plant in two and offered me one section, nibbling at the other with every evidence of enjoyment.

I shook my head. I was sure I could not force his half from him. But to mouth that strange thing myself I could not.

He chewed and swallowed. "But it is good!" he urged, plainly surprised at my refusal.

"You can have it. But save some room for real food." Again my hand went to my tunic front to reassure myself I carried what he needed there, though how long that small store could last, I did not know. It was probably only a matter of time before I would be driven to consume just such a thing as that Oomark now relished.

We found a resting place. I thought it safe, for we were in the open, with no cover more than a boulder waist high to me—and I could see on all sides. Oomark was willing enough to halt there.

As he sat down on the ground, he pulled at the seals of his boots. "My feet hurt. They feel as if my boots don't fit any more. I'm going to see why—"

His buoyant return to normalcy after his fright still amazed me a little. I would not have believed his recuperative powers so great, but I was thankful this was so.

As he unsealed his boots, I took out the various containers I had crammed into my tunic. And though I could really have eaten all in sight, I opened only one package, breaking the thick slab it contained into two portions. It was one of the fruit-protein cakes, giving high energy level. The taste was very good.

Yet when I picked up my portion and held it to my lips, I found its faint odor offensive. It was necessary to force myself to chew and swallow, and I took no pleasure in its taste. I remembered Oomark's earlier aversion to the choc. And I wondered if, having sampled the food or drink of this world, one was left with a strong dislike for one's natural food. Stubbornly I ate the chunk. And the longer I worked at it, the less obnoxious it became, so that the last bite or two was normal tasting.

"This is yours." I held the other half out to Oomark.

He shook his head. "Don't want it. It's spoiled or something. I can smell it's bad clear over here. You oughtn't eat a mess like that, Kilda. It might make you sick."

And he absolutely refused to sample any of the supplies I had. Since I could not feed him by force, I had to accept that he had been sufficiently satisfied by the plant he had eaten.

Perhaps later, if he found no more such and was really hungry—I slipped off my outer tunic and made a bag of it that I could attach to my belt. The storage bag must remain a weapon. The air was warm and caressing against the skin of my arms. Though I had on only an under tunic, sleeveless and low-necked, above the waist, I was not cold.

The gray light seemed to give my bared skin a new color. I was not gray as Oomark; rather my naturally brown skin was even darker and more ruddy brown. It had a gloss as if polished with oil. Yet to the touch it felt normal. I wished for a mirror, and ran my hands over my head and face in its lack, trying to guess by touch what I looked like.

The result was not instantly horrifying as it had been when I had faced that terrifying reflection in my bedroom, but it was startling enough. In the first place, my hair, which had always curled so tightly that I had trouble dressing it and so kept it cropped closer than fashion dictated, was now in straight strands. I pulled one loose—not dark brown any more, but green. Unmistakably so!

Under my touch my eyes, nose, mouth were, as far as I could guess, as always. For so much I was thankful.

"That's better!" Oomark had pulled off his boots, tossed them to one side, as if he never wanted to see them again, and stretched his legs out before him.

His feet—no! At that moment I could have screamed denial of what I saw, except that I was too frightened to utter any sound at all. They were no longer human feet. Rather the toes had grown together, so that what I looked upon was something midway between a deformed foot and a cloven hoof, while the furry hair above it was much longer and thicker.

"Oomark—" Though I shrank from doing so, I made myself reach out and touch the horny section of hoof and slide up to the fur above it. I had hoped, wildly, that this was an optical illusion, that I would feel a normal foot.

But it was not so. Oomark's hoofs, his haired legs, could be felt as well as seen—just as my green lank hair had been real when I plucked it from my scalp.

"I can walk a lot better now," he announced. Apparently the sight of hoofs did not in the least bother him. He might have expected to see such when he pulled off his boots. He kicked out his feet, as one might do when released from punishing restraint.

As I surveyed him closely from those hoofs to the top of his head, I saw something else. Those bumps on his temples were appreciably larger. They were no longer round or covered with skin. Instead, they were curved, tipped, a cream-white—they were horns!

There comes a time when one has been faced by too many shocks, and thereafter the not-to-be-believed can be accepted passively. I had somehow progressed to that point. Or else I was in such a state of shock that I found nothing abnormal. Strange, yes, but it did not add to my fear.

When we started on, I again had that feeling that we were followed. But the veil of mist was so thick that I could only make sure, by frequent glances behind, that whoever or whatever skulked there was not in close range.

Oomark did not pick up his discarded boots, but left them lying where he had thrown them. Twice more he jerked the purple plants free of the soil and munched on them, each time offering me some. I wanted none of them. The one time I took a bit to examine it more closely, I found the smell as offensive as he seemed to find the supplies. Even the touch of its leaves against my fingers made me brush them back and forth across my breeches after I had thrown it away.

"How far are we from Bartare?" I demanded when it seemed there would come no end to our journey. This country was open meadowland with thick, lush grass, not even a bush to break the open lines of it. The grass had odd peculiarities, for there were circles seemingly exact in their marking. Their rims were indicated by a taller and noticeably darker green growth. I saw that Oomark avoided stepping on any of those darker bands when he crossed them. And I followed his example, partly because inborn wariness suggested all precautions were good.

We were in the middle of one such when I asked my question. He had taken the lead. Now he glanced back over his shoulder, his horns even more evident. Also I saw his once small ears were elongated, rising to a very noticeable point at the top.

"I don't know. She is there—" He pointed ahead into the mist with confidence.

But where was "there"? He seemed to have no idea and finally became sulky when I pressed, saying that he could not tell—that he only knew she was ahead and, if we went far enough, we would find her. I eyed the mist uncertainly. Though I had no way of measuring its advance, I was quite sure that I had had a far greater range of visibility at the beginning of this journey and that the outer veil was moving in restrictingly, which was not pleasant to consider, the more so when I firmly believed we were being trailed. Suppose that drifting stuff circled about us as thickly as some fogs I had seen, so we were lost in it? Then we would be easy prey for anything.

It would be better to find some shelter and hole up until the fog lifted or cleared to the point it had held when I had come out of the woods. But before I could suggest that, Oomark moved closer. His nose, appearing larger than natural, with wide, flaring nostrils, was turned to the left, and he seemed to be testing for scent.

"Best we stay here, in a ring of the Folk," he said. "There be others abroad." Not only his appearance had changed; his speech was also odd, the choice of words different. Now his actions surprised me, for he went to his hands and knees and crept about the inner perimeter of the circle, his head close to the ground, plainly sniffing gustily as he went. When he had completed that circle, he squatted back on his hoofs.

"This is a fair place." He patted the ground on either side with his hands. "The others cannot break a ring, you know. We bide here now till outdraw comes again—"

I sat down so I could closer study his altered face, hoping that the expression there might help me.

"What others are there, Oomark?"

"The others—the Dark Ones. They and the Folk are never one. But here one of the Folk is safe, unless it is lot time and he is the sad-chosen." He shivered as might one thinking of some well-known terror.

"And who are the Folk?" I continued gently. The Oomark I had known was almost gone, lost in this alien child. I longed to somehow catch and hold fast a last poor remnant, but how I might do that, I did not know.

"The Folk? Be you mist-witted, Kilda. All know the Folk—you—me—"

"Bartare—the Lady?"

"All, yes, all." He nodded.

"And the others? Was it one such who chased you?"

I thought he looked a little puzzled. "He was not—not of the Dark Ones, nor of the Folk. He is One Between." He made of the word "between" a species name. "As you will be, Kilda, if you don't watch out!" He shot that last at me like a threat.

In fact, I glanced at my own arms and hands to be sure there was no harsh growth of hair showing on them, that I was not changing into a monster like the one I had wounded with my bag of stones. But my skin, though dark and shining, was still smooth.

"How will I become that?"

"If you do not accept, you will not be accepted." He said that solemnly. He might have been uttering a rule of law.

"Halfway you have come. But more than halfway must the journey take you. Take off your boots, put your feet to the earth—feel!"

I hesitated. Oomark had shucked his foot covering to display hoofs. If I pulled mine off, would I be fronted by a similar distortion? I tried to wriggle my toes—was sure I felt them move. But I must know! I drew off my boots.

My feet! No, I did not have hoofs, but they were not as I had always seen them either. The toes were longer, thinner. They appeared to uncoil, to show an extra joint on each as I released them. And they were far more prehensile than any human toes should be. These new, flexible ends curved down without my willing it and dug into the soil.

And throughout my body I felt a shock, as if those toes, in so sinking into the ground, had encountered therein a source of energy that flowed back through them up my legs, into my body. I jerked them free, trying to force on my boots again.

But that could not be done. The longer toes might not be accommodated therein without such crippling as would mean I could not walk. And they wriggled independently as I tried to crowd them together and fit them into those coverings, as if they had a life of their own and were determined to return to the soil.

Finally I ripped loose the inner lining of my boots, and these strips I bound around and around my feet with a vindictive tightness. I might not be dealing with my own flesh and bone, but with rebellious entities that fought me.

Once they were thus bandaged so that none of their bare surface could touch the ground, they became quiet. And I could almost believe those wrappings hid a normal human foot. I would have to go on without my boots, but the wrappings were a safeguard I dared not relinquish.

"That was not a clever thing to do, Kilda," Oomark commented. "It is better you come into the paths of the Folk, lest you be lost, for you are not of the Dark Ones—"

"I am Kilda c'Rhyn," I said defiantly. "I am not of this world! Nor are you, Oomark Zobak!"

He laughed then, and something in that laughter was not in the least childlike.

"Oh, but you are, Kilda, as am I. And there will be no denial left in you soon. None at all."

EIGHT

At that moment I wanted no argument, for there was something about Oomark now. Though he was still a small boy, in some ways he was secretive, older. I did not like those sly glances he sent in my direction now and then—gloating—satisfaction at my difficulties, a searching for a change in me?

Once more I took out food. But he would have nothing of what I offered. I ate, a much smaller portion than I wanted. But I must ration myself. These supplies could not be renewed.

It began to rain, or else the mist, which had grown thicker and thicker, condensed on our bodies. I could see no farther than the outside of the ring in which we sat. Oddly enough, the heavy moisture did not make me uncomfortable.

There was a strange sensation in my scalp, and I raised my hands to discover my hair was not plastered to my skull by the damp but stood erect, and it could not be forced flat save by keeping a hand pressed upon it. The wet on my skin and in my hair took away my thirst.

When I glanced at Oomark, I saw him licking the down on the back of his hands (for it grew there now), even up his arms, just as a cat might perform its toilet fastidiously when wet, though he did not appear uncomfortable.

Then, with a jerk, his head snapped up, and he stared over my shoulder. I pushed around to gaze in the same direction.

At first I could see only the billowing mist. Then I was aware of a darker shape that did not drift with that mist but pushed against it. Though I could not hear the slightest sound, it was padding about the circumference of the ring. Was it what had followed us?

I reached for the weighted bag. How I longed for a stunner, though a laser beamer would have been best. However, the thing, whatever it was, was never more than a dark shape.

Oomark slewed around, following it with his eyes as it moved. I wondered if he could see more of it than I did.

"What is it?"

"A Dark One."

His nostrils expanded as if to test the air, and then he added, "It cannot come within the ring. Also"—his head lifted a little higher—"there is something else out there."

At that moment I smelled enough to make me turn my head in disgust, a nauseating odor. Long decay and filth blew a puff of stench across our refuge. I must have uttered an exclamation, for I heard Oomark say, "That is the Dark One. Always do they smell so. But the other thing—"

He stood up. The dark shadow passed before him on its round. But Oomark continued to look into the mist ahead of him. A moment later he shook his head.

"It is there. I think it watches, but I do not know what it may be, save it does not stink like a Dark One."

What more he might have said was drowned out in a high, carrying sound, which made me shiver. And that clarion call or trumpet summons was answered—from so close by that I thought it might be that shadow beyond the ring wall. The answer came as a low, snarling growl.

Once more the call, surely a summons, a demand, so imperative was it. The growling followed, a protest, a sullen whine. But on the third sounding of that horn, there was no growl, rather a deep, carrying bellow, perhaps the answer demanded.

Oomark squatted down again, his arms about his knees, balling himself as if to make as small a target as possible to escape notice. I saw his shoulders shake in a series of shudders. His head rested now on his knees, so I could not see his face.

Though I searched the wall of the mist, I could no longer sight that dim shadow, nor did the stench of it linger. Off in the gray billows the horn gave another blast. Now there was no questing note in it, rather a gloating, a promise of worse to come. Before its echoes died away, there was a yapping, a noise that sent my hands in an involuntary gesture to cover my ears. I wanted to sink into the earth and pull protecting sods over me.

"What is it?" I asked Oomark in a half-whisper. He seemed to know so much of this place, and his fear was now so apparent that I thought he could set name to the nameless.

"The *hunt!* Ahhhh—" His words lapsed into a moan of pure fear. "He hunts—"

"Who?" I grasped Oomark's shoulder. He aimed a blow at me in return, as if in his present state he did not know friend from enemy. "Who? Tell me!" I shook him.

"The driver of Dark Ones." Those strange yellow eyes through which Oomark surveyed this alien world were fixed on the mist wall. His tongue licked his lips. "He calls his pack to a hunting—"

There was nothing to reassure one. Still holding to Oomark, I listened, straining to pick up any sound in the dank mist. But when the horn peeled again, it was fainter, farther off, and the hideous yapping that answered it was barely audible.

I felt Oomark relax a little. Once more he licked his lips. He sniffed the air.

"The dark hound is gone," he reported.

I knew that I must have out of Oomark all he knew or suspected about this world. To travel on blindly, not knowing from which side and at what moment danger might leap, was too great a risk. Knowledge was my hope.

"Oomark, you must tell me what you know of this world—of things such as the Dark Ones and the hunter—"

Again he looked at me cornerwise, slyly.

"Please, Oomark. If we are to go on, I must know what dangers lurk here."

He shrugged. "It is of your choosing that you do not understand for yourself. You would be of that other place, not wholly of this."

I rebelled. "I am not in the least of this place! I would return to my *own* place."

"See?" He spread out his hands in a gesture of bafflement. "You choose to be one in the middle. And the hunter of Dark Ones—

and such as he—can therefore hunt you. You ask to know— The means are before you, but you will not take them."

"Oomark!" I drew on all my store of patience. "Tell me what you can."

The boy hesitated. I thought, "If he does refuse, what means have I of forcing him to it?"

Then he said slowly, "I do not know everything, save that when something such as the hunter's horn sounds, then here"—he touched his forehead—"there comes knowledge. I know what can be eaten and drunk, what we may meet on this road, and whether it be friend or foe. But before it happens, I do not know, truly. It is only what I see or hear—"

That he spoke the truth, I did not doubt. Now before I could urge any more out of him, he raised his head a little and pointed with his chin.

"The One Between, who was by the rocks, he is here."

"What does he want?" Oomark seemed so certain, as if he could actually see the hairy creature.

"He hungers—"

My mind made a horrifying guess. Were *we* the prey the thing trailed? I tightened my hold on the bag and prepared to do my best in our defense.

Oomark touched my arm and shook his head. "Not us. His is not the way of the hunter. No, he hungers for what you carry—the food from the other place."

"Why?"

"I do not know, only that it draws him. He wants it so badly that it means the whole world to him. He can think of nothing else, only that. So I can in turn feel his great hunger in me." Oomark put his hands to his middle, rubbing himself.

But why? Why would a creature of this world want my few supplies? Not that he would get them, I told myself fiercely. I had that bundle safely under my hand, and the bag was also ready for any attack.

"Yes, that is what he wants. He will follow as long as there is strength in him. He is hurt, you know. When you struck him, he was hurt. Here." Oomark fingered his own shoulder, lightly, as if dreading to put pressure on some wound.

"Still he is very strong—" I remembered only too well the bulk of the creature, and I had no desire to face new attack.

"He is tired, and he hurts. Now he has found another ring and rests in it. But when we go on, he will follow." Oomark reported confidently, and I believed him. So it would be up to us to lose or discourage that follower.

Oddly enough, though I had been tired when settling in this ring, I had no desire to sleep. Nor, it seemed, did Oomark. Though we talked but little thereafter, we spent the passing of time (and how much time, I could not calculate) as if we were waiting for some signal. However, it was not a waiting that made me uneasy or impatient. Rather it was a languid, quiet period between two bouts of action.

We heard no more sounds. Nor did any shadows move now in the mist. Finally I became aware that the curtain was lifting, that I was able to see more. Oomark got to his feet, or rather his hoofs.

"It is the period of outgo. Let us be on our way. I am hungry."

I made as if to open the supply bag. He shook his head.

"I want real food—not that which makes one sick to smell! Come on!"

With that he gave a bound that cleared the darker green of the ring rim, his small hoofs clattering on a stretch of rock beyond. I looked at my boots. It was plain I could not put those on again. The bandaging must serve me for foot covering. And there was no reason to burden myself with useless things. So I left them lying as I moved after the boy.

The lifting of the mist came more swiftly. The ground where we had halted was level and had many rings of various sizes across it. Not too far away one of those rings was occupied. The hunched figure now getting awkwardly to its feet was that of the creature who had hunted Oomark. The tatters it wore for clothing fluttered in a breeze. It had turned its head in our direction. One arm hung by its side. But the other moved, and it extended its empty hand, palm up. I could see the mouth working as it had before when the creature tried to speak.

Again that effort was mighty, convulsive, until my fear was touched with a trace of sympathy. Even I could see it meant no harm, at least for now; it was pleading with us for that which I carried. Why would it so want the food Oomark disdained? The slit mouth worked, spatters of spittle showing in the corners. And the hand, trembling as if it were an effort to hold it so, stretched beseechingly to me.

"Come on!" Oomark had drawn ahead. He looked back impatiently. "I want food."

"Foooood—" The word was a distorted mockery of the boy's, but the creature had uttered it.

I held the supplies tight to me in the crook of my arm while I swung the weighted bag with my other hand. Yet still I hesitated. And in that moment I knew that I could not do what all good sense told me was safe. I took the thong of the stone bag between my teeth, holding it ready. Then I thrust my hand in among the supplies. Without looking, I grabbed what I first touched. It was a choc piece.

Without watching, lest I grow more generous than I dared to be, I threw that in the general direction of the creature and ran on after Oomark.

But the boy had halted, and when I caught up with him, he was scowling.

"Why did you do that?"

"Because—I was sorry for—"

"For *that?*" He laughed in a way I did not like as he pointed.

I turned, to see the creature crouched low to the ground, pulled in upon itself as Oomark had been at the sound of that dread horn. It was making no move to follow us.

"What—what is the matter?"

"You were sorry." He mocked me, his lips grinning in a smile that was not pleasant, which reminded me of—Bartare! "You were sorry. But he is sorrier now!" The boy stabbed a finger at the quiet figure.

"Why?"

"You gave him food—now look at him! It hurts and hurts and hurts. And he deserves that hurting! He is neither one thing nor the other. Maybe he'll be nothing at all shortly."

"Oomark—" I tried to catch his arm, but he eluded me, laughing hatefully. "That food—did it poison him?"

"If it did not, he'll wish that it had. You will, too, Kilda, you will, too. Look at yourself—just look!"

It was his turn to grab my arm and swing it up before my eyes in a hold tight enough to bruise.

That brown shine on my skin had increased. There was a kind of hard shell developing from my flesh. I jerked away, refusing to look.

"You cannot stop it, you know." Oomark lost some of his mockery. "Look at me!" He danced from one small hoof to the other, turning so that I could see him from every angle. His hands pulled at his tunic, loosening it. Now he threw that and his under tunic from him so he was bare to the waist. Bare—no! His small body was completely covered with a soft gray down. It was thinner on his arms and shoulders—I could see through it to his skin—but at his waist it grew longer and thicker.

"Put on your clothes!" I tried to give that order my old authority.

"No!" He kicked at one of the tunics. "No!" He stretched wide his arms and capered in a grotesque dance. "Those are hot. They scratch. I do not need them any more—ever!" He went skittering away, as if he feared I would catch and try to clothe him by force. Unlike the discarded boots, I did not leave them lying. Rather I rolled them tightly and stuffed them into the top of the stone bag.

"Come on!" He beckoned to me. But I glanced back once more at the hairy thing.

Was Oomark right? Had the food the alien begged for so piteously indeed proven poison? But if our natural food had been fatal to it, why had it—or he—wanted it so badly—dogged us, begged? And if our food was poison to a creature of this world, would it not follow that native food would be so to us? I had eaten nothing save from what I carried. But Oomark—

I put all thoughts of the stricken creature out of my mind to run after the boy, determined that this time I would not allow him to take such a risk.

But it was too late, for he stood beside a large bush or small tree planted at one end of a mound. It was heavy with golden berries, and Oomark was not the only feaster. From some of the branches hung those gauzy-winged things I had seen in the woods. And in the grass were small animals.

Neither winged things nor animals took any notice of Oomark, nor did they when I approached. They were too intent upon feeding. The berries were large, perhaps the size of my thumb, and so full of juice that they spattered widely when their skin broke.

Oomark pushed them into his mouth three and four together, so the juice trickled down his chin, dripping into the hair on his chest.

"Here." He held out a sticky hand, three of the globes on it. When I shook my head (and it took determination to do that, for they made me long to taste), he grinned. Then he shrugged and popped the refused berries into his own mouth.

I drew away, realizing I had no chance to stop him, afraid I might yield to temptation. I made special note of the mound by which that bush grew. It was odd to find it in that level land, and it gave the impression of being purposefully humped there for some forgotten reason. Also, it was only the first of a series of such that were erected in a straight line. I counted nine within the visibility limits of the mist.

Each of these had a bush or tree planted at one end. But not all of those were alike. Three were of the yellow fruit. Three bore larger spheres, which would fit into the palm of my hand, and these were a dark purple-red. At them no feasters crowded. In fact, there was something repellent about them. The leaves of the trees there were also not uniformly shaped, but irregular and of a green so dark as to be near black.

The other three trees had a much lighter foliage—a silver edge to long ribbony leaves of a very pale green. Their slender trunks and branches were not covered with rough bark, but smooth and of a silver shade also. They had no fruit, only clusters of white flowers, which swayed gently, even though there seemed to be no wind. Now and then I caught a whiff of a fragrance so sweet that I longed to run and bury my face in one of those clusters. But, like the purple fruit, they seemed to ward off touch, though I did not have the same distaste for them as I did for the dark fruit.

These trees were all planted in a pattern: first the golden berries, then the purple spheres, last the silver flowers. Then they began all over again, through the same series twice more. So I was very sure this was of a purpose. What were these mounds? Graves of rulers or priests now long forgotten? There hung about them an aura of age, of settling into the earth, which did not come only from passing years, but also from the weight of centuries. Or were these the remains of buildings, soil-encased, perhaps the last of some ancient fortress?

It would seem Oomark had had his fill, for he came away

from the bush to kneel and rub his hands in the grass, pulling up a tuft to smear the juice from his face, though his efforts at cleanliness were not too successful.

Then he turned about to face the mound and lifted both hands. Holding them palm out, he spoke, certainly not to me, nor to the hopping and flying things still feeding.

"My thanks, Sleeper, for the bounty of the table, the richness of the feast."

The words had the ring of ritual, a form of invoking the invisible. Once said, he did not linger, but came to me as one prepared for brisk action.

"Who is the Sleeper?"

Oomark looked puzzled and glanced back to the mound. "I don't know."

"But you said—"

"I said that because it is right and fitting. Don't be asking, asking, asking all the time, Kilda! If you would eat, you would know—you wouldn't have to ask!"

"I would know if I ate. Is that how you know, Oomark?"

"I guess so. Anyway, I know you thank the Sleeper after you eat here. The Folk always have."

He started away on a course that paralleled the first of the mounds, passing the purple fruit, coming to the silver flowers.

"What about these?" I still tried to add to my store of knowledge. "There are more fruit—"

"No!" He averted his gaze from the purple spheres. "You eat those—you die. Not all the Sleepers have kind thoughts for the Folk. You don't eat these, and you don't *touch* those!" He pointed to the flowers.

"Are they so deadly then?"

Again he seemed puzzled. "No—not in the same way. It is—they might serve the Folk if they could, but it is not in them to do so." His frown of puzzlement grew deeper. "I really don't know, Kilda. The fruit is bad because the Sleeper there hates us. But the flowers—they are not enough like the Folk to be touched."

Three grades of Sleepers, I deduced—those offering the berries for refreshment, those dangerous and evil, and those too unlike the inhabitants to make contact. Or was I being fanciful now and reading too much into what I had seen and Oomark's words?

As we passed the mound with the silver tree, its clusters of flowers and the long banner-like leaves began to ripple. A wind of high force might have been tearing at them. Yet the trees at the flanking mounds showed no such troubling. Finally that tearing snapped a small branch heavily weighted with a ball of flowers. It did not fall to the ground, but rather whirled over and over through the air until it was thrust as one might thrust the pointed head of a spear, the splintered end down, into the ground at my feet.

Oomark cried out and backed away. On impulse I stooped and caught at the branch under the nodding flower cluster. It was like grasping a rod of ice, so cold was the sting from it that ran up my arm. Yet I could not let it go. Instead I pulled it from the grip of the soil.

The gale that had broken it free from its parent tree and brought it to me had ceased as if it had never blown. And—my fingers—!

The brown, hard crust over them was cracking, flaking away like a dusty powder. The flesh so uncovered was still brown, but it was the skin I had always known. Though my hand was still cold, I had no desire to throw the branch from me. Instead, I made it fast to my belt.

Oomark retreated again. "Throw it away—back to where it came from!" He gestured to the now quiet tree. "It will hurt you!"

I flexed my fingers and saw with awe and gratitude the normal flesh. "Such hurt I will take gladly. See, Oomark, my hand is now as it always was!"

He cried out and ran from me as he had fled from the hairy creature. I might now have been a horror, hunting him.

NINE

✦

He easily eluded me and sprinted away, paying no attention to first my commands and then my pleas. Rather, he sped as if with a definite refuge in mind. I was seized by the idea that his desertion could cut two ways: not only would I lose the child for whom I was responsible, but I myself would be lost without a guide as well.

Somehow I managed to keep sight of him, passing the last of the mounds. Beyond were more earthworks. Only they were not as sharply defined as the mounds, being more rolling.

Oomark did not avoid these, but ran into the midst of them. Well grown with grass, they raised on either side, now hiding him. I speculated, even as I ran, as to whether I was now in what might have been the last remnants of a great city. If so, very little remained to mark its walls and buildings.

Here and there, sometimes growing in small thickets, were stunted trees bearing the evil purple fruit—although that was shriveled-looking. Much of the harvest had fallen and lay rotting in the grass, a stench rising from it to plague the nostrils.

In fact, as more and more of such trees came into view, I found myself choking and coughing, having to slacken speed. Now I had lost sight of Oomark, who had gone beyond the barrier of the mist.

I started to run again, as fast as I could, calling out his name.

Only the echoes of that, distorted as if mouthed back to me by lips never intended to utter human speech, came to my ears. Then I heard a flapping sound, a croaking, and I looked to the left.

There stood several of the fruit trees. In them, under them, waddled, perched, and fed some feathered creatures. Or at first I thought them feathered until I saw better. They had the clawed, scaled feet of some domestic fowl. But supported on those were yellow bodies ending in long, supple tails. Necks, not so long but as limber, ended in pointed heads crested by four horns or growths of white, giving the creatures the appearance of wearing a small crown. The eyes were red and seemed to glow. Sharply pointed wings were feathered with broad yellow quills. And the creatures were ill-tempered, lashing at one another with those tails, threatening with beak and claw as they fought over the rotting fruit.

Though they were not large, there was a malevolence about them that promised ill for one attracting their attention. I stopped calling abruptly, hurried by, watching them carefully even after I passed, since I had an uneasy feeling they were only pretending to be so engrossed in feeding and were ready to trail me.

It must have been during those moments when I was intent upon the flying things that I lost my last hope of catching up with Oomark. Only a short distance beyond I faced a split into three of the ways I had followed. It was impossible to see any track on this thick turf to tell me which I should take.

Both the mist and the height of the barrows and mounds limited my sight. And, in addition, two of the ways, the one ahead and the one to the left, curved a little beyond, hiding their direction. Perhaps that made me decide upon the right fork, which seemed to run straighter.

Only, as I continued, those piles of turfed debris, or whatever the mounds might be, grew taller, until they were well above the level of my head. And the road did make a curve. I paused to listen now and then, hoping to pick up some sound to assure me that my choice had been right. It was during one such pause that I sighted a scraped place where the turf had been torn off a stone—a trace that someone, or thing, *had* passed that way.

It caught my eye because the stone under it glowed so that it was noticeable even in this half-light that was dusk among the mounds. I approached, hoping to find a footprint, and the glow deepened into a silvery radiance.

But it was only a scuff mark, having nothing to tell me, save that it was new done, and I wanted to believe Oomark had left it.

Having taken the first curve, I saw that my road became a baffling twist of in and out ways between towering mounds, much of it shadowed murkily. I began to fear that I had no hope of ever finding one who wished to remain hidden here. The way branched again, and again it was a root from which innumerable small rootlets sprang. Then it, too, narrowed and grew less.

I halted. The mounds that walled me in were perhaps twice my height, and the dusk in which I stood was almost as great as the danger period of indrawn mist. I did not like what I saw ahead—better go back to the original branch and take one of the other ways. It would perhaps not put me on the boy's track—I could not hope for such good fortune—but it might take me out of this haunted place.

Haunted it was—I would have sworn to that. I was sure that things flitted just beyond my range of sight or lurked spying on me. Sometimes I heard a ghostly, far-off twittering, like the rustle of breeze through dried leaves, which made me think of alien voices whispering. Also, though nowhere else in this world had I been conscious of a change of temperature, here there was a rising warmth. Only it carried no comfort with it. Rather it made me feel that I walked a thin skin of safety over consuming fires.

I licked my lips and thought of water. My feet moved almost of themselves, scuffing the earth, those long, thin toes writhing within the bandages, as if to free themselves and dig in, seeking the energy that had so frightened me when I had first taken off my boots.

But when I turned to retrace my way, I discovered the full extent of my folly. All the winding ways looked alike, and I could not be sure which had brought me here or even of the general direction from which I had come. I felt trapped, and with that realization came panic, shattering my control. I ran along the nearest path and, when it split, went right, and when it split again, left, my heart pounding, my mouth dry with fear, my wits so overborne that I would have been easy prey in that moment. That I was in a place inimical to my form of life, I no longer doubted, just as I did not doubt that I was watched, with a dreadful sniggering anticipation such as I could not put name to, nor imagine form for.

The hardest thing I have ever done in my life was to make myself halt, gasping for breath, really look ahead, and force my brain to override emotion. It was true all ways looked alike, but I fiercely battled panic. I could not keep my feet still. They pounded and dug at the soil, as if they had a life of their own and were no longer under my command. And the desire to tear off the wrappings I had adjusted with such care, to feel the soil, was such an agony that I do not know how I held out.

Then a whiff of scent reached me, and I remembered the branch in my belt. Though it had been some time since I had picked it up, yet there was no wilting of leaves or blossoms. It might have been freshly broken from the tree. I touched its stem, and from that contact spread a feeling of clean cold—nowise else can I describe that sensation. Just as the heat generated by the land about me bore with it a sensation of filth and long decay, this cold was a knife to cleave to sanity and straight thinking.

On impulse I took the branch from my belt, and I leaned over, to sweep it lightly over my tormented feet. Though the bandages kept it from touching my flesh, the toes stopped writhing. They no longer dug into the soil. So it was that when I went on, I carried it, fastening my food package to my belt in its place. In my other hand I still swung the weighted bag.

What I fronted as I rounded the end of the next mound was nothing that a stone-heavy bag could menace. For a single instant, a very short one, I thought that I had caught up with Oomark. Then I knew that the thing fronting me was not Oomark, even in transformation.

It was much larger, a little taller than I, and with a lot more bulk. The likeness to Oomark was in general form, for it balanced on two hoofed feet. And since it wore no clothing, the hairy growth on its flanks was free to hang in rough tangles, matted with clots of mud and sticky masses. Hoofed as it was, it was also a biped and walked erect. There were unmistakable hands on the ends of its forelimbs. And with those it scratched busily in the hair of its flanks. Its head was long and narrow. Perhaps once it had been more humanoid, but now it was like some grotesque mask, for the nose was broad and there was very little chin beneath its loose and working lips.

Since it slavered a little, a thread of moisture pended from its mouth and wet the tuft of beard waggling on its chin. Above the very large eyes, horns, much larger and more curved than those Oomark had grown, spread up and back. The skin of its face was yellow-brown. And from its body arose such a stench as made me sick. It regarded me unblinkingly, and—what was worse—it regarded me with manifest intelligence and malignant purpose.

I backed away. The thing continued to scratch and stare. Then it advanced, stumping along as if it had no need to hurry, as if the outcome of any contest was already decided in its favor. And I knew that it was enjoying my fear and disgust.

I dared not turn my back on it to run. I had a feeling that I must face it squarely and that as long as I could do that, I had some small advantage on my side. It was purposely using the effect it had on me to break my nerve. So I sidled along, swinging the weighted bag in my hand, though that was a pitiful weapon to use against this.

It watched me with a contemptuous satisfaction through strange eyes. They had no dark core or pupil, and they were a full red, like those of the flying things I had earlier passed. As I crept back and it stumped forward, we came into the darker shadow of the mound, and those eyes suddenly blazed with fire, like twin torches in the murk.

Seen so, there was no impression of blindness about them. Though they appeared as opaque ovals of fire, yet it was plain they were still organs of sight.

I continued to back away, just as it relentlessly followed, though it made no move to attack. Then my shoulders struck against one of those turfed rises, and I staggered, struggling to keep my feet. I tried to slip along, one shoulder braced against the mound, with the very small comfort of knowing that side of me protected.

The creature lifted its horned and ill-shaped head and gave voice to a series of grunts. And to my shuddering horror, those were answered from my right, as if another such monster were only waiting there for me to reach it. I stopped, afraid to turn my gaze from those blazing eyes to look.

Once more my adversary grunted and this time was answered by a squawking as two of those flying things I had seen guzzling the fruit flapped down. The thing threw out an arm, and one of the flyers used that as a perch. The other kept to the air, soaring and dipping, its supple neck twisting as if there were no bones in that length, thrusting its head first toward the monster and then leveling, with the neck in a straight line, as if about to aim itself at me.

But that was not the end of the company gathering to hold me at bay. There came a thudding, the pounding of something running, and a black shadow pushed up beside the horned one. It was very large, its spine ridge equal in height to the first one's shoulder, and it went four-footed. A tail as thin as skin stretched over bones (as might well be, for it was not smooth but knobbed at regular intervals) swung at its haunches. And its head was but a skull covered with skin, with no flesh underneath for padding. It had great dark pits for eyes, and deep in those I could see a flicker of the same fire as in the horned one's. Jaws gaped wide, taking up two-thirds of its head, set with a double row of fangs that were phosphorescent. A great black tongue showed between them. It had small ears set very close to its skull, and in contrast to the hairiness of the horned one, its skin, so tight in places, but sagging in disgusting wrinkles about its bloated paunch, carried no fur at all.

It squatted down on its hindquarters, flanking the horned one. I knew that I could not turn my back on this company, nor even look away from them long enough to see what might lie ahead if I continued to slip along the wall of the mound. To retreat was impossible, nor did I have even the faintest hope of victory if they rushed to bring me down.

What followed was so total a surprise that I jerked back against my support of earth and again nearly overset myself. I heard words, though they meant nothing to me.

"Skark, Skark! Shuck, Shuck!"

The four-footed thing leaped, whirled, and planted its forefeet against the mound opposite me. Its skull-head went back, and from its open jaws came such a sound as might make all hearers shudder.

The horned one also faced in that direction, tilting back its monstrous head to see aloft the better. At the same time it gave a toss to set the winged thing off its perch on the arm into the air, as if signaling it to search out the source of that call.

The hoarse voice was continuing. "Skark, Skark! Shuck, Shuck!"

I was so startled that it took me almost too long to realize their attention was caught by that call and that now I had a slim chance for escape. I reversed my way and pushed along the side of the mound in the opposite direction to the sound that had warned me. There one of the side paths opened, and into this I slipped, then ran on, keeping some watch on my back trail.

The continued sound of those words, called over and over, drowned out now and then by the baying of the four-footed enemy, somehow reassured me. Could I believe that someone— something—in this maze of horrors had deliberately intervened to save me? Oomark? Yet that voice had not been his. It was deeper, hoarser, no child's cry.

"Skark—Shuck—"

Now that I was away from the immediate vicinity of it, I could not be sure of the direction, save that it was behind. The words echoed among the mounds, now sounding so loudly that I feared some ill chance had brought me circling back to the spot, now so faintly that I could hardly distinguish the separate words, encouraging me to believe I was well away from danger, though I would not allow myself to rely on that.

If I could only get free of the mounds! I stared about me, hoping against very faint hope that I could see something that would suggest I was retracing my original path. However, each way was so like the other that they told me nothing.

A whiff of evil smell was my first guide. I was sure that that was what I had scented at the fruited trees, and it came from a new trail to my left. Since I had no other guide, I might as well surrender to that of my nose.

The stench grew stronger, and I came out at last, not by the trees where I had seen the winged ones eating, but rather at an open space in which there were far more of these growing. They marked each side of an open corridor or road that led to a pool or small lake that was triangular in shape, too even not to be artificial.

Seeing that water, I thirsted, but it was not for me. Water into which fell the fruit of such trees, for I could see the rotted spheres floating in it, would not be fit to drink. So I turned along the narrow space between the mounds that ringed this area and the tree grove. Soon the trunks and branches made a thick wall between me and the water. The faint echo of the calling had ceased, urging me to a tired trot. If the things had been released from whatever hold the voice had on them, they might be already sniffing out my trail.

It was while I was pushing to my greatest efforts that I came across a trail. Surely those hoof slots in the earth had been made by feet much smaller than those of the nightmare creature and were more like those Oomark would leave. Heartened by that belief, I turned to follow them. But I kept ever on the outlook, listening for hunters. I heard a distant baying, though not such a cry as the one the four-footed thing had given in answer to the call from the mound top. This sound held a note of ghastly triumph, as if it were close to the kill in some chase. I gasped and tried to run faster, wanting to reach the open.

Chance, or perhaps something else, played in my favor, for I stumbled past a mound to see open grassland ahead. Not only that, but again those small hoof marks were deep printed in a patch of uncovered soil. I knew, or thought I did, that Oomark had come this way.

I burst into top speed, putting the sinister collection of mounds behind me, though I feared at any moment to hear, too close, that baying on my trail. When it did not come, I wondered what it had been hunting. The why and wherefore of that opportune intervention I could not guess.

What had moved to my rescue back there? The thought of that shaggy creature who had begged for food and dogged our way suddenly occurred to me. Perhaps it was so intent upon getting its hand paws on the supplies I carried that it would save me from its fellows in order to gain all the loot for itself. That idea was enough to add more speed to my pace.

How long I had wandered in the mound maze, I had no way of telling. In fact, as I considered it now, time within this alien world did not appear to be measured in any way I understood, though it might be that those periods when the mist closed in and those when it withdrew might parallel the night and day of more normal existence. If so, I would have to face, sooner or later, another indraw time. And past experience warned me of the advisability of finding one of those rings of refuge that Oomark had shown me. But though I searched the ground in every direction as I ran, there were no telltale rises of darker green.

The need for water and for food gripped me. I began to feel

such fatigue as I had not known since my too limber toes had drawn sustenance from the ground itself. The bindings around my feet were wearing and loosening. Very soon I would have to improvise substitutes. I had seen no more tracks and had no idea whether I was still following Oomark or not. All in all, my case was a hard one, and I could not keep on going much longer.

It was one of the foot wrappings that settled the matter at last. It flapped loose, caught between my ankles, and sent me sprawling. I lay, jarred by that fall, and then pushed up—to see I must rebind my feet, sacrificing more of my tunic to the business.

I was also certain, as I looked about me, that the mist was closer than it had been when I broke from the mounds. Soon it would shut down completely.

The branch! It had been in my hand when I had fallen. I looked for it quickly. The long stem was snapped in two. But the unfaded leaves and the unwithered flowers were all right. And the grass under my touch was moist, as if the mist was a gentle rain for my refreshment. I laid the branch on the turf and brought out my supplies. So little! It was only the fact I had packed generously when we had left, thinking to share some of the sweets with Oomark and his friends, that gave me as much as I had. I mouthed a single wafer. It was a torment instead of an alleviation of my hunger, making me so avid for the rest that I had to bundle it away in a hurry, lest temptation utterly overwhelm caution.

Making that bite last as long as I could, I unwound the raveled and worn coverings on my feet. I had tried to place my feet on the bag of stone so that they would not touch the ground. But again I had no control over them. Before I could reach for the flowered branch, they wriggled to the turf.

I could not free them then. The toes had turned down, digging into the soil in a way that nailed me fast. I fought fiercely, tearing painfully at my own flesh. Then I was overcome by my body, for once more that energy spread up from my toes. Such a feeling of well-being followed that I surrendered weakly.

But only for a time did I cease the struggle. Perhaps I was able to use my returning strength to good purpose. I picked up the branch, holding it against me breast high, bending my head over it. When I did that, my mind seemed to clear, and I could feel again the resolution that would not yield. To allow my body to command would, some instinct told me, mean the end of me, Kilda c'Rhyn, as I was and had been. And that I would not allow.

So bolstered, I was able to touch my feet with the flowers, then drag my toes from the ground and rest them on the bag of stones. But it frightened me to see, as I rubbed away the sticky earth, that my toes were very dark and even longer and thinner than they had been the last time I looked at them. I hated to touch them, as if they belonged to someone who had contracted a loathsome disease.

I tore at my tunic, a hard task without cutting tools. In the end, I achieved two doubled layers of cloth. Between those I laid, smoothed and flattened, pieces of coverings of the food concentrates, doing all I could to toughen the improvised foot coverings. These I bound on with the greatest care, fearing lest they might come loose and I find myself barefooted on the ground. When they were fastened with the last knots, I tested them gingerly by setting my right foot on the soil. The toes remained quiescent. It would seem I had successfully isolated them.

But all this had taken time, and though I was stronger than when I had fallen, the mist was well closed in. I was averse to wandering blindly through it. I listened, but I could hear nothing. However, the lack of sound was in no way reassuring. And my imagination was very quick to supply me with disturbing suggestions—I could perhaps be visible to the normal inhabitants of this world and might at this moment be the focal point for some stalk.

I curled myself together, the branch once more resting on my knees, where the perfume from it soothed my overwrought nerves. The supply bag was fastened to my belt, my weapon under my hand. I waited, though for what—save disaster—I could not have told.

TEN

✳

I did not sleep. In fact, I was aware that I had not felt sleepy
for some time now—a tiring of the body, yes, but no desire
to sleep. But I could not move until the mist lifted, so I had
only thoughts to occupy me. I had some small tatter of memory
nagging deep in me—perhaps something I had learned in Lazk
Volk's storehouse of knowledge.

Lazk Volk—my past on Chalox now appeared so remote that
I might have been looking down a long, long corridor to a half-
open doorway at the far end. But somehow, remembering him
brought my thoughts more into focus. I tried to imagine I was
sitting before him, about to report on some study tape, marshal-
ing my words into order, ready to make my points of weight
and value.

What were the facts I had discovered? Oomark's aversion to the
food I carried, his change, his fear of the flowering branch.

But—I had begun to change also, though I had not eaten as
he did. How? Why? I carefully traced memory. I had drunk!
On my awakening here I had drunk at the pool. Therefore, I
had taken into my body some of the natural products of this
world. Then why did the flowering branch bring my skin back
to normal? And what of my hair? I tugged loose at least two of
my hairs to look.

They were not as green as they had been, I was sure. And

some of their curl had returned. The flowers had done that. Was that why Oomark feared them? Did he know they would halt his alteration, perhaps return him to his old self? But he should want that! I shook my head and recalled the old cry from Volk's computer—"Not enough data."

There was no use speculating over Oomark. I had better confine myself to what I thought, felt, and knew for myself. I could well believe that eating and drinking here resulted in bodily change. The hairy creature—if my premise was correct, then he—it—she—might once have been human! That would explain (somehow I thought of the stranger as male) his frantic attempts to get off-world food, in the hope it would aid him to change back. But the flowers worked for me—why not for him? Perhaps he had reached an alteration state that prevented their use. I could guess and guess and guess, but I could not be sure of the truth.

I started, my head up, my ears straining to hear. There was something moving in the mist. I watched that faint shadow. Too well I remembered that which had prowled around the ring when Oomark and I had refuged there and what I had encountered among the mounds.

A shape, dark, coming straight toward me! I arose, the weighted bag ready. To run blindly through the mist was useless. It was better to face danger as best I could, but I had little hope if what came for me was of the caliber I had met.

The figure came on slowly, lurching in its walk as if hurt or maimed. Then I could see it as clearly as this stage of the fog allowed. The hairy thing! I swung the bag in warning, and he halted.

There was a torn bandage about his chest that might cover a wound. But—he was changed! At least I did not remember him so manlike. His head was more erect, his shoulders less hunched. Nor did his hair covering appear so dense.

"Friend—" The word was distinct, as audible as if Oomark or Bartare had uttered it. Once more he showed me both hands empty in a gesture of goodwill. Dare I trust him? If I could find partnership, have a guide through this nightmare countryside, then I could better reach the children, perhaps force a return to the normal world.

"Who are you?" I demanded.

He hesitated, as if not knowing whether to approach, and then shambled on a few steps. I saw that those rags he had twisted about his body bore a dark stain in one place, and I added, almost involuntarily, "You are hurt!"

He cupped one hand over his bandaged wound. "Shuck has fangs." His voice held a tired note.

"Shuck—Skark." I echoed the cries that had drawn the attention of the monsters, allowing my escape. "Did you call so from the mound crest?"

"They must answer to their rightful names. It is the law." He gave me an oblique answer. "That is why they guard their names so well, that they may not be bound by the naming of them."

Perhaps that would have made sense had I known as much as he. But at least this creature must have saved me from what prowled the mounds. So I could not believe, as he stood thus before me, that he meant me any harm.

"What do you want?" Perhaps that sounded cold and hard. Yet I was not ready to welcome so strange a fellow traveler.

"You have—food." He licked his lips.

"Very little now," I was quick to answer. "And why do you want it? There seems to be plenty here."

"If you eat that, you become part of this world," he said slowly. "You can then have no hope of going back."

"*Is* there a way back?" I seized upon that eagerly. "Where?"

"*They* know, the Great Ones of the Folk. And there are ways they can be tricked into telling. But that I learned too late. I was then—like this. I was tied here. But if you eat true food, then you have a chance of breaking their spells. He pointed to the flowering branch. "You could not handle that if you were one of them. They fear the notus because it counteracts their power." He staggered, as if he could no longer keep his feet, and went down, his arms outflung to reach to me and what I carried.

Prudence warned me to leave him alone. But in that moment sympathy outargued prudence. I knelt beside him, tugging at his heavy shoulder until I was able to roll him over on his back. His eyes were closed, and he breathed shallowly. The stain on the bandage was dry, so I did not try to shift it to examine the wound beneath, lest I do more mischief than good.

This time I was close enough to see those few rags of clothing were remnants of ordinary fabric, and one scrap had insignia worked upon it. I knew that mark. This scarcely human creature wore a Survey badge!

Survey! To touch that link with the past was a prod into action, strengthening my determination to stand against the menaces of this land. It was a link, indeed, with sane and normal living, though it would appear he who wore it had had little luck in remaining himself.

He stirred, and his deeply sunken eyes opened. I was not even sure he could understand me, but I must know.

"You are Survey—who?" And I think I would have shaken it out of him had he not answered slowly.

"Jorth Kosgro, First-In Scout, Twenty-fifth Division, Argol Sector—"

Only one thing meant much to me now—Argol Sector. If he had operated out of there, he could have come to Dylan. But why? Dylan had been on star maps now for more than a hundred years. And the scouts penetrated far out into the unknown. Unless he had been sent here for some administrative reason, he was very far from where he should be.

"I came from Dylan. How did you reach here?" If he could answer that, perhaps I would have some clue for our return. His talk of those among the Folk who might be tricked into revealing a way did not mean much. I wanted solid facts.

"Jorth Kosgro, First-In Scout, Twenty-fifth Division, Argol Sector—" His mechanical repetition was exasperating.

I leaned closer. "Jorth Kosgro!"

He stared back up at me, and I had the feeling he did not see me at all. Frustrated, I sat back on my heels. Perhaps it was the effects of his wound, or perhaps he was so changed that his memory of the past was clouded. I wished I had water—perhaps that flung in his face might—

But what had he said? He wanted the food I carried. I opened my supply bag. I had three blocks of choc left and the rest of the package of wafers. And something else—a tube of dewberry jam meant to be squeezed out on the wafers, and one of a meat extract for the same purpose. I chose the meat now as the most sustaining.

Yet I hesitated for a moment before loosing its cap. The supplies were so limited. I would have to take care, or I could not keep normal or help the children. The children—they were my first duty. On the other hand, this stranger knew the dangers here. He had already saved me once, and he might provide our way out. I gave myself such reasons, but among them was also the fact that I could not turn my back upon one who had come to me so, who was basically of my own kind.

I slipped my arm under his shaggy head, lifted him up a little so he rested against my shoulder, and put the end of the tube between his half-open lips, squeezing the soft paste into his mouth. I did not give him much, knowing that it had to be guarded.

I saw him swallow, though that seemed to be a difficult and painful process. Then he moved as one striving to sit up, and I steadied him. He leaned so far forward that I thought him about to fall on his face, but he was holding his middle and his mouth twisted in pain.

"No—matter—" He got out the words in gusty breaths, fighting for control over what racked him. "It will be better—soon."

But the moments he fought that battle seemed very long to me. Finally he straightened up. There was the glisten of sweat in his facial hair; he brought up one hand to smear it away from his eyes.

Then he looked to the food, and I put out my hand quickly to cover it. He could have so much, but no more.

"You are right." His voice was firmer. "It must not be wasted." Then, turning his head with visible effort, he pointed to the branch.

"Let me—the notus—" Once more his voice was hesitant, and he regarded the flowers almost apprehensively.

What he wanted, I could not tell, save that I knew the change they had wrought in me. Perhaps he hoped for the same result. I bent my head to their scent as I handed them to him.

Only he turned his head away sharply, as if the perfume I found so stimulating was to him a foul stench or acrid fumes.

I could see the great effort he made, forcing himself to hold his head steady, to lean toward the branch and breathe deeply. He gasped, choked, as he expelled that quickly. His hands came up slowly, so I was minded of a man putting out his fingers to grasp a searing coal, nerving himself to the task because some will or duty demanded.

And he took the branch and held it, though he writhed and twisted as if under torture.

"I can—no—longer—" There was a dark bead of blood on his lip where his teeth must have cut flesh. He tossed the branch from him and sat, his shoulders slumped, his whole attitude so desolate that I was moved to ask, "What was it that you hoped?"

"I have gone too far— After I lost my rations, it was eat of their food or starve, though I would not surrender all my will ever!" He sat staring down at his own body, as if he both loathed and feared what he saw. Then he might have faced some fact squarely and won out, for his head came up again and he looked to me, ready to face what lay here and now.

"One does not go forward by looking back." That might have been a quotation. "And to us now the going forward must matter. Are you old Terran stock?" The change in subject surprised me.

Then I laughed because it was a foolish question. "Who is nowadays, when even where Terra lies is in dispute? My father was of the scouts. He made a planet marriage on Chalox, of which I am issue. How do I know how many hundreds of generations back now Terra lies?"

"Terra unknown? But that is impossible! Why, I have on my ship Terran tapes. I am only fourth generation from First Ship on Nordens."

It was my turn to stare. I had never met, even among all those far rovers who drifted in and out of Lazk Volk's quarters, anyone who had any real contact with Terra. For generations it had been a legend. There were stories it had been destroyed in some galactic war. Those I knew were either a mixture of cross-planetary strains like myself, or could and did, with undue pride, trace their families back to a First Ship. But that ship, in turn, had lifted from one of the crowded inner worlds, not from Terra.

"I have never met anyone who had contact in any way with Terra." I wondered if he were telling me the truth or trying to impress me for some reason.

"It does not matter. What does is that Terra has very ancient legends of a place such as this—" His hand indicated what lay about us. "But then it was a part of Terra."

Now I knew he must be insane, so tormented by his stay here that he babbled nonsense. "This is Dylan!" I retorted. Only of that I could not be sure. It was certainly not the Dylan I had known.

He who called himself Jorth Kosgro shook his head. "You say you came here from Dylan. I know that I came from an unknown planet where I set down my ship. And Terra has legends. The tapes are in my ship now, concerning all this. They tell of a People of the Hills who lived underground and tried to entice mortal men to visit them. If you ate or drank of their food and drink, you were bound to them. Skark—they had legends of him, too. I have even seen on tridee a very ancient statue of his like. And Shuck—he was said to roam parts of Terra at night, bringing misfortune or death to all who sighted him. All the people had strange powers of mind, so they did things that seemed impossible to mankind. Even the rings of safety, those were sometimes seen on Terran ground. And it was considered ill fortune to step within them, doubly so in any way to destroy them."

His words carried conviction. At least it was evident he believed what he told me. But this could not be Terra—it could not! And I said so.

"Perhaps not Terra, but something else. It may be in another space-time existence, a world that does not obey the laws of matter as we know them—but that at intervals is able to touch one of our planets so there is communication between them for a space. All the legends of Terra were very, very old. And it was true they belonged to an early time when that planet was thinly populated and mankind were few. Such crossings back and forth were far in the past. So it might be that the tie with this world had been severed in some manner and this, or Terra, moved into a new position. Thus when a gate was then opened, it was upon a new world."

"But why do they want to cross, to bring us here?" Things were beginning to make better sense to me. "Bartare— She wanted to come here—she was guided in a way. But why would they want her?"

"Bartare, who is she?"

Keeping my tale as brief as I could, I told him why I had come and how, and that I must find the children.

"A changeling," he said. "It is another tale of the People of the Hills, that for some reason they needed new blood at intervals and must draw upon mankind for recruits. They either enticed adults or tricked them into entering their domain, or they exchanged children with humankind when they were very young, though the latter story might have covered some other activity. It is plain your Bartare knew well what she was hunting, and she found it here. And—if she is of their blood for sure—" He shook his head. "I do not think you will get her to return willingly."

"Willing or not, she must go back," I said with a determination I secretly wondered I could continue to hold.

"I wonder—" he began, and when he did not continue, I prompted him.

"You have some idea as to where I may find her?"

"Perhaps. Her calling would be the work of a Great One. You would have to go to one of their cities to find out. And since those have their safeguards, those you sought would be warned of your coming. Do not underrate them, Kilda c'Rhyn, for while our kind depend upon machines and the works of men's brains to do their bidding, they have that which is totally alien to our way of thought and our powers, yet it is the more mighty here."

"But you can show me—take me there?" I brushed aside his warning.

"If you wish. It would seem there is little choice in the matter."

What more he might have said was lost, for we heard then, afar off, the horn that had frightened Oomark and me. And this time we had no ring to bring us safety. My companion moved with more speed than I thought he had left. He was on his feet, facing the mist curtain; his two wide and flat nostrils puffed in and out, as if he would use the sense of smell to locate menace.

First he turned in the direction of that sound. And this time I could not deceive myself—it was closer. Then he looked to the right and once more sniffed.

"There lies running water—" He pointed as if he could see it. "If we can reach that, we have a chance."

Why water meant safety, I did not understand. But I must trust one who knew more of this world than I did. So I fastened the supply bag to my belt and caught up the branch and my bag of stones.

He pointed to the branch. "That can slow them. Do you, every time I say 'Now,' turn and brush it across the ground where we have passed. The hounds will be baffled for a space."

Thus we started on, curtained in the fog. Every time he said "Now!" I turned and swept the ground behind. We could hear the horn calling at intervals, and a yapping answered it. Sometimes it sounded nearer, and then my heart pounded and I felt the cold of fear rise in me. Then, mercifully, it would fade again, though whether that could be some peculiarity of the fog, I did not know. What I did see was that my branch, which had resisted such long handling and usage, being apart from the parent tree, was beginning to fray and lose blossoms. So I feared it would be gone soon. I said as much to Kosgro, but the only comfort he gave me was the hope we could find another of the silvery trees—since they were not rare.

"We are close now—hear?"

Hear I could the gurgle of water. Under our feet was bare gray ground in which white stones glowed dimly. Kosgro went down on one knee to grub out several of these, cupping them in his hands. To my surprise he examined them with care, as if we had all the time in the world to play some childish game. When he had selected nine of them, he waved me on. We slid down a bank, and there was the stream, which was not only a swift-running one, but also one with murky water. I had no liking to wade out into that.

"Here." He took the stones one by one, spat on each, and mumbled something in so low a voice that I could not hear. As each was so treated, he threw it into the water, first near the shore, then each a little beyond, as if he could so make a bridge. When I was about to demand an explanation, I was shocked into silence.

Could I really believe the evidence supplied by my staring eyes? Out of the rippling water, on the very spot where each of those small stones had plopped out of sight, there arose a white block, offering a series of stepping-stones. But it must be all illusion.

"On!" He still held three stones, but with his other hand he gave me a shove to emphasize his order. It was plain he was willing to trust the blocks. I might have rebelled, only the horn sounded—far too close.

So I crossed to the nearest, sure I would not step on any firm surface but plunge into water. Only there *was* solid footing under my bandaged feet. Thus heartened, I tried the next and the next. I could not see through the mist to the other bank of the river, nor did I know how wide was the expanse so bridged.

I came to the sixth stone—and still water ran before me. Kosgro crowded up beside me and studied for a while before he threw the seventh stone. Then he said, "Wait here, until I can be sure how close we are to the far bank."

He leaped to the seventh stone, and from there he threw the eighth. He was in the fringe of the fog now, and I could not see him clearly. I waited, shivering as the spray from the water being driven against the block on which I stood wet my feet and legs.

"—on—" His call was muffled, but I thought he wanted me to come. So I went to the seventh, the eighth, and finally the last. There still water ran ahead, too much of it. But the mist could not hide Kosgro standing waist-deep, holding with one thick arm to a fallen tree that lay out over that flood. He motioned me to jump so that he could reach me.

Making sure that the bag of stones and that of supplies was securely fast to my belt, I thrust what was left of the branch into the front of my tunic, leaving my hands free. Then I took that final jump.

The force of the current was such I would have been swept from my feet, bowled over and under its surface, if a hairy arm had not caught me. Somehow we both splashed and fought our way out on the bank and lay there gasping.

Again the horn sounded, so close that it must be now on the other side of the river.

"The blocks—they can cross—"

"Look," he told me, and I did so.

There were no blocks, and at least two of them should be visible to me.

"That spell does not hold for long, nor would it hold for any I did not will to use it. There is some advantage in spying on the Folk, you see. I have lurked and skulked and watched them all I could as they go about their lives apart from their strongholds—hoping to learn enough to be able to force my return or to drive some bargain with one of them. They will give me no heed, for I am One Between—neither of the Dark Ones, nor of their company—since I would not surrender to their ways. My only hope has been learning what I could. But at least one of my hard-won scraps has served us well this hour!"

Though I could still hardly believe that he had brought us

across the stream in such a strange fashion, I could not deny we were there.

The horn gave a wild, threatening note. I leaped to my feet, ready to run. But Kosgro showed no haste.

"Running water." He pointed to the stream. "That will halt any of the Dark Ones until they find a bridge somewhere, which will bring them over. For a space we are safe from them."

ELEVEN

"**B**ut we shall not stay here!" No matter how far away such a bridge might be, I wanted to be well away from here, though to move on in the mist also brought problems.

"No." He shook himself, as might an animal, to free his body from water. My clothing clung tightly to me. For the first time I wanted heat, a chance to see the sun and to be warmed by it.

I was willing to let him choose our way, for I had no guide. I might well blunder back to the river in this blindness. He was again sniffing the air, as if he would so smell out our trail.

Then he said, "There is a safe place of the Folk not too far away."

He strode off as one who sees a clear road. I hurried to catch up to him and demand, "How do you know?"

"Can you not smell it?"

I could smell the scent of the bruised flowers I bore, and that was all.

"The Folk use growing things in their spells for doing and undoing. Where they grow, the scent hangs heavy."

"Such as this?" I touched my bedraggled branch.

"No, that is something else. I do not know who planted those. But the Folk do not use them. They are from an earlier time, perhaps another people—"

"Those mounds where these grew—was it once a city or a burial place?"

"It could be either, or both. If any know the history of this world, it is only the Great Ones of the Folk. And they guard their knowledge jealously. There is ever rivalry between them and the Dark Ones. And also some rivalry among themselves. Then, there is something else—" He paused as if he did not want to continue.

But I pressed him, for what I learned, each little scrap, might be an aid toward our return to a world I knew.

"What else?"

"I do not think that the Folk are supreme, though it is true they manage to hold those of the Dark in check. But I have heard enough to know that there is something *they* fear, that they pay a tribute to at intervals. And they pay that tribute in living creatures—which is also one of the reasons why they must recruit from other worlds."

"The children!" Had Bartare been summoned for such a reason? If so, there was all the more need for me to find them—and speedily.

"I do not know." It seemed he did not greatly care.

I had a flare of anger at that, until good sense snuffed it. After all, why should he? The children were nothing to him. And perhaps all that tied him to me was the food I carried. Only—if that were so, why did he simply not knock me out and take it? I had no doubt that his strength and fighting skills were superior to mine, and he could take the supplies with little trouble. Yet from the first he had asked and not forced. And the puzzle he presented continued to plague me.

"The mist is thinning."

I had been too intent upon my own thoughts to notice that until he spoke. But now I could see the circle of vision was, indeed, wider. And moments later we came to a road. This was not merely a turf-grown cut such as that which had led into the place of mounds, but had a pavement of blocks fitted well together. And some of those blocks had the same pale glow as the stones my companion had used to form his strange bridge. Others were red or yellow or even black. And though they were scattered here and there, with no discernible pattern, yet it was possible to advance along stepping on only one kind if you took time and watched carefully.

"Wait." Kosgro's arm rose as a barrier before me. "This is one of their travel places."

"A road, as I see—"

"More than a road. It does not run to any one place but many. Oh, I cannot explain it, for I do not understand its workings. But I have seen it used. And it works this way—each color of block serves one destination. If you are not careful where you step, it will either not work at all or take you where you do not want to go, for the Dark Ones use it also. Since you seek special persons, choose the glowing blocks. Step only from one to another of those, and with each step hold in your mind the face of the one you would see. Concentrate upon that with all your strength—it will then lead you to him."

"But there are two children—Oomark and Bartare."

He shrugged. "It would seem that you must choose."

Choose? Bartare was with the mysterious Lady who had brought her—and us—here. And since she had come willingly, perhaps she was as safe as anyone might be in this place of many dangers. But Oomark had run off into the unknown. And thinking of the hunt, those I had seen in the place of mounds, I thought I had no choice after all—it must be Oomark, and I told him so.

"As you wish. The glowing stones then, and think of him as you saw him last."

I was surprised, for he spoke as if he had no interest in where I went. Did this mean we parted company here? I asked, and he made a noise that might have been a harsh laugh.

"Leave you? Not while you carry that which is life for me. But one place is as good as another if we can keep out of the reach of the Dark Ones. I still have thin hopes that something more will come of our meeting. However, since yours is the seeking, you must take the lead here. Only hold my hand, for I have no mind picture to aid me and must depend upon yours."

For a moment I was inclined to refuse, to be free of Jorth Kosgro. My old suspicion stirred. But finally I held out a hand, and he took it in firm grip.

If any one had witnessed our advance on the road, he would have seen an odd sight. In order to step only on the glowing blocks, I wove a very zigzag way, sometimes forward, sometimes, of a necessity, back. I tried to shut from my mind all but Oomark as I had seen him last, running from me because I held the branch.

My back and forth path brought us away from the point where we had first stepped on the pavement. Now I could see, as the mist retreated, that the road ended abruptly only a short distance from where I paused to study the remaining blocks. So far we had gained nothing, and I was ready to abandon this and demand Kosgro strike away—overland.

"Think of the boy!" It might be he read my thoughts and was urging me back to strict concentration.

Obediently I again held Oomark's face in mind and took the last three steps on the pavement, towing Kosgro. Then, I seemed to be running, and yet under me the ground also moved forward, so I needed my own speed to keep on my feet. There was a whirring on either side, a blur as if our speed befogged the country through which we were passing.

Then I fell, or rather the sensation was that of being tossed from a moving way, so that I struck a hard surface with some force and lay gasping a moment or two before I sat up to see where we were. I heard a groan and looked around.

Kosgro lay a little away, his hands pressed to that bandage about his chest as if he were in pain. Then he struggled up so we sat side by side, able to see where that odd method of travel had deposited us.

There was a wide stretch of green sloping gently down from our landing place. The meadow was the same rich green, but there were none of the darker rings marked on it. Rather, there were pale flowers, white and cream, and bushes heavy with those golden berries Oomark relished. Around each of these were gathered flying and hopping things.

Not far away moved larger creatures, either eating from the wealth of berries or lying in the grass. Oomark? No. Was that Oomark—or that—or that?

I could see little difference in them from this distance. They all walked on cloven hoofs and were hairy and horned, like the boy. There were only some very slight variations in size when two moved together. I could not tell one from the other. If I called—would Oomark come?

Three seemed to be playing a game, tossing from one to another a ball-shaped object. Another nursed a small animal, petting and smoothing its fur. None wore any scraps of clothing such as Oomark still had about him. But remembering how easily he had discarded the boots and his upper tunics, I could not count on his not having thrown away the rest of his other-world garments.

"Can you tell him?" Kosgro wanted to know.

"No. I can call—"

"No!" He was emphatic. "It would be wise not to attract any more attention than you must."

"They—they aren't Dark Ones?"

"No, they are of the Folk—lesser beings. But they are full of mischief and would do nothing to help you. Just the opposite. You had better try to locate your boy quietly."

"But they all look alike! Except some seem a little taller than others. It is like expecting me to select a single grain of sand out of a stretch of gravel." I had been counting. There were ten of them, and I could not distinguish differences.

"It poses a problem certainly," Kosgro agreed. "Is there anything to which he was greatly attached, which you could speak of now to attract his attention? If you know of such, we can move closer. You can then mention it and wait for response. The others will seek to hide him, but your speech might bring some betraying response."

"Bartare? I could speak of her—"

Kosgro shook his head. "She is deep in the affairs of this world by your account. They could know of her. And they could counterfeit a response to baffle us."

"You seem to know a lot about them."

"I do. When I first came here, it was they who stole my food when I was trapped in a bog hole. They ran out of reach, tearing open my bag and scattering what it held. When I managed to get loose, I trailed them, until I learned that anger draws the Dark Ones, too. And I discovered I must control my emotions for a shield. These beings change from one moment to the next, never holding to any course of action for long. I believe they are all children who have been recruited from other worlds over the centuries—"

"Centuries! But they could not live so—"

His head turned so he faced me fully. "Save for the killing the Dark Ones do now and then, there is no death here."

There are races in the galaxy whose life span is infinitely greater than that of my species—the Zacathans, for example. But even they know death in the end. A place with no natural form of death had never been found, though such does exist in the legends and myths of many peoples.

"Do you know what will interest Oomark—a name, something of the sort?" He pulled me back to the matter at hand.

I thought—his mother's name? His father's? I could not be sure. That of some friend on Dylan? Then it came to me—Griffy, over whom he had been so shaken.

"I can try—"

"You will not have very long," he commented. "These can show such speed that we shall not be able to find them again if they run."

I could have done without a warning, which put even more strain on me. They were looking at us now, and I feared they would turn and make off. So I acted quickly, looking down into the grass as if searching for something and holding out my hand as I called, coaxingly, "Griffy, come! Griffy! Griffy!"

I dared not look up to see if I was making any impression on the group before me. Instead, I added what I hoped would be the crown of my performance.

"Griffy? He *must* be here somewhere! Help me find him—Griffy!"

"Griffy!" I had not called that time. It was a younger, shriller voice. "Griffy—here! Where—where is he?"

One of those hoofed figures burst from among the rest to run toward me. Two others started, as if to head off their fellow. But they swerved aside and ran back as Kosgro tackled the small body, which immediately began to fight. Then the others broke and ran. And they moved with such surprising speed that I knew I could never have caught up with them.

Kosgro mastered his captive with some effort. He was panting as he stood holding Oomark, while the boy's hoofs kicked and tore at the ground.

As I came to them, Oomark shrilled, "Let me go, let me go! You lied! Griffy isn't here. Let me go! I'll call Bartare. She'll get the Lady and make you sorry—very sorry." He was all small boy now. In his fury he had lost that strangeness of speech that had come with his change in appearance.

"I want Bartare, Oomark. If you call her, I shall be most grateful—"

He stopped his struggles so suddenly that I was suspicious. I hoped that Kosgro would be, too, enough not to relax the hold he had on him.

"You don't want to see her. She'll make you awfully sorry—She and the Lady. They know how to do a lot of things to make a person sorry. You'll see!"

"I want to see Bartare. And I think you know where she is. You said you did—you were taking me there."

"That's not my place. I have the free Folk—they're my people now. Let me go with them." He stood quietly and now was ready to plead for freedom rather than fight for it. Only there was a slyness in the gaze he kept on me, which promised that we had better not trust him. Those in whose company he had been had now vanished from sight.

"Oomark, you are not of this world," I began, and then I saw Kosgro shake his head. I thought I knew he meant that the boy could not be moved by that argument. No, but perhaps anger might work.

"I do not believe you really know where Bartare is. You were only saying that. If you did, you would prove it—"

If he refused to cooperate, I did not know what we could do. We might keep him prisoner, but we could not force him to lead us. Or if he volunteered to do so, we could not be sure that he was leading us right.

"You'll be sorry, very sorry!"

"Very well, I shall be sorry. But still I must see Bartare."

"She is with the Lady. I don't like the Lady. I don't want to go there—"

Perhaps his distaste for Bartare's dream companion was such that no argument might move him. I could only keep on trying.

"You want to be free to go with your friends. Take us to Bartare. Then, if you still wish, you will be. But until you do, we shall keep you with us."

Perhaps enough of the old Oomark still existed in that shaggy body to let him feel the weight of adult authority, and by habit he responded to it.

"All right. Anyway, I won't be sorry about you—either of you—after the Lady sees you."

"We'll go now," I said.

Oomark grinned. "Better for me. Then I can see the end of

you!" And there was more than childish malice in his tone. As with Bartare earlier, I caught the feeling he had dipped into such knowledge as no child should ever have. That alien part of him was again in command, his human side covered.

He looked up and around at Kosgro. "You can let me go, Between One," he said, with the force of an order. "I shall not run from you. Do you wish me to swear that by Turf and Leaf?"

Kosgro stepped back. "I accept your promise."

"If you *will* come, then let us!" Oomark was all impatience as he started on, looking back at both of us.

We followed. He led, and he held to a pace that made us trot to equal. As we came among the bushes where the berries hung, I heard rude noises. Bits of soft earth mixed with squashed berries came out of nowhere to bespatter us—until Oomark threw up one arm and gave a crowing cry. After that there was nothing, and his fellows, who might have planned to lay an ambush, let us be. When I looked back once, I saw that they had not deserted Oomark, but had fallen into a compact group, trailing us.

That we were moving into one of the great dangers of this world, I did not question. Nor did Kosgro's demeanor in any way lighten that foreboding on my part. He kept glancing from side to side, as if awaiting attack. Oomark's friends had dropped so far to the rear that they were half hidden by the mist.

"How far is it?" I asked at last.

Oomark sent me one of his sly looks. "How far is it? If Bartare does not want you, it can be doubly far." Which made no sense to me, but seemed intelligible to Kosgro, for he stopped short. Oomark turned around.

"What are you waiting for? You want to see Bartare. If you want to see her, come on!"

"Not if you take us by the dale way," Kosgro returned.

Again I did not understand. But I was ready to let him argue since it was apparent he did.

Oomark shifted from one hoof to the other in a dance of impatience. "I would not waste time. Come—or let me go!"

"Not by dale way."

Oomark answered that with a flare of temper. "What do you know of the ways? In ways, out ways, dale ways, straight ways? You're one of the Between. Less than the things that burrow in this!" His kick freed a lump of soil, which flew to strike Kosgro on the knee. "Betweener!" Oomark hooted, making of that word an insult.

"Not by dale way," Kosgro said for the third time, his tone quiet and unruffled. It held the authority of one who had been obeyed, and expected without question to be so obeyed again.

Oomark's head dropped as if he could no longer meet the other's gaze. He kicked loose another clod, but this did not reach Kosgro as he had intended it to.

"All right!" he cried at last. "I take you the out way!"

"That is better." Again Kosgro's calm reply had its effect. I could see that his winning this point had once more brought Oomark back to more his human self. And with Oomark the boy we could deal better.

He came and held out his hand to Kosgro, who took it, and at the same time offered his other to me. When we were so linked, Oomark started on. But this time he did not trot in a straight line as before, but rather wove in and out through the ankle-high grass. So I was reminded of the way I had stepped from block to block on the road that seemingly went nowhere. Here there was no pattern to be followed.

So we traveled in a weary way, which appeared to lead to no goal, but rather to be some senseless game. Yet since Oomark had only agreed to this under pressure from Kosgro, I knew it had importance.

I was so busy watching the twists and turns of those two that I had little attention for anything else. But at length I saw that the grass was thinning out. There were long stretches of silver sand strewn with flecks of fire, though those flecks were green not red. They grew thicker and thicker until the sand appeared formed of jewel dust.

When there was no longer any grass to be seen, only this gem sand, tall things arose out of the mist. At first I thought them giant trees; then I could see they were pillars of faceted crystal, milk-white or cool green. They were towers with carving on their sides. That is, so they seemed when we were yet a distance from them. But the closer we came, the less they were like that, being huge worn pillars instead. Still always ahead was the semblance of towers and more towers.

Very close at hand all illusion vanished, and there were many winding ways at the roots of those pillars. To pass along those made the wayfarer feel small and lost.

Even here Oomark did not walk straight, but wound from side to side down one of those ways. Twice he turned completely around, as if starting out again. Yet somehow he brought us deeper into the maze. I grew fearful, thinking we might come upon such as had fronted me in the mounds. Perhaps the mounds had once been like this, but the pillars there had crumbled.

The illusion that this was a city continued to hold, save that it was a city without any inhabitant on its streets, no heads at the windows, no sign that any living beings save ourselves moved here.

In me grew a longing to call out, to learn if we were alone. But there was an awe-inspiring silence. And all I could hear was a whispering from Oomark; he could have been repeating words in a singsong chant. Perhaps he had been doing that since we began this odd method of progression. But I had not been aware of that before.

He halted, so quickly that Kosgro bumped into him, and I, in turn, brought up against the other's broad shoulder. We could see the city ahead, the pillars around us, nothing else. Oomark was grinning again, that unpleasant, unchildlike grimace that was not born of goodwill.

"There is a wall now," he reported.

I could see nothing of the sort. Kosgro dropped my hand, though he retained hold of Oomark, and stretched out his arm. It was very apparent that his fingers flattened against some unseen surface. He felt up and down, exploring it.

Oomark tried to pull away from him. "There is a wall," he repeated. "The way in, the out way, can't take us past it. I've done all I can do. Let me go now!"

"We have not reached Bartare," I pointed out.

He scowled at me, openly hostile. "You can't now. I'm not a Great One. I can't break through that."

"No, you can't," Kosgro agreed. I was dismayed, not only because he agreed, but also because I realized that I had come to depend upon him, perhaps too much, to the threatening of what I must do.

"We can't, but perhaps she can." Kosgro moved a little to let me face that invisible barrier. "Try the notus."

TWELVE

I looked to the branch. It was fading fast now, the flowers yellowing, drying up, and the scent was no longer so strong. But as I took it from my belt, Oomark cowered away.

"No!" I think he would have tried to run, only Kosgro caught him.

"Touch the wall," the latter ordered me, restraining the boy.

I felt—my finger touched a smooth surface. It was warm, and my fingertips pricked as they slipped across it, as if some current of energy flowed there.

Then I held out the branch. There was a blast of light, a crackling. Energy might be short-circuited so.

"Yes." Kosgro nodded. "I thought so. That is why they fear the notus—it destroys their power creations. And since they spin the energy from themselves, this may recoil on them now. Let us go on."

Oomark wanted none of that. He had stopped kicking and struggling, but he hung his head sullenly and refused to talk when Kosgro questioned him.

"Can't we just go straight on?" I was impatient.

"I think not. This is one of those places that is overlaid with their illusions. Unless—" Kosgro looked to the branch again. It was shriveled badly, flaking into gray ash when I moved it.

"Are any of the flowers left?" he asked.

I examined it carefully. In the very center were six, withered but still intact.

"Give me three. You take the others," he said. "Rub them across your eyelids."

I hesitated. Sight is very precious. I had no mind to endanger mine, for I remembered only too well how I had fared in the place of blazing geometrical forms.

"If you want to find a road here"—it was his turn to be impatient—"then this is your only chance. I tell you their form of illusion holds too well. We can be entangled and held prisoner by it."

He believed what he said—that I knew. Slowly I raised the crumpled blossoms, closed my eyes, and rubbed the lids with those bruised petals. Held this close to my face, I could still sniff that scent, which, as usual, gave me a feeling of well-being.

I opened my eyes—

There were no tower-pillars about me. I gasped, for it would seem I was back among the mounds where the monsters prowled. About me were heaps of tumbled blocks cloaked with growth of turf and bramble, while the way, which had run straight ahead before, was only a narrow path winding in and out amongst those blocks.

"What do you see?" Kosgro demanded.

I glanced at him, then away quickly—almost ill, dizzy. The hairy figure that I knew wavered, was sometimes this and then that, until I could not be sure of anything about it. Did I see a human man, misty and ill-defined? Or the haired creature? Or even—in flashes—a huge purple triangle?

"Don't!" I held out my hand in appeal, in hope that he might settle down into a stable form.

"What do you see?" Again he asked.

"You—you aren't stable. What—what are you?"

"Not me!" That voice came out of that bewildering swirl of shapes, which flowed from one into another. "What do you see around you?"

"Mounds—ruins." I studied now what did appear to be concrete and fixed.

"There is a road?"

"A small path."

"Then lead us along it—and don't look back!"

I was only too ready to obey. To keep my eyes ahead steadied me, and I began to recover from the panic that had filled me upon witnessing what had happened to Kosgro.

"What do *you* see?" I asked.

"Just as before. I have not used the notus—yet."

Perhaps he was right. Were he to have the double, triple sight of me, of Oomark, it might lead to trouble.

"You have the boy?"

"Yes. What lies ahead?"

I did not quite know why he wanted that information, but I gave it to the best of my ability, describing the crumbling mounds. Yet one was so much like the next, there was very little in the way of landmark. Only the path was trodden, so it seemed in regular use. There were marks like hoof slots, and others not far removed from booted feet. Always I spoke to Kosgro of what I sighted, but he asked no more questions.

This maze of mounds appeared to extend a long distance. Finally Kosgro did break silence.

"What lies ahead?"

"Nothing but more mounds."

"Yet *we* see a taller stand of towers. I think we must be close to the heart of this place."

As if his words turned a key, I did perceive a change, for we passed around a curve in the path and before us was an erection that had suffered less from passing time. No turf greened its sides. The blocks of its walls were naked, and the path we followed led through a massive open gateway in that wall. If it had been dark within that gate, I do not think I would have so readily entered. But beyond streamed light, brighter than anything I had yet seen in this mist-shrouded world.

So we came into what must be the heart of that place. There was no roof overhead. Set about the walls at spaced intervals were rings of silver metal, and those held balls which glowed. These were no stronger than the moonlight of a normal planet, but united, the radiance was considerable.

We stood on a pavement akin to that of the road Kosgro had mastered. It was made up of blocks of various colors of stone, some silver, some green, some crystal. But there were none of black or red as there had been in the road.

The pavement was a square about a platform raised the height of two steps above it. This was all of crystal and emitted a soft light of its own, a thin haze, which, at the four corners, rose in trails as if fires burned there.

On the platform, at its center, a haze gathered and ebbed, then gathered again, to form vague masses, only to disappear, and then reform. To watch that ebb and flow held one's eyes and—

"Kilda!" A jerk at my arm turned me away, and I heard such urgency in Kosgro's voice as brought me aware of him quickly. Nor did I need any more warning. This was a place in which to be ever on guard.

But if his cry had shocked me out of a half-drawn spell, it also caused a change in the weaving mist. That thickened into concrete shapes.

"Bartare!" For the first time since we had left the place of ringing rocks, I saw her. In her, too, there were changes.

Her hair was much longer, covering her to the waist like a cloak, until she swept it back. Her face was thinner, making her eyes appear larger. She stood with hand to chin, her fingers tugging at her lower lip, watching us as one who must make an important decision. And there was a daunting air of assurance about her.

She smiled as if she could read my mind and knew my growing uncertainty, for this was no longer a child over whom I could assert that small shadow of authority I once had.

"So you have come, despite all warnings, Kilda c'Rhyn," she said. Her voice was still high and light, that of a child, yet she was no human child now. "And what have you come to do, Kilda? Wrest us back into that small, small world where I was nobody, nothing? Do you think I will go—or Oomark—now that he has known what it is to be of the Folk? Has he not asked his freedom? We have broken out of the shells your kind made for us. This body was of your world, yes—" She ran one hand from her breast to her thigh. "But the spirit it houses has come home! And now the body becomes the proper casing for it. We cannot return—nor shall we!"

She had moved out from the center of the platform and now stood close to us, looking down, playing with the long ends of her hair. Still there was in her a portion of the human she had been, even as it came now and then to the surface in Oomark, and I saw that she was enjoying the belief that she was in control here and now.

"We are free!" she repeated. "And you cannot make us unfree, Kilda."

Bartare was the center. If we were ever to return to the sane world, it must be through her.

"Are you free, Bartare?" I chose my words with care. "Who stands behind you—there?" I pointed to the dense pillar of curling mist still occupying the center of the platform.

She lost her half smile and came closer. "Do not call me 'Bartare'! I am not Bartare. I am who I was meant to be. You cannot control me by naming that name."

"And if you are not Bartare, then who are you?" I noted that she eluded my question concerning the other occupant of the platform.

Now she laughed. "Not so will you catch me, Kilda. My name cannot be named by you. I am free of any bonds. You understand, Kilda—I am free!"

"I do not believe it," I returned flatly and boldly.

She stared at me, then for the first time glanced back at the mist. When she returned her attention to me, she laughed once more, but not quite so confidently. Perhaps the use of the notus had heightened my sense of intuition, so I was able to know her unease.

"Ask of *her*"—I pointed to the mist—"if you are free."

It seemed to me that Bartare's Lady must be here. And my words brought about a change in the mist. It thickened and darkened. Finally it was a form, taller than any human, yet humanoid in shape—a woman, as I had guessed, and one who was majestic, awe-inspiring. Her black hair rippled down to her feet, and it was tossed free over her shoulders as Bartare now wore hers, though a band of silver set with white stones was about her head. More silver and white stones formed a collar wide and deep across her green gown, a point of which extended in a narrow line between her breasts to unite with a belt at her waist. The green of her robe was that same green Bartare, even in our own world, had favored, and it flowed about her as if she was not clothed in fabric but in some living substance that caressed her body. As with Bartare her black brows formed a bar above her eyes, and her features were clean-carven in a cold beauty that repelled.

I saw her so for an instant, long enough to engrave her in my memory for all time. Then, as with Kosgro, she shimmered and was changed into something else and else and else. So quickly were those alterations that nausea gripped me, yet I could not look away.

Once more Kosgro saved me from the snare of illusion, if illusion it was. He called my name sharply. I started and was able to break the hold her eyes had fastened on mine, to look back to Bartare.

"Ask it of her," I said. "Let her say you are free."

"I do not need to ask." Bartare's voice was heavy with pride. "I am of her kind—her spirit daughter! I am a changeling. Do you know what that means, Kilda? Once your species did know well. I am one of those planted among human kind to learn their ways and draw with me into this world some of their stock. She has given me now the right to show myself truly of the Folk—proving to you also that I am not one to be lightly used. You think me a child, Kilda, to do this and do that as you say. I played that game while I must, to reach the gate. But a child in this world, one of the Folk, is not such as you can lay any command upon.

"Because you—because you—" She hesitated, repeating herself. Once more she glanced to that thing behind her, though I resolutely kept my eyes from following the direction of hers. Whatever she would have said she decided against. Instead, she waved her hand.

"Look you—the Folk and those who are one with them. They are coming to see me prove my right to stand here thus—with this!"

From where she had gotten it, I could not tell, but suddenly she was holding a narrow-bladed sword, not of any metal, but fashioned of wood so newly cut that it had a clean whiteness to it. Using that as a pointer, she flashed it from side to side, calling to our attention the fact that we were no longer alone at the platform. Others had come to stand quietly watching.

Indeed, that was a strange gathering. There were those like Oomark, perhaps of the very group that had trailed us. There were women, slender, with thick green hair waving back and forth on their heads, their skin shining brown, wearing scant coverings of leaves. There were men and women humanoid in appearance, more so than these, and all had black hair and wore green. And there were others, some beautiful, some ugly, with now and then a head or face so grotesque as to seem out of a nightmare. They gathered around three sides of the platform, but facing Bartare there remained only the three of us.

"You have stayed Between, Kilda, as has this sniffing monster who shuffled hither at your bidding. And Oomark." Her eyes turned to her brother, now crouched at my feet. One of his hands held to my breeches, but his head was bent, and he did not raise his eyes.

"Yes, Oomark. I owe him something, for he helped to open the gate—though he did that because I willed and not because he wished to aid me. But it would seem that now he clings to you, Kilda."

I dropped my hand to rest upon the short curled hair now covering the boy's head.

I found words I had not consciously planned to say. "Because he is not yet entirely lost to what he once was."

"So? If he has chosen, then shall he abide by that choice. Now I shall bind you three to our purposes, and then you shall serve as tribute this time to the Outer Dark. You shall be a lock on that other gate through which have been swept far too many of the true blood. By the power in me—"

"Kilda!" That was Kosgro. "Give me your hand! Give, but do not look at me. Look rather—there!"

As if his words had been a pointing finger to aim my sight, I looked. What he had cast upon the ground were two of the three blossoms of the notus I had given him. They were yellow and limp, but very noticeable.

His hand closed on mine so tightly that it might have brought a cry of pain from me had I not been too aware of something else, for there was a strength in him that was not only of the flesh, but also of the spirit. Something in me answered to that strength and was drawn to it. Had I wished now, I could not have raised my eyes from those two blooms. Oomark crowded against me, clutching at my legs, hiding his face.

"Put your hand on what is left of the branch!" Again Kosgro's order sent me groping for those fragments of stick, leaf, and flower. Part of the small bits left now crumpled into a dry dust upon which my fingers and palm curled and held tightly.

Only dimly was I aware of a chanting in Bartare's child voice.

The words were strange. I tried to shut my ears, realizing that to hark was to further the illusion she spun.

So I looked only at the crumpled flowers. And in the punishing grip of Kosgro's hand, I read the effort that held him tense, into which he was pouring all his energy.

Then—the blossoms wavered in my sight, even as had Kosgro and the woman who was not a woman. There were no flowers lying there—but lasers, much like those I had seen many times on my own world.

Kosgro broke grip with me. I watched him stoop and catch up those weapons of another space. One he held in a hand that no longer assumed any other shape. The other he gave, butt foremost, to me. This I gripped, though I had never held such before.

"Stop her!" He made, I thought, to fire at Bartare. But I had another idea and stepped ahead of him to the foot of the platform. I hurled the ashy stuff of the dead flowers straight into the girl's face. Some of it reached its mark. The rest shifted down in a cloud of particles, looking far more than the scant handful I had thrown.

She screamed horribly. The sword-wand fell from her hand, struck the edge of the platform, and broke in two. Bartare swayed, her fingers clawing at her face. Then she took a tottering step or two straight for me and leaned over, her other hand still shielding her eyes, as if to grope for her broken sword. Instead, she fell almost into my arms, and I held her fast.

Beyond her that pillar of mist whirled madly, and I tore my gaze from it. Still holding the girl, now limp in my arms, more of a burden than I could support for long, I backed away. She did not struggle. For that I was thankful. I could not have compelled her had she fought.

"Back!" That was Kosgro. He moved in between me and the others there. His form was stable now, the same hairy humanoid he had always been. He held the laser at firing ready.

The crowd continued to eye us in utter silence. Not one moved in our direction. I could not believe in such continued good fortune. Were they just going to let us walk out with Bartare?

Oomark was still huddled on the ground as I had left him when I had shaken free to attack Bartare. Now he began to crawl on his hands and knees, as if he lacked strength to get to his hoofs. I longed to help him up, but I could not manage both children at once.

There was a flapping in the air. The whirling mass on the platform had sent out a long strip of green to fly at us. I saw the bright flash of the laser cut it through. And the cut-off portion fell to the pavement. But it did not lie still. Instead, like some evil life form, it wriggled toward us.

Kosgro fired again and split it in two. Now both portions made reptilian advances. Still no one in the company moved. Their faces were impassive. It might be that any quarrel we had with the entity on the platform was none of theirs. For their curious neutrality I rendered thanks, but we dared not build on its holding.

We were under the arch of the wall opening now. And it would seem that, save for those crawling green ribbons, we were to be allowed to retreat unopposed, unless some danger waited outside—

But beyond the gate were only the mounds— Mounds? No! The glitter of the crystal spires evolved from dissolving mounds. That clear sight given me by the notus was wearing off. I cried out.

"What?" Kosgro was quick to ask me.

"I see the towers again."

"We were lucky it lasted as long as it did, but perhaps our luck has run out."

I knew what he meant. Not having clear sight, I might not be able to lead us out again. But if I could not—what of Oomark? He had come to me again and was holding me in the tight finger lock of a terrorized human child, though he wore the guise of the furred creature still. Bartare was limply unconscious.

"I cannot carry her much farther—"

"No. Let me have her." Kosgro took her from my aching arms and swung her over one of his thick shoulders, steadying her there with his left hand. The right still held the laser.

I drew Oomark to his feet. He moved unresisting in my hold. Leaving the rear guard to Kosgro, I swung the boy around and faced him toward a road that seemed to run straight out between those lines of towers.

"Oomark, you must lead us!"

I looked at the palm of the hand that had held the ashes of the notus. There was a little film of stuff still there. It might help, so I smeared it across my eyes.

What I faced now was a wavering world, first one thing and then another. It took all the strength of will and purpose I could muster to keep my eyes open and not shut them to that sickening mingling of changing forms. I steered Oomark with one hand on his shoulder toward the road I saw only in bits. He began to walk, staring straight ahead, as if he had no will of his own but moved by mine only.

I saw enough to use my laser. A green thing had curled out to entangle our feet, and a second snapped out of one of the mounds. Both times the things I fired at were parted but not destroyed, the sections wriggling after us.

"Do they follow?" I called to Kosgro.

"No."

A small part of my mind wondered at that. But I concentrated mainly on our road.

In and out we went, while about us tower became mound, mound tower. But once more the tower part became more solid and lasted longer, and I guessed that the dust was now failing me also.

However, Oomark kept moving, even when once more I saw only the illusions, and we had to pin our escape hopes on him. He had not spoken since we had passed the unseen barrier coming in, and he moved now in what seemed to me a trancelike state.

Whether we were following the same road we had come, I did not know. The need to be free of this place was so great that I would have run if I could. But Oomark could not be urged to a faster pace, nor could Kosgro keep to it carrying the burden of Bartare.

Then came a moment when the laser vanished from my hand. I heard an exclamation from Kosgro and guessed that his weapon was also gone. Like the other gifts of the notus, the weapons had only been loaned us for a space. But at least they had started us on our escape. Now I looked to either side fearfully, dreading to see one of the green ribbons in ambush.

That journey seemed to go on forever. Fear chilled me. Yet the emotion was a goad to keep me moving. And Oomark marched so determinedly that I held to the hope he would bring us free. In the end he did, out into the open country.

I threw myself on my knees and pulled him to me, holding him close in thankful embrace. Then I looked to Kosgro.

"We made it—we're safe!"

THIRTEEN

He shook his shaggy head. "Far from it. In fact, we have moved into greater danger."

Such was his tone that I felt frozen, as if an ice wind had curled lash-wise about me.

"But we are out of that city!" I protested.

He shifted Bartare's limp form on his shoulder. "Do you not remember what she said about our being intended as a tribute to the Outer Dark?"

"And what does that mean?"

"If what I think, it is serious. The Folk are not supreme here, though they try to boast that they are. Two ways war in this world, and the Dark Ones take their toll. I have heard it whispered that even the Great Ones of the Folk pay a price to keep what they rule. And I think they have marked us for that price."

"If—if we can get back—"

"Yes, our only hope is escape to our own world. And these two children opened a gate once. We must hold to the very thin hope that we can learn from them how to return. But we must not linger here."

"Where then?"

"Where there is neither dark nor light, as known to these people—a neutral ground."

"That being?" It seemed to me that our chances were shrinking fast.

"There are such places, marked by the growth of notus. Both influences avoid those."

"Where do we find one?"

"That is it. I cannot be sure. But to keep moving is one small defense. If we hesitate in any one place, we may be the prey of either light or dark."

I could have raged aloud with anger now. He had dashed my hopes, to give me little in return. To blunder across this haunted land, I thought, was the plan of a madman.

He might well have read my mind at that moment for now he said, "I give you the truth, for to hide the worst is to spread perhaps another net for our trapping. We shall be hunted as perhaps few have been before, and we can depend on none other than ourselves. But the sooner we leave here, the better."

He did not even wait to see if I followed. Settling Bartare against his shoulder, he started off into the mist. Seeing no other way, I took Oomark's hand and trailed behind. Luckily the boy did not dispute my hold nor refuse to go, though he still moved in a daze.

We recrossed the expanse of emerald sand and then passed onto the turf. But always the mist held, and I did not see how Kosgro could be sure we were not wandering in a circle that would eventually bring us back to the very site we fled. He did not run, but kept to a walk that Oomark and I could match easily. Now when we were out of the worst pressure of fear and need, I felt hunger, and I knew we could not go on much longer without rest and food.

The even spread of turf began to be broken by a growth of bushes. Finally Oomark tugged loose from me and sprinted to one loaded with the golden berries. When I would have run after him, Kosgro stopped me.

"Let him be. He will eat whether you try to keep him from that food or not. We must save the other world food for us—"

So heartless did that sound to me that I turned on him in surprise and anger. Doubtless he read it in my face.

"It is so. The children will not eat your supplies now. To force that upon them will waste it, for their bodies will reject such food. But we need the strength it will give us. If we surrender and eat here, then we are dead to what we have always been. Do you want that, Kilda?"

Perhaps his logic made good sense. But I rebelled against it, as might Oomark against the food I wanted him to have. Kosgro laid Bartare on the grass and squatted down on his heels beside her. I hesitated. I wanted to go to Oomark, fast stripping the berries from the branches, spattering himself with their juice as he crammed them into his mouth.

Only, watching him eat, I knew Kosgro was again right. I would not be able to control the boy. And manifestly Kosgro would give me no aid. So I sat down and leaned over Bartare, for the first time wondering at her condition, she lay so still.

Under my questing hand her heart beat steadily, and from all appearances she might have been peacefully asleep.

"Bartare!" I laid my hand on her shoulder. Kosgro's fingers closed about my wrist, drawing it away.

"Better leave her so. If she wakes, she may not be willing to go with us, and we cannot battle with her—"

"But—what is the matter with her?"

"The notus shocked her. I have seen it happen so. It does not last. But in this land all men or things fear lack of consciousness, because then what they hate may creep upon them unseen."

I had to accept his words, though I chafed inwardly at depending so much upon this stranger. However, again his logic made sense, for if Bartare was hostile (and we had good reason to believe she would be), then, indeed, she could hamper our journey.

"We need food." Kosgro broke bluntly into my thoughts.

Again I wondered a little at his forbearance. Long ago he might have wrested the food from me, even taken it to leave me adrift here. But he had not done so, and he asked instead of taking. By so little was I assured that I could depend upon him.

I opened the bag and surveyed the pitiful remains of our supplies. A wafer between us? Or a square of choc broken in two?

But he was continuing, "We must have more than before—"

"No!" I held both hands to guard my store. "There is so little—it will not last!"

"True. But neither shall we if we do not get the strength it will give us. And we need our full strength now."

I was still unwilling. And I watched Oomark longingly. To have food about and deny it to one's starving body was double pain. How long before we would be reduced to what grew here?

"We must have strength to go on," Kosgro repeated.

My hand shook a little as I brought two wafers out of their wrapping and held one out to him. He ate it as I did, making each small bite last as long as possible. And so that we might not be tempted further, I once more rolled up the bag and made it fast to my belt.

Oomark returned, wiping his sticky hands across his flanks, his tongue licking his chin where juice had dribbled. He looked down at Bartare and then to me, and he was alert now, with much of the old slyness back in his eyes.

"The Lady wants her. She'll come for her," he remarked.

Such was the effect of his certainty that I half turned, expecting to see trouble close at our backs.

"That shall be as it shall be." Kosgro stood up and stooped to pick up Bartare. "Best be getting on—"

"Where?" Oomark asked. "We'll be meat for the hunters at the next indraw of the mist."

Kosgro looked at the boy as intently as if searching out in him some answer to an unasked question. And then he said, speaking to Oomark as he would to an equal, "Where would you shelter from the hunters?"

I thought Oomark was surprised. But now there was more of the human to be seen in his small face.

"There is only one place—if we can find it."

Kosgro nodded. They shared some special knowledge, shutting me out. And that I would not have.

"If you know—both know—then where?"

"Where the notus grows," Oomark returned, but still he looked to Kosgro.

"But I thought—" I remembered how he had raced away from me when I had taken up the branch, as if what I held then was deadly.

"There is safety, from the Dark Ones, from the Lady." But I saw him shiver as if such safety would be hard bought.

"It is safe," Kosgro repeated in a way that made me think of a promise given. Since they would so shut me out, my irritation grew, and now I demanded loudly, as if to shake them out of that unity, "Where do we find it? Is it close?"

"We search," Kosgro replied. "And we hope that we are favored by whatever fortune remains to us in this world. We can scent it—"

He turned as if to go. I reached for Oomark's hand that we might walk as we had before. But he eluded me, to forge ahead of Kosgro. Since they appeared to believe that scent alone could win us safety, I, too, began drawing deep lungfuls of air in search of that fragrance.

Though we plodded steadily ahead, I could pick up nothing to aid us. My impatience and bitterness grew stronger. I was sure this was a fool's quest, depending far too much on chance, and yet I had nothing to offer in its place.

Turf grew only in patches now, and there were fingers of rock rising higher through the green. It was gray, and on it the mist left runnels of moisture, which I began to regard longingly, running my tongue over dry lips and remembering more and more the fine feeling of water in one's mouth.

Then there loomed out of the veiling about us a rock that was different, for in some distant past this had been shaped by hands. Nature could not have left it so. It was a pillar, squared. And down its foreface, so deeply carven that even erosion had left enough pits and lines to be read, were characters. But these were of no language I knew, nor had I ever seen the like even in Lazk Volk's collection of long dead galactic tongues. On the left face of the column, partly turned toward us, was a figure in half-relief. On the face, if it had ever had such, the features were worn away. Only the roundness of the head and the length of a humanoid body, though that body was also equipped with mantling wings, remained.

It had been carved to lean forward, gazing down at its own feet or else the foot of the pillar. There rankly tall dark green grass grew, such as that which formed the rings of shelter.

Kosgro halted. With one hand he pointed to the grass.

"A guide, if it will work for us."

"A guide—but how—?" I did not finish, for he was continuing.

"Get a clump of that, Kilda, a fair-sized one."

Though I could not see the purpose, I went to the foot of the column, gathered a bunch of the grass in my hand, and pulled as hard as I could to free it from the soil. But it did not give

way. Instead, the resisting blades cut my flesh, making me let go
and cry out in surprise.

"Not that way!" Oomark came running. "You do not take—you
ask. And if there is a will in our favor, it will come."

He shouldered me to one side and looked up into the feature-
less ball of a head.

"Give me your hand." He did not wait for me to raise it—he
grabbed it. And before I could protest, he smeared the open
palm, where blood had gathered in those cuts, across the stone
breast of the carving.

"Paid in blood!" he cried. "Paid in blood! Now pay in kind,
by old bargains—let this be so as we ask it!"

So did he influence me, I half expected that ball of a head to
show us an open mouth, speak, either agreeing or denying. But
there was no such happening. And, Oomark, having loosened his
hold on my wrist, allowed my hand to slip away from the rock,
leaving dark smears behind.

"Now pull," he told me.

I was nursing my wounds. "I have open cuts—you do it."

"I can't. You paid the price, not I. If the bargain is made, it
is with you alone."

He did not explain, only stepped away, leaving the action to
me. Once more I started to grasp the grass, this time with the
other hand.

"No!" Again Oomark halted me. "With your right hand, or
else it is no true bargain."

I winced as I bent my cut fingers around the grass. I did not
jerk at it now as I had before, but tried a slower pull. After a
long moment of effort, it yielded. The roots were not fine and
threadlike, but rather the whole bunch I had plucked grew from a
single gnarled and thick length, which came forth from the ground
with a shrill squeak of protest. I sat back on my heels waiting for
Kosgro to tell me what he wanted done with this treasure.

"That has power of a sort. If any notus grows near here, it will
point the way. Hold it loosely, keeping just enough control so it
will not slip from your grasp. As we go, it will tell us the way."

Since this was all of a piece with the other alien matters of
this world, I made no protest. I got to my feet, and as we went
on, I held that bunch of grass with its stiff, much curved root a
little away from my body.

"Indraw comes soon." Oomark walked between us, as if he had good reason to want protection. He was right. We were fast entering into one of those periods when our way would be too hidden to follow.

But at that same moment the tuft of grass and root in my hand turned to the right. And though I strove against it, it stubbornly resisted and continued to point so. I called their attention to it and heard a sigh of relief from Kosgro.

"The indraw—" Oomark reached up to catch at one of those rags of uniform that still clung to Kosgro's body. "We cannot keep on."

"We have no choice, I think," the other answered.

I saw that now he hunched even more under Bartare's weight, and he pressed one hand to the bandage lapping his chest, as if his wound troubled him.

"The notus may be far off—" Oomark protested.

"Stand where you are," Kosgro told me. He then put out his hand to the root, testing its rigidity, jerking his fingers away quickly and rubbing them up and down his thigh.

"I don't think so. In any event, we shall have to risk it. There is no possible shelter here."

We had come to a place of many rocks, which I did not like the look of in the least. Here ambush would be easy, and my imagination stationed some enemy behind each we passed. Oomark might want to hide here, but to me it did not offer safe cover.

The grass root shook and altered direction in my hand as I made detours around those boulders. It was necessary to go slowly as the footing was bad, consisting of small rolling stones and places where one could trip.

During our travels those bandages I had set around my feet were wearing through fast, and I knew that unless I was able to renew them soon, I would be left barefoot—a condition I dreaded, so that I pushed forward at times with reckless speed until some muttered warning from Kosgro slowed me.

The indrawing of the mist was almost complete and so slowed even more our going. We did not hear any warning horn this time. The presence of a lurking menace came to us first by a breath of air carrying a sour stench, strong enough to make me gag.

Yet Kosgro drew in a deep, testing noseful of the effluvium. He had paused, even as I, and now used both hands to adjust the lie of his living burden. I saw Bartare's face, her closed eyes, her slow, even breathing.

Unfortunately, the root pointed us directly to the source of that foul odor. I clung to a rock support and glanced at Kosgro. Did he know what lay ahead? Was it something we dared face?

He might be measuring odds. Twice he sniffed deeply. Oomark crouched between us, once more seeking the protection we could afford his small person.

At last Kosgro shrugged. "We have no choice. Sooner or later it will detect us, even as we do it. Then we have no chance of escape."

"What is it?"

"One of the fell-worms, I think. But that does not greatly matter—all of the Dark Ones stink in some manner. That is one of the safeguards the Folk have, since ofttimes they do not seem to know that they so betray themselves to those they would hunt. On it is—"

I wanted to refuse, to stay where I was, for the stone under my hand seemed now an anchor to safety. But as always, I must depend upon his superior knowledge.

With the root pointing, I squeezed between rocks and went on. The loathsome smell grew stronger. But though I listened with all my might, I could hear nothing moving. My other hand went to the weighted stone bag I carried still, slung at my belt. Could I use that if I were suddenly confronted by some monster? I freed it, ready to swing.

The reek of vile corruption tortured my nose. I wanted to cough, but I dared not. Oomark had both hands pressed to his nose and was breathing through his mouth.

There was a swirl in the mist. It was plain that something now moved there. Fingers caught at my shoulder. I was slammed painfully against another of the tall rocks. Then Bartare was shoved into my arms, and Kosgro twisted the weighted bag from my hold. He moved out before us, swinging it as if to test the weight and balance of that poor weapon. Oomark crept up beside me.

The movement in the mist had a dark core. But so thick was the indraw that if we waited to see what crept there, it might be far too close. I did not need any warning from the others to freeze into immobility, wishing I could deaden the beating of my heart, the sound of my breathing. It seemed to me both of those were alerts to pull the thing down upon us.

That darker spot in the fog grew more defined. It neared the edge of the curtain. Then there broke through a narrow black wedge, aimed at Kosgro like the spearpoint of a weapon. For a second or two I thought it just that.

Then it was too close to mistake. The thing was ringed, and between those ridges of gristle it contracted and expanded. This was no weapon, but part of a living thing, though I could not detect eyes, mouth, nose—saw nothing but the black flesh.

It hovered so for an instant or two, and then it darted at Kosgro. He swung the bag against the side of that cone-shaped head with such force that it bore the cone before it against the rock to our left, smashing it between the stones in the bag and the unyielding surface of a boulder.

There was no sound, but a thick, viscid stuff spurted out. Then, in a wild lashing, the whole of the terrible body was upon us, writhing and whip-flailing. Kosgro struck and struck again, though never with the same luck as the first blow. Twice it had its loops around him in crushing force. Yet, as its battered head flopped about limply, he was able to tear himself free.

I could do nothing to help him, and I feared. The thing was perhaps three times his height in length, and his blows seemed to rebound, leaving no sign of wound behind.

Mostly he battered its head. Once or twice I thought him finished when those loops encircled and tried to drag him from his feet. And I could see he was tiring. If he had given it its death blow with his first lucky attack, it was a long time dying.

Twice more I saw him allow the coils to take him as he concentrated on the oozing head. Then that fell to the earth, to lie still, though the rest of the worm coiled and uncoiled. He turned to look at me. And there was that in his face which made me push Bartare against the rock and look about wildly for some weapon.

Only stones! I pushed the guide root into the front of my tunic and caught up one so heavy that it needed both my hands to lift it as high as my knees. Gripping this, I somehow covered the ground and brought my burden down on the active length of the worm. It landed squarely, though I had had no time to aim. By some chance of fortune it must have hit a sensitive spot, for the coil still holding Kosgro gave a convulsive shudder and loosened so that he could pull free and jump over it to safety before it knotted again.

He scrambled to catch me and pushed me back just in time, for the flopping became frenzied. It beat the ground and the rocks in a wild lashing of the unmarked end of its body. I could hear Kosgro's heavy breathing through the thud-thud.

"We—must—get—up—" He steered me back to the children. Then, bespattered with the thing's blood, reeking with its awful stench, he stooped to lift the girl.

"Up!" His eyes blazed, as if by the very force of that uttering he could lift us all.

I caught at Oomark, who was already scrabbling at the surface of a boulder, trying to find some toe—or hoof—hold as an aid to climbing. I raised the boy until he could catch at the top. Then, somehow hardly knowing how I did it, I was beside him.

There was a range of ledges ladder-wise beyond, and Oomark was already seeking the next. I turned and was able to lift Bartare as Kosgro supported her from below. Then he joined me.

The rest of that wild climb remains a blur in my memory. That we made it was as great a stroke of good fortune as Kosgro's first blow in that battle. But that struggle had taken its toll of him. He tried, even with my help, to raise Bartare to his shoulder and failed. So we somehow got her along between us until we reached a site well above the level where we had met the worm.

Below, how hidden in the mist, we could hear the continuing struggles of the creature. It would seem far from dead. And Kosgro said, between gasping breaths, which seemed to hurt him, "Must—get—on— It will be—heard—draw—hunters—"

On we went, slipping, pulling at one another and at Bartare, who continued as if asleep in her own bed, until something within me wanted to slap her awake, so I had to set controls on my exasperation.

Finally Kosgro collapsed and half sat, half lay, on a ledge that was wide enough to give us a perch. We could not see below, above, or even far along that. He seemed to be content to lie, breathing heavily. And I, in little better case, crouched beside him. Oomark huddled just within our range of vision, his head turning from right to left, as if he listened with terrible urgency.

FOURTEEN

The thrashing of the worm was a distant drumbeat. But there were now other sounds. That world, which when the mist drew in had always seemed so locked in silence, now resounded, though I thought all such noises came from safely below our perch. I could not identify them, nor did I want to.

Oomark moved closer. "First came the small, now the larger. Soon they will finish the worm, and then they may follow us—"

"True," Kosgro agreed. "Time for us to move." He eyed Bartare and once more felt, with a delicate touch, his bandaged side.

"Your hurt—it should be tended."

"Later. We have no time now," he told me with authority. "But it is true I may not be able to carry her for long."

"How far yet?" Oomark demanded. "Look to the root, Kilda. How far?"

I had forgotten our strange guide. Now I brought it out. Once in my hand, it snapped to a point along the ledge. Kosgro touched it with a fingertip.

"Rigid enough. We cannot be too far away. And while I can, I shall carry her."

As if heartened by what he had read in the root, he arose and let me help hoist Bartare into her old position across his shoulder. Then once more we set out along the ledge. I needed no warning for caution. I was only too aware of those sounds. And

I could guess what might happen were we to attract attention of those who feasted there. We had been overwhelmingly lucky in our meeting with the fell-worm. We could not possibly hope for such good fortune a second time.

The ledge grew narrower, and I began to wonder how we could manage if we had to climb or descend the cliff wall. With Bartare a dead weight, I doubted if we could make it.

But fortune once more smiled, for when the ledge did end, it was in a series of projections like the steps of a giant stair leading up, and these we could manage.

It was a hard pull, and once more we collapsed, panting and gasping, at the top. At the summit the root turned in my hand, pointing down at an angle to say we were above our hoped-for refuge. So close were the mist walls about us that I feared any advance in this blinding fog might send one or all of us falling over some unseen edge.

"Down, eh?" Kosgro hunched above Bartare, looking to the root. "But if that is our road, we cannot take it—yet." He sighed as one who has made a great effort to little purpose.

"Also," he continued after a moment, in which I had time to realize just how great the danger was, "there is the matter of food—"

Food! I clutched tightly that bundle. But I could not deny I was hungry. Hardly any of my longing had been assuaged during that mockery of a meal we had shared by the berry bush. If the very thought of food made me faint, how much worse it must be for Kosgro, who had not only carried Bartare, but also had expended so much energy in fighting the fell-worm.

Reluctantly I unwrapped the supplies and knew once more the chill of viewing so little. Once this was gone, our last hope of remaining in part ourselves would be reft from us.

I smeared protein paste on wafers and kept the smaller portion. And to the larger I added a choc cube for Kosgro. He did not demure accepting the larger share. Good sense dictated such a decision.

Mouthing my wafer, I quickly rewrapped the food, hiding it from sight and temptation. Then I began the rebandaging of my feet. More of my tunic must be sacrificed to that effort.

I winced when I looked at them, so alien had they become. The toes were abnormally long—like—like roots! Rooted feet, shining, hardened skin like bark, green hair—I put my hand to my mouth and I did not cry out, but still I shuddered as I hurried to wrap those feet, trying not to think.

Suppose I had obeyed the impulse that had ridden me to throw aside the wrapping and burrow with my toe roots into the soil? Would such action have led to my becoming a shrub, a tree, something firm fixed in this world for all time? I must be careful that did not happen, that I did not allow my toes to touch ground.

Oomark had been walking up and down. Now he came clattering over the stone.

"We must go! There are many Dark Ones below, more coming!"

Kosgro sighed again. "He is right. At the indraw they hunger the most. The worm will not be enough."

I picked up the root, hoping that it might have in some way modified its signal. But it still pointed down.

"Where do we go? If we follow this, we must return."

"And that we can't!" Kosgro flexed his arms. "We still have to move along this level as long as we can and hope for some small favor from fortune."

Once more he carried Bartare. But now our pace was a crawl with frequent stops for rest. Then the root made a sudden shift in my hand. I stopped to display the backward shift to my companions.

"We have passed the place."

Kosgro laid down the girl. Together we went to our knees and crept to the left very slowly and cautiously, hoping to come to the lip of the heights on which we stood and so gauge what lay below. Then, just as the stench of the fell-worm had been a warning, so now a wave of that invigorating fragrance of notus was a promise of hope. Kosgro exclaimed, his slit mouth stretched in a grotesque parody of a human smile.

"It does not sicken me this time!"

"What does not?"

"The notus scent! I can stand it." He pounded one big hairy fist on the stone. "Don't you understand? The food has helped. I am now less a part of this world. The notus does not warn me off!"

I could understand his exultation, for I had felt it when my skin had softened as I picked up that earlier branch. Together we lay, shoulders touching, trying to see below the rim of rock. But so heavy was the indraw, there was little we were sure of. The trees we sought could be very far or near, but still well hidden.

As my root toes had drawn some form of energy from the soil, so did now the scent bring me another. The hunger that had been a cramping pain in my middle was gone. I felt at peace and, not only at peace, but also as if there was nothing I could not accomplish—that I could command fate and make it subject to my will.

"It does not seem too difficult a descent," I said. What we could see of the rock was broken and pitted to offer hand and footholds.

"Where we can see," Kosgro agreed, but he added, "It is what we cannot see we must fear. If we had a rope, any form of climbing aid, we might—"

Was he going to give up! Astounded, I levered myself to a sitting position. "But we must go down!"

"I agree. But tell me how."

A moment of sober thinking told me he was right. Three of us might well make it. But with Bartare there was no chance—not for all of us. Already I was facing the only solution. I alone had the ability to handle notus without discomfort. That a branch was a powerful aid here had been proven. And we must have that aid to survive. Therefore, I must make the descent, get a fresh branch, and return with it.

I said so and prepared for some protest from Kosgro. He was silent for a long moment, then said, "I suppose that is the only way."

"You sound doubtful."

"I cannot help but be so. We do not know what lies below, even if the rock is climbable beyond the short distance we can view. To go down into the unknown is perilous, and you are the least well prepared to face such dangers."

"From what we can smell, there must be more than one notus tree in bloom. And how many of the dangers of this world can approach such? Or am I wrong in believing it a cure for many of the local ills?"

"No. And you are right that you alone may be able to handle it. I can only say keep your wits and senses alert and take all possible care."

After what we had been through, I needed no such warning. Once more I checked the coverings on my feet to be sure the bindings were tight. And before I slid over the rim, I did something else. I untied the food bag, thus giving him the greatest trust I had. He did not move to touch it; rather he looked at me searchingly and said, his words very sharp and clear, "If you expect ill fortune, then do not go. There is something in the very air here that can pick up and enlarge on any lack of confidence, forcing upon one the very fate he would avoid."

I forced a laugh, hoping I did not show his words had shaken me. "So you think I believe myself ready for disaster? But you are wrong. It is just that I do not wish this bumping against me. Now I lay upon you a dire warning in return—it may be that our lives rest upon that bundle."

He nodded. "Do you think I do not already know that? Be sure it will be well guarded."

I did not look up again as I swung over, but kept my full attention for the rock wall with its many useful breaks. In spite of the tight binding, my feet were more supple and able to search for holds and cracks than they would have been in boots. But I inched along, testing each hold before I used it as an anchor.

My world narrowed to that strip of wall, water-slimed by the concentration of the mist. The secret was, I quickly decided, to live in the present moment only. Thus I clung and hunted for holds, clung and hunted, and each time I changed position won a little farther. The fragrance of the notus grew stronger, heartening me, when I dared to think about it—to the belief that the tree or trees could not be too far away.

At last my feet touched a surface, and I held on, still facing the wall, not yet daring to turn, while I slid first one and then the other back and forth, to make sure I had firm footing. I kept one handhold and very slowly edged to face outward.

There was solid stone under my feet, running out level into the mist. And a green rim of turf was there, too. I hesitated before moving out, for I was not sure I could return to this same spot. But the notus could not be too far away, and hesitation solved nothing.

I began counting my paces aloud, hoping thus to have some clue for a back trail. So I reached the turf, which was soft and springy underfoot. And I stooped and tore a portion loose, though the tough growth resisted, so that I was able to leave a mark. I continued ahead, leaving gashes behind me every five paces.

Thus I reached the first of the notus trees. There was more than one—in fact, a small grove of them. And I stood breathing deeply, rejoicing in the feeling of headiness and well-being.

The blossoms hung in thick clusters, but they were not the clear white of those of the first branch. Some were gold-tipped at the edge. And others detached, to drift groundward, where there was already a rich shifting of them on the turf.

I walked carefully under the nearest tree, looking up, determined to select the freshest of the branches, for it would seem that the flowers were now past their bloom peak and in the last stages of their life.

Having made my choice, I raised my hands to wrest that branch free. But when my fingers touched it, it was snapped up out of reach, as if the tree realized what I would do and was resisting. That startled me into jumping back, for I had an odd idea it might lash back at me in return.

Was this another case similar to the tuft of grass? Must I give some sort of weird payment in return? I examined the cuts on my hand. They still smarted, but they no longer bled. I drew a deep breath and went to the trunk of the tree, putting my torn and grimed hand flat against that shining silver surface.

Why I should do this, I do not know, but it somehow seemed right. And I spoke to the notus as if it were a fellow being who might conceivably be stirred to aid were it to understand our deep need. I asked of the tree whatever it would give me, saying that I would not try to take if it refused, for I remembered now how that first branch had been borne to me by the wind, that I had not reft it from its setting.

Over me the ribbon-narrow leaves rustled, and the bunches of flowers tossed. That movement had not come from any wind, but it passed on to the next tree, and the next, growing louder and louder.

About me fell in a shower those blossoms now fading, dislodged by the tossing. They caught in my hair, in the folds of my under tunic, clung to my arms and shoulders as if their petals had adhesive coating.

There was a sharp split somewhere over my head. When I leaned back, my hands still on the tree bole, to see what had happened, a branch fell with odd precision across my two arms. It was Y shaped, with a cluster of flowers crowning each arm. And, to my delight, these were not as well developed as those being shed, so they might be expected to last for some time.

I spoke again, giving my thanks to whatever power had brought me this gift, being awed and moved by the response to my plea, ashamed of my greedy action in trying to break off my choice earlier. Under the palms of my hands the bole seemed to be sweating, or else moisture condensed there. I longed to lay my lips to that, to lick to my dry mouth the heavy glistening beads. So great was that longing that it tempted me past prudence, and I did embrace the trunk and set my lips to it.

The moisture was not water—it was too sweet. But it brought warmth and a feeling of good and hope. Also, though it was not a full drink such as I was used to, it refreshed me greatly. As I started away from the tree, I again gave thanks. Nor did it seem strange to me to do so, for the notus was plainly not just a tree—though what it was I did not know.

With the branch safely tucked into my belt, I went back to the cliff. The climb was not as bad as the descent, for now it was easier to look up to the holds, and secondly, the moisture had refreshed me, readied me for more exertion.

The blossoms that had fallen on me still clung to my skin. Nor did I want to brush them off, for their scent and the soft touch of them on my flesh were good.

Just as the climb was less demanding than the descent, so did it take me a shorter time, for which I was glad. And when I pulled up and over the rim, I was eagerly trying to devise some method by which we could all descend to the grove. I looked upon that as the ideal haven for rest and refreshment.

The indraw was beginning to lighten as I reached the top. Bartare lay there, apparently as deeply asleep as ever. Oomark squatted some distance away, as if playing sentinel. Kosgro sat by the girl, his shoulders hunched, his hands dangling between his knees, his attitude one of exhaustion.

He lifted his head as I waved the branch triumphantly in the air.

"We must get down somehow," I told him. "There is a whole grove of notus. And—"

My waving of the branch had at last dislodged some of the

petals clinging to my skin. They floated through the air, and a few fell on Bartare, her face and breast.

For the first time she stirred—not only stirred but also regained consciousness with the speed of a sleeper roused by danger. Her hands brushed at her face. We were too startled to move. For so long she had been more or less an inanimate thing that perhaps we had begun to accept her as such.

Kosgro reached for her, too late. She slipped away from his grasp with the desperate speed of an animal trying to evade capture. One of the petals from her face stuck to her fingers. She cried out, beating her hand against her body as if she must wipe away some tormenting thing.

"Bartare!" I moved toward her, and she gave a scream that brought me to a halt, throwing up her arms as a barrier, as if in me she saw some monster she could not face.

Kosgro might have reached her then, save that Oomark cut across in front of him. The man jarred into the boy, stumbled, and fought for his balance. Bartare, gaining her feet at last, gave us one last look of horror and defiance and ran—out into the mist, away from the edge of the cliff into the unknown.

Unthinkingly, I raced after her.

It was only when the mist held me that I realized my utter folly, for now we might all wander without hope of meeting. We could call and so perhaps establish contact. But such cries would certainly also attract notice we did not want or dare to face.

As soon as I was aware of my grave mistake, I paused to listen. I could hear ahead the thud of feet on the stone—Bartare. Yet when I moved, I lost that sound. So I dared not take it for a guide. I looked at the notus branch. The root had led us to it. Now could the notus lead me to Bartare? I no more than harbored that speculation when it did turn in my hold so that the fork with its double burden of flowers pointed. And I was sure that had not happened by any act of mine. I had no choice but to follow its guide.

I did as Kosgro had instructed when he hunted Oomark. I concentrated on the girl's face in my mind and let the notus point the way. It led me on, out and away from the cliff.

Once more I passed from stone to a downslope of sand and soil, stunted bushes breaking raggedly out of the mist, to be swallowed up again. Often I stopped to listen. But if Bartare still ran, she had outdistanced me so far. I could not pick up that faint drumming of feet. No, I could not hear that. But there were other noises enough to make me sure I was not alone in the veiled countryside. Things passed to and fro there on business of their own.

I was chilled, thinking of Bartare perhaps coming face to face with one of the monsters of this land. Whether the girl could summon her Lady to her aid, I could not guess. And it might be I would have to face them both when I found her. But I dared not let that thought deter me now.

Then I heard a calling, which was not really a full sound but rather a vibration in the air, to be felt also. And since the branch pointed me in that direction, I believed Bartare was trying to summon aid. The ground fell in a sudden drop before me, and the grass and moss that clothed it was slick, so I slipped and slid to the bottom.

One of the turf-covered mounds ended my journey as I came against its wall with some force. I heard an excited laugh and looked up. Bartare knelt on the crest of the rise, staring down at me with the satisfaction of one who sees an enemy in difficulties. Then she raised an arm and signaled to something I could not see, while she called clearly, "Come and be fed, runner-in-darkness!"

I had so little warning, I was not yet on my feet, though I did reach my knees before that shadow became terrifyingly clear. It was Shuck, or enough like that monster to be its twin. And it bore down upon me slavering, but in grim and horrible silence, its fangs displayed between gaping jaws.

"Eat! Eat!" Bartare's voice no longer held a human note in its shrilling. Then she added, "A last thanks to you, Kilda. For once you are serving me well. Play with Shuck, and he will forget me."

Though I was still on my knees, I raised the flowered branch and pointed it at Shuck.

"Shuck!" I put all the force I could into that.

The creature stopped so short that it skidded, its paws cutting furrows in the soil as it tried to stop before it overran me. I then used the branch as a whip, lashing out. Shuck tried to dodge but was struck on head and shoulder by the flowers.

It leaped back and away, snarling and giving tongue in deep

coughing notes. And it flattened to its belly against the ground, striving to creep at me from another angle. But I was ready for that also.

"Shuck!" I took the initiative, advancing toward the cringing monster. I waved the branch above my head. It gave ground before me until at last it flung back its head and gave a mighty howl, enough to make one's ears ring with its discordance. Then it flashed away into the mist.

I ran up the mound as fast as I could. Bartare had gone down the other side and stood at the foot. It was plain she was undecided and had not yet run into the unknown. Before she could move, I was over and down and had locked a handhold on one of her wrists.

She pulled and fought me, though only to free herself. It was plain she was in deadly fear of any touch from the branch. And though she protested every step, I dragged her with me, the mound to my left shoulder, watching ever for any attack out of the mist. So we struggled back around the end of the mound to the side I had first approached.

I had Bartare, and I thought I could keep her prisoner, at least for a space. But whether we could ever now find the others, I did not know. And the possibility that we were indeed lost was an added burden. Bartare's struggles continued, and finally I rounded on her hotly.

"If you do not be quiet, I will use this!" I waved the branch in her face, so she averted her head as far as she could.

I was in such a state then between fearing the return of Shuck, perhaps with reinforcements, and the loss of Kosgro and Oomark that I meant it. She must have read the determination in my face, for the fight went out of her instantly.

FIFTEEN

"You do not know what you would do!" Again her voice was not that of a child. "With that you can destroy me!"

"As you would have destroyed us," I reminded her. "Were you not leading an attack against us in that city?"

She sent me one of those sly, sidewise looks such as Oomark used when farthest from his human self—only this was even more alien—to chill me anew.

"But"—shrewdly she grasped the flaw—"you do not want to kill me. You want to keep me prisoner. Therefore, you will not use that—"

I both saw and felt her body tense as she prepared to renew a struggle, so I was quick to answer her, hoping both my voice and expression would carry conviction.

"No, I do not want to kill you, Bartare. But I can use a light touch, and I think it will govern you—or make you helpless and unconscious as you were before."

I advanced the branch, and she shrank back. But she was not yet conquered.

"You cannot tell me to do this or that. I am of this world as you are not. And if you try to drag me back to that other, be warned, I shall fight you to the end—you and that sniveling creature who calls himself my brother. Brother—! As if I am kin to him! And that Between who crawls and begs and will do anything to be allowed to lick crumbs from your food bag. You three—to think you can stand against the Folk!"

"As we did when we brought you with us?" I reminded her. But my heart was heavy. I did not see how we could continue to drag her with us if she remained so defiant. As for finding out how to escape—unless— A thought rooted in my mind to grow.

"You can be truly rid of us for all time—"

"As we shall"—she flashed—"when Melusa brings you to an accounting." She laughed. "Do not think to put a spell on her by shouting aloud that name? It is not her true one, any more than Bartare is mine. You cannot so control us."

"You can be rid of us and suffer no hurt by it," I told her. "But if we have to defend ourselves, we shall, as we have already proven. Show us a way out of this world, and we will give you no more trouble."

"You, maybe, and perhaps the Between one. Oomark—he is too much one of us now. And, besides, I have no key to any world gate—not from this side."

I felt a stab of fear. What if the gates could be opened only from the other side?

"But your Melusa does. How else could she have found you over there?"

Bartare licked her lips. She no longer pulled against my hold. "And if Melusa does this, you will truly go and trouble us no more?"

"That is certain." The last thing I ever wanted to see again was this nightmare world. But neither did I have any intention of leaving Bartare. I could not honestly believe she was of unearthly blood, left on Chalox for some purpose of their own. Rather when the time came, I had every intention of seeing she went with us. It was the old, old space law that had operated since my kind had lifted from their parent world—that legendary Terra. It did not matter if your companion was your blackest enemy—you did not leave him behind on an alien planet. You fought to the death to get him free and off.

I had no affection for Bartare, but neither would I leave her here if we ever did have the great good fortune to find a gate. How I would manage to transport Oomark in his changed state and her, I did not know. Now it was enough to make a pact with her to keep her less a burden.

"I do not altogether believe you," she said. "However—" What she might have added, she did not say. Instead, her expression changed, and I had only that much warning to turn and face what crept there.

Shuck had managed to summon a partner, or else he now had a thing to dispute his prey. As one who had had access to Lazk Volk's library of weird wonders, I thought that nothing could astound me, but this gibbering monstrosity was the worst I had yet seen.

My species has an inborn aversion to the reptilian, though since we have taken to space, we have managed to modify it in the case of such races as the Zacathans and one or two others, whose ancestors wore scales when ours wore fur. But enough of that primeval horror was in me now to hold me for what might have been a fatal second or two.

The thing was a nauseous mixture of humanoid and reptile. It had a green-skinned body studded with warts and swellings. Its outstretched hands were four-fingered with a disk sucker on the inner side of each digit. The body was bloated, mostly hanging stomach, its legs short and bowed as if by the weight of that paunch. The head was large and round, with eyes planted well to the top and very large. There was no sign of ears, but a mouth gaped, and from the inner part of that—

Instinct, perhaps heightened by all that had gone before, saved me. At the moment of attack I held up the branch, and that long, slippery cord of a tongue that whipped out, dripping evil yellow slime, touched one of the flower clusters.

It snapped back instantly into the mouth, which also clapped shut. The thing, with a curiously human gesture, brought both of its hands over that mouth, staggered back and away, tearing at the thin bands of darker green that marked its lips, shaking its bubble head from side to side, plainly in agony.

"Come!" Bartare pulled at me. I went, though in part I faced the creature as I retreated. It had fallen back against the mound and was still tearing at its mouth, for the moment seeming no longer aware of us.

We scraped along the earthen wall as fast as we could. But what if Shuck waited beyond? After a last wary glance at the green thing, I looked ahead. No black form there. However, were we to head into the mist, anything might come at us unseen.

And besides, how could I find Kosgro and Oomark without any guide or landmark? Or—I looked to Bartare.

"Can you find your brother?" If he had been able to trail her across this world, surely she ought to be able to do the same.

When she did not answer at once, I wondered if I could ever force such information out of her. My hold over her, if I had any at all, was very slight.

"You have that which will keep off Dark Ones," she said at last. "But not all of them can be controlled. I do not think, your being what you are, you will go and leave them with me. That is not the way of your kind. And—perhaps I have been in a small way changed by living with your people after all. Yes, I can find Oomark—and if he is with the Between one, that one also. Come!"

I had no recourse but to trust her, though it was a wrench to leave the illusion of safety the mound at my back gave me. Yet that was no real defense against Shuck or the warty thing. My best weapon I carried ready in my hand, and I must be ever alert, not only to any hostile move from Bartare, but also to what might move within the mist.

We faced that slick slope down which I had come, and it was hard to climb this. So engaged, I had no hold over Bartare. If she took off again, I would be lost.

But at last we reached the top and had the graveled rise before us. Then, remembering the trick Kosgro had taught me, I turned every few steps and swept our back trail lightly with the notus, hoping thus to ward off pursuit.

"The mist lifts," Bartare observed, which was true, but I was tiring, and all I could think of was that we must find a place of refuge. The safest was, certainly, the notus grove—if we could force Oomark and Bartare into it. Once there, perhaps Kosgro could play some trick with illusion that would serve to solve our problem temporarily.

Now we were back on that expanse of rock at the crest. And—all was well! Kosgro had not gone searching for me, but sat there with Oomark, now almost as thickly haired, leaning against him within the circle of his arm.

They arose as we joined them. I saw a questioning look on Kosgro's face. Familiarity with his brutish features had taught me to recognize the small changes of expression. But he asked nothing until I turned to give a last sweep behind.

Then he did say, "Company?"

"Yes, and such as I do not like at my back."

"Then it is well to move on."

"Down there." I pointed to the cliff. I expected some dissent from Oomark, but the boy said nothing. He had remained close to the man, holding to one of the big hands.

But when Bartare came to the rock rim, she balked. Perhaps the notus scent was a warning.

"No! I won't!" Her protest was now in the voice of a stubborn child.

I did not know whether to threaten her again with the branch, but Kosgro faced her.

"You will!" he said, with confidence. "Or else you shall remain here—alone."

Since she had already run into the mist, seemingly without fear, I could not see in that any threat to move her. But again it appeared the other three shared knowledge denied me.

Kosgro held up his hand. "Listen!"

We did. The clamor from the site of the fell-worm's death, which had been muffled by the mist, sounded louder. There was snarling, growling—worse I could not identify.

"They have finished what chance gave them," Kosgro was saying to Bartare. "Those who came too late will have their appetites aroused and naught to answer. It will not be long before they cast about and pick up our trail—"

She interrupted him. "The Dark Ones hunt only during indraw." She was like some small creature at bay, darting quick glances right and left in search of escape. So I moved between her and the way we had just come.

"When they hunger, they will hunt at any time. And below lies the only safe place. They will not go there, not even under the lash of some power."

"We can't! I can't!" Her protest was a cry. She had lost the assurance she had shown with me. Perhaps, because Kosgro was more of this world, she saw in him a more formidable opponent.

"We can, you can," he returned. "It is that or face that which will come. It will come hungry and not be turned aside. And you know well, Bartare, that to flee such when they hunger is merely to arouse them to greater efforts. You run—if you run—to no good end. There is no refuge here, save that below."

"But the notus is death also!" She twisted her hands together.

"Not so. You have tasted of the notus, when Kilda broke your spell. Has it killed you?"

She hesitated before she answered. "It made me sleep—dream. I do not want such dreams! I will not have them!"

"The notus touched you. But you can shelter in its shadow and not touch it. Neither can those others touch you."

I do not believe she was convinced, but somehow he had mastered her. She shrank. I cannot otherwise describe what happened to her better than to say she shrank into the girl child she must have been meant to be.

When he beckoned, she went, even though it was plain she dreaded each forward step. And I knew a vast relief as she slipped over the rim, Oomark close behind. Kosgro signaled me. I shook my head.

"I last, and I shall brush the way with this." I shook the branch, for I thought not only of the unseen menaces by the worm site, but also of the warty thing. Had it recovered from its tongue wounding, it might be following. And there was something about that creature which made it, to me, worse than Shuck or Skark. I never wanted to face it again.

"Well enough." He lowered himself over the rim awkwardly, as if he found movement difficult. I wondered about his wound. Had his recent exertions opened it? He had never permitted me to tend it, and I could not urge such service on him against his will.

True to my promise, I paused wherever the handholds allowed and swept with the notus. As had been true of the earlier branch, this one showed no signs as yet of wilting or fading. And I made up my mind that when we moved on from the grove, I might try for a second such to hold in reserve.

The scent was strong. I drew deep breaths of it, relaxing. When I turned at the foot to face the grove, I saw Kosgro a little ahead, an arm about each child, urging them on, though it was plain that to walk under the branches there was an ordeal for all concerned.

We went on until we came to an open space where no tree stood, and over us was only the mist-silver of the sky. There Kosgro released the children, and they dropped down, stiff and silent. One might have believed they were pent in the midst of some great evil.

I went to put my hands on the trunk of the nearest tree, feeling once more that most welcome moisture. I ran my wet palms across my face, which revived me as if I had drunk my fill at some streamside. Then I pulled loose my under tunic and tore a strip from its edge. This I patted against the bole, soaking up all the liquid I could find. With it well dampened, I returned to the others.

I had found that moisture so reviving that I could not help but believe it would aid Kosgro. His head was forward on his chest, so I could not see his face, and both hands were pressed to the bandage about him. I knelt and put as gentle a hand as I could on his shoulder.

"You must let me tend your hurt," I told him. "If it becomes infected, that means disaster, not only for you, but all of us as well."

He gazed at me dully, as if he did not hear, or if he heard, as if he did not understand what I said. I laid the dampened cloth across my branch, thus supporting it free of contact with the ground, and I pushed aside his hands to unfasten and unwind that stained and dirty cloth. Under it, along the arch of his big chest, was a puffed red line. I knew little of wounds and their tending, but it seemed bad to me.

His head had fallen forward again, and he did not raise his hand in protest. I took up the wet cloth and began to touch it to the red puffiness, keeping my fingering as light and delicate as I could.

He winced and started. Then, as one who steels himself to some necessary pain, his body tensed. Twice I went back to the trees to wet my swab, returning to dab at the wound. The third time I leaned back on my heels. I was astonished by what I saw, nor could I believe at first that my eyes reported correctly. The inflammation was clearly less. It would appear that the notus had more than one virtue for those who could accept it.

For the third time I wet the cloth, and then I wrapped it around him, making it fast with the same pin he had used to secure the first bandage. It was a collar badge, discolored, but still of a First-In Scout. He gave a sigh when I had done, his body relaxing.

"How bad is it?" he asked.

"Bad, I thought. But the tree dew has helped. It is not so inflamed now."

Cautiously he flexed his muscles. "You must be right. There is far less pain now."

I sacrificed more of my tunic. This was the last length I dared rip from it. Once more I wet that patch at the trees and took it to Oomark.

"Let me wash your face." He jerked and would have dodged. But Kosgro held him. Again I touched delicately, knowing the child's fear of the notus. He did not cry out as I thought he would, but endured what I did to him, his body trembling.

Once more I collected the precious moisture. When I came back, Bartare was on her feet, scuffling with Kosgro.

"Don't do that!" she shrieked as I advanced on her. "If you do, you'll be sorry! I can't find your old gate for you—I'll, I'll be Between—Between!" So frantic were her struggles and cries that I stopped.

"But you'll need water, Bartare, and I've discovered this dew is the same as having plenty to drink."

"Make me do it then," she flung at me, "and see what happens. The notus makes the Folk forget if they use it. I tell you I'll forget everything—all you need me most to remember!"

It was plain she believed what she said, and I dared not take the chance of proving it. If Bartare needed water, she would have to wait until we were able to travel on and could find some pool or stream.

But I folded the dampened cloth I had not been able to use and tucked it between my belt and my skin under the curtailed length of my under tunic.

Kosgro untied a bundle from his belt, our food. When he passed it to me, I opened it—so much less than we needed. I offered some to the children. Bartare refused with exaggerated gestures of revulsion. But to my surprise, Oomark accepted a wafer. He ate it in small bites, which he chewed as if he mouthed something bitter, but still he ate.

Watching him, I felt a small spring of hope. Perhaps the notus had wrought something of a change. That he had taken a step back along the right road I was sure.

The portion Kosgro and I shared was very small indeed. But

somehow my body did not crave more. Then I inspected the wrappings on my feet. The strips frayed and wore through so fast. I must have something to protect them better. I was examining what I did have ruefully when Kosgro spoke.

"Why not try those?" He pointed to where a drift of the ribbon-like leaves lay under the nearest tree. They were yellow and sere, but when I picked up a handful and pulled and twisted it, I discovered that the leaves were unbelievably tough. Straightway I gathered a lapful of them.

"Let me." Kosgro took some, and though his fingers jerked and muscles quivered as if he found the occupation painful, he began to braid and weave them together with more skill than my fumbling attempts could equal. I followed his example until together we had achieved two sets of mats, four in all, thick as the width of my thumb, and some rough cords also twisted out of leaf fibers.

The sandals I bound on my misshapen feet in the end were no master works of art, but they certainly gave me protection, perhaps better than any I had had since I had discarded my boots. I sat surveying them with no small satisfaction while I tied the last cord firmly.

How long they might last I did not know, but in any case I must be prepared for when they did give out. I set about making a bundle of leaves, laying them straight and tying them together, intending to carry them with me.

I regretted the bag of stones that Kosgro had dropped at the site of the worm struggle. Not only was it our only weapon, but I had also stuffed into it Oomark's discarded clothing, which might have had good use now. I began to think about it.

"What do you plan now?"

I was so startled at what seemed a reading of my thoughts, or rather of very hazy intentions, that I stared at Kosgro. That he would agree to trying to retrieve the bag, I thought unlikely, but I did want it.

"We left the bag back there."

"And you propose to go after it—a bag weighted with stones?" He laughed harshly. "You think it a treasure worth returning for?"

I was stung. "It served you well enough with the worm. If it had not been for that, you—we'd all be dead!"

"You have no idea of what is back there now."

"I have the notus—"

"Do not become overconfident because of that. There is such a thing as ambush. You do not know the kind of things that lurk here. Such senses as we have to serve us are not able to alert us in time to protect against some prowlers. Notus or not—" He threw up his hands in an odd little gesture. "But if one cannot argue with you—if you must face fate—"

Oddly enough, it was his surrender, the feeling in his tone that I could not identify, which decided me. I have always believed that the foolhardy is no hero, and sometimes far worse than a coward. The few advantages that the bag might have given us would not outweigh embroilment with monsters. I remembered vividly that it had been only the surprise in Bartare's eyes that had saved me from the warty thing stalking behind my back.

"You're right."

His big gash of a mouth smiled. "May the fates witness this historic moment—a woman admits she is wrong."

It was my turn to laugh. "Not so! I did not say I was wrong—I said you are right."

"So that is your way of dodging the issue, Kilda? Well, even so much will satisfy me. Do not grieve for your bag of stones. I may be able to turn up some better weapons and a lot less clumsy, too."

He stood up, flexing his thick arms. It was plain he could move with more vigor than he had when we had reached the grove. Seeing that, I grew more confident.

Then he began to move around the edges of the clearing, stooping to search among the fallen leaves, covered in some places by a snow of faded blossoms.

SIXTEEN

Having made a circuit of the clearing, he returned with a gleaning of sticks, fallen branches of trees. Now he tested them. Two broke under his flexing, but three held. Two of those were as thick as two of my fingers laid together, but the third was of greater size and, at one end, had stubs of branchlets protruding.

Kosgro switched the three through the air and thrust in and out with them as I had seen swords used in tridee tapes made on primitive worlds.

"Not much compared to a laser," he commented, "but an improvement on your stone bag." And he sketched a gesture in my direction, which, made by a less brutish body, might have been the formal bow-of-courtesy of an inner planet man.

Puny and weak those looked when I thought of them being employed against any of the monsters. But they were of notus wood, which might give them more value than mere wooden rods.

"You can handle these," I observed. "But earlier, when you tried to touch the branch—"

"Yes! It is true the notus no longer bothers me. The food—this"—he touched his new bandage—"are all working!"

I had noted no outward change in him as had occurred in me when I first took up the notus. But then I had not been so long nor so deeply under the influence of this world.

"This and this, I think." He dropped one of the thin branches, but kept hold on the other two. "There is something else we may try."

Back he went to the trees, gathering up handfuls of the withered blossoms. Again it appeared he could now handle such without danger as he brought them back to me.

"We rub these along the sticks," he said, sitting down cross-legged to use half his harvest for just that purpose, while I followed his example with the other branch.

Mashed in my hand, the flowers became an oily pulp. The odor was very strong, too sweet. But I rubbed with a will, and the mess in my hand seemed to be absorbed by the wood so worked upon. Also the white bark glowed with phosphorescence, so that when we shook the last sticky fragments from our hands, we had not only crude weapons but also torches of a kind.

Kosgro sent his in a whistling slash through the air, and there was a cry in answer. Bartare, who had been sitting in sullen silence, whom I had ignored, thinking her best left alone for a space, cowered away, although that blow had not come anywhere near her. She did not get to her feet, but began to retreat, her face turned to Kosgro, as if she dared not look away as she crawled from him.

"Proof of the effectiveness of these," he observed. "We may have something as good as lasers."

"No!" When I would have gone to her, concerned by her plainly abject terror, she threw up her arms. I could have held a lash ready in my hand. And I was ashamed of arousing such fear.

I dropped the stick I held and put out my empty hand.

"See, I don't have it, Bartare. Don't be frightened."

She peered out from under those sheltering arms and then lowered them. Her green eyes were very large in her small face. And it was in that moment that I realized how little physical change there had been in her.

Her gaze was wary, and I said, "We would not hurt you, Bartare. Why do you fear?"

"Accursed!" She half screamed, making a gesture that included not only the notus about us, but also Kosgro and me. "For the Folk accursed!"

"Why?" I prodded.

"Before the Folk, of those who came before. The Folk entered through a gate, and they were few. The others here gave them refuge and let them be. But those others, they did not use the treasures of this world. They did not want to summon powers and rule them. And the Folk found that they could. Then at last the others said that they must not do such things and that a gate would be opened and the Folk must leave through it to a new world again. But the Folk did not want that, for if they so went for any length of time, they grew old, their power dwindled, and they died.

"So they warred with the others. And they won, for their powers were strong. But the others, they had their own ways," she intoned, as if she were chanting some ancient saga or half-forgotten history, "and they left checks upon the powers. Though most of the others used their gates and went away, there were some who chose to stay—"

Kosgro went down on one knee before her, listening as if this was of importance to us all. "Are they still here then, Bartare, these others who war with the Folk?"

She shook her head. "That is not known. They set barriers in some places that the Folk cannot pass. But since, after long watching, nothing has come forth, the Folk believe they are either dead or gone. But the notus they left, and it cannot be rooted out or killed by the Folk. And it is bad!" Her face contorted into an expression of loathing. "It hurts, it destroys, and it makes one lose power and forget the rituals. It is an enemy like the Dark Ones. And now you take it into your hands—and you will use it against the Folk!"

She began to cry, such crying as is rooted in a desolation of spirit and depth of sorrow no child should experience. I went to her, taking her in my arms, holding her young body, racked with sobs, close to mine. And I spoke as soothingly as I could.

"Bartare, we shall not use these weapons against anything except that which attacks us. The Folk themselves fight the Dark Ones, do they not? So shall we. We mean no harm to those of this world. All we want, as I have told you, is to be safely back in our own place once again."

I did not know whether she was so lost in the depths of her misery that she could not understand or even hear me, for there was no response. Then I was surprised by Oomark. He came to us and took, timidly, his sister's hand from where it lay limply on my knee and held it between two of his.

"Bartare," he said, "you do not need us, do you? You will be glad if we go. The Lady does not want us, not truly."

She gave a hiccupping sigh and turned her head on my shoulder so she could see him. "They want to take you—me—back with them!"

"They want the most to go back themselves," he answered her. "And the Lady, she can stop them taking us, if she truly wants to."

Something in that shadowy doubt acted upon Bartare as a goad. She pushed against me, moving apart.

"She wants *me!*" Bartare flashed, though I noted she did not add Oomark's name to that. "She won't let me go! All right." Once more in command of herself, too quickly to be normal, she spoke more to Kosgro than to me. "All right! I'll take you to a gate—if I can find one—and then you can go through. And we'll be glad, glad, glad!" With each "glad" she pounded her fist against the ground as if beating an enemy.

"How far from here?" Kosgro wanted to know.

She shrugged. "How can I tell in this place? The notus shuts off mind-search. I shall have to be out of this place before I can sense it."

So we would once more have to depend upon a guide we could not trust, and I did not like it. And Bartare would be even less to be trusted then Oomark. Could we use him for a check on her?

The indraw having lifted, we at last left the grove, though I hated to see the last of that sanctuary. We did not turn back in the direction of the fell-worm's ending, but struck off at an angle. Since there was no way of checking compass points, I never knew whether we headed north, east, south, or west. In fact, I always feared that we might wander in circles.

Bartare led through a side valley or canyon. She set a fast pace at first. I think she was very eager to be away from the notus. Then she came to a halt as the last of the fragrance vanished.

"Leave me—stand away!" She made an emphatic gesture at us and climbed to the top of a tall rock. There she stood, her eyes closed, before she began to turn slowly. Three times she so revolved. Then she raised her hand and held it out as she started that turn for the fourth time.

Her hand shot out and stiffened into a point. Now she opened her eyes and beckoned to us with her other hand.

"That way."

She was plainly certain. But whether she was guiding us to a gate or rather to some stronghold of the Folk where we would be captured, we could not be sure. I only hoped Oomark's reasoning had decided her.

Once more we came out of the rocks into a wide stretch of turfed country that had rings growing in it. And shortly we came upon one of the thickets of yellow berry bushes. Bartare sped ahead, stripping the berries and eating them avidly. Oomark started after her and then paused. But when he made up his mind and joined her, I noticed that he did not feast with the same relish he had displayed before. He took only a handful and ate them slowly.

Bartare was at last satisfied, and when she joined us, her smile held much of the old sly insolence. She was fast recovering from her breakdown in the grove.

"It is too bad you will not eat of the food of the Folk," she remarked. "Why do you want to be Between, Kilda? Is it because you are afraid?"

"I am afraid of not being me—Kilda c'Rhyn," I told her.

"As if Kilda c'Rhyn is so great a thing!"

"To me it is. I was born so—I wish to remain so."

"Yet you think of *me* as a child! And I am so much wiser than you shall ever be. It is like one picking an apple of the Sun, to eat only the skin and throw away the inner part."

"There is such a thing as too much knowledge—of the wrong kind," I replied. For some reason she was trying to provoke me. If she had been malleable in the grove, she was now her old difficult self. And that alarmed me, for she could well be preparing to lead us into a trap.

"You!" She swung now to Kosgro. "Has being a Between been so good a life? Do you also want to be yourself? But what now *is* yourself?"

"Suppose you tell me," he countered. "You say you are of the Folk and I am Between. Does that not make me beneath your notice altogether?" As he spoke, he swung his length of notus, and that she eyed, losing a little of her assurance.

She did not answer him, but said rather to all of us, "Your gate lies ahead. Come if you wish to find it."

Once more she set off, and we followed. But my misgivings grew the greater with each step.

The green turf made a carpet for our feet. My sandals of dried leaves were more comfortable than the wrappings. I felt as if I walked on cushions.

Finally we came to a place where stood a mound taller than any I had yet seen, covered thick with turf save on the side facing us, where that green had been cut away to show gray ground in the form of a symbol taller than a man. Against the green it was such a signpost as none could overlook.

Bartare halted at the foot of the mound, gazing up at the symbol. Then she turned to us with a triumphant smile.

"I promised to bring you to a gate. And that I have done. But opening it is another matter, and one I can*not* do. So now how will you manage?"

Kosgro was a little behind her, also studying the symbol. I thought it must have some meaning for him. However, Bartare had hammered home our helplessness. We could be well within the power of reaching the sane world of Dylan and still find all our struggles worthless.

"What—" I began when Kosgro waved me into silence. There was that about him which suggested dawning excitement. Did he see some way out of our dilemma?

He raised the notus and pointed its tip at the symbol. Bartare cried out and would have sprung at him, her hand outstretched to catch at the arm supporting the rod. I moved, setting my own thinner branch before her as a barrier. She fell back, her face convulsed as she babbled words I did not understand.

Kosgro moved again. With the tip of the notus staff he traced the lines of the symbol, painting them in the air, for that literally happened. The tip left a shining line in the air, copying in miniature the greater drawing on the mound. Though he dropped the rod, that shining in the air held steady.

Then, raising the staff again, he balanced it as a man might balance a throwing spear. He shouted two words aloud and hurled the notus through the center of the symbol in the air. On and up it went, until it struck the center of the mound cutting and stood there quivering.

The words he had shouted were repeated and repeated again by such force of echo as I had never before heard, until the separate sounds made a single thunderous roll. From the quivering rod aloft burst a bright column of white fire.

The noise stilled. Bartare had folded into herself on the ground, her arms over her head for protection, Oomark similarly balled near her. But Kosgro stood erect facing the fire he had so oddly kindled, and I was shoulder to shoulder beside him.

I longed to ask what he was doing. Did he have the "power," or whatever was needed, to open the gate? However, when I saw his attention so fixed upon the fire, I dared not speak.

No gate opened. But with another blast of sound, something appeared between us and that flaming rod. Kosgro reached out, though he did not look to me, and caught out of my hold the second notus rod, dropping its point a little, but holding it as a man would hold a weapon.

The whirl of light solidified. Once more we fronted the woman, if woman she truly was, who had been with Bartare in the city. She did not move or make any gesture, only watched us, her beautiful face expressionless.

That she was beautiful was true. And I think she was one who delighted in using that beauty as a weapon. But if she thought to do so now with Kosgro, she must have been disappointed.

"Melusa." He greeted her briskly as one wanting to bargain and not waste time about it.

"That is one of my titles," she replied, her words, though quietly spoken, carrying as clearly as the horn of the dark hunter. And they were as chilling as that sound also. She might be of the Folk, but to us she turned the face of a Dark One.

"What would you?" She came to the point as directly as he had done.

"A gate opened."

Now a faint shadow of smile curved those too perfect lips. "Ah, little man, you know not what you ask, or you would not demand it of me."

"I ask return for myself, for these who are not of this world. We have no proper place here—let us go."

"Or what will you do?" She was an adult, amused by the importunities of a child.

"Use this." He raised the rod he held a fraction higher. "And that—" I guessed what he wished and shook the flowering branch I carried.

"You use what you do not understand, perhaps to a purpose you will not wish. You are not an adept, nor even of the Folk. What you have rashly seized upon can destroy you the quicker."

"It has served us well so far. I think that you are the one who needs to fear it the most. We ask little of you—an open gate—for we are not of your molding and making."

"One is." Her voice was a little sharper. "She was sought and shaped to our needs. We do not bargain for our own."

"Your own? Yet she could not stand against us when you bade her show her powers. You had her shaping, yet she failed the test you set her. Look upon her! Is she yours to her heart?"

"Melusa!" Bartare was on her feet. Now she ran past us and began to climb the mound, her arms outstretched as if to embrace the woman who waited there. But Melusa made no answering gesture in welcome.

"So"—she spoke over the child's head to Kosgro—"with you is it all?"

"It is. Nor do you wish that which is flawed in your eyes."

"Melusa!" Bartare's cry was one of pain. She had tried to reach the woman of the Folk. Now she swayed and beat with both hands on what seemed an invisible wall between them.

"If she was of your true kin, could she not pass the protection?" Kosgro continued. "You have set that up against any danger to you. Why, then, does it keep out one you have named 'daughter'?"

"Melusa!" Bartare was screaming that name now. She had slipped to her knees, but still she beat on that surface we could not see, walled away from the woman.

"You argue with a serpent's tongue!" flashed the woman. For the first time her calm cracked.

"I do not argue, I state such facts as we can all see. Bartare has not betrayed you, but it seems that you or yours stand aside from her. Would not your protection allow her past if she really was of your kith and kin?"

"She was one of our chosen ones, long schooled and waited for." Melusa looked down at the girl who could not join her. "Why should the protection reject her?" She pointed one hand at Bartare, who lifted her head, her eyes streaming tears, in silent pleading.

There was a long moment of silence broken only by Bartare's sobbing. Then Melusa spoke again.

"I know not why or how. But it seems she is not one of us.

You have done this then—!" There was about her such an aura of menace that I clutched the notus branch more tightly.

Once more she pointed her hand, this time at Kosgro. From the tips of her long fingers there shot a ray of green light. But as swiftly as she had moved, so did he counter by crossing that with the notus rod, which cut it as cleanly as if the ray were solid and a knife had sliced it. The portion that was so deflected fell back at an angle to the ground, where a curl of smoke arose from a rapidly widening patch of black charring.

I was half expecting her next move and had the branch ready, for now she pointed to me. The heat of the ray she directed I could feel since, though I held the branch well out, it did not give me the length of reach Kosgro had. But he whirled half around and slashed at the ray held at bay by my frail shield and again deflected it.

"You see"—his voice was calm and confident—"we cannot be handled so. I know that the Folk are not of those who battle fruitlessly against odds. Let us go, for if we remain, we shall ever be a center of conflict. And your world has too many such now, for if we are still here when you open the gates to recruit, who knows what may happen? Like attracts like. We can sweep into our company those answering your beckoning. What would that do to your plans and needs?"

How much of his threat was possible, I did not know. But perhaps neither did Melusa. However, she made one more trial of us. This time she reached out her arms to Bartare and called, in a softened voice and one utterly beguiling; "Bartare, come to me!"

And the girl tried with all her might, throwing herself against that invisible barrier until she sank down, still feebly beating at it with bruised hands. Yet it held fast. And at last Melusa's arms fell to her sides, and she spoke to Kosgro.

"If the protection holds against her—then she is useless to us. It seems that in some manner you have corrupted her. Therefore, she is yours. You ask for a gate—well enough, you shall have it—"

"No!" Kosgro interrupted her with an authoritative note in his voice. "I did not ask for *a* gate. I asked for *our* gates—the one through which I entered and the one through which these others came. We will not have another strange world set before us but those which were our own before we were drawn here."

How was he to make sure of that? We could be deceived even now. I wondered what safeguard we could summon against treachery.

"Your own gates? Very well." That shadow smile I did not like grew stronger and I liked it even less, for it made her beauty even more sinister. "You shall have what you ask for, though you may find that it shall profit you little and that even being Between is better."

"By the Seven Names you will swear—by Archeron, by Balaf-mar, by—"

Her face held lines of horror, and she raised her hand as if to hurl some ill fate at him.

"Do not sully those powers with your tongue. You are filth, muck, less than nothing! It is not allowed for such as you to call upon *them!* You have so profaned great things and deserve—"

He silenced her for a moment, but no more, by raising the rod. "Filth am I, and muck, and such as dares not recite your names of power? Yet I hold this which is of a greater power, and I am neither blasted nor overborne in the doing of it. I have learned some of your secrets, Melusa. And such as I have learned, I have held against this hour when I might force one of you to do my bidding. Therefore, I say to you, swear by those names when you say you will return us to the worlds from whence we came."

She had herself under control now, but red hate burned in her eyes. "I cannot return you to those worlds. I can but open the gates. The going through must be yours."

"So be it. But first you swear."

And she swore, though the names were sounds not clear to my hearing, but they seemed to satisfy Kosgro. When she was done, he nodded.

"Well enough. Now the gates, Melusa."

I reached down and gave one hand to Oomark. He caught it in a tight grip. Then I went to Bartare. She tried to jerk away from me, but her strength was so spent that she could not resist my hold. I was determined that we three be so linked as to be together when we went back to where we belonged.

Then I looked at Kosgro. Now that the time had come when we would separate, I was confused and unhappy. There was so much I wanted to say but no time left in which to say it. Suddenly I did not want to go without him. Yet that was what he had asked, and by his choice I must abide.

He was still watching Melusa.

"We are ready, Lady."

"Go then, and get what peace you can out of it!" she cried. She stamped her foot on the turf. From that impact a crack opened and spread with great speed, as if the mound were being riven apart to form a dark archway.

"Come on!" For the last time I would hear Kosgro say that. He marched into the dark, and reluctantly I followed, drawing the children with me.

SEVENTEEN

We were caught in a darkness that was also movement. There was a sensation of being whirled this way and that. I was no longer conscious of my body, if I kept hold of the children, if I had been reduced to a wisp blown by some storm. Then the darkness was entire, and I was at rest.

Such contentment did not last. In me grew a nagging, urging me to effort. And that I could not escape, so I opened my eyes.

Here was no dark. Sun was warm, hot on me, blazing down to set me blinking, half-blinded—a natural, normal sun, what I had so long missed in that place of eternal mist.

I sat up to look around, to make sure I was back in a world like that of my birth. There was a stretch of sand on which I had lain, beyond red rocks among gray ones. Seeing those, I found memory stirred, a small prick of fear. Red rocks—? There was a good reason to fear those.

Within touching distance lay a small body. It wore only rags of breeches, but it was human! No horns showed on the forehead, and its bare feet were feet, not hoofs! I gave a sigh of relief. Oomark was a boy again, not the changeling the other world had made him.

Oomark— But where was Bartare? Had she escaped me during the transition, remained in the gray land? I looked around. No—there lay a huddle of green, with thin, pale legs and arms outflung, as if she had not fallen there gently but had been carelessly tossed aside, a toy for which some giant child had no longer any desire.

It was to her I crawled first, turning her over, raising her in my arms, fearing in those first moments that she did not sleep but had left us forever. Her eyes were tightly closed under that black bar of eyebrow, and her face was pale, as if she had suffered some long and wasting illness. But she breathed evenly and lightly, as if she lay in normal sleep.

"Bartare!" I called her name softly, resting her head against my shoulder. "Bartare!"

She stirred. Her lips shaped words too low for me to hear. Then she opened her eyes and looked into my face. For a moment I read no recognition in them, only hazy bewilderment. Then memory must have returned, for her face mirrored such desolation I thought no child could feel. She began to cry, not in noisy, protesting sobs, but with a depth of silent sorrow. So her tears gathered and ran down her cheeks, her mouth worked, and yet she made no sound. The sight of that awoke all my sympathy. I held her even closer, rocking her back and forth, crooning with my lips close to her tumbled hair, trying to give her all the comfort she would accept from me.

"Kilda?" Oomark sat up and looked at us. There was a shadow of fear in his face. He crawled across the sand and gravel to my side and threw his arms about both me and his sister, burrowing as close to us as he could. We might have been the only point of safety in a hostile world. I loosened part of my hold on Bartare to put an arm about him also, holding them both.

"It is all right," I repeated over and over, making singsong of the words. "It is all right. We are back, back where we belong."

This was the place where our adventure had begun, the stretch of dried river valley with the sounding rocks that had opened the gate between worlds. How long had we been gone? Time measurement escaped me. I could only guess that it must add up to days, and we must have been the objects of a search. Perhaps such searchers were still about, and I could find them. My body ached with a depth of fatigue I did not remember ever having felt before. I looked to my feet wearing those crude sandals—the branch— For the first time I remembered the notus and looked to my belt, where I had made it fast before I had caught at the children by the symboled mound. But it was gone. However, my feet—they were my feet again with proper toes. So I must be all human once more, even as Oomark was.

"I'm hungry and cold. I want to go home!" Oomark cried.

"We shall, oh, we shall. Bartare, my dear, do you think you can walk a little? If we get back to the ranger station, we can get home quickly."

"I was home—you brought me away." Her voice was small, crushed, woeful. Now she pushed away from me.

"I want to go home now! Please, Kilda, I want to go home!" Oomark stood up, tugging at my hand.

I arose, surveying the valley and the air above, hoping to sight some searcher who would spare us the trip on foot back to the station, for my body protested every movement as if I had been put to some severe strain.

But there was no sign of anyone else. We might have been on a deserted world. Kosgro—on what planet had he awakened? Would he return to his ship and rise on a new voyage of discovery with his ordeal in the gray country only another incident in an adventurous life? Would he try to trace us and our fate through some official channel—or could I do so for him? But that thought I put from me now. The important thing was to get back to the station and then to Tamlin.

Bartare did not protest. She appeared to accept that there would be no return to the other world. But her silent, woeful crying continued. Now and then she smeared the palms of her hands across her cheeks, wiping away the tears.

We had reached the top of the river valley cliff when I realized that the trip back to the station was going to be even more difficult than I had thought. My aching body resisted each new effort I demanded of it, and the children were lagging. I had no strength to carry them. We leaned against some rocks for support, while once more I searched the skies and the country for some sign of life.

"Kilda! There—someone's coming!" Oomark pointed, not at the sky but out over the tumbled rocks. Only it was not a ranger combing for us. A single figure advanced, slowly, pausing often with one hand or the other braced against a nearby boulder, as if that support were badly needed.

I waved both my arms and shouted, "Here! Here we are!"

There was a gesture to acknowledge my call, and that other turned his slow march in our direction. He must be in trouble or hurt, he made such an effort to reach us.

As he came closer, I saw that he was a young man, and he was not wearing a ranger's uniform. Tattered remains of breeches did cover part of his body, and around his chest was a bandage. The skin of his hands and face was very dark, the space tan of a starfarer, but on the less exposed parts of his body it was ivory-white. He had no sign of beard—another indication he was a spacer, since facial hair for them was eradicated on first showing. Dark red hair was cropped very close, a mere stubble on his skull, though his brows were as black as my own. His face was drawn and gaunt, the bones standing out clearly beneath the stretch of dark skin. It was plain he was in no better shape than we.

My attention centered on that bandage—I stood very still, hardly breathing. Could it be—? But Melusa had sworn to return us to our own worlds. Why would Kosgro be here? He had landed his scout on an uninhabited planet, then fallen through a gate by chance. This was Dylan, for over a hundred years a known and settled world.

I took a step or two to meet him, and I made a question of a name: "Jorth Kosgro?"

He halted, holding to a rock with his left hand, brushing the right across his eyes, as if he were in doubt of seeing clearly.

"So she broke oath after all," he said. "She sent you after me."

"No! It was the other way around!" Though Melusa had willingly or unwillingly betrayed him, I was glad, in spite of knowing what this must mean to him. "This is Dylan—she sent you with us!"

He stared at me. "It is"—he answered me slowly, spacing his words as I might have done if I had been trying to impress something upon a child's mind and that child was only half attentive—"the planet on which I made landfall. It is not on any map—I discovered it."

"It is Dylan!" I countered. "This is the way we came—" I gestured toward the hidden station. "Why, there is a ranger station just behind those ridges. They should be out hunting us now. And we are a short flitter flight from Tamlin, a port city."

He balled the hand resting against the rock into a fist and brought it hard against the stone. "I tell you, I planeted on an unknown world. I have not yet sent in a report—I can take you to my ship—prove it—"

It was delirium, of course, born of his wound. I surveyed the bandage I had adjusted. There were no fresh stains on it. Even if the wound had not broken open, he must be under great strain. We had had very little food. As soon as we could get to the station, they would be able to give him proper care.

"Come on!" Oomark ran back to catch Kosgro by the hand. "Please, we're so hungry. It isn't far to the station, really it isn't. And they'll give us something to eat."

Kosgro looked down into his small face. "Where is this place?" he asked, as if the boy's answer was very important.

"Well, I don't know exactly where this is," Oomark began to my dismay. His hesitation would only feed Kosgro's delusion. "We aren't very far from the Lugraan Valley and the park where the flitters are. Gentlehomo Largrace brought my class from school. And Kilda and Bartare, they came with our families for the picnic. We were to watch the Lugraans and write a report. And the rangers said for us to keep together and not wander. I'll bet they'll be awfully mad when they find us. Kilda, will they be so mad that they'll tell the commandant and have him punish us?" For the first time since his return, he looked apprehensive.

"I think when Commandant Piscov knows the whole story, he'll understand," I hastened to reassure him.

Kosgro glanced from one to the other of us. There was a stunned expression on his dark face. But when Oomark pulled at his hand again, he came.

"I want to see this ranger station, this flitter park. Show me!" he said.

We went very slowly along the rough way. I was more than a little worried. The fact we had met no searchers bothered me. Surely the rangers would have maintained a lookout on one of the higher points with distance glasses, as a check. Yet, save for some flying things, the world might have been as barren of others of our kind as Kosgro insisted it was.

Coming to the top of the slope, we looked down at the track that led from the valley platforms to the flitter park. Such a well-worn way would convince Kosgro at once.

But there was nothing—save faint indications that such a cut had once existed. I had made no mistake—this was where

Bartare and her brother had left and I had followed. Right over there was the rock on which I had left Lazk Volk's recorder. But not only was that box gone, but the rock—when I looked for it—had vanished.

"Kilda, where's the road? What happened to the road?" Oomark cried.

"Yes, where is this road?" Kosgro sounded triumphant, as if he were proving his point. Yet I had sighted too many still unchanged landmarks to be mistaken. And if one looked closely enough, the remains of the road were still visible.

"The road ran there. And you can still see part of it! There! There! There!" I stabbed my finger to indicate the places. But that it had changed from the well-marked way to this was very hard for me to accept.

"I want to go home, please, Kilda!" Oomark sounded frightened.

"We'll go down to the flitter park." I took his hand. "This way." Resolutely I slipped and slid to that faint gash that should be our link with civilization. Not far now—just two turns more—

My feet hurt. The rocks, so different from the turf of the gray world, cut through the flimsy sandals. But I hobbled on.

The flitter park—yes, the remains of it! But no craft stood on the cracked surface, its edge roughly scalloped where chunks of it had broken away. It had been hardly used, and there were no attempts at repair. How could this happen in just *days?* It all looked as if years had passed since anyone walked here.

The ranger station was only a shell. The roof had crashed into the interior; the building was plainly derelict and must have been so for some time. I think I must have cried out, not being able to believe, yet aware that this was no dream. It was as real as the wind blowing about me, the grit that chafed my feet.

A warm hand slipped under my elbow to steady me. I clutched at Jorth Kosgro, clung to him, just as Bartare and Oomark had clung to me.

"Please!" My voice was small and frightened, too. "What, oh what has happened? This—this was the park, that the station. It was, I tell you, it was!"

"There is only one explanation. I didn't want to believe it. But you're right. This was once just what you say it was."

"Then what has happened, what *did* happen to change it? We can't have been away for more than a few days—"

His arm was about my shoulders, and the warmth and strength so near to me was steadying. I shook uncontrollably and I felt as if I would never be warm again.

"There is another part to those tales from old Terra—the ones about the changelings and the world of the Folk. I didn't really think of that before. Now it seems that it must be true also—"

"What—what do you mean?"

"That some of those who went or were taken into that gray country did return after what seemed a day, or a month, or perhaps a year. But when they came to their own place again, they discovered that years or centuries had passed—"

"No!" Such a thing seemed utterly beyond reason. I closed my eyes and refused to look at the desolation about me, to believe that it was indeed the work of time and that we had been lost for years upon years.

Then he held me a little away from him, his hands heavy on my shoulders. He even gave me a small shake as if to summon my full attention, so that I was forced to open my eyes and meet his level, penetrating stare.

"Kilda, when you entered the gray world—what was the date—galactic, not planet time?"

"It was—it was the year 2422 After Flight—"

"The year 2422," he repeated. "But, Kilda, when *I* planeted here, the year was 2301 After Flight."

"One hundred twenty-one years earlier! I don't believe it!" I wanted to deny it, I had to! Yet when I looked about me, the evidence was plain. Now I met his eyes fearfully. "What—what can it be now, then? How long?"

"We cannot find out here—that is certain. We shall have to reach some settlement."

"They didn't reach this far." I ran my tongue over suddenly dry lips. "We are a long way from Tamlin without a flitter."

"But not from my ship," he countered. "And even a hundred and twenty-one years will have had little effect on a Survey scout. Let us go."

I was willing enough. The less I saw of this place, the better, until I could adjust to the thought that time had been our enemy. But I saw Kosgro as a young man, tired and worn-looking certainly, but young. And the children, they were as they had been when we had gone through the gate. My own skin was smooth, with no sign of age. I ran my fingertips over my face. I could not be sure, but by touch the skin there was as smooth and unfurrowed as that of my hands and arms.

"Where do we go?"

"Back there—"

"Kilda, where are the flitters? Why is this all broken?" Oomark broke in. "I want to go home."

Bartare rounded on him. "There are no flitters, and maybe no city," she shrilled. "It's all, all gone! You would come back—now see what's happened!"

"Stop it!" For the first time in a long period I spoke to her harshly. "We are not sure of anything, Bartare. Oomark, we shall go to Kosgro's ship. Perhaps he can take us in that, or else his scouting flitter, back to Tamlin."

But though we tramped at a faster pace, all of us being eager to reach the ship, we did not find it. Instead, we came to an open space, and there Kosgro stopped short, swinging about, plainly looking for landmarks. When he turned to me and spoke, his voice was dull and empty of emotion.

"It is gone."

"I know. It is in the museum park at Tamlin."

We both looked to Oomark. "What?" "How do you know?" Our questions intermingled.

" 'Cause when Gentlehomo Largrace flew our class out here, he made a swing over here to tell us about the mystery ship. When the settlers first came, they found a scout finned down here. It had been here a long time, 'cause it had a shape they didn't use any more. But they never found out anything about it—it was locked. So finally they moved it in town to the museum. He promised to take us to see it on our next observe trip."

"If it's in the city, we'll have to go there."

"How? We have no supplies, and it is a long trek through wilderness country to the nearest holding, if the holdings are still here."

"Do we have any choice now?" he asked, and I knew he was right. We did not—save of dying where we stood. And tired as we were, that was not our choice of an ending.

The rest of that nightmare passage exceeded anything we had

faced in the gray world. Not that we were menaced by monsters
out of a mist, but hunger was our constant companion. Kosgro
used his survival training, and it was only his skills that kept us
alive.

We lived on meat from animals he snared, brought down with
a well-aimed rock or knocked over with a club. He fought animals and birds for berries that were already half dried up. The
rags of our clothing became tatters that did not cover us, and
we wove very perishable substitutes out of grasses and reeds. Our
feet grew sore and then slowly toughened, and we lost all track
of time, save we could count the days since we had first found
the ruined ranger station.

And in all that time we saw no flitters, no evidence there were
still any of our kind on this world. I could not think what had
happened. When I had left Dylan, there had been a small but
steady flow of emigration. More and more plantations and grazing
land had been in use each year. Now we several times saw herd
animals but quickly learned to avoid them. They had gone totally
wild and were smaller, more wiry, and very alert, as if they had
learned to defend themselves in order to survive.

On the twentieth day of our wandering, we came to the first
sign that man had once tamed part of this land. Tangled vines
grew around a hill, and the fruit they bore still hung in dry and
withered bunches, decimated by birds and insects, plainly never
harvested. We broke the shrunken, wrinkled things to eat. They
were bitter and much smaller than the ones I remembered, but
they were food, and we not only ate our fill, but also made bags
of leaves pinned together with thorns to carry some with us.

The vines had overwhelmed and half buried buildings. So
entangled and covered were those walls that we did not try to
get inside. It was evident nothing remained we could use.

But even with this evidence of the collapse of civilization on
Dylan, I held to the hope that there was still a city, a port. If
we could reach that, we could find people—if not those we had
left—how *long* ago?—then still people.

Oddly enough, the farther we traveled, the more Bartare lost
whatever she had brought with her out of the gray world, the
more she became a normal child. Though Oomark had asked
troubled questions at first, he, too, came to accept this strange
thing that had happened. And I thought that both, being young,

could better adapt than could Kosgro and I. For me it was an endless nightmare, and I struggled to wake from it.

Luckily for my sanity and perhaps for Kosgro's equilibrium also (though by the nature of his training he was better prepared to meet strange strokes of fortune), the very mechanics of keeping alive and moving and seeing to the well-being of the children filled our days. But I nearly broke as we worked our way through more of the derelict and overgrown holdings and came to the outskirts of Tamlin.

Here the too luxuriant vegetation had not yet wreaked so great a havoc. The houses stood intact, though here and there a roof was missing, or there were other signs of long neglect and abandonment. It would seem that through some chance or disaster Dylan had been left to silence and emptiness. We came to the house we had left to go to the valley. I went into the courtyard to face closed doors. Hesitatingly, I called. As I expected, there was no answer. Still I went to open the door of Guska's room. It was empty even of furniture.

"Kilda—it's all gone—my clothes—my byny shell—everything! It's all gone!" Oomark came running from the room that had been his. Bartare had not even tried her door. She stood by the dried pool.

"Of course it is!" Some of her old impatience was back in her voice. "Everything's gone—it's been gone a long time!"

Perhaps the meaning of all we had seen had not really struck Oomark until that moment. He turned very pale. Then he went to Kosgro, and his voice shook as he asked, "It's real then—we've been away a long, long time?"

Kosgro made no attempt to soothe. Instead, he answered him as he might a much older boy or man. "It's real, Oomark."

"I wish—I wish they had left my byny shell," he said. "Father, he had it when he was a little boy. He wanted me to keep it always. I just wish they had left that."

He walked slowly out toward the gate before he turned to ask, "If there's no one left here, what are we going to do?"

"We haven't been to the port yet. If there is anyone left, that is where we should find him—or them."

We did not visit any of the other houses. Now we hurried along the streets of the city. And there was only silent ruin about us as we passed.

So we came to the apron of the landing site. No ships stood down there. I had not expected that they would. The burn scars left by deter landing rockets still marked the field, but those could remain visible for years.

"Headquarters tower." Kosgro spoke as if to himself and headed purposefully across the end of the burned apron to that building which had been the heart of an active port, filled with computers and com devices. Perhaps if we *had* been abandoned here—my spirits took a sudden leap—there would still be some off-world com left working so we could summon help from the stars.

I quickened pace, and the children began to run, keeping up with Kosgro's lengthening strides. We reached the central door of the tower—to find it closed. But the admittance circuit was still working, and it opened for us.

Kosgro called out—his voice seeming a thunderous shout in that place—"Anyone here?"

EIGHTEEN

A moment later I wished that he had not made that call, for
his voice echoed so hollowly, coming back in an eerie moan.
I did not expect any answer, so I was startled.

The words "Who's there?" in an authoritative demand came out
of thin air. For a moment I could believe we were back in the
gray world where such happenings were not extraordinary.

"Scout Kosgro and party," my companion returned. Then he
went to one of the inter-com screens and fingered the controls
so that we would appear on any open screen in the building.

I heard a muffled exclamation and then, "Flight deck lookout.
Take the grav and come up."

A door slid back in the right wall to display the open shaft
of a grav. We stepped in, caught by the energy beam, and were
carried aloft. Inside me a tight pressure band relaxed. So we were
not alone on Dylan after all. Whatever had happened since we
went on that fatal expedition to the valley had been drastic, but
at least it had not finished off our species here.

The grav deposited us on the lookout of the tower. As soon
as the door slid back, we saw three men awaiting us. But there
were no familiar faces among them. I realized my hope of seeing
Commandant Piscov, who would believe our story because of the
very fact we did appear now, had been a foolish one.

The trio were not young, and they were in uniform. But their tunics were patched and threadbare. Two had the insignia of planet militia, the third was a ranger. They had lasers ready, which they restowed in their belt rings as we stepped out.

"Who are you?" the leader asked.

"First-in Scout Jorth Kosgro, Kilda c'Rhyn, Bartare and Oomark Zobak." Kosgro answered for us all.

"Your ship—where did it crash?" The ranger pushed forward a little. "Are you refugees?"

"By the look of them they are near beat." The officer waved the other back. "They can do with food, I would imagine. Sit down. And, Brolster, bring out the rations."

So we found ourselves sitting in the places for those monitoring in and out space ships, eating such food as I had almost forgotten existed. Whatever had changed here, they still had ever-heat containers full of what must be savored slowly bite by bite.

However, when my first sharp hunger was satisfied and I looked around that chamber, I could see it was not a working place any longer. Many of the devices were shrouded and sealed in protecto, as if they had not been used for a long time. In fact, only the tall ledge of buttons and levers, before which the man who had introduced himself as Section Commander Weygil had taken his seat, appeared to be in use.

His companions were Patrolman Brolster and Ranger Cury, Cury being the one who eyed us almost as if he held some suspicion concerning our purposes here.

"You did crash, didn't you?" Weygil asked when we finished the food.

But before Kosgro could answer, Oomark went over and put one of his small, much scratched, and grimy hands on the section commander's arm.

"Please, where is everyone? They—they were all here—yesterday—" He looked back to me. "Was it yesterday, Kilda? How long were we in that place?"

"I don't know." A time long enough to frighten me if I allowed myself to dwell upon it, I guessed.

"What—" Cury interrupted impatiently.

Then once more Weygil held up his hand. "Not now!" he ordered, before he gave Oomark a gentle, encouraging smile. "The people have gone, son, most of them. Did you have someone here you wanted to see?"

"Mother—she was sick. And there was Randulf and his poohka Griffy, and Gentlehomo Largrace, and Commandant Piscov—"

At that last name I saw Weygil's eyes narrow and knew he had recognized it.

"And you expected to find them all here?"

"Sure. They were here—everybody was here when we went to the valley. And now—everything's different. All our things are gone out of the house. Even my byny shell Father gave me—everything!"

"It's been forty years since Commandant Piscov was transferred," the patrolman said in a low voice. "His name was in the records we sealed last week. Forty years!"

"What was the date—when you went to the valley?" Weygil asked Oomark.

Oomark frowned a little and glanced at me. "Kilda, when was it?"

I did not want to tell them, but I had no choice. "The fourth of Adi, 2422 After Flight."

They stared at me. I saw incredulity and then suspicion on two faces. Only Weygil appeared unmoved.

"This," he said slowly, "is the twenty-first of Narmi, 2483 After Flight."

"No!" Perhaps it was my cry of horror that convinced them.

Cury's hand had gone back to the butt of his weapon. But at my cry his fingers relaxed. I had suspected, but I had not been sure. More than fifty years! Yet I felt no older, the children looked no older than when we had gone into the gray world. Then I remembered—for Jorth it was now more than one hundred and eighty years!

"It's a trick!" That was Cury. "They're spies sent to trick us." He drew his laser and pointed it at Kosgro, probably deeming the scout the most dangerous of our company.

"Listen!" Weygil had been studying us, but he spoke to Oomark.

"You went to school here?"

"Of course!" Oomark was impatient. "I was in the fourth group—with Randulf and Furwell and Portus—"

"Who else?" Weygil prompted as he paused.

"Well, Randulf and Furwell and Portus—they were my friends. But there were some girls—and there was Buttie Navers and Cleeve.

Why—his name was the same as yours! He was Cleeve Weygil! Is he your little boy? He never said his father was a soldier—"

"He wasn't," the section commander answered slowly. "Cleeve Weygil was my older brother."

Oomark shook his head. "He couldn't be. He's a little boy like me and you—you're an *old* man!"

"They've been planted, filled up with a wild story and planted!" Cury broke in again. "Probably sent to beam in some snake-landing party. Best burn them right now."

"Be quiet!" This time Weygil's bark was sharp. "Oomark Zobak, his sister Bartare, and Kilda c'Rhyn." With his forefinger he pointed to each of us in turn. "But—I remember now! They searched for months and never found any trace of you. The matter was only dropped when the war broke out. After that no one had any time."

"What war?"

He told us, and his voice sounded as if he were aging years in the setting out of facts as the few remaining on Dylan knew them. There had been the sudden attack of an alien task force aimed at outer ring worlds. That had been defeated in a battle near the Nebula, but it was only the beginning. The destroyed force was but a scouting arm for a vast armada. Raids and more attacks followed. When the strangers were finally beaten, this whole section of the galaxy, once civilized, had been left in a state of chaos in which the strong lived and the weak were swiftly gone. There was no communication left between separate solar systems, even between worlds. Strange diseases spread deliberately or by chance left some planets charnel houses.

Dylan had been hurriedly evacuated by all save a guard force in the third year of the war. For a while the field here at Tamlin had served as a refitting station for smaller fighting ships. Then ships ceased to come. Five years ago the small garrison sent out their own last scout ship to discover what had happened. It had never returned. Luckily, there was still a huge dump of supplies housed in warehouses around the port.

The holdings, the grazing lands, had early slipped back into the wild. The few remaining families on Dylan had withdrawn to one quarter of the port and were housed in buildings set aside for the military command. They still kept up a constant monitoring for off-world coms, hoping to pick up news. Only they had heard nothing at all for a long time.

"Now," Cury said as Weygil finished his somber report, "where *did* you come from? Are you refugees? Or plants sent in to take over?"

Bartare had come to me. Now her hand slipped into mine. The spell that had held her in thrall was gone. She needed what little reassurance I could give her.

"Go on!" Cury urged. "Where did you come from? And don't tell me out of time fifty years back! If you were sent in by some raiders, it won't do you any good. We have repulse fields working still, and we'll see you don't turn them off!"

"Kilda?" Kosgro spoke to me. Perhaps he thought I might be more readily believed, though the more I thought of our tale, the more impossible I knew it sounded. However, we had nothing to offer but the truth. And that I told them, cutting my narrative to the bare facts as they had happened to me, to Oomark, and to the rest of our small company. Even so, the telling seemed to take a long time and to sound very strange.

When I was done, Weygil spoke first. "Another space-time continuum linked at intervals with other worlds," he said.

"You mean—you believe them?" demanded Cury.

"The theory is known," his superior returned. "And it fits what I do know about the disappearance of these three." He gestured to the children and me. "What about you?" He spoke to Kosgro. "When did you enter that world and how?"

Once more Jorth told of his planeting as a First-In Scout, of his accidental entrapment in the gray world, and of the year when that happened.

"The year *2301!*" Cury's disbelief was sharp.

"Yes, 2301," Kosgro repeated. "And I think I can furnish you with proof. Oomark says that a scout ship was discovered here and moved to a local museum. You all know the peculiarity of those craft. They are on special personna lock and will open only for the one who sets that. If the ship is still here—it will open for me and no one else."

I had forgotten that safeguard of a scout ship. Not only could it be placed on personna lock at planeting, so it could not be entered and could serve as a refuge for the scout if the need arose—but inwardly it was constructed so that its engines responded to one man alone, he who was signed to it. There was no better way for Jorth to prove his identity than to enter that ship.

"Museum?" Weygil repeated, and then excitement colored his voice. "Of course, it would still be there. There would be no reason to move it."

"Then take us there—now!" Kosgro urged.

"Stay with the com," Weygil ordered Brolster. They kept a day-night watch, hoping some whisper out of space would tell them one day they were not wholly forgotten.

We descended the grav and came out on that apron seared by rocket fire, but which had not felt that hot breath for years. We did not walk back to the ghost city. Weygil had a ground car parked nearby, and though it was small, we all crowded in. The sound of our passing echoed far too loudly as we sped along the empty streets. And I liked less and less the look of those blank windows and the dust and dried leaves and wind-blown debris that drifted about the buildings. So well built were they that they might well stand here not fifty years, but a hundred—more—a monument to a dead colony. And how many more such worlds swung around suns, some without even a handful of inhabitants to pass through echoing cities? Some must have been burned off and remained dead cinders, others been visited by plagues that left unburied dead lying where they fell. I tried not to think of that. Let me concentrate on the fact that if we had come back to a largely empty world, it was one we knew and not that gray monster-ridden one that had held us prisoners.

Finally we drew up before a two-story building. Pointing skyward beyond it was the nose of a ship poised on its fins, ready to seek its element—space. It was far smaller than the liner that had brought us to Dylan, than even a medium-sized free trader. But it was a ship, and seeing it gave promise that with it mankind was not altogether exiled from the stars.

We passed through the outer court of the museum, Weygil burning off locks with his laser, hurrying on to the outside enclosure that held the scout ship. Kosgro trotted ahead to stand at the foot of one of the fins, dwarfed by the tall rise of the ship, small though it might be for a star traveler. For a moment he surveyed it. Then he spoke aloud, slowly. His words were meaningless to me, yet I knew they must be a lock phrase, some sentence he had set in as a signal.

As easily as if it had been only an hour ago that he left it, a hatch opened on the side. Through that came the boarding ladder, thudding on the pavement at the scout's feet. He grasped it, ready to climb aboard when Cury moved, throwing himself in a tackle that did not carry Kosgro to the ground, but rather pinned him to the ladder. I think he was so startled by that attack that he did not struggle.

It was Weygil who cried out. "Cury! What are you doing? He's proved his point. He certainly is the man he said he was. The ship would not have answered him otherwise."

"Don't be a fool!" shouted the other. "He's a pilot. This is a ship which may be navigable. He can take off—leave us! Leave us to go on rotting—" Cury's face was a mask of fury. "He's not going to take off and leave us!"

Kosgro fought now. What he did to the man pressing him to the ladder I did not see, but suddenly Cury reeled away and back. The scout faced him, his bare hands poised in formalized invitation to unarmed combat. Cury reached for his laser, but the weapon was at the wrong angle for a quick draw, and Kosgro sprang, chopping a blow with the side of his hand at the other's neck. The ranger slumped at the foot of the ladder. Kosgro rounded on Weygil, his hands ready for defense.

"Relax. I'm not Cury." Weygil was calm. "Did you kill him?"

Kosgro was surprised. "No. Why should I?"

"He would have killed you." The section commander produced a tangler and showed some skill in spinning a restraining cord about Cury's wrists, binding them firmly together.

"More than Tamlin has changed." He did not look at us while he spoke. "We are too few. We have waited too long. For some of us that is not too difficult. We made our adjustments long ago. Others, by their temperament, cannot live with what is left. Cury is ridden by the belief that if we can only make off-world contact, Dylan will come to life again. He cannot accept the fact that no one off-world has tried to contact us, which either means that we no longer have anything to offer or there is no one left who remembers we are here."

Weygil sat back on his heels. "He is secure now. I'll take him back to the barracks, give him a chance to cool down. By the way—*is* your ship operable?"

"I can see." Kosgro swung up the ladder and vanished through the hatch. It seemed a very long wait for us. Oomark drew close on one side, Bartare on the other.

"Kilda," the boy asked, "where are we going to live? There's no furniture, nothing in our house any more."

Weygil smiled at him. "Don't you worry about that, son. We have a home for all of you. I've a young grandson about your age, and there're a couple more like him in the barracks, some girls, too," he added, for Bartare's benefit. "Our families chose to stay, and we're not badly off. There're fifty of us, and we have the resources of a whole city, plus about a hundred bursting warehouses, to see us clothed, fed, and taken care of."

"Colonies have spread planet-wide," I observed, "from less seed."

"Very true. Most of us realize that. We go through the motions of standing watch at the port. Some of us, like Cury, have to believe that the situation is only temporary. The rest—" He shrugged. "We don't cherish false hopes. We have a lot, a great deal more than many ship-crash survivors who have started out on a new world. And we're growing—ten of our company are children, with more on the way. We'll make out."

With Sector Commander Weygil in charge, they probably would. But what about us—where would we fit in? Were we again doomed to be Between, neither of one world or the other?

Kosgro appeared on the ladder. As he reached the pavement the ladder was drawn up swiftly and the hatch clanged shut.

"It's operable—but it needs a new fuel core. That's exhausted."

"Good enough. Now—let's get back to the barracks. Brolster will have been on the com to the rest, and they will be impatient to meet you."

Cury was still unconscious as they packed his limp body into the ground car. Once more we drove through those silent streets, heading back to the port and the barracks buildings flanking it on one side.

A mixed group was waiting to greet us with excitement. Bartare, Oomark, and I were swept off by the women. I had forgotten the sheer delight of soaking in a fresher, losing the grime left by long days of tramping, standing in spray that healed my scratches and bruises. To look in a mirror again was strange; to put on whole garments, lightly scented, which Weygil's daughter offered me—that was wonderful. To know that I was no longer weighted by the fears and responsibilities that burdened me—that was the best of all!

Our story was a wonder almost as great for our listeners (for we told it now in detail) as their history was for us. With Weygil urging, though it would never now reach Lazk Volk's library (How had Chalox fared—was Volk's collection still intact, to be drawn upon by whatever civilization still existed?), I began to record our story in full. Then I got Oomark to add his part, but when I approached Bartare, she did not even answer at first.

Though she did not keep to herself as she always had when with her contemporaries before, yet neither was she completely akin to Alys or Wensie in the barracks. She gazed a little beyond me when I asked for the second time, "Will you do it, Bartare? You know so much more than we of the world of the Folk—"

"Why should I?" she asked flatly.

"Because it is knowledge, and all knowledge should be preserved for the future." I gave Lazk Volk's creed in which I had been trained as a girl.

"They think it is a story." She made a gesture to include the inhabitants of the barracks. "A lot of them want to believe it is. In a little while that is what it *will* be, just a strange story. Who is going to care about your record anyway? Your Lazk Volk will never hear it. He must have been dead for a long time now."

"Very well. I can only ask you, Bartare. I can't make you."

Then the mask she wore shattered. "She doesn't come any more," Bartare said in a whisper. "She will never come again!"

"Melusa?" But I did not need confirmation. I knew of whom she spoke.

"She—she said I couldn't reach her, back there on the mound— and I couldn't. So I never was her real daughter—never at all!" The words came faster and faster. "I always had her before—now I haven't anyone!"

"You have me, truly. Bartare, you have me!" I offered what I could.

She shook her head. "You want to do that, Kilda—give me something because you are sorry for me. But you can't. You are you and I am I, and we are too different."

She was putting into words what I had always felt.

"No. She won't ever be back again, Kilda. And already I've forgotten so much. I lie awake at night and try to remember the call words and the things I used to do to make this or that happen. But they are slipping out of my head. And pretty soon this will just be a story to me, too. When that time comes, I hope I won't care any more. That's the worst, Kilda, in a way—to hope that I won't care!"

She took my hand. "Don't ask me to record, Kilda, because if I do, then maybe someday I'll want to read it. And I'll remember a little bit, but never enough, never enough!"

I understood. Bartare had made her choice, since in the gray world another had been made for her. If she must put aside all that that had meant to her, she must do it now. So I never asked her again, though there was much that might have gone into record had she agreed. I thought what pleasure it would have given Lazk Volk. But, as she had baldly stated, he was not able to have it now.

From that time Bartare was more and more like the other children, perhaps trying consciously to be so at first. But soon there was no apparent strain in what she did. Her one-time unseen companion was long gone.

No, it was not Oomark or Bartare who could not join fully in the life of Dylan's tiny colony. I was the one. I was more than fifty years out of step, and I could not catch up, though I believed honestly that I tried as hard as Bartare to fit myself into the society of which I was now a member. I had thought that when I returned from the gray world, everything would be all right. Now I found that false.

Weygil kept me busy as a recorder for the official tape banks to be sealed at the port. If the colony did not survive (and there was always the shadow over us that a sudden epidemic, a raid, some natural catastrophe might wipe us out), then our records would be protected for generations to come. But this activity could not occupy all my hours.

As a lone woman I was courted and pressed hard for marriage by five of the unattached men of the company. And I knew that sooner or later I would be forced into the mold of the others of my sex on Dylan—husband, children, a narrowing of the future. And I could not yet accept that. I strove to hold off the need for a final decision for a while yet.

In the meantime, Jorth worked on his ship. Fuel cores existed in plenty in the warehouses but were meant to be fitted into warships. It meant a long and delicate task to shave one down for the refitting in the much smaller scout. He was given every aid the colony could offer, for they saw in him their last chance to establish contact off-world. As Weygil had told us, a goodly portion of the colony did accept matters as they were, had given up hope of stellar contact, and were using their energy to make the best of that around them. But there were others not so resigned.

Cury, from wanting to fight Kosgro, became his most eager aide. I could guess that the ranger was determined to be in the ship when it finally lifted.

In the meantime, I saw very little of my late companion. He worked hard, and when he returned to the barracks, it was mainly to eat and sleep. But the climax of both of our problems came on the same day.

Matild, Weygil's wife, took me aside in midmorning and spoke her mind bluntly. I was a matter of discord. There had been a fight between two of the unattached men, neither of whom I favored. In fact, I had been most careful, once I knew the situation, not to favor any one of them, staying among the women all that I could. But the mere fact that I had made no selection was becoming a source of trouble. Since it was necessary for the good of the whole colony, this must not occur. I must choose at once.

That she spoke good sense, and that it was best for the group, I could not deny. Yet that I would be forced to do this—my inner rebellion was such that I went out of the barracks and into the silent city. Where I went did not matter. I wandered up one street and down the next. There were five unattached men, and to none of them was I in any way drawn. I did not feel part of the colony. I did not want to mingle my future with theirs.

I paused in the garden of the house that had been Comman-dant Piscov's in the old days. The untended growth was a tangle that had long ago broken out of the formal beds in which it had been planted. The weaker things had been smothered out of existence, but the ranker and hardier ones flourished. They had fought for life, and in them I read a lesson. It was fair and peaceful. I only wished I could stay there, forgetting all outside the half-open gate.

A metallic clicking aroused me. Startled, I thought that perhaps one of my persistent suitors had trailed me. But it was Jorth who stood there.

He wore a uniform from the warehouse stock. His space boots with their magnetic plates had caused the clicking. But his tunic was unsealed, and his hands were red from much scrubbing to remove the last traces of the work he had been doing.

"I saw you come here—on the ship's visa-plate," he said, almost as if he were accusing me. "She's ready to lift."

"They'll be excited."

"They don't know. They think I still have a day—two days—"

"Why?"

He did not answer. Instead, he walked to me. His freshly scrubbed hands fell on my shoulders in a grip tight enough to be painful, yet one I welcomed gladly. And he drew me up, close to him. Then he looked into my eyes squarely, and I knew there was no more need for words between us—this was what I had been seeking and needed.

"You'll come." That was not a question, but I answered as if it was.

"Yes!" And then I added, "When?"

"Now. I have supplies on board. Cury helped."

"He thinks to go."

Kosgro shook his head. "I made no promise. There is only one I would take from here. I'll carry their message. That I would have done in any case. And, Kilda, I do not know what waits out there. If we rise into complete chaos such as Weygil thinks exists—then it may be far worse than anything you can imagine."

"After the gray world, nothing can be worse."

"We can't take the children."

"No. But they have chosen their own way. Oomark is happy here. And I think Bartare will be. She has lost that dread companion who urged her to other ways."

"But you have found one—though perhaps not a dread one. And I shall urge you—"

I laid my finger on his lips. "You urge me to nothing! I, too, have chosen. Where you go, there will I be also, even unto the end of all stars!"

So it was we slipped through the dead city to the ship. And Jorth brought me into the only home he would ever own, which was to be mine thereafter. Gladly did I exchange the safety of Dylan for whatever might await the two of us beyond.